A KISS IN THE WOODS

"Have you ever been to Greece, my lord?"

"Not yet, but it is an ambition of mine to see the places about which one reads in school, to see temples to gods and goddesses who no longer walk the earth, to walk where the fathers of philosophy trod the markets— yes, I hope to travel there. And you, Tacye Adlington?" Worth asked. "Do you dream of faraway places?"

"My dreams stopped in Italy. I've read all I could find of the wonders to be seen there."

"Perhaps some day you will see them," he said from behind her. He reached for her and turned her. "I think," he mused softly, "I'd rather enjoy seeing them with you . . ."

This time when his hands clasped her waist, Tacye gasped softly. But she didn't pull away. When he tugged gently she stepped closer and when one arm circled her and his other lifted her chin the small bit necessary for their lips to meet, she allowed it.

His mouth touched hers, lifted, touched it again. Tacye wanted more and pressed into him, lifting her hands to his shoulders.

When his lips touched hers again, slanted slightly, pressed warmly, her arms slid around his neck, holding him close.

ZEBRA REGENCIES
ARE
THE TALK OF THE TON!

A REFORMED RAKE (4499, $3.99)
by Jeanne Savery

After governess Harriet Cole helped her young charge flee to France—and the designs of a despicable suitor, more trouble soon arrived in the person of a London rake. Sir Frederick Carrington insisted on providing safe escort back to England. Harriet deemed Carrington more dangerous than any band of brigands, but secretly relished matching wits with him. But after being taken in his arms for a tender kiss, she found herself wondering— *could* a lady find love with an irresistible rogue?

A SCANDALOUS PROPOSAL (4504, $4.99)
by Teresa DesJardien

After only two weeks into the London season, Lady Pamela Premington has already received her first offer of marriage. If only it hadn't come from the *ton's* most notorious rake, Lord Marchmont. Pamela had already set her sights on the distinguished Lieutenant Penford, who had the heroism and honor that made him the ideal match. Now she had to keep from falling under the spell of the seductive Lord so she could pursue the man more worthy of her love. Or was he?

A LADY'S CHAMPION (4535, $3.99)
by Janice Bennett

Miss Daphne, art mistress of the Selwood Academy for Young Ladies, greeted the notion of ghosts haunting the academy with skepticism. However, to avoid rumors frightening off students, she found herself turning to Mr. Adrian Carstairs, sent by her uncle to be her "protector" against the "ghosts." Although, Daphne would accept no interference in her life, she *would* accept aid in exposing any spectral spirits. What she never expected was for Adrian to expose the secret wishes of her hidden heart . . .

CHARITY'S GAMBIT (4537, $3.99)
by Marcy Stewart

Charity Abercrombie reluctantly embarks on a London season in hopes of making a suitable match. However she cannot forget the mysterious Dominic Castille—and the kiss they shared—when he fell from a tree as she strolled through the woods. Charity does not know that the dark and dashing captain harbors a dangerous secret that will ensnare them both in its web—leaving Charity to risk certain ruin and losing the man she so passionately loves . . .

A Lady's Deception

Jeanne Savery

ZEBRA BOOKS
KENSINGTON PUBLISHING CORP.

ZEBRA BOOKS are published by

Kensington Publishing Corp.
850 Third Avenue
New York, NY 10022

First Printing: June, 1995

Printed in the United States of America

Chapter 1

Early Summer, 1815

Tacye Adlington strolled into the front parlor and paused, hand in pocket, to stare across the room at Damaris. Damaris was worth staring at, thought Tacye. She'd been a remarkably pretty child, but the last two years had touched up the picture amazingly. At nineteen she'd become a perfect pocket Venus—as the saying went.

Blessed with light brown, naturally wavy hair, a bright smile and the training proper to a young lady, Damaris Adlington was a finished piece of perfection, indeed. Or so Tacye had overheard someone tell the new—and unwed—vicar only last Sunday.

The "piece of perfection" looked up from the chemise into which she was setting tiny embroidery stitches. It was her turn to stare. Horror widened her blue eyes. "Tacye! You cut your hair!"

Tacye shrugged, feeling again the pang of regret unexpectedly experienced when the first waist-length, mahogany brown lock had fallen. "It was a nuisance."

"But it was beautiful."

"A man doesn't need beautiful hair, Damaris."

Damaris pressed her lips together, relaxed them. "That again."

"It's the only way."

"Tacye, I cannot like it. It cannot be proper."

"For an older brother to take his sister to Bath for the summer? Who could possibly object?"

"*Everyone*—the instant you are discovered to be a woman!"

Tacye cast a wry look at her nearly flat chest. "I'm twenty-five, love. If I were ever to show myself female, then I'd have done it by now. Besides, I've often gone to market dressed this way. All those years no one ever knew I was not what I appeared to be."

"Yes, but then it was only for the day and you had good reason. You were selling crops or buying horses for Terence or . . ."

Damaris turned a trifle to the side. A tear formed, rolled down her damask cheek. Surreptitiously she lifted a finger to wipe it away.

Tacye trembled, her emotions as overset as her sister's—more so, actually. "Don't cry, Damaris. Please. I didn't mean to remind you. Truly I did not." A desperate note could be faintly heard in the slightly too quick delivery of the words. She stepped farther into the room, moving toward her sister—stopped, uncharacteristically indecisive.

Damaris dabbed openly at her eyes. "It is you who should cry, Tacye. You and Terence were so very close. You meant so much to each other in a way others could never understand, I think." She frowned daintily, perhaps a trifle accusingly. "I don't know why you haven't howled away your grief to have lost your twin."

Tacye turned toward the windows, conscious of the hard knot of black sadness deep within her. It was simply there. It never went away. It was part of her now. It occupied that portion of her which was her missing half, her missing twin brother. Terence had bought his commission in '08 and died five years later at San Marcial. How pleased Terence would have been if he could have known when his men crossed the Pyrenees into France and that Napoleon was, finally, banished to Elba.

Not that the monster stayed there. Waterloo was over now and the would-be French emperor would not escape again. This time the allies would be sure of him!

Tacye had forced herself to think of recent history in order to avoid remembering the day Terence died, but—not unexpectedly—the memory slipped by her guard, welled up in vivid detail. . . . They'd been given oranges from a neighbor's orangery and she was helping Cook prepare marmalade when, suddenly, it was as if she'd been rammed in her middle by a pole. She'd doubled over, dropping knife and fruit, grasping her tummy as if to hold it together.

A few moments later she'd understood: Terence had been shot. Minutes more and Terence was dead.

She was alone.

The pain had never faded. It merely congealed into a hard heavy ball, a weight she carried everywhere, everyday, all day. For the most part, she was occupied with other things, too occupied for full awareness, but it was there. Her grief was still an open sore, a pain she allowed no one to touch, couldn't bear to touch herself. . . .

On that day two years earlier, no one had understood why she'd gone into mourning for her brother. No one believed that life-loving joyful Terence could possibly be dead. Even those who knew there was a special bond between the twins found themselves losing patience with Tacye in the weeks which followed that terrible day in the kitchen.

Then official word arrived and Damaris cried, noisily, for her big brother, sobbing out her grief. Aunt Fanny's blind eyes had welled at odd moments, the tears tracing a path down her cheeks, only to be firmly wiped away.

Tacye had never cried. Had never been able to cry.

She looked across the salon to where her sister sat, sewing in hand. She smiled the odd half smile, the other half of her twin's. "He's gone, Dammy. I can do nothing about it. Certainly, tears will change nothing. Besides," she said, shoving her hands more deeply into the pockets of the trousers she wore by preference, "do you think Terence would approve of tears? Stupid waste of time, *he'd* say, and so you know." Tacye forced a cheerier note. "Besides, I've told you and told you that Terence made me promise I'd not cry if he died." The rock of pain expanded unbearably, shrank again to manageable proportions. "I promised him, Dammy. So I can't."

A brief pause ensued. Damaris pouted, but gave into Tacye's calm steady look. The younger girl dipped her head to study her embroidery, reached for her sewing basket and carefully chose a deep pink with which to thread her needle. By default, she allowed that subject to drop—returning to the other sore point. "I still don't think you should have cut your hair."

"It is done," said Tacye shortly, hoping this might be the last time the subject of Terence arose between them. "Done is done, Damaris. So, do let us forget that and discuss what must *still* be done before we leave for Bath."

Damaris looked up. "But do you truly think it fair to Aunt Fanny . . . ? To let her think . . ."

"I haven't exactly lied to her, Damaris. I received a letter from Anne. My old friend hoped she would be in Bath this summer. If she didn't exactly invite us to stay with her . . . well, do you think Aunt Fanny would be happier knowing I mean to take lodgings?"

"I don't see how that makes it right," repeated Damaris.

Tacye ignored her sister's pettish comment. She'd been planning this sojourn for years, doing without luxuries, postponing necessities, and saving carefully from the household budget so that, when the time came, she could give Damaris an opportunity to see and be seen, a chance at a better marriage than could be achieved here in an area where eligible males were so scarce as to be nonexistent.

Something must be done. Already the sons of nearby farmers were arriving, shy and unsure, on the doorstep. Far worse, the two eldest sons of the local profligate, a nearly destitute baron, were at each other's throats in their rivalry for Damaris's attention. The Lambourn temper was a byword in the region and Tacye didn't wish to exacerbate the boys' rivalry and unnatural brotherly hatred by adding Damaris to the already boiling pot—although she feared it was too late. And then there was the new vicar. But that wouldn't do. Not when his sister was determined to keep the poor man in her own pocket!

"You should be pleased that I heard from my friend, Damaris. It is because she may be there that I choose to go this summer. You see, I'd rather wondered how I'd achieve invitations for you, but now I may write a letter of introduction which you may give Anne and *she'll* introduce you around."

"Why don't you just introduce me to your friend yourself?"

Tacye raised her eyes to heaven and then glared at her sister. "If I am not there," she asked, overly politely, "then how may I introduce you?"

Damaris looked confused. "But you will . . ." She remembered. "Oh. You must remain in the character of my brother. I wish you would not. I cannot like it that you mean to pretend to be a man. I cannot think it proper."

"Damaris, you *promised* me you'd not complain again, on that score. You said you understood why I am to become Tobias—or Toby, if you prefer."

"I promised and I will keep my promise, but I do wish we did not have to lie to Aunt Fanny. Even if she *is* blind, she is the kindest, most marvelous woman I know—and it is not nice of you to take advantage of her as you do!" Damaris pointed at her sister's trousers. "You know very well she couldn't possibly approve such attire and what she'll say when she knows about your hair, I cannot say!"

"What she cannot see will not harm her," said Tacye almost absently.

The argument concerning her preference for dressing in male clothing had begun the instant Damaris first recognized her own femininity and become shocked by her sister's eccentricity. It was such an old argument Tacye could recite the words in her sleep. She jumped directly to the clinching argument. "None of the servants would tell her and no one else sees me to know me, when I'm dressed this way, as you well know."

As usual Damaris was silenced if not convinced. Tacye wandered to the window and stared at the garden, aburst with color in the sunlight. Silence followed her and for a bit she felt almost at peace as her eyes roamed the garden, which promised summer, and the greening park land beyond where lambs frolicked and their dams nibbled happily.

"Not too long now and we'll be in Bath, Dammy. Doesn't the thought excite you at all?"

"I guess I'm just not so adventurous as you, Tacye. I know I'll enjoy the parties and new dresses and all, because I do enjoy such things, but, well, I'm perfectly happy here just as we are. Do you truly think we should go?"

"Go? Yes, of course we must ..." began Tacye. Her glance turned sharply toward the main gate as movement caught her attention. *"Hell* yes!" she exploded in a manner fitting her attire, if not her sex. "We most certainly must go. In fact, we should have departed *yesterday.*" She turned and grinned. "Here come the Most Reverend Ralph Connors and his busy sister Bridget." The grin widened. "Just think, Dammy! Once we've left for Bath, we need not be polite to Bridget!" She strode toward the door. Reaching it, she paused, turned, frowned. "Will you be all right while I change?"

The thought of facing, all by herself, the portentous but already enamored vicar and his waspish sister made Damaris blanch. "If you would just ask Aunt Fanny if she's available ..." Her faint voice trailed off.

"How nasty of you to make use of our poor defenseless aunt that way," teased Tacye, mimicking Damaris's earlier chiding.

Her grin widened as she removed herself into the hall before Damaris could find something near to hand to throw. Damaris was far more ladylike than Tacye had ever been or wanted to be. Even so, Damaris had a surprisingly accurate eye when it came to throwing things!

Tacye was halfway up the stairs when she heard the tap-tap that indicated her blind aunt was on the move. "Aunt Fanny?" she called, taking the rest of the steps two at a time.

"I'm coming, dear."

"How did you know ... ?" asked Tacye.

"Mary was helping me sort my drawers. She looked out the window and saw the vicar's gig. Now, hurry, my dear. It would never do if the Connors were to see you dressed in the pantaloons you are no doubt wearing!"

Tacye's mouth dropped open. Her aunt *knew*. . . .
"Aunt Fanny!"

A tight little smile of repressed amusement lit her
chaperon's face. "It is very simple, Tacye if you'd only
remember there is nothing particularly wrong with my
ears. I just heard you coming up the stairs in a way you
never could have done if you'd been wearing your
skirts."

"You don't object?" asked a bemused Tacye.

"Well, it's difficult," said her aunt, teasingly. "You
see, I often dressed that way when alone with my husband. One can do so much more and do it much more
easily, can one not? My James hated twaddling women.
He'd have been impatient with a bride who was too
missish to throw a leg over the bare back of her horse
and gallop off or to go climbing in the fells with him
whenever he took the mood or . . ."

On the words, Fanny's mouth closed with a snap.
Her teasing stopped abruptly. That last thought was not
a happy one. Fanny's husband had died in a climbing
accident.

After a moment, Fanny forced a smile. "I often hear
the way you stride about, Tacye, something one cannot
do in skirts—as I well know. Do hurry, Bright-eyes," she
added coaxingly. "If we are very lucky, perhaps the
Connors won't stay above a moment or two."

The cane's tapping sound resumed and Tacye heard
her aunt mutter, "Not that we're likely to be that lucky,
of course. Miss Connors will very likely have a budget
full of complaints about the parish. Really, someone
should have a word with that poor man about his sister's
tendency to interfere. . . ."

Tacye listened to see that the cane's tapping reached
the right door on the ground floor, heard a pause and
then heard Fanny enter the salon. How her blind aunt
could find her way around the house and grounds was,

Tacye thought, a miracle. She was so good at it, that anyone who did not know her would never guess she was blind!

Another miracle—and not such a pleasant one—was her aunt's ability to discover one's secrets, thought Tacye on a much dryer note. Had Fanny *always* known Tacye wore trousers? Known that Terence gave her her first pair when they were mere children and kept her supplied as they grew older? Known that Tacye still wore trousers whenever she thought it safe? Which was far more often than Damaris approved! But Damaris had never tried them, didn't know the freedom they gave one . . .

And Fanny *had* known and never said a word . . . ?

Ah! Enough of that. When there was no one to respond, such questions were unproductive.

Besides, something else was bothering Tacye as she stripped out of her unsuitable garments. It occurred to her to wonder what else Aunt Fanny might know since she knew all about the trousers. Suddenly Tacye had new reason for hoping the Connors were making a round of visitations and would stay only a moment: she must question her aunt about the Bath adventure. Carefully, of course, but closely. Somehow it didn't seem so much of a lark, taking Damaris to Bath in the guise of a brother—not if her aunt had guessed her plan!

Tacye followed their old butler into the salon in time to hear Bridget slyly teasing a rosy-cheeked Damaris: "I truly think it quite naughty of you, child. You should put those poor dear boys out of their misery, should you not? There is something terrible in the notion of brother fighting brother. Rather biblical, if you think about it. . . . So, child, do tell. Which will you have? Herbert or Hereward?"

Damaris, her mouth drooping, turned wide hurting eyes toward Tacye. Tacye's lips firmed and her eyes nar-

rowed. Had this been going on for long? Why had
Fanny allowed it? Ah. The vicar had her cornered and
was discussing, again, her aunt's support of a Sunday
School of which he strongly disapproved. . . .

"My sister will, of course, have neither Lambourn,
Miss Connors," said Tacye, her voice tart. "But then,
I'm certain you do not seriously suggest that *any* inno-
cent be allowed to ally herself to *that* particular family."

"But if she is not to have a Lambourn, then will she
have Farmer Johnson's boy?" Bridget eyed Tacye's hair
through which she'd threaded a ribbon before Tacye
came down stairs. "Of course he *is* a big manly sort
of . . ."

"Lout," inserted Tacye sweetly.

". . . lout," echoed Bridget unthinkingly, still wondering why Tacye Adlington had cut her magnificent hair.
She blinked. "No, no, of course not. That is not at all
what I mean."

"Whatever you mean, my sister has no interest in
Johnson's heir. Have you a reason, Miss Connors, for
making yourself so busy about my sister's affairs?"

"Do not be so teasing, Tacye," inserted Fanny, her
soft voice somehow making itself felt. "I've been telling
your brother, Bridget, that my nieces are off to Bath one
day soon. They'll spend the summer there. I'm sure,
pretty as she is, our Damaris will have all the young
men wooing her and, among them will be one, I hope,
who will catch her eye." Fanny paused a significant moment. "You really needn't concern yourself, Bridget,
about Damaris's matrimonial intentions."

If there was a bit more acid in the tone of the last
sentence than was proper, all ignored it—although the
vicar's ears showed a rosy color.

Satisfied with knowing her brother was safe from the
chit, Bridget complacently turned the subject. The visit,
however, lasted quite another twenty minutes, but at last

the Connors—the vicar lingering a trifle longer than proper over his adieux to Damaris—removed themselves to their gig and trotted off down the lane to disappear out the gate.

"I thought they'd never go. Why," asked Damaris, "is Bridget so nasty to me?"

"She's afraid her brother will offer for you, of course," said Fanny promptly.

"Reverend Connors?" Damaris' eyes widened. She looked to her aunt. "He might offer . . . ? For me . . . ?"

"He, like every other male creature within miles, is smitten by your undeniable beauty," said Tacye. "I believe the difference, which his sister is too dense to understand, is that the vicar takes his duty to his parish seriously and will not marry to its disadvantage!"

Damaris worked her way through that teasing comment and, looked up, her outrage clear. "Tacye Adlington, I would too make a good vicar's wife!"

"Oh? Have you a tendre for our vicar and I not know? Should I follow and call them back?"

"You know I do not," insisted Damaris, "but I *would* make him a good wife if I *did.*"

Fanny chuckled. "Your sister is teasing you, Damaris, my dear. Can you not hear the laughter in her voice? Of course you will be an excellent wife to whomever you wed, whatever his station in life. But I hope, my dear, that you'll lose your heart to someone who will love more of you than your beauty in return."

Damaris's cheeks heated to a brilliant rosy red. "Tacye teases and you lecture. It is too bad of you!" She gathered up her embroidery, rose to her feet. In moments she'd left the room in a swirl of pastel pink skirts.

"Did we overly upset her, Tacye?" asked Fanny after a long moment's silence.

The older woman groped delicately among the things on the tea tray before her until she'd located the teapot, the sieve, and her own cup. Tacye watched in silence while her aunt manipulated these items. Fanny lifted her newly filled cup of tea and, awaiting her answer, turned her blind face toward where Tacye sat.

"We said nothing which shouldn't be apparent to her," said Tacye on a sigh. "If she hadn't made the connection between Bridget's spite and Connors's interest, then it was as well she be made aware of it." She frowned, her voice more thoughtful when she continued. "As for your, hmm, *lecture,* Aunt Fanny, she's very conscious her beauty draws attention and has already come to realize it is not the right sort of attention. I know it has begun to concern her."

"I see." Fanny was thoughtful as she sipped her tea. "Tacye, about this sojourn in Bath . . ."

"Yes?" Tacye encouraged when Fanny's voice trailed off to nothing. She waited, impatient, but knew it was best not to press her aunt too quickly.

Finally her aunt drew in a deep breath and let it out slowly. Looking sightlessly, into somewhere only she could see, she asked, "I've been wondering why I have this awful premonition you plan something outrageous?" She quested in somewhat the manner of a hunting dog casting for a scent, a mannerism she'd acquired since going blind.

"I'm insulted you could say such a thing!"

Fanny chuckled. "But not that I might think it?"

Tacye's aunt waited a moment, expectantly, but Tacye said no more. "You do not deny it, Tacye." The older woman sighed, a lugubrious sound verging on martyrdom—although her eyes twinkled. She waited again, then sighed again, this time an almost silent sound of true concern. "I think I must insist that I, too, go to Bath, Tacye."

"We'd be very happy to have you," said Tacye smoothly, "but I cannot allow you to suffer the disorientation which ensues whenever you are forced to make such a move."

"That is very kind and thoughtful of you, Tacye. And it didn't take you long to think it up, did it?" Fanny's mouth compressed, tightened still more, relaxed. "But it will not do. I soon make myself at home again, do I not? Ah!" Fanny's brows arched, her mouth priming. "You have managed to do it to me again, have you not?"

"Do what, my best of aunts?"

"You've avoided speaking of your outrageous plans." Her glare was directed only a very little away from Tacye's face. *"What are they?"*

"Bluntly asked, my aunt."

"Deftly avoided, my niece." Silence settled between them and still again Fanny sighed. "I am," she said, "named Damaris's guardian in my brother's will and have, therefore, authority over the child's movements." She paused for emphasis. "Tacye, either you tell me your plan or I'll forbid Damaris's removal from this house."

"Blackmail? I wonder if you would."

"Try me."

"Aunt Fanny, you are bamming me."

A muscle jerked in the older woman's cheek. "No, Tacye, I am not." Again she paused. "Tacye, I'll be very blunt indeed. I will not allow your unhappiness or your impatient nature or your need for adventure or whatever it is this time, to bring *scandal* down on that child's head. I would be shirking my duty to Damaris to allow it."

"Scandal! My sister . . ." Tacye rose to her feet, staring. She lost what little color she had. Always pale, even when spending much of her time out of doors, she whitened and felt prickles under her skin and wondered if she would, for the first time in her life, faint. "Aunt Fanny, I love my sister. You know I would never . . ."

"My dear," interrupted her aunt, "ever since Terence died you've become more and more restless. It is just as it used to be when you and he would build to a major rebellion every two or three years and go off half-cocked—as the expression is!" Color tinged Fanny's neck at her use of the cant term. "Come Tacye, you remember when the two of you joined the drovers. You were halfway to London following their herd of cattle before we found you. Then there was the time the two of you tried to go to sea. Remember that? Thank goodness you didn't reach a port city! Or what of the time . . ."

"Enough! Surely I'm too old for such tricks and you need not concern yourself to this extent."

Fanny shook her head sadly. "Tacye, one of your many redeeming characteristics is that you do not lie—or at least only by omission. You are old enough you *should* know better, but I have a very good understanding of your nature, my bright-eyed Tacye! *Tell me your plan for Bath.*"

Tacye sighed. She'd tried very hard to avoid this, but it seemed she would be harried and hassled until she gave in and it was such a bore, squirming this way and that to avoid it. "I mean to take the name of Tobias Adlington. I will become Damaris's brother. We will take lodgings—in fact I've an agent looking at available rooms this minute. As a man I'll escort my sister and be there to protect her. That is all."

"You did not receive an invitation from your friend Anne whatever-her-name-is."

"No." Tacye repressed a desire to sigh. "Anne is unlikely to even be in Bath. Her letter saying she hoped to be allowed to go—she's not well, but her husband is something of a tyrant—set my plan in motion. I've since received another saying she doubts very much that she'll be there."

"Ah. Then it is still more important that I go, is it not?"

"I thought I said you mustn't do that to yourself!"

Fanny chuckled. "Tacye, I've been saving my little income for five or six years now—except for tithing and for what I simply could not avoid buying. I've a nice little nest-egg to add to the one I suspect *you've* put together. Between us we should be able to give Damaris a very nice summer in Bath. No—" Fanny raised a hand. "Don't say anything until I finish. There are occasions when it is far more proper for a woman to chaperon a girl. Morning calls, for instance, would be more comfortable for Dammy if I were there and when shopping for her wardrobe she'll need to be seen with a woman. We will take along my Mary who has a very nice taste in style and color and she'll give me the hint if Damaris tries to order something unsuitable. Besides, even though Bath is no longer so popular as when I was a girl, I fear it may be far more expensive than you've guessed. We may very well *need* my bit to see us through."

"But I'm *not* mistaken in how much you dislike finding yourself in new places, how difficult it is for you."

Fanny smiled. "Tacye, as much as I love you, you are not the best of escorts for a blind woman. You are far too impatient and stride out with far too long a stride— even when in your proper attire! Damaris, on the other hand, does it very well, warning me of obstacles and guiding me over the smoothest paths. Too, she has a very nice trick of hinting to me when someone is nearby, done so that it is not embarrassing but clues me to necessary social behavior I would otherwise not realize was necessary because of my lack of sight. I'm quite comfortable with Damaris and as for new rooms"— She shrugged. "I'll soon learn my way around, assuming we may train any new servants that they must always leave the furniture in exactly the same spot!"

"I had thought to take one or two from here," said Tacye absently.

She was silent for a long time. Fanny began to worry she'd perhaps said too much—or not enough? Something. Finally Tacye rose to her feet and strode toward the windows. Fanny followed her movements by the sound of the younger woman's rustling skirts. The not-so-very-much-elder aunt folded her hands and waited. Finally the rustling noise neared and, after another moment, Tacye reseated herself.

"How, my dearest of aunts, have you managed to fool me so completely all these years you've had charge of us?"

"Like most people, you have tended—quite unconsciously—to believe that because I'm blind I cannot hear or think! It is a habit people have when dealing with the maimed."

"I've never thought of you as maimed!" insisted Tacye, outraged by the suggestion she had.

"No. But you have thought of me as not quite so able as a sighted person. Admit it. You and Terence often attempted to take advantage of that indisputable fact."

There it was again: Aunt Fanny had again mentioned her twin just as if he were not dead, just as if he would walk in the door with that old gleaming look in his eye, as if he would pull her hair and whisper adventure in her ear. . . . How dare she! How dare she speak of Terence so offhandedly!

"I don't think you should come with us," insisted Tacye. "Despite the logic of what you say, I think it cannot be good for you to suffer—as you know you will— all the problems of travel, a new home, a new town in which you must move and make decisions and then, too, you will suffer because of idiots like myself who think you less than a normal person."

Fanny chuckled at her niece's acid tone. The chuckles turned to outright laughter. "Oh, my bright-eyed vinegar-tongued Tacye. What sweet revenge you must have felt to say those words to me! Now, love, come down off your high horse and use the excellent mind I know lives behind your eyes. You are not one with more hair than wit, as the saying goes, but you must not just possess the *ability* to think. As the tutor you shared with your brother would say, you must also *use* it!"

More hair than wit! Wouldn't be difficult to have more wit than the little hair left since cutting it that morning, thought Tacye. She sighed. It was quite bad of her aunt, not to get angry and enter into a rousing good argument. Maybe some of that restlessness to which Fanny had referred would go away if she could only indulge her penchant for arguing ...

But only Terence had understood that problem. Only he had ever given as good as he got and would give her no quarter and always, once the argument was over, no matter who won, they had both felt lighter and freer and ... more at peace. Tacye sighed again.

Her aunt added another point in favor of her going. "Tacye, you mentioned your friend Anne would very likely not be there. Have you, then, heard that some other person with whom you can claim acquaintance will be in Bath this summer?"

"No. I pray nightly that Anne comes and that she is willing to introduce Damaris to a few people who may set her feet on the proper social path. I've recently written to explain the situation to her, but have yet to receive her response. As I said, I doubt she'll be there ...."

"Then," said Fanny with decision, "I *must* go. It is very likely I'll meet old friends or acquaintances now residing in Bath. I've not kept up with anyone, but we're not such an ancient generation, after all and not *all* of us will have gone to our maker, surely!" Her lips pursed as they did when she wished not to laugh. "Perhaps *I* will discover someone willing to give our lovely Damaris her chance. Tacye," she added, when her niece remained silent, "you don't really wish to try this adventure alone, do you?"

Tacye frowned. "I'll admit to a concern that I might not know enough about proper society, that I might allow Dammy to meet someone she should not or that I might make some grievous error against propriety which would destroy Damaris's chances forever. In that respect I would be glad of your company—but only so long as you are willing to accompany Damaris and her brother Tobias."

Fanny's frown drew straight brows down into a tiny vee between her eyes. "Tacye, if I'm there, do you still think it necessary that you pose as a man?" she asked cautiously.

"You yourself just mentioned that it is not uncommon for people to take advantage of your blindness. With Damaris at your side you'll draw men who, looking for an easy conquest, plan to take advantage of a beauty who is known to have no male protection." Tacye again rose to her feet. She stared down at her aunt who stared up, blindly, toward her niece's face. "I think it is not just necessary, Aunt Fanny, but *crucial* that I take the part of Tobias. . . . You cannot know how *very* beautiful she is, my best beloved of aunts," Tacye finished softly.

Fanny's frown remained in place for a moment longer. It faded. Then, wrinkling her fine straight nose, Lady Tamswell smiled wryly. "In that case, Toby, m'boy," she said, looking down her nose in the manner of a hoity-toity dowager, "just how soon do you think it will be before we can make ourselves ready to be off?"

It was Tacye's turn to be startled and a surprised

chuckle escaped her. "I assume calling me Toby means you agree?"

"Oh yes. I reluctantly accept your condition because I do see *some* sense in what you say. I only hope your masquerade does not become more of a bane than a boon!"

In London at very nearly that same hour Lucius Bernard Julian Mereworth, Marquess of Worth, laughed at the ton's newest Earl, James Ethan Cahill.

"But you don't understand how it is, Worth," said Cahill, peering around the tree behind which he'd just hidden himself. "I can't see. Has she gone?"

"She's gone," said Worth soothingly. "You're wrong, you know."

"That Lady Mary's on the hunt?" asked Cahill, a hopeful note clear to be heard.

"Not that. Of course Lady Mary is out to wed you if she can. As long in the tooth as poor Mary is you shouldn't be surprised that she's chasing you. New and presumably not so wary blood, don't you know?" Cahill shook his head and Worth chuckled once more. Worth sobered. "What I meant is that you are wrong that I don't know. I too have suffered from matchmaking mamas and their predatory daughters. I sometimes wondered if they weren't one reason I bought my commission and followed Wellington all over!"

Cahill peered around the tree trunk again, uncertain if he could trust the Marquess not to tease him about the lady's presence. "Got any advice to someone new to the game?"

"Wear well-fitting boots so they won't pinch when you run," responded Worth promptly. This witticism brought a chuckle from Cahill. "Why don't you leave

London?" Worth suggested in a more serious vein. "That, I'd think, would be the simplest solution."

Cahill grimaced. "Can't. Promised my aunt. Lady Lawton, you know? She wants to bear-lead me through a season here and then, still worse, wants me to escort her to Bath when she leaves London and prays that I'll stay there a while as well."

"Bath. I didn't know that anyone of Lady Lawton's status still summered there."

"The Bath season is deteriorating, she says, but she's always gone and even owns a house there. She claims she cannot abide sea air and that Brighton is unbearable. Bath's a comfortable town, she says."

"The Queen of the West," murmured Worth.

"I've heard Bath called that," nodded Cahill. "Which must mean it's worth a look-in. Besides, I, too, have property near there," he added diffidently. He was still new to his unexpectedly gained honors and still found admitting to the ownership of an estate embarrassing— and he now had more than one to which he must admit! "I agreed to escort Lady Lawton when she reminded me I should look into it. She tells me my uncle set up a rather good race course there. He was sporting mad, you know. And my cousins as well. I feel a trifle guilty I am not."

"You did the right thing, selling off most of his hunters and certainly his racing stables would have been a burden when you've no particular interest," soothed Worth.

"You're the first to understand that. Thank you. Others look at me as if I were a guy."

"Only particular friends of the late earl, I'm sure."

"I'm not *totally* unsporting," said Cahill. "I'll keep up the coverts there for the hunting which I'm told is excellent and I think I'll organize a race meeting while in Bath. Would you come down for it and, perhaps, an

evening of cards with old friends?" he asked, again with
that barest touch of diffidence.

"Bath," said the Marquess thoughtfully. "I don't think
I've been there since I was in short coats—but, if joining
the Regent in Brighton is the alternative, then Bath
might be very good indeed!"

"Brighton does sound like more of the same of what
we've suffered this season, does it not?" Having reminded himself of the purpose of the London season,
Cahill looked around warily, checking that no other
woman with marriage on her mind had noticed him.

"Exactly." Worth grinned, showing white teeth in a
sun-darkened complexion, his dark auburn hair glinting
with a few sun-lightened streaks. Worth brushed his
hand over it, pushing a wind-ruffled tuft back behind his
ear. "Of course, Bath will be more of the same as well,
but perhaps a trifle less of more of the same?"

Cahill grinned. "You were always a bit of a wit,
Worth. I'm glad you've not changed."

Worth, who could see around the tree, said, "Thank
you. As for you, I think you might consider yourself
safe. For the moment, that is. Those Beacherton girls
have a speculative eye on you, however, and will, before
this fete is over, find someone willing to introduce you to
them!"

"It is the very devil, Worth," said Cahill sadly. "Are
you fully aware that not one of these young woman
would have given me a single look last year at this
time?"

"A title and wealth have their disadvantages. You'll
find they also have a few advantages, so chin up my
boy. Buck up and face your world!" Worth bowed the-
atrically, and ushered Cahill from behind his tree.

"But you will come to Bath?" asked Cahill again, just
before joining his young Lawton cousins.

"If you wish it, I'll come to Bath," promised Worth

and moved off to saw hello to Lady Lawton who told him all about how she wished she could find a young woman to interest her nephew, that Cahill must marry and have children as soon as possible and it was desperately worrying that the boy seemed to be put off by every young woman to whom she'd so far managed to introduce him and what was one to do?

Worth, murmuring appropriately soothing comments, decided that his promise to go to Bath was one he'd not forget. Poor Cahill obviously needed him! Besides, there was less likelihood of finding marriage-minded misses in Bath these days. They all flocked to the far more popular Brighton. Which was all to the good, was it not? Worth, after all, also knew what it was to be chased by marriage-minded misses. He, too, was exceedingly tired of it.

Yes. Bath, with its slowly decaying gentility, sounded just the thing!

Chapter 2

Mr. Grenville Somerwell shifted his long lanky body in his great-aunt's landau and wished she'd give the order to move on. They had blocked traffic in Bath's busy Milsom Street for far too long while Lady Baggins-Keyton lectured the little Templeton chit on her flirtatious ways.

Not that it wasn't true that the girl had made a fool of herself during the ball at the Upper Rooms the previous evening, but it wasn't his aunt's place to scold her. Besides, the poor child was so mortified, Grenville idly wondered if she'd survive or if she'd expire right there in Milsom Street.

Pretending he'd no notion what his great-aunt was up to, Grenville sucked on the head of his cane and watched a lumbering, old-fashioned, traveling coach move ponderously along the street toward them. It was forced to pull up behind the Templeton's equipage, the grizzled driver waiting patiently for the blockage to open up. There was a rider coming along beside the coach who waited with far less patience, noted Grenville, a youngish man, bending to look at someone seated inside.

The gentleman had a familiar look and a faint degree of interest surfaced in Grenville. Then the rider's horse, the least patient of all, danced on its front feet in a most peculiar manner. Tension filled Grenville. His head reared back and his eyes widened as he indulged in painful thought. No one, so far as he could recall, but Lieutenant Terence Adlington had ever wasted time training his mounts to do that ridiculous little dance.

But Adlington was dead—was he not?

It couldn't be Terry Adlington—could it?

Grenville wished he dared raise his quizzing glass and try for a better look at horse and rider, but his hands were trembling and someone might notice and that wasn't to be thought of. It was scary, however, seeing that horse dance that way. Could there possibly be two men in the world who would train their mounts in that foolish fashion. Could there?

Grenville's great aunt settled back. She tipped her parasol and poked the ferrule in her driver's back, her usual means of informing the man he should drive on. The other carriage pulled away and the heavy coach started forward as well.

As they passed each other Grenville chanced a quick peek and saw, staring from the window, the wide-eyed bemused face of the most beautiful girl he'd ever seen in all his life—and then the coach passed on by.

The horse and rider followed closely. As the rider pulled alongside the Baggins-Keyton carriage Grenville gave *him* a quick but searching look as well, turning away instantly.

Grenville's hands clutched the head of his cane, his knuckles hurting, and his knees had that trembly feel to them which he'd suffered, off and on, since the Battle of Waterloo earlier that spring—a sensation that made him think they'd knock together if he weren't very careful indeed. It irritated him that he must spend far too much of his time taking care they did not!

And now . . . but it really couldn't be. Could it? Lieutenant Adlington *had* died at . . . Grenville couldn't quite remember, but it was one of the major battles in the Peninsula war. He was certain. Yes he was. He knew *that* much, at least . . .

Or, was he only pretty certain he knew? Maybe he was wrong. In fact, he quite desperately hoped he was wrong. How could he find out?

Another thought entered Grenville's rather thick skull and he relaxed. Worth would know. According to the Master of Ceremony's visitor's book, which everyone who was anyone at all signed upon arriving in Bath, Worth had arrived late the preceding day. *Worth* would know if Adlington were dead. All one had to do was ask him . . .

Grenville sighed deeply with the relief of remembering he knew someone who could tell him he was wrong to think he'd just seen the ghost of Lieutenant Terence Adlington. Someone who could tell him, as was likely, he'd done no more than confused Adlington with someone who *had* been killed and that Adlington was as alive as he was himself.

Unlike so many.

Grenville shuddered at the thought of all the lost friends, the dead and buried. God knew, enough *were*. So very likely he'd only erred. He did that. Often. Erred, that is. So that was all right. He'd *not* seen a ghost. Not this time. Worth would settle the point once and for all.

Grenville nodded to himself—and, blinking, found it was his turn to be poked by the parasol's pointed end. "Yes, Aunt?" He swiveled around, turning his whole body since his heavily starched overly high shirt points made it impossible to simply turn his head. Blinking, he discovered his aunt had again had the carriage stopped.

"Are you deaf?" said Lady Baggins-Keyton in the overly loud tone of one who was. Deaf, that is. "Run into the shop and bring me out a fresh pastry to eat with a nice cup of tea when we arrive home." She turned her pop-eyed stare on him. "Well, nincompoop?" she asked before he'd time to gather himself together to move. "Must I do it myself?"

Grenville stifled a sigh and wished Great-aunt Bagsy were not *quite* so wealthy. If she were only moderately rich surely she couldn't get away with being the family bully and utterly nasty to all and sundry—even her nearest and dearest. Himself, that was. At least he hoped he were dearest as well as nearest! It was because of Lady Baggins-Keyton he'd come every summer to Bath since he was a mere child—excepting, of course, for the years he'd been in the army.

Actually, it was in order to avoid Bath and Great-aunt Bagsy that he'd nerved himself to buy his commission. Only after Waterloo had he decided *anything,* even his great-aunt, was better than war. But if he continued to suffer thusly at his great-aunt's hands and eventually found she'd not left him a nice little fortune in her will—well it would be just too bad of her . . . !

It crossed Grenville's mind that thinking of his aunt's preposterous demands made it impossible to think about ghosts and his tendency to see them! So, although it wasn't a much better alternative, he'd think of his aunt. Now, if only she didn't order one about so, or point out, over and over, all one's minor infractions . . .

The lumbering vehicle which had caught Grenville Somerwell's eye halted just beyond the foot of Milsom Street before a four-story building which, of a morning, would stand very nearly in the shadow of the Bath Abbey's bell tower. Its windows were escalloped in the new way with wrought iron balconies which were painted a bright green and the windows themselves shone sparkling clean. Tacye looked over the building and decided it was, if nothing else, well cared for, which seemed promising.

John, the coachman, climbed down from his perch and opened the door, pulling down the steps. He held out his arm and Damaris Adlington climbed stiffly to the flagstones. She looked curiously around herself as John spoke softly to Fanny.

"Lady Tamswell? If you'll move forward about a foot, I can reach your arm. That's right. And the doorway be maybe a handspan before your toes now. Very good. That's right," he said as she stepped down. "And here you are," he finished, helping her to a position on the pavement before the building's entrance. "You're only a few feet from the steps, my lady," he finished softly. "Miss Damaris will surely see you right now, while I see to the luggage."

Her eyes skimming the first floor row of balconies, Damaris was saying to her sister, "I agree it looks well enough, but Tacye, there must be a reason the rent's so low on so much space."

"I don't doubt it," said the medium-tall mannish figure at her side. "But to whom are you speaking, my dear? No one named Tacye here."

Damaris giggled—an embarrassed shrillness marring her usual dulcet tones. "I'll never remember to say Toby," she whispered. "I'll use the wrong name and ruin all. Perhaps that's why I'm so fearful of what you do . . . ?"

"Shush, Dammy." Tacye raised her voice a trifle, and said, "Well, Aunt Fanny? Shall we go in?"

"Yes," urged Damaris. "Let's do."

The younger girl took her aunt's arm and Tacye watched, eyes narrowed, as her sister spoke quietly and calmly, explaining there were three steps and a landing before the door. They made the distance with Fanny stumbling very slightly only when she reached the bottom step. She achieved her goal with no other difficulty.

Tacye, dressed for her role as Damaris's brother, took
the steps lightly and lifted the knocker. A motherly looking woman opened the door and peered out. "The
Adlington party, madam," said Tacye. "I believe we're
expected? We'd like to be shown to our rooms now if it
is not inconvenient?"

The woman, wiping her hands on her apron, nodded.
She turned and started up the inner stairs. "I'm Mrs.
Armstrong, young sir, your landlady. Now if you'll just
follow me . . ."

"Will you wager the rooms are on the top floor despite what your agent said?" asked Damaris softly.

"I don't believe the agent would lie about such a
thing as that," said Tacye, wondering, herself, just what
would be found at fault. Something surely. She'd expected to pay far more for lodgings.

Tacye followed the landlady and again listened to
Damaris tell Fanny what to expect. Again Fanny made
the distance with only one trifling stumble and this also
when she and Damaris reached the steps. Tacye made a
mental note to suggest to Damaris that she give their
aunt that last little cue so that Fanny need not even fear
the stairs!

It had been enlightening, listening to John and
Damaris when they led Fanny into inns along the way
or helped her in and out of the carriage. Why had it
never occurred to Tacye to help her aunt to "see"
through her ears that way? She sighed. Very likely it was
because she and Terence had never had time for anything but each other and since Terence's death, Tacye
hadn't broken the habit of self-sufficiency. A habit which
had, perhaps, resulted in a trifle self-centeredness?

Or, more kindly, and according to dear Aunt Fanny,
the twins had been made of quicksilver and were never

apart for more than they could help. Then Terence had
gone to war and Tacye had had time for nothing but
her concern for him—and then, worst of all, he'd died.
From that point on, she'd been so wrapped up in keeping her unhappiness under control she'd still had no
thought for anyone else.

Tacye was very glad to set aside such self-chiding
thoughts when the landlady, having unlocked a door
near the head of the steps, handed over the keys. Tacye
tossed them into the air, boy-fashion, and caught them.
As they entered a small foyer, she stuffed them into her
pocket. Mrs. Armstrong opened a second door leading
from the square entry into a room which overlooked the
street.

"This be the sitting room," explained the landlady.
"As you see, it has a grand view down Milsom and, if
you've a mind to it, you can watch the people coming
and going and—" She smiled, her eyes twinkling.
"You'll know when your friends go into a library or
have set their minds to buying a new hat. It's not a *big*
parlor," she said a trifle defensively, "but 'tain't so very
tiny."

"I'd say it's a trifle larger than the small dining room
at home, would not you, Damaris?" asked Tacye in an
off-handed manner. She'd vowed to do better by her
aunt in future. Hinting to her about the rooms was no
more than a beginning.

"Oh, yes. A trifle, I think. In any case, it is adequate
to our needs, I'm sure. I'd like to see the bedrooms
now," said Damaris, still searching for flaws.

After giving that order, Damaris turned to the landlady without releasing Aunt Fanny who was beginning
to show signs of strain—as she always did in new surroundings until she'd had time to explore in her own
fashion.

The landlady didn't seem to notice, but returned to

the foyer and opened still another door which led into
an inner hall. Three largish bedrooms opened off it, two
on one side and one on the other along with two very
small rooms which Mrs. Armstrong said were suitable
for servants if one didn't mind having such quartered so
near—extra rooms at the top of the house were for rent,
of course; if they preferred. The Adlingtons did not.

That settled, the landlady disappeared through a door
at the end of the hall and into the "offices"—as she
called them. A barely adequate kitchen took up one side
and on the other was a room which appeared to be a
combination butler's pantry, storage, and linen closet.

Damaris and Tacye looked at the small kitchen,
looked at each other. Could this be the flaw? Cook
would be contemptuous of such inadequate facilities and
might even indulge in a tantrum if she could not be cajoled into seeing the necessity of putting up with the
poor conditions. That coaxing, thought Tacye, should
be done *before* Cook saw the rooms in which she'd be expected to work!

The Adlingtons and Lady Tamswell followed the
landlady back toward the parlor, taking a longer look
into the three main bedrooms. Tacye immediately chose
the smallest and plainest for her own.

Damaris, about to object that the elder sister should
have the larger room, caught her "brother's" eye. A delicate color flooded her cheeks and she immediately
chose for herself the bedroom which seemed the most
complicated to move around in.

Fanny said she'd look at her own room later which
the landlady accepted with a nod. The Adlingtons, however, knew this meant hours, perhaps, of careful memo-
rization as Aunt Fanny learned how many steps and in
what direction would bring her to wherever she wished
to go, whether that be from her bed to her wardrobe or
from the dressing table to the door. It would take a great

deal of time and was not a process with which Aunt Fanny allowed anyone to help.

Perhaps, thought Tacye, no one *could* help.

"So. Here you are," said the landlady. They had returned to the parlor and Damaris tactfully seated Fanny in one of the comfortable-looking although rather faded chintz-covered arm chairs.

"Everything seems to be very much as our agent reported," agreed Tacye. "You received our first payment, I believe?"

"That's right, young man. It covered your first month. Now, if you've any questions or if all is *not* as you like it, then you just come tell me and I'll see what can be done. Any questions about where you should go or what to see or about signing the book at the Pump Room, for instance—" She said this last with very slight emphasis. "—Then you just ask. That'll be your man with your boxes and trunks," she added, hearing a knock at the door.

John was loaded with part of the luggage, the rest scattered at the top of the stairs. Tacye directed him as to where things should go, carrying some of the smaller items herself. Before they'd quite finished bringing things in from the outer hall, Mary and Cook, who had come by stage, arrived, but Tacye was occupied with her coachman and couldn't catch the later for the little talk she'd planned—one she'd hoped would prevent the cook's walking out in a huff!

John, whom she couldn't escape, was using the freedom of a life-long retainer, to express his views of her masquerade. Tacye heard him out and nodded. "When disaster strikes, John, I'll allow you to say I-told-you-so. Once. Then I don't ever want to hear about it again, is that understood?" She glared at him, hoping to silence him. It did no good.

"Ye're going through with it then?"

"I believe I must, John. Damaris is too beautiful not to have male support during her stay here."

"So?" The old man's chin tilted belligerently. "What if some scoundrel offers her insult?" John looked up at his mistress from under shaggy brows. "You plan to challenge him to a duel, maybe?"

Tacye chuckled. "You do dream up the worst possible situations, do you not? John, you mustn't worry so." She grinned, shaking her head at his ridiculous suggestion. "The mere existence of a brother will assure such does not happen, can you not see that?"

John obviously *did not* see, but forbore to argue more, knowing it would do no good. "I'll take your nag around to the stables that agent spoke of and then I'll just be on my way." He busied himself checking that Tacye's gelding was firmly fastened to the back of the coach. "You'll send notice of when I'm to return?"

"Yes. It'll be about two months from now, John— unless Damaris is within an inch of a good match, in which case we'll stay on another week or two—but yes, I'll write."

"Shouldn't take *more'n* a week for some fine gentleman to fix his interest in our Miss Damaris," said John loyally. "You'll be coming home where you belong in no time at all. I'll see the nag properly settled, then, before I leave for home . . ."

It took another ten minutes to settle the old coachman's fears and get him moving. The argument and cautioning and sheer repetition had Tacye forgetting the problem with Cook. John finally gone, she returned to the parlor where Damaris was, once again, plaguing her aunt for information concerning Bath.

"But my dear," Aunt Fanny was saying, "you must remember how long it is since I was last here. Our landlady's comment reminded me, however, that the very first thing to be done, is for Tobias to go to the Pump

Room and sign the Master of Ceremony's visitor's book. Everyone must sign it and the sooner the better."

"By 'first thing' do you mean tomorrow or that we should go immediately, Aunt?"

Aunt Fanny smiled, but there was tension visible in the little lines near her eyes and the tautness of her lips. "Tomorrow would be fine, dear boy. But whatever *you* decide to do, I mean to stretch out on my bed and sleep. I can't imagine anything I'd like less than a stroll to the Pump Room." A brief smile crossed Fanny's thin face. "Damaris, on the other hand, would very likely . . ."

"Damaris is quite capable," interrupted that young lady, "of asking Ta-*Tobias* to take her for a walk!"

"I can sign for all of us?" asked Tacye, already finding herself uncertain in her role as Tobias.

"Yes. As newcomers you'll be met by—" Fanny's tiny frown deepened. "—Fiddle. It's been too many years, and I can't for the life of me remember his name, but you'll be asked if you'd care to sign."

"Very well, because I haven't a notion where this precious book is kept or, for that matter . . ."

Suddenly talk became impossible. All conversation was drowned completely by a not too dissonant clangor as nearby bells rang out. Far too near! It went on and on, the runs and repetitions becoming very nearly unbearable. Finally, the carillon fell silent. There wasn't a sound in the parlor either.

Aunt Fanny rose to her feet. "I think," she said in a dry voice, "we've just discovered the expected flaw."

"Yes," said Tacye. "and exactly why the rent on these rooms is kept so low!"

Mr. Grenville Somerwell was finally able to escape his aunt when visitors arrived at her elegant address on the Royal Crescent. As the distant bells tolled he checked his intricately tied cravat, resettled the padded shoulders of his wasp-waisted coat, and, taking up his hat and amber-headed cane, walked out into the clangor. At this distance the noise did not jar *too* badly on Somerwell's ragged nerves which had never completely healed after the terrors of Waterloo, but nevertheless he'd be very glad indeed when this visit ended and he could leave Bath. Sudden loud noises had bothered him from the moment the last gun stilled at that last horrendous battle.

Where, wondered Grenville, as he walked down the hill from his great-aunt's house, was he to find Worth? Not at the Pump Room. The proper hours for promenading and gossiping in the Pump Room were long past. Nor was it likely that Worth would be in any of the card rooms the town boasted. Worth was no gamester, although he'd take up a hand or two of an evening, along with a congenial group of friends. Nor did Worth drink to excess, so the public rooms of an inn or hotel were an unlikely milieu for the Major—the Marquess, that is . . .

Grenville drew his cane to his mouth and sucked on it as he strolled, thinking. A library, perhaps? Now that was a distinct possibility since the late coaches would have brought the newest journals from London and a man of Worth's character would wish to be in touch with what went on in the world. Grenville made a mental list of Bath's libraries and bookstores and, immediately upon his arrival on Milsom Street, full as it could hold of shops of all sorts, entered Joseph Barratt's circulating library. Worth was not there.

In James Marshall's, the third library Grenville tried, he found his quarry, although if he'd not been thorough in his search he might have missed him.

"Why are you sitting way back in this corner where you can't be seen?" Grenville asked the Marquess of

Worth a trifle querulously. "I almost left without finding you myself which would have been altogether too bad when I've been hunting all over town for you."

Worth peered over the top of his paper. "Perhaps, Somerwell, I'm sitting in my corner because I'd no wish to be found?"

The younger man cackled. "Always the jokesmith, ain't you? I've a question for you."

Worth sighed. "Then ask it. The sooner you do and the sooner I answer, then the sooner I may return to perusing my paper, is that not so?"

"Bit difficult."

Worth's left brow rose. "A delicate subject?"

"You might say that."

Both brows climbed Worth's forehead. "Don't know that I'm the one to ask in a case like that. Never been overly much in the petticoat line myself." The brows came down to their proper level and snapped together. "In fact, Grenville, I hadn't thought you to be."

Grenville waved his hand. "No, no. Not a petticoat question. Nothing of that nature."

Worth eyed his former junior officer and remembered that it had always been a trifle difficult to bring the lad to the point. "Perhaps you shouldn't attempt to prepare me, but should just ask."

"You sure?"

Worth nodded. Firmly.

"Sad-making question, perhaps," warned Grenville. Worth continued to stare impassively. Grenville studied the face before him for a few moments and evidently decided to accept the hint. "Been trying to remember. Did Lieutenant Terence Adlington survive the war or did he not?"

"Terry?" A vision of the medium tall officer with the funny quirk to his smile filled Worth's mind. "I didn't know you were a friend of his."

Grenville shrugged. "Not *especially* close, but I knew him pretty well. At least I think I did. If he's the one I'm thinking about, that is. Just needed to know if he stuck his spoon in the wall—or not."

"A bullet with his name on it found him at San Marcial. He was a great loss to the regiment."

"Thought so. Couldn't recall the battle, but was almost sure . . ." Horror darkened Grenville's visage. "But that means . . ." His color faded and he shook his head as if denying something, and then, abruptly he turned on his heel. With no words of thanks or of goodbye such as propriety demanded, he wandered off, headed vaguely in the direction of the door.

"Somerwell!"

The younger man didn't respond. It was very much as if he'd not heard. His reaction bothered Worth. He remembered how shattered Grenville had been at the end of their last battle and decided he couldn't allow the younger to go off in such a perturbed state. With a sigh of regret for the unfinished article—which covered a debate on the proposed corn law bill, a subject which he'd found of interest—Worth lay aside the paper and followed Grenville from the library.

Out on the flagstones, Worth looked both ways, discovered his prey, and set off. "Somerwell," he called again, striding rapidly to catch up with the dawdling fop who strolled blindly forward sucking on the end of his cane. "What *is* the problem?"

"What? What's that? Problem?" Grenville remembered how friends had reacted in the past when he'd admitted to seeing a ghost. He was very tired of finding himself the center of so much hilarity. "Problem?" he repeated. "Oh, nothing. Nothing at all, I'm sure."

"Something led you to ask about Adlington. I haven't thought of him in some time, but now I do, I remember him with a great deal of affection. What brought him to *your* mind?"

Grenville peered sideways at Worth. Very obviously his interrogator was *not* going to go away and leave him be. "Thought I saw him today," he mumbled. "Nonsense of course—just that the fellow's horse did that funny little dance on his front feet. Like Adlington's always did? If it *was* Adlington who trained . . . oh," he added when Worth nodded, "you remember, too, do you? Odd to see it again. That's all." Grenville picked up his pace. "Don't want to hold you up, Worth. Talk to you sometime when you ain't reading your paper, hum?"

"But I'm not reading it now." Worth's longer legs easily kept pace. "Tell me where you saw this animal?"

"The horse? Very nice black gelding. Maybe a trifle short in the back," added Grenville after thinking about it, ". . . but only a trifle, mind. Looked a fast beast, I'll say that for it. Spirited creature." He glanced to see if this would pacify the Major—the Marquess, that was.

"Where," said Worth, simulating patience as well as he might, "did you see it?"

"Where? Oh. Here. In the street." Grenville waved his hand in an airy fashion. "Where else would one see a horse?"

"And the rider looked like Terry?"

"*Damn* like," said Grenville, his skin paling at the memory. He looked around as if fearful of seeing him again.

"Hmm. All alone, the rider and horse?"

"Don't think so. Think they were following the carriage."

"Ah. We progress, do we not? Tell me, Somerwell, what sort of carriage would that be?"

"A demned great awkward traveling coach, don't you know? Haven't seen the like since the last time I visited my grandfather. Not that I *could* visit him recently. Been dead this age, you know."

"And *in* the coach?" said Worth, ignoring Grenville's comment.

"Hmm? *In* the coach?" For the first time Grenville remembered the beauty peering from the window. "The most glorious face you ever saw!" A bemused expression crossed the younger man's features. "Think I'll write an Ode to the Vision in the Window . . ." His eyes unfocused and he almost walked into a lamp post.

Worth caught his arm and guided him around it. "Later, Somerwell," he said.

"Hmm?"

"Write your ode later. For now, why do you not describe your vision."

"Describe . . . ? The beauty you mean?"

Worth nodded, wondering if he'd managed to finish this conversation without doing damage to the fop walking at his side.

"Oh. Perfect features, don't you know?" said Grenville fervently. "Hair like in a portrait by that painter who did my grandmother—the one with flowing draperies and wide brimmed hat and baskets of flowers and what not."

"I suspect you mean Gainsborough," said Worth.

"I do? I do not. I mean m'grandmother." Grenville cast a look of half bemused lack of understanding and half outrage at Worth when his companion chuckled.

"Tell me about your vision, Grenville."

For half a moment the fop looked as if he'd walk off in a huff, but once again a mental picture of the beauty put all else from his mind. "Well, now. My vision's pale brown hair was all wavy and loose and glinting in the light like in one of those pictures, don't you know? And her face a perfect oval and her eyes large and well lashed and . . ." Again he almost walked into a lamp post and again Worth steered him around it.

"And?" asked the marquess when no more was forthcoming.

"And?" Grenville blinked. "Ain't that enough? Better be, 'cause that's *all*. Sitting in the coach, don't you know? Couldn't very well see if she looked that good . . . er—" Grenville blushed. "—Hmm . . . er, down farther, don't you know?"

"I was wondering if anyone else might have been in the carriage," said Worth softly.

"Didn't have a chance to see, did I?"

"Didn't you?" Worth eyed him. "Perhaps not. Not if the young lady is half so lovely as you claim. In fact, in that case, it's perfectly reasonable you saw no one else. But, did you, perhaps, notice where they went?"

"No." When Worth seemed to wish more, he added, "I was with my Aunt Bagsy. Lady Baggins-Keyton, that is."

Grenville's mouth drooped. It occurred to him he'd best get home and rejoin his dear Aunt Bagsy before he'd been gone so long he'd earned a lecture on the proper behavior of the young toward their elders which would, if he were really late, be followed by another favorite, the one on punctuality.

"Speaking of my aunt," he said, "better be off and see if she wants me for anything. Goodbye now." Somerwell turned at the first corner and started up the hill.

For a long moment Worth stared after him. A mount that danced on its forefeet. A man who reminded Somerwell of Adlington. To quote Somerwell, was *damn like* Adlington, and a beautiful maiden. A mystery?

Hmm. Worth raised his eyes to the sky, but didn't see the scudding clouds which hinted at rain later that evening. His mind had turned back to long hours of night-talk around small campfires, to Adlington's fond tales of

his sisters . . . the young one he believed would grow to
be a beauty, yes, but especially, the tales of his twin who
rode like a devil and could shoot better than he did himself. A sister who didn't flinch at language better left in
the stables, who would follow him on any adventure—
assuming she wasn't leading it herself! A sister, more-
over, who preferred to wear Terry's cast off trousers
when out and about . . .

But surely not in Bath!

Would she dare?

Worth headed for the Pump Room. If by some far-
fetched chance, the Adlingtons *had* arrived in town one
might assume they would, like other new arrivals, make
the Pump Room their first stop, there to put their
names down in the visitor's book.

Five minutes later Worth scowled at the names carefully inscribed in a firm hand: Lady Fanny Tamswell—
that, he recalled was the blind aunt. Miss Damaris
Adlington—that, the sweet young sister Terry predicted
would grow into a beauty and Somerwell had certainly
described a beauty. Last but not least, Mr. Tobias
Adlington—a cousin perhaps?

Worth thought not.

This Mr. Tobias Adlington had some explaining to
do, thought Worth, as he returned to his suite in the
York hotel. In fact the young man's mere existence
posed something of a problem, because Worth distinctly
remembered Terence's concern that if something happened to himself, there would be no male relative to
whom his sister could turn for help. Not that his twin
would do so in any case, according to her doting
brother—which fact had appeared to sooth Terry's guilt
somewhat although Worth had thought it should not.

But if she wouldn't turn to a male for help, then just
who was Mr. Tobias Adlington? And where was Miss
Tacye Adlington? Did he dare a guess . . . ? Suddenly,

life, which had become rather flat of late, took on a new interest. Worth, with a well-concealed twinkle in his eyes, found himself looking forward to meeting Bath's newest residents.

The following morning Cook appeared in the parlor where, at a round table in one corner, the household was to take its meals. "I can't do it," asserted Cook, crossing her arms over her chest.

Cook had already complained long and loudly about the kitchen on the preceding evening—and their meal had underlined her problems. Tacye had argued her out of that eminent tantrum, but now foresaw the need to do it all over again. Before she could speak, however, Fanny took a hand.

"You must do it," insisted Lady Tamswell, a tiny frown marring her fine brow.

Cook answering scowl made Fanny's look mild indeed.

Tacye rose to her feet and moved to Cook's side. She put an arm about the plump body and led the woman from the room.

"Don't listen to my aunt, Cook," she said as they walked out. "Of course it is impossible. I knew it would be the moment I saw the limited space in which you'd be expected to work."

Tacye opened the hall door and pushed Cook along toward the second small bedroom where she deftly maneuvered the overly plump women through the door.

"Now," she continued in a soothing voice, "you just pack up your things and I'll see about getting you an inside seat on the stage and you can just go back home where you belong. I should have guessed, really, that there would be inadequate facilities in rented rooms for a real cook to spread out and prove her expertise. We'll be sad to see you go, of course, but we'll just have to find someone who is used to the terrible conditions and who has learned to manage them—although she'll never be so good as you. There will, though, be someone, and I won't tell them you found it impossible, of course. That would be disloyal to you, would it not, Cook?"

"Now stop your shoving, *do*. I didn't say I *couldn't* cook a decent meal in that pokey little kitchen."

It was exactly what she *had* said, but it wouldn't do to remind her. Tacye hid a grin at the success of her tactics!

"But," said Tacye, hoping she'd not over do it, "it would be cruel of us to ask it of you, would it not? It is really too much. I should have realized before." Tacye moved around the room, looking under the bed and atop the armoire. "Now just where did you put your portmanteau . . . ?" She turned to look at Cook.

"I *won't* go." The scowling cook crossed her arms. "What if Lady Tamswell should come down with one of her heads?" she asked, triumphantly. "Who would there be to prepare one of her special tisanes? No one," Cook answered herself, a brisk note entering her tone. "I didn't say I *couldn't* cook there," she reiterated, ". . . but it isn't going to be easy," she finished with just a hint of uncertainty.

The battle was won and Tacye suppressed her glee. "Is there anything which might help?" she asked.

"No. I'll have to do things a bit differently, that's all." The cook sat down on her narrow bed with a sigh. "A little old to learn new tricks," she said warningly.

"Don't you worry. We'll be very patient with you because we know you will figure it out. You don't think we *want* to find another cook, do you? Why, we'd never find one who understood our little quirks and what we like and—more important—what we dislike, the way you do."

Tacye went on in this fashion for only a little longer before the cook heaved herself from her bed and returned to her totally inadequate kitchen determined to show her family she could overcome even such odds as these. Tacye returned to the table and looked at the cold ham and the congealed eggs which had been overdone to begin with. The ham, she decided, was edible. Taking two slices of cold toast, she stuffed the ham between them and carried the result to the window. She stared down into the street as she chewed.

"Toby, come sit down," scolded Aunt Fanny, her sharp ears allowing her to interpret what Tacye had done. "You are no longer in the country where you may act the veriest ruffian, my boy. Here you must obey the rules of proper behavior and the rules state you sit at the table to eat."

Tacye turned and noted the twinkling look her aunt could not conceal. "You are determined to reform me?"

"I am. If you are determined to play the fool, then you'll play it in such a manner you are unlikely to be unmasked. You will obey the rules, Toby, or I will burn your wardrobe and you'll be forced to return to your skirts, will-ye nill-ye."

"I don't understand why obeying stupid rules will prevent me from being unmasked."

"It is quite simple, really," said Fanny with a patently false patience. "Every time you do something odd— such as walk away from the table while still eating—you draw attention to yourself. The more you draw attention, the more likely you'll be discovered for what you are. Have I made myself clear?"

"Too clear, my dearest of aunts. In fact, reluctant as I am to admit it, I see no possible hole in your logic through which I may squirm. I will try to comply with all the ridiculous strictures society decrees."

"So?"

"So?" responded Tacye, turning again from where she'd gone back to staring out the window.

Her aunt sighed. "You have not finished that disgusting excuse for breakfast—or have you?"

Tacye chuckled. "I would like a cup of hot coffee, best of my aunts," she teased.

"Then you may just come over here and get it yourself."

"And when I've done so I may also sit myself down to drink it?"

"You may." Fanny chuckled. "It isn't often I manage to get the better of you in an argument."

"No." Tacye grimaced, but mildly, and added, "For Damaris I will grit my teeth and accept the necessity of playing the idiot."

"Society's rules do not make one idiotic."

"You'll never convince me of that, my dearest of aunts. I've said I'll play my proper part. Surely you won't insist I must like it as well?"

The chuckle this time was near to a laugh. "Tacye, I wish I'd not lost my sight. I wish we'd been financially able to take you to London for a proper season. If only I might have introduced you into circles where your wit and eccentricities would have been appreciated—" She paused for half a breath. "—So that you'd not have been so lonely or so alone these past few years."

Tacye stiffened. Terence going off to war and leaving her behind had been bad enough—but then he'd died and that was worse. Fanny's comment was obviously brought about by a thought her aunt had carried in her mind for a long time. It had burst out now with no notion of hurting Tacye but only of expressing Fanny's wish that things were otherwise than they were and Tacye knew it.

She bit her lip. Hard. She must not explode, must not rant and rave, must not berate her loving aunt for even suggesting someone, *anyone* could fill the part of her left empty by Terence's death. *She must not upset her aunt.* Tacye rose to her feet and again walked to the window.

"Toby?" asked Fanny quietly, realizing what she'd done. "I won't apologize."

"No, why should you?"

"It's true, what I said. Every word. If you'd had friends who understood you, friends who loved you, you would not have suffered for so long or so deeply."

"Enough."

"You don't believe me. Sometimes I wish you were not quite so sure of yourself, Toby, my boy. I fear me that you'll come a cropper one day when you discover for yourself that it is possible to have a friend other than your brother—possibly more than a friend . . ."

"*Enough,* Aunt Fanny." Tacye whirled to face her aunt. "We will not discuss Terence, do you understand me?"

"So cold." Fanny hugged herself, but a grim look indicated her determination to speak now that she'd broken the ice. "I'm not a servant who cannot answer back. Nor am I Damaris who will cringe away from an argument. I am determined you will overcome your grief and live—as Terence would have wished you to do!"

Tacye trod to the door and opened it. She was about to leave the room when her aunt said, softly, "How unlike you to run away, Tacye—*Toby,*" she corrected herself. How very unlike you."

Tacye hesitated, then, ignoring the charge of cowardice, she slammed the door behind her and opened the door to the stairs. She slammed that too, and went down the steps three at a time, almost running into Mrs. Armstrong at the bottom. A quickly exclaimed "excuse me" and Tacye strode on out onto the street.

There Tacye drew in a deep breath, stuffed her hands into her pockets, and, shoulders hunched, stalked away

from the Abbey Arms toward the edge of town. A long
walk in the country would calm her. A very long walk,
she feared.

But how dare Fanny talk to her in that fashion? How
dare she suggest anyone could ever fill the void left by
Terence's loss? How . . .

The thoughts roiled and boiled and heated her brain
dangerously. Tacye hadn't the least notion where she
roamed. In fact, later, when she finally looked about
her, she immediately realized she was lost, but she was
in luck. From across a field a rider approached. She
waited.

The horse neared her and the equestrian noticed her
standing near the stile she been about to climb. The
man waved, changed his course the trifle necessary to
come up with her, and, as he approached, peered at
her.

Sudden horror distorted Grenville Somerwell's visage.
He reined in his mount, took another look at the slim
male figure with the well-known face, shook his head violently. "No, no, no," he said.

Wrenching violently at his horse's mouth, he turned it
to one side and raced his animal toward a five-barred
gate. They jumped it and turned onto the road at which
point they galloped off, hell-for-leather, to the left.

Why, wondered Tacye, had that rider rushed off like
a frightened hare when he'd obviously approached with
the intention of speaking? Tacye pursed her lips, her
eyes widened in confusion. What had gotten into the
silly creature? He'd flown off on a tangent as if he were
chased by the devil himself!

On the other hand, perhaps the rabbit, dressed as he
was with his shirt points so ridiculously high and those
even more ridiculous white tops to his boots—perhaps
he'd solved Tacye's immediate problem? Surely one

might assume a fop such as he would raced off toward Bath?

Tacye climbed the style and looked down the tree-shaded lane. Assuming the idiot on the horse had not totally lost his wits, then one might follow and see where the way led. Tacye grinned. Even if one could not rely on such a half-wit, then perhaps the half-wit's guardian angel would see him safe?

So. Perhaps one wasn't quite so lost as one had thought. Tacye set off, taking the direction the equestrian had inadvertently pointed out, and, after walking for something over a mile, saw, with some relief, the spires of Bath. At that point Tacye easily found her way home.

Chapter 3

"Feeling ready for your first visit to the Pump Room, Aunt Fanny?" asked Damaris three days later.

One could hear the excitement in her voice, the anticipation. Every morning Damaris had hoped to start making the traditional daily visit to the Pump Room at the proper hour of the morning when all of Bath's best society gathered there to drink the prescribed three glasses of the ill-tasting waters—but more importantly, one went to see and be seen. Each morning she'd been put off. Until now.

Damaris twirled happily. She stopped, facing the room, her arms wide. "Our very first visit!"

"It won't be *my* first visit, child. Only the first in more years than I care to admit."

"I don't see how it can have been more than ten, Aunt Fanny," said Tacye, from her favorite lounging stance by the window. She turned to look fondly at her aunt. "You came to us immediately after your husband died. I distinctly remember Father saying you were far too young to be widowed. . . . Twenty-four? Is that right?"

"Which, if you turn your mind to your governess's instruction, makes me thirty-four and an ancient," responded Fanny with the dry humor for which she was noted. "Every year of which will look to be two when I'm seen to stumble over my own feet."

"We won't let you stumble, Aunt Fanny," encouraged Damaris.

"No, of course you will not. I'm being foolish."

"I think you've learned to get around our rooms very well indeed. And very quickly, too."

"Damaris, you needn't treat me like a child who has learned his lesson more rapidly than expected." This time there was a rather acid note in Fanny's voice. "You've forgotten to take into account that there is very little I must learn. The space is limited and the furnishings are rather more minimal than one would have if one did the rooms up oneself." She pushed herself to her feet and adjusted the fit of one glove. "Are we ready?" she asked, looking around sightlessly.

"We're ready," said Tacye.

Even Tacye who, to her chagrin, had discovered herself to be a trifle insensitive, could hear the bravado in her aunt's tone.

"You may *feel* an ancient, my best of aunts," she said, "but you look as young as you did when you first came to us. Here is my arm," she went on before Fanny could respond to that bit of flattery. "We're facing the door to the entry hall, as you know, and the stairs are only four feet beyond that. I'll pause before you are to start down."

Tacye had learned *her* lesson quickly and well, too. She could now guide her blind aunt with a tact which Fanny appreciated to the point she'd actually begun to prefer her new escort.

Damaris, on Tacye's other arm, was glad Tacye had taken over the responsibility for leading Aunt Fanny. She knew that, now she was in Bath, she was far too excited, far too easily distracted, to take proper care. First of all, there were the many strollers in all sorts of colors and only the very latest styles.

Damaris bit her lip at that, wondering just how out of date her own simple dresses would be seen to be. At least, as a girl just being introduced to the ton, she would not be expected to have more than the plainest of styles and she'd managed to retrim this gown, at least, so that it didn't look too far from the norm.

But, besides the pedestrians, there were the shop windows to glance into! The hats, in particular, were almost impossible to pass by. She'd spent ten whole minutes staring at a golden straw with yellow roses when out the evening before with Mary, Aunt Fanny's maid, for chaperon. Someone would buy it soon, Damaris thought, and wished it might be herself, but she daren't say such things aloud or Tacye would dip freely into her savings to do so and it wasn't fair, thought the younger girl, that everything be spent on herself. Damaris sighed the softest of little sighs.

Luckily, they were soon away from such temptation and approaching their destination. They entered and, suddenly shy, Damaris feared to look around. She stood quite still, her hand on Tacye's crooked arm, her head bent as she studied her toes. Tacye didn't notice. She had never been shy in her life and had, from the moment they came through the door, studied the room with its tall windows overlooking the Roman baths and, more importantly, taken a quick glance around at the occupants.

"Aunt Fanny," she said after a moment, "there are several empty chairs to our left, if you'd prefer to be seated. Hmm." Her voice dropped to a murmur. "There is also an interesting looking gentleman raising his quizzing glass and . . . and how strange. He's studying *you*, Aunt Fanny, instead of Damaris!" How boorish, thought Tacye. "He's coming this way now. What do you want to do?"

"Fanny Tamswell!" said a pleasantly deep voice before they could do anything at all. "So, you've finally returned to civilization, have you?"

Tacye thought his voice expressed a great deal of satisfaction at that thought and wondered about it.

For a moment Fanny didn't respond, then, tentatively, she asked, "Lord Seward? Can it be?"

"At your service, my lady. Will you stroll with me?" he asked eagerly, adding, "I must hear what you've been doing while in your self-imposed exile. My dear, I would like nothing so well as to get to know you again."

"I am not alone, Lord Seward," said Fanny, blushing. "I wish to introduce to your notice my niece, Miss Damaris Adlington, and my nephew, Mr. Tobias Adlington."

Damaris peeked up at the tall, thin, slightly balding peer. She decided he didn't look too frightening and managed to answer politely when he asked how she liked Bath. Tacye was polite but taciturn in her turn and Lord Seward turned back to their aunt.

"Lady Tamswell? Fanny . . . ?" he asked, hopefully, "Will you take my arm for a stroll around the rooms?"

"My aunt expressed a preference for a seat among those chairs, my lord," Tacye interrupted in a soft voice, but with such firmness that she would not be gainsaid. "Aunt? Perhaps your friend would join us there?"

Lady Tamswell paused for a moment before saying, "Please, Lord Seward. I admit to a preference for stillness."

His brows arched in smooth dark curves upon the wide brow resulting from his slightly receding hairline. "You? I can't imagine you being still, my old friend. It was the one thing about visiting you and Gerard which

I always found so difficult. The two of you were *never* still!"

Fanny sighed. Softly. "You will find I've changed a great deal, my lord."

"Ah. I thought perhaps it was surprise the first time! But you used to call me John, did you not? I remember being made free of your name not long after your marriage . . . Fanny."

"It has been so very long . . . John." Fanny looked flustered. "I cannot believe you still remember."

"I remember everything."

Aunt Fanny looked alarmed and Tacye immediately intervened, pressing lightly on the trembling hand which was still tucked in Tacye's arm. "If you will only step this way, Aunt, you may rest yourself in those chairs. Yes. It is only a few feet, after all, and here we are. I will set this chair so the sun won't get in your eyes," she added, laying Fanny's hand on the back of the chair. She scrapped the chair around, gently rubbing the arm and front against her aunt.

Fanny reached for the arm and Tacye pushed the seat against her legs. Fanny sat. And heaved a sigh of relief.

Tacye noted that Lord Seward's brows were again arched. She caught his gaze and held it steadily. He quirked a look that asked a question. Tacye compressed her lips, nodded only the barest of nods. Seward's expression immediately turned to one of pity which Tacye knew would be the last thing her aunt would wish.

It was her turn to sigh—also in relief—when Seward merely shrugged and seated himself in a chair he pulled near.

"Now, my dear, I want a detailed report of all you've done in—dear me. Has it truly been so much as a decade?"

Fanny, relieved by the belief she'd not given herself

away, chuckled. "Fully ten. Who comes?" she asked, hearing footsteps.

"My friend, the Marquess of Worth," he said softly. "I can't recall if you ever met?"

"I believe he was with the army."

"So he was. Ah, Worth. Well met."

"Seward. Will you introduce me?"

"Of course. Join us, will you not?"

The introductions were made. Worth studied the closed emotionless face of the so-called Tobias. If it were Tacye, he decided, she would not be easily unmasked. And, if it were, it was as Terence had said: she made a very good boy. Assuming she *was* the boy! Finding the answer to this mystery might be more difficult that he'd expected.

Again Worth studied each member of the small family. Deciding the beauty was the weakest link, he turned to Fanny and asked, "May I take Miss Damaris for a stroll around the room? Perhaps we'll meet friends to whom I might introduce her."

Fanny gave her permission despite Tobias's cautioning hand on her shoulder and the pair strolled off, shy Damaris seemingly content to go. Tacye stood behind her aunt, but ignored the bantering conversation between Fanny and Lord Seward. She watched Worth talking to Damaris, watched Damaris come out of her shell of shyness and, strangest of all, watched her sister actually chuckle at something his lordship said! Tacye studied the medium tall man with the dark auburn hair and bright blue eyes. Would he find himself smitten with Damaris? Would he be the one to make an offer? Would her sister accept?

Tacye found she was frowning and immediately smoothed her expression. Why should she frown? Wasn't that exactly why they'd come to Bath? To find a suitor for Damaris? But, surely not one so *old*. The man must be in his thirties and surely far beyond finding a chit just out of the schoolroom a proper bride.

Tacye pulled herself up short. For all she knew Worth was married. She must discover whether he was eligible, if he were wealthy enough to support a wife and, if he were, whether he was a gamester, if he was the sort who was polite in public but a veritable monster in private. . . .

Tacye closed her eyes. When she'd blithely decided to come to Bath with her sister, the details and problems she'd face had not occurred to her. Suddenly it was startling clear to her the project of finding her sister a husband was a far more complicated business than she'd envisioned! Just how *did* one discover the information necessary to such a situation?

Across the room Worth glanced down at the beauty and then, ruefully, around at the Bath quizzes who were watching them and wondering behind their fans who the young woman might be—and more, of course, what she meant to him. Such gossip must be nipped in the bud and there, decided Worth, after another look around, was just the man to turn speculation from himself.

"Will you meet a friend of mine, Miss Damaris?"

"I would be pleased to meet anyone you call friend, my lord," she said without the least sign of coyness or flirtation.

Her composure pleased him. She would not embarrass him or herself, he decided and led Damaris to where the Earl of Cahill sat among aunts and cousins. He introduced her first to Cahill's eldest aunt, the formidable Lady Lawton. He was glad to find that Damaris could say all that was proper without blushing and that her curtsy was graceful and the right depth. In fact, she didn't blush until she faced the earl who had risen at their approach and then, again, her eyes dipped to look at her feet.

"James," said Worth, "you will be pleased to meet Miss Damaris Adlington. She is the younger sister of one of my best men in the Peninsula and is in Bath for her first foray into the far more difficult battle we call polite society."

Damaris glanced up at Worth, suppressed a quick chuckle and looked back at the floor.

"Miss Damaris, will you be pleased to greet one of my oldest friends? Lord James Ethan Cahill, Earl of Cahill?" asked Worth gently, encouraging her as well as he could.

"Very pleased," she murmured. She peeked at the earl and looked quickly away, her blush deepening.

Cahill had noted her appreciation of Worth's joke about society. He'd also noted her ease of manner when introduced to her ladyship and his other aunts. It did her no disservice in his eyes—or in his aunt's if truth be known—that she was shy when introduced to the male of the species. He took her hand and studied her features with more interest in a proper young lady than he'd felt for a long time.

"Are you staying long in Bath?" asked Lady Lawton who had noted the approving look her nephew gave the girl.

"We've taken rooms at the Abbey Arms," Damaris answered. "We are to stay for two months."

"Ah. Well, child, I'll send around an invitation to my next informal ball. I've dozens of young nieces and nephews, as you can see—" The crowd of young people around her chuckled or giggled. "—And their favorite entertainment seems to be a dance. We hold them often in the summer months. Those and pick-nicks and card parties and fetes and other entertainments of a like manner." Lady Lawton peered at Damaris, a sharp questioning look. "Will you be able to attend, my dear?"

"As my aunt permits, my lady, and I know of no reason why she would not."

"Ah." Lady Lawton relaxed—not that she'd believed Worth would introduce someone totally ineligible to her notice! "I wondered. You have an aunt for chaperon?"

The family situation was soon explained and when Worth took her off to continue their stroll, he was pleased he'd set the little Adlington's feet on the proper path. It was, he felt, the least he could do for Terry who had been a good friend as well as an outstanding officer.

Besides, as he was well aware, Lady Lawton wanted Cahill married. She would encourage any young woman who, even momentarily, took his eye and Miss Damaris had certainly done that!

"I didn't know you knew my brother, Terence," said Damaris when they'd moved away from the others.

"I was his senior officer, Miss Damaris."

"Then you were there when . . ." Tears welled in her eyes and she had to pause to bring her emotions back under control. "I'm sorry," she whispered when she'd blinked them back.

"It is not wrong to miss a beloved brother, Miss Damaris. From what I remember of his conversation, it is my belief his twin must miss him still more?" he asked in a kindly tone few of his acquaintances would have recognized.

Damaris glanced again at his face, but it was impassive and seemed to be asking no more than politely—so why did she think the answer important to him? "Tacye has not ceased to mourn deeply. I think it is impossible for her to stop. It is as if some essential part had been removed by the surgeons and she can no longer function as before." She raised her eyes and studied the man beside her, her mien serious. "Do you understand at all what I mean, my lord?"

"Oh yes," he said casually, and then added, "At least, if I do not exactly *understand*, I know to what you refer. There was a very special closeness between the two, was there not? I remember one time when Terry and I joined a chase—coursing hares was a popular winter sport in the Peninsula, my dear. Suddenly Terry pulled up his mount, practically fell from the saddle and sat on the damp ground cradling his leg as if it pained him dreadfully. When we talked about it later he was rather grim. He said your sister had broken her leg? It would have been the winter of 1811, if I remember correctly."

Damaris nodded, her eyes wide but staring rather blankly. "She slipped when helping my aunt from the carriage. . . . So what Tacye says is true?"

"I do not know what it is that Miss Adlington says."

"She knew exactly when Terence took the shot which killed him. She knew the instant he died—it was weeks before we had official confirmation. Was he shot in the bel—" She flushed crimson at the word she'd about let slip. ". . . Er, the, er, torso?"

"Somewhat below the ribs," said Worth, using as polite a form for gut-shot as he could manage. Worth, not wanting to think of the horror of that sort of wound, turned grim, stalking on silently until he realized this was hardly polite. He slowed his steps. "You must forgive me, Miss Damaris."

Damaris blinked. "You had returned in your mind to those years of battle, my lord. I do not take umbrage because you are deeply bothered by such thoughts and do not wish to play society's games. I am very sorry to have reminded you, but, on the other hand, I cannot help but wish to know what happened to my brother."

"He died very quickly and didn't suffer for very long," said Worth, not wishing to go into greater detail.

"I have one question and then we'll turn the conversation to happier topics, please. When your sister realized your brother had been hit, was it because she'd felt his pain as he had when she was hurt?"

"Oh yes. At the very least *something* rather terrible happened because she frightened Cook so badly that the poor woman came into the front of the house screaming for help and insisting that someone must ride immediately for a doctor. It would have been quite humorous if it hadn't seemed so serious. Of course Tacye pretty much immediately recovered herself and refused the doctor. At first she wouldn't tell us what had happened, but she went around in such a daze that Aunt Fanny insisted. When Tacye said Terence was dead, we didn't believe her. Or maybe we didn't wish to believe her?" Damaris looked up again at the man by whom she walked. "It is very strange," she added. "I don't know why, but I feel you understand."

He patted her hand absently. "Was there no one beyond your aunt to whom you could turn for help?"

"Oh no. It is quite ridiculous, but we seem to have no relatives at all. Single children married single children for several generations and, until our paternal grandfather, there was only one child in each generation. Absurd, is it not, that in a society where everyone appears to be related to everyone else—at least our aunt has told us it is so—that we should be so very much alone?"

"Perhaps when you marry, Miss Damaris, you should choose a man who has a very large family. You will acquire all those much-needed relatives at the time you wed."

She giggled softly. Smiling up at him, she said, "Perhaps I should. I will rely on you to tell me when a man has a suitably large family so that I may consider him carefully."

"Ah, then I should begin my duty," he said in a teasing voice, "by explaining to you that Cahill has far too many relations for him to know what to do with them all. He would, I think, happily allow his wife's family to adopt as many as they would wish for themselves. In fact, he would very likely encourage the exchange!"

She blushed again, but delightfully rather than painfully. "Lord Cahill is not married then?" she asked, shyly.

"No. He became earl unexpectedly something over a year ago. His uncle, the then earl, *his* heir, and the heir presumptive were killed in a fluke boating accident. A sudden squall no one could have predicted overturned their boat. Poor Cahill had settled quite happily into a country vicarage and expected to rise gradually in the church hierarchy—with the help of his extensive and influential family, of course. It has been difficult for him to take on the role and responsibilities of his new position."

"I'm sure it must have been, poor man. Why, he'd have had no training for it. Nor would he have been made known to the people who must now depend on him and that, too, must make his new position difficult. Oh, I do feel sorry for him!"

"Do not allow him to know that!" said Worth with a chuckle. "He detests pity and would not care to know that so beautiful a young lady was feeling it."

"Oh no," agreed Damaris, turning her head to look up at him from under the brim of her bonnet. "It never does to allow a gentleman to see that you feel sorry for him. I wonder why men must always reject compassion as a somehow weakening emotion. Can you tell me, my lord?"

Worth chuckled, finding this demure young miss far more interesting than most her age. Cahill, he thought, would be a lucky man if he were to win her! And then he wondered why he himself was not attracted in that way, but put the thought aside. The chit was, after all, very young—too young. "I will think about your question, Miss Damaris, and if I find an answer I'll explain it to you, but now I believe it time I return you to your aunt."

They crossed to the chairs which had become filled by various of Lord Seward's acquaintances. Worth greeted friends, was introduced to one woman he most particularly did *not* wish to know and then made his escape, but before he left he gave Tobias one more long and searching look. When Adlington noticed, Worth nodded curtly, and walked away immediately.

Tacye followed him with her eyes. She wondered about him, wondered about his feelings for Damaris and, with a trifling touch of bitterness, wondered why she was wondering! But it was strange behavior, was it not, his singling out Damaris to walk with while he ignored every other young woman in the room?

The gossip flying around the circle surrounding her aunt indicated how exceedingly unusual a thing it was for Worth to escort a very young woman anywhere and several sly voices, teasing Damaris, wondered if his lordship had been caught, at long last, by the Adlington girl's beauty—and perhaps, suggested Mr. Grenville Somerwell somewhat pompously, also by a feeling of responsibility toward her. Mr. Somerwell had done his best to look in any direction from that where, silently, Tacye still stood behind her aunt.

One woman, Mr. Grenville Somerwell's aunt, pooh-poohed the insinuation. "And why, you silly chump, would you suggest such a thing as that?" asked Lady Baggins-Keyton of her nephew, her unwillingness to accept a notion she'd not thought of first driving her to belligerence.

"He knew Miss Adlington's brother." For half an instant Grenville looked toward the silent Tacye but hurriedly away again "Well, come to that, so did I. So did lots of people."

"It is not unlikely that lots of people knew young Adlington. What is that to the point?" insisted his aunt, poking him with her umbrella.

"He was Terry's senior officer, that's what," said Grenville a trifle belligerently himself.

"Yes. That is true," Damaris inserted in her soft but clear and carrying voice. "I asked him to tell me of my brother's death. He was kind enough to do so, although I fear it upset him a great deal to remember how it had been."

Tacye felt a deep stabbing hurt at the mention of her twin's death. Would she never be allowed to forget? But, surely she didn't wish to forget? Of course she did not!

After a moment the speculation began again. Not only sly voices caught Tacye's attention, however, but also sly looks turned on the pouting young widow, Mrs. Diana Lovett, to whom the marquess had had to be introduced. From what was said, Tacye got the impression the widow had set her cap at Worth and the other members of the group would not be unhappy to see her fail.

From Tacye's viewpoint, the woman's obvious jealousy was merely one more difficulty of which she must be aware. The daggers-look cast Damaris's way would only be the beginning. If the woman was that determined to reach her goal, she'd not allow a mere girl to stand in her way! Mrs. Diana Lovett was possibly a power to be feared.

Tacye discovered she wasn't enjoying their first visit to the Pump Room half so well as she'd hoped to do!

The first invitation from Lady Lawton was not to a ball. In fact it was a note arriving only hours later suggesting the three newcomers join a pick-nick expedition to Cahill Manor, a minor holding of the Earl's a few miles north of Bath. The party had been arranged for the following day and Lady Lawton apologized for giving Lady Tamswell no more notice, but had just had the thought that Miss Damaris might enjoy meeting other young people in such an informal setting where it wasn't always necessary to mind one's tongue and speak only of those topics acceptable to a drawing room.

"A pick-nick? Oh dear," muttered Fanny, "if it were to turn into a romp it could instantly destroy Damaris's reputation. Before she'd ever had an opportunity to establish that she's a modest, well-behaved young lady. I wonder . . ."

"Wonder away, Aunt, while I write this acceptance to Lady Lawton for Damaris and myself." Tacye seated herself at the small ladies' desk in the corner. "I will deliver it and go on to find a conveyance I may rent. Even a gig will do, I suppose . . ."

"Usually the person doing the inviting expects to pick up the guest in her own carriage or to make other arrangements concerning transport," said Fanny absently, obviously worrying about something else.

"Much better. I've got a decent mount so I may join the cavalcade in an unexceptional manner."

"So you may. But what of myself? You know I'll not willingly put myself to the terror of managing over rough ground."

"I'll chaperon Damaris. You'll remember that I intended doing so all along?"

"But her first outing . . . I don't know, Toby. It would cause talk if I am not there."

"Listen to my note: *Dear Madam, My niece and nephew would be pleased to join your pick-nick outing assuming you are willing to help chaperon my niece. Much to my regret, I myself will be unable to partake of the treat due to a prior engagement.*

Your ladyship's obedient servant, and so on. Will that do?" asked Tacye.

"Hmm. It *is* rather short notice. . . ."

"So it's very likely you might have a prior engagement."

Fanny chuckled. "You're a menace, Tacye Adlington!"

A knock sounded at the outer door just then and a few minutes later Mary, Fanny's maid, announced Lord Seward. He barely allowed the door to close behind him before saying, "I'm a nuisance, am I not? But it occurred to me only after you left the Pump Room, Fanny, that I hope you'll join me in my carriage for a country ride. Tomorrow, I mean. Please Fanny? Don't say me nay automatically as I think you are about to do . . . oh, you there, my boy?" he asked, suddenly noticing Fanny wasn't alone in the sitting room. A spot of red appeared on each cheek. "And Miss Damaris . . ." He bowed.

Tacye affected not to notice his embarrassment. "I'm here, yes, and I think it a very good thing if my aunt were to accept your invitation. You know how much I dislike prevaricating, Aunt. Especially when there's no need," added Tacye in an aside.

"Prevaricating?" asked Seward, his ears more sensitive than Tacye expected.

"We received an invitation from Lady Lawton to join her pick-nick party tomorrow, but my aunt has no love of such outings. I have written a response in which I say that my si—er, cousin and I would enjoy it immensely, but that my aunt has a prior engagement. . . ." Tacye handed over the invitation and the note as casually as she might have done if Seward had been a friend of long standing rather than an acquaintance of mere hours. After she'd done so, she wondered at her trust in him. But then she noted the warmth with which he studied Fanny and decided that anyone who felt that deeply about their beloved aunt—and had done so for a full ten years—must be exceptional.

The notes were returned as silently as they'd been given over. "I see just how it is. Yes, Fanny, I agree with your nephew. You must accept my invitation or be made out a liar by Adlington's note."

"Surely if I remain here in our rooms no one would know. . . ."

Seward chuckled. "Don't ask me how it is, Fanny, but everyone knows everyone else's business in Bath. In fact, it often seems as if one's business is known before one knows it oneself! Let me give you an example. The newest word is that Worth will announce his engagement to young Miss Damaris before the week is out—"

Damaris blushed red, her brows closing together in irritation.

"—And all because he strolled around the Pump Room with her on his arm this morning. So, my dear, given how addicted to gossip the Bath quizzes are known to be, you must come, don't you see, or it will be all over Bath that you did *not.*"

"I come so that you may be the next source of gossip? Surely they will deem you, at your advanced age, to be more cautious. They'll surely think it'll take more than a week before you allow yourself to be caught in the parson's mousetrap!" teased Fanny and then blushed and tried to hide her hot cheeks behind her handkerchief.

Seward chuckled but his tone lacked any hint of an echo of her teasing note when he responded, "My dear, I've waited ten years. If you demand it of me, I suppose I may wait another week or two."

Fanny, startled, jerked back in her chair, her eyes showing the whites for a moment. She turned toward where Tacye had been standing, turned back and didn't know where to face to avoid the man who hinted at something she must deny, must avoid ever hearing again, must make him understand. . . .

"I believe you have shocked my aunt into speechlessness, Lord Seward," said Tacye smoothly. "Congratulations. It is not easy to accomplish that feat as I know to my sorrow."

"Are you suggesting I talk too much?" asked Fanny, her voice pitched a trifle too high due to her unsettled nerves. She twisted the handkerchief around her fingers.

"No such thing, dearest of my aunts; only that you always have a response no matter how deftly I try to achieve the last word. Aunt, I believe if you ask it of him, your friend will not repeat the error of his ways. I believe he is fearful you will send him away and deny him your company. In my opinion that would be unfair and, too, it would make you unhappy, would it not? It has been too long since you've had a friend who knew your life before you came to us? Perhaps if he were to promise to be only your friend . . . ?"

Seward scowled at Tacye. Tacye shook her head at him. His lordship's lips tightly compressed, he turned to stare at Fanny who had now wound the abused handkerchief into a tight twist from one end to the other as she thought what she should do.

"Fanny," said Seward softly when she didn't speak, "if I have unsettled you or made you unhappy, I apologize. I will willingly be your friend as I was in the past. I would support you and help you and make your visit to Bath as pleasant as may be possible. Do not send me away, my dear."

She stared at nothing at all. "I cannot allow you to say anything . . . suggestive . . . ever again."

"I will not suggest anything ever again," said Seward solemnly and was rather pleased at the instant but momentary scowl his words brought to his love's brow.

Obviously, even though she'd asked it of him, she was not totally pleased that he'd promptly agreed. Seward smiled to himself. He would not, when he next proposed, *suggest* they marry—a damn fool thing to have done so soon after meeting her again in any case. He would choose the next occasion carefully and make it next to impossible for Fanny to deny his *demand* that they be wed as soon as possible!

"Well, Aunt Fanny?" said Tacye artlessly. "That sounds a fair offer to me."

"Fair! T-*Toby* you know nothing about it—but you are correct that I cannot bring myself to send away a friend of such long standing." Fanny drew in a deep steadying breath. "And I will enjoy a ride in your carriage if you still wish it after I tell you that I am blind and can only embarrass you, over and over again, with my awkwardness."

There was a dare in her voice and Seward didn't hesitate. "I have watched you walk across the Pump Room. I have seen you glowing among a group of nattering women, none of whom would merit a man's attention for more than a moment. I have seen you leave the Pump Room with dignity and grace. When is it that I will find you embarrassing me or yourself?"

"I had Toby and Damaris by me. They've learned to cover my disability."

"You think too much of it, my dear. I assure you no one guessed."

Seward shook his head when Tacye raised her brows, reminding him he'd guessed. Actually, he'd not *guessed*. He'd already *known* and had only forgotten. After all, he was present the day his friend fell from a rock face and Fanny, who watched from a distant vantage point, had turned away covering her eyes, screaming that she hadn't seen that, that Gerry hadn't fallen, that it wasn't true. . . .

A short time later it was discovered she was blind. The doctors were baffled. Then an old wise woman, locally imputed with having witchy ways, had come to the house and insisted on examining her ladyship. She'd gone away muttering about how the mind played such silly tricks on itself and, when asked, had told of a woman who couldn't walk although no one could find a thing wrong with her legs and a man who had lost the use of his hands immediately after he realized he'd killed his best friend in a fight.

The old woman insisted there was nothing wrong with her ladyship's eyes. Her ladyship simply refused to see and if she ever desperately needed to see, if it were ever truly important enough, then she'd very likely allow herself to do so. But until then . . .

Before Seward could truly assimilate that information, let alone act on it in some way, Fanny disappeared from society, never to be heard of again. Lord Seward had gradually put his life together after losing not only his best friend but the woman he envied his friend for winning.

Now he had a second chance with her and nothing would be allowed to interfere this time in his pursuit of his one and only love. Not even Fanny herself would be allowed to refuse him, however much she wished to play the martyr—as she was very likely to do, given the situation.

No. Not this time . . .

Chapter 4

The day dawned beautifully clear much to everyone's delight. Damaris was helped into the Cahill carriage by Lord Cahill himself, an honor some felt was not the due of Miss Damaris Adlington, even if she were Bath's newest beauty. Nor, according to her immediate detractors, did she deserve the further honors of facing the horses *and* a seat beside Cahill's favorite cousin. But so it was and other young ladies who had angled for the position quietly gnashed their teeth at their failure.

Tacye, after seeing that Damaris was comfortable, moved to her gelding and crossed him so easily that Worth, who'd been watching, wondered if, after all, he was wrong in his belief that Tobias Adlington, unmasked, would prove to be the female twin, Tacye Adlington. He waited until the cavalcade had left Bath by the Lansdown road before he casually maneuvered into position beside his quarry at the end of the string of carriages.

"You hold yourself somewhat aloof, young man. Is it because you've not been introduced and don't yet know people?"

"I fear I am not a social creature, Lord Worth, and am content to stay to one side and observe. I've come to Bath for one purpose only and that is to see that

Damaris is known to have a male relative who can protect her. It is so easy, is it not, for a beauty to find herself in grave difficulty through no fault of her own? If it may be avoided, I'll not allow that to happen to my . . . sister."

"Her friends will help you," said Worth. "She'll not be allowed to fall into difficulties, although it is better that you are here as well, of course, to deal with the many requests which will be made for her hand." It immediately occurred to the marquess that Adlington might misinterpret that comment and consider it indicated an interest he himself did not have in the girl. "She is a delightful child, is she not?"

"Child, my lord?"

"Oh, definitely a child, I think," Worth reiterated and smiled to himself when tension in the youthful figure riding beside him seemed to ease. Wishing to test his theory concerning this member of the Adlington clan, he asked, "When you suggested you shunned society, does that include such occasions as the private races planned for later this week? They'll be held on this same estate to which we go today."

"Races?" Tacye, already sitting straight in her saddle, seemed to straighten still more. "I have heard nothing of any races, but then we may be said to have barely arrived, may we not?"

"I'd forgotten you've had no opportunity to learn about the occasion. That animal you ride looks a strengthy beast."

How far, Worth wondered, would Terence's sister go in her masquerade—assuming this was Tacye Adlington and not a suddenly acquired relative. A half-brother, perhaps, from the wrong side of the blanket? It was a possibility, of course.

"Do you challenge us?" Tacye gave a scornful eye to the easy gait of the lanky roan Worth rode.

Worth grinned. "Not with this creature. Poor Hyacinth was never my fastest mount, but she's got stamina and an easy gait and that, when one is on maneuvers, is far more important than speed. She's an old favorite," he added, "although I now save her for jaunts such as this. No, I was thinking of matching your black to my Jackass."

"Your . . ." Tacye sputtered with laughter. She turned twinkling eyes toward Worth and met the silent laughter revealed in his. "What a ridiculous name!"

"So I've been informed. More than once! What do you call that black?"

"Numbskull." Tacye grinned. "Jackass versus Numbskull. Now there is an *excellent* match, is there not? I think I must take your challenge for the simple pleasure of hearing the announcement!" Tacye heard her easy words and realized she'd been coaxed from her preferred role of observing others. She backtracked. "But will I not be thought a thruster if I am entered on such short notice?"

Worth's chin rose and his visage was one of stern reproach. "Since you'll have my patronage, you'll be accepted," he said in a particularly sweet tone but with a faint hint of arrogance that made the little half-smile so characteristic of Tacye appear at the corner of her mouth.

The half-smile had been equally characteristic of Terence and reminded Worth of him. "Adlington," he said abruptly, "I will say once how very sorry I was when Terence was lost at San Marcial. If you've questions or wish to talk about him, I'll be happy to do so. He was a friend as well as a damn good junior officer and I still miss him."

The half-smile deepened and, with difficulty, Tacye controlled a response which was confusing to her, containing as it did both a positive and negative emotion.

After a moment she turned to Worth and looked at him, curious. "You knew Terry well?" she asked cautiously.

"As well as anyone, I believe." Worth wondered what response that would bring and impatiently waited to see.

"Ahh." Again Tacye held silence for a long moment. "Then you are wondering at my existence, are you not?" she asked. "You *know* Damaris hadn't another brother. At least," she added on sudden inspiration, "not one acceptable in polite society?"

Again Worth wondered if he were wrong. Could any female—even the Tacye Adlington Terence had described—make such a statement without the least hint of a blush? "You mustn't be embarrassed by a rather irregular position—or at least, from what I know and what you've just said, I assume you have been . . ." Worth sought for words and ended, ". . . shall we say recently adopted as a full member of the family?"

"You would spread word of my birth?" asked Tacye, hiding a grin at the notion she'd be known to have been born on the wrong side of the blanket. Her father would have shouted with laughter at such a notion—and then punished her for suggesting such a thing!

"I see no reason to do so," said Worth, returning her attention to himself. "If your sister and aunt accept you, then society will do so on their behalf."

"I see."

"Do you?" He gave her a curious glance and wondered what it was she thought she saw.

"You will watch me and see that I keep to certain lines of behavior. Racing your Jackass is acceptable, but accepting the attentions of that little blonde in light blue who has been flirting with me off and on since we joined you at the Abbey Arms, would not do?"

A muscle clenched and then relaxed in Worth's jaw. He was wrong. He must be wrong. A female would never have noticed the blonde's behavior—or at least

would not have been attracted by it as Adlington
seemed to be.

"My lord?"

"I set no limits to your behavior. I said and I meant
that if you are acceptable to Lady Tamswell, then society can have no complaint."

"You surprise me."

"I have seen enough of you already to believe you
have the instincts of a gentleman—which is more than
can be said for some of those born to the role." Worth
nodded toward a dark-browed rather Byronic-looking
figure who rode far too close to the carriage in which
Damaris was seated. "Just a hint, Adlington. That *gentleman* is one of those who is *not.*"

"Not a gentleman? I thank you," said Tacye quietly.

She mulled over possible ways of indicating to the
gentleman that he was unwelcome to Damaris. As she
cogitated Cahill rode up and, insouciantly pulling rank,
took the man's place beside Damaris.

Worth chuckled. "For the moment I see no problem,
but you must tell your sister she's not to encourage
him."

"There is the smallest of problems with that advice,
my lord. Damaris never *encourages* anyone. She is polite
and friendly to all, but never anything more. Unfortunately, her reserve has never stopped a single male from
falling headlong into love with her and pestering the
daylights out of her. Even more unfortunate, she has not
learned the trick of turning a cold shoulder."

"More's the pity. The child should be taught discrim-
ination."

"So she should." Despite his comment he thought her
a child, Tacye wondered at Worth's true view of
Damaris. Twice now he'd made a comment which
could be seen as more than casual interest in a newly
met acquaintance. "Since the task of teaching it seems

beyond her aunt or myself, would you care to take it on?" she asked, wishing to test her suspicion.

Worth looked horrified and Tacye chuckled.

"You were bamming me, of course," he said. "I would very soon be bored to tears in Miss Damaris's company however nice a girl she is, and, very likely, I'd strangle the chit if she were to say *but Lucius,* even once in response to a suggestion refining on her behavior. I am not altogether a patient man, you see, and mere sweetness does not appeal," he finished softly, again casting a look to see how his new acquaintance would take his comment.

"Sweetly mawkish, you would say?" Although Tacye smiled, it was her turn to slant a curious look in Worth's direction, but she could see nothing to indicate those last words had been the warning she'd first thought them. And why should he give her warning in any case? He could not have penetrated her disguise, surely, or he'd not have asked her—a mere female—to race.

"Tell me about Jackass," she suggested, deciding a change of subject was in order. "I would have thought it an insult, calling a horse for a he-ass bred for hard work under difficult conditions."

"Jackass, I assure you, has worked exceedingly hard under very difficult conditions. He was my third and last horse at Waterloo, for instance, and saved my life at one point, standing over me and allowing no one near when I was creased and unconscious for a few moments. He will always have a home—even when he becomes too old to work at all. But he is no where near that age!" Worth tipped his head and studied the points of Tacye's horse. "I'll bet you he can beat that long-legged Numbskull of yours by a full length."

"Nonsense. Not only will your Jackass not win by a length, he'll not win at all." Was she, she wondered, being foolish? It was some time since she and Numbskull

last raced. In fact, not since ... since Terence's last
leave. Tacye stifled her fears. "You've not seen the turn
of speed of which my gelding is capable," she offered.

Worth felt sudden qualms. This was, possibly, a
young woman and not the young man she seemed. He
had no business urging such behavior. "The course is
rather rough with several tricky jumps. Perhaps you
should go over it before we decide anything?"

"I will certainly wish to go over the course, but I am
perfectly happy with your challenge."

"And what will you bet?"

"That I win? I am not a wealthy man, Worth. The
bet will have to be token and the race the thing."

"But if you are certain you'll win ..."

"There is always the possibility of a stumble, is there
not? Or that Numbskull shy at a blowing leaf. I'll not
risk much," said Tacye firmly.

"Very well." Worth, wondering about the Adlington
finances, suggested, "Shall we say a hundred pounds?"

Tacye drew in a deep breath. "I was thinking more
along the lines of ten, my lord."

"Not worth the work, is it?"

"You never race for the sheer joy of it?" Tacye patted
her black's neck. "Numbskull will be disappointed."

Worth laughed. He'd thought to give Tacye—if it
were Tacye—an easy win, giving her her winnings as
well, which he suspected would be welcome in a household with what he suspected was a limited budget, but
Tacye—at this instant, given her caution concerning the
bet, he was almost certain it was Tacye who had too
much pride for such a ruse. "Very well, bantam. I'll not
push you any harder. Ten pounds it is. Tell me," he
added, "about your aunt. I once knew a groom blinded
by a kick in the head. He had some of the same man-
nerisms as your aunt. Is she blind?"

Tacye's turned a quick probing look his way. "She is

and hates to have the fact known. I'm sorry you guessed."

"I don't think anyone else noticed. Except Seward. John knew her before?"

"He was Lord Tamswell's friend and appears to have carried a tendre for my aunt through the intervening years." Tacye grinned, her eyes flashing at the memory. "I think he's already flustered her a great deal by his attentions!"

"Seward has shown no interest in any eligible miss for as long as I've known him," mused Worth. "Of course I was out of the country much of the time, but his reputation is that of a misogynist."

"Then he doesn't frequent the muslin company either?" asked Tacye a trifle tentatively.

Worth felt his ears heat. It seemed he wasn't as easy with Miss Adlington's masquerade as he'd thought. At least . . . damn. Whenever he became certain he was a she, she would say something which led him back to wondering if he were a he after all. And given her—his—last comment, he was again of the opinion she was a he!

"My lord?"

"What?" Worth searched his mind and retrieved Tobias's last question. "Oh. I've heard no rumors indicating such tendencies."

"You find my query impertinent," said Tacye with a certain diffidence, "but it is difficult to know just how to find answers to such points. Since you offered the information that yon rake should not be encouraged and since I must have a care for both my sister and my aunt, I assumed you would not object if I elicited information which will help me determine those who are proper companions for them."

"I am sorry if you thought I'd pokered up at your question. It was another thought entirely that intruded.

I will gladly help you with such information as I may have or may discover for you at any future time you request it."

That, thought Tacye, was one of the more generous apologies she'd ever heard—especially when an apology was not really required.

"Now, about that race," added Worth, who hoped such questions *could* wait for a future time when he'd adjusted a trifle to his role as mentor in what was the oddest situation he'd ever thought to be in—assuming he was the she he sometimes thought her to be! Worth silently groaned at the thought of how tangled one could become when dealing with pronouns! "I will call for you early Thursday morning if that is all right? About ten?"

His words roused Tacye to a chuckle. "It is well you added that last. I must, I see, do something about my countrified expectations." She noticed that Worth's brows arched, queryingly. "You see, my lord, when you said early," explained Tacye in a gentle voice, "I assumed something closer to eight."

"My boy, it is well I'm a tolerant and understanding man," huffed Worth in mock outrage. "I suggest you not allow anyone else to hear you admit to such parochial notions. Eight o'clock indeed! Why, it's the middle of the night." Worth looked ahead and sighed. "I've enjoyed our talk, but it appears that we've arrived. Cahill asked that I oversee the disposition of carriages and horses while he took his aunt's guests in hand, so if you'll excuse me?"

Tacye nodded and Worth rode to the head of the cavalcade. Tacye rode forward until she was by the carriage in which her sister sat. She was still there when she noticed the strange young man she'd last seen in the Pump Room where he'd done his best not to recognize her existence. Now he stared at her—much as if she were a ghost. Tacye shrugged and turned back to watch her sister, but the thought of eliciting such a strange reaction bothered her and she turned toward the foppish stranger again before turning back to Damaris when her sister's delightful laugh floated into the air.

Mr. Grenville Somerville and several other young men had ridden out ahead of the rest of the party. Their aim was to look over the ground and, with luck, learn the trick of the maze so they might impress some young lady by their astuteness when the major portion of the guests arrived. Grenville had enjoyed himself, exploring the gardens and laying bets on some of the races which were to be run on Thursday.

Grenville also believed he'd discovered the trick of the maze, but was telling no one else, because he hoped to ask that little blond Cahill cousin to explore it with him, assuming he could find the courage and could manage to do so where she wouldn't embarrass him in front of others if she turned him down. She was a cute little thing and too young to be a danger to one's freedom. Very likely she'd not be officially out for at least another year and was only tolerated in the family parties that Lady Lawton loved to organize.

Therefore, in the midst of happily planning a mild round of pleasure, it was a great shock to Grenville to find the ghost was again following Miss Damaris's carriage. One thing had become clear, however. Now that Grenville knew who the girl was, it made sense that Adlington's shade hover around the little beauty. But why did the ghost look at him with such a fishy eye and why did he look from Miss Damaris to himself and back again?

Grenville shuddered and turned away. It was too much. His much anticipated outing, a day free of his aunt's over-bearing self, was ruined and it wasn't *fair*.

Why couldn't Terence Adlington stay in his grave like any decent ghost would do? And why did he chose to harass Grenville in this fashion—or was that explained by the simple fact that Grenville was one of the very few people who could actually see a ghost? It had, after all, been forcefully brought to his attention that most people could *not* when they'd laughed at him for telling tales of his sightings.

Grenville sighed. It was a talent he'd gladly give up in an instant if he could. But he couldn't. And, obviously, Adlington's ghost wished something, couldn't rest until it was accomplished—but what could it be? Not that Grenville really wanted to know, of course.

Grenville wandered off to the terrace where servants had set up a keg of ale as well as an urn of lemonade. He took a good quaff of the nutlike brew and sighed. It really *wasn't* fair of Terence to appear just when he been set for nothing more than a light-hearted day in the sun. Now he must spend the whole of it avoiding Terry's ghost.

Grenville wasn't about to complicate his life by getting himself involved in solving Terence's problem—whatever it might be! No. Never. He wouldn't do it. Grenville sought another ale and gulped it down. Carrying a third, he wandered off feeling exceedingly put upon.

Tacye saw her sister go off in the midst of a group of young women, laughing and giggling and very obviously enjoying herself a great deal. As usual, girls who began with jealousy of Damaris's beauty soon succumbed to her very real charm and equally unfeigned interest in others. The younger Adlington would be safe enough among so many.

So, seeing all was well, Tacye turned her mount to

the side and followed a gig to where vehicles were being parked and horses taken off by competent looking grooms. She followed along, satisfied herself that Cahill's arrangements for the care of the horses were all they should be, and wandered on still further, wishing to explore on her own.

Tacye had told his lordship she was not a social creature. That was true even when she could play her normal feminine role so that now she was quite content, strolling along through a heavily wooded area leading away from the house. She poked gently into Cahill's coveys which were well populated with young birds and sighted a fox's brush disappearing into a tangle of brush. At one point she nodded greetings to a surprised looking keeper.

Eventually, her stomach giving her her marching orders, Tacye returned to where the main party had gathered on the terrace to partake of Lady Lawton's version of a pick-nick. This included long buffets loaded with food which was served to one by uniformed servants. One pointed to what one wanted and healthy servings were added to what was soon an overflowing plate. This the servant then carried to one of the myriad of small tables dotted around the terrace and the guest was carefully seated before the servant returned to a place behind the serving table where he would aid another guest.

Tacye, not wishing to join a group of people she didn't know, didn't follow convention as written by Lady Lawton. Instead, she took her plate from the servant and moved to where a low wall separated the slate-paved terrace from a much larger, if slightly overgrown, rose garden. She was joined there by Worth much to her surprise.

"I'd thought you a sort of unofficial host along with Lord Cahill," she said.

"I've done my duty by at least a dozen schoolroom misses and I will not put myself out again until it is time to see them all into carriages. Enough, Adlington, is quite enough and friends should ask no more of one!" Worth ended on a faint note of humor. "Where did you disappear to? Ah ha! You are faintly flushed. A touch of the sun? I see how it was," he teased. "You couldn't face the social melee and bolted!"

Tacye's sun-touched face took a darker hue and she explained, "I enjoy country living, my lord, and merely spent a quiet hour or so wandering." In an attempt to once again turn the subject from herself, something Worth often made a trifle difficult, Tacye said, "Lord Cahill has surprisingly large coverts, does he not?"

"The late Lord Cahill liked a good shoot come fall. He was very particular about his birds and I'm amazed you got close enough to check them over. The preceding lord's gamekeepers were trained to be very protective and the young birds are not allowed to be stirred up and I thought Cahill had kept them on."

"I'm sorry if I trespassed. However, I saw only one dour old man. Came on him rather suddenly, actually, and I guess he did seem a trifle startled by my appearance, but then he nodded and didn't move so I supposed I was free to go where I liked."

"Bald, with his skull brown and spotted?" asked Worth sharply. Tacye nodded. "You have been honored, my boy! Old Stemper is very careful indeed whom he lets near his birds from early spring on into late fall!" Worth looked around, saw his friend and motioned him over.

He told the tale of Tacye's invasion of Stemper's domain and Cahill, who had not really noticed Miss Damaris's brother gave him a thorough look. "Stemper let you have your head, did he? Amazing. You actually got within a few yards of him before he noticed you?" Cahill's eyes widened. "Truly amazing. Worth? Wouldn't you agree? Stemper is very proud of his woodsmanship. And you are whom, my boy?" he asked, realizing they had not actually been formally introduced.

Worth shook his head. "How rude of me." He made the introduction and then added that he'd laid another challenge for the races Thursday. His Jackass again Adlington's Numbskull. "It will have to be worked into the schedule," he added.

"If there is a difficulty we may have our race another time over another course," suggested Tacye.

"Quiet, bantam. The more races the happier the Oxford and Cambridge crowd will be. They have a great deal of excess energy at that age and must rid themselves of it somehow. A long day's racing is just the thing to settle them down for another week or so."

Cahill looked vaguely shocked. "Worth, you forget," he said in a low voice. "Adlington must be very much that age himself and you insult him when you insult the others!"

"One matures more quickly in my situation, Lord Cahill," said Tacye quietly, not pretending deafness. And, she thought, let him read into that whatever he wishes.

Cahill reacted only by giving her a sharp look and then said, "Ah yes. Responsibility for one's womenfolk does age one, does it not?" He looked around. "And speaking of your womenfolk, there is that unspeakable Questerman making up to your sister again. Excuse me." Cahill stalked off with no more than that terse excuse for a goodbye.

"Perhaps I should go, too," said Tacye.

"Let Cahill handle it. As host, he would do the same for any young woman so you needn't worry it will lead to gossip." Worth frowned. "Actually, I wonder who had the nerve to invite Sir Davey. Lady Lawton must have had the vapors when she learned a guest of hers had the bad judgment to include him in their party."

"He has that rather arrogant look to him that suggests he might not have waited to be included in someone's party," suggested Tacye, eyeing the quiet confrontation between guest and host.

"Then how . . . ?"

"You are not truly so naive, my lord."

Worth raised a questioning brow.

"It is very simple, is it not, my lord?" asked Tacye kindly. "He very well may have invited himself."

Worth glanced to where the rake had moved when he'd been routed by Cahill from the group surrounding Damaris. The man wore a scowl which boded ill for someone. Worth vowed to keep an eye on the man.

Cahill had the experience and courage to handle the cully. Young Adlington might very well have the courage, but he—or she as the case very well might be— couldn't possibly have the experience and if, by chance, Adlington turned out to be the she he rather believed her to be, rather than the he she pretended to be—in his mind Worth paused at that point and again attempted to become clear on all those hes and shes but decided it wasn't worth the effort. What was important was that Sir Davey Questerman *not* be allowed to carry things too far.

Worth had no wish to think of exactly what he might mean by that last ambiguous phrase, but there was that vague but persistent rumor that Questerman had not acted quite honorably in a duel some years previously. . . .

At about the time Lord Worth decided it was necessary to keep an eye on Sir Davey, Lord Seward arrived at the Abbey Arms in his sister's phaeton. After giving careful thought to the problem, he'd decided the lady's phaeton's low lines would make it easier for Fanny to enter and leave it gracefully. Nor was it one of the truly light phaetons which had practically no body work. She should, he believed, feel secure with the woven side and back enclosing her. He threw a coin to a loitering boy to watch his pair and took the stairs up to the Adlingtons' rooms with a lightness of foot of a boy half his age.

He was admitted by a curious Mary who studied him closely—this man who was showing interest in Lady Fanny. After all, Lady Fanny, although the kindest of mistresses, was blind. It seemed strange to the girl that any man would show interest in a blind woman and she wished to find out what sort of creature would do so.

"Ready, Fanny?" he asked.

"No." Fanny grimaced. She settled more deeply into her chair. "No and I never will be." She cast a look in his general direction and asked, hopefully, "Perhaps I should remain here after all?"

"I don't think that very polite when I've gone to much trouble to see to your comfort."

Fanny was silent for a long moment. "One would not care to be considered rag-mannered, so I suppose I may as well make the attempt, had I not?"

"Yes. Please do," he coaxed. He paused. "For me, Fanny?"

His voice was much nearer on the last words and, startled, Fanny looked up, moving her face a trifle from side to side, searching for his presence. "John?"

He touched her shoulder lightly. "I'm here. You must teach me how to help you, Fanny."

She was silent for half a moment and then sighed in resignation. "If you will hold your arm where I may reach it." She scrabbled for a moment at air, but soon had her hand tightly around his wrist and then rose to her feet. "Now turn us to face the door." He complied and Fanny told him how to cue her as to what to expect. When they exited the building Fanny raised her face to feel the sun on her skin. Then she sighed and raised her parasol.

"I don't care if you get a little brown. I well remember how you loved the sun," teased Seward. "In fact, I too like to feel the heat or a gentle breeze against my face."

"But any of the old tabbies who saw me allowing the sun on my skin would natter the news all over town about how uncivilized the Adlingtons' aunt has been discovered to be. It wouldn't do, John."

"No. I don't suppose it would," he said gently. "I'm driving a low-built phaeton today. You should find no difficulty getting in or out of it. This way, my dear?"

He soon had her seated and went around to take the reins. Happy to have Fanny to himself for awhile, he drove as rapidly as he could along Great Pultenay Street, around Sidney Place and on out into the country. Very soon they trotted along the macadamized London road.

"This is a comfortable carriage, John."

"Do you like it?"

"I'll admit that too often in an open carriage I fear I might fall out. This is different in that I know it is low to the ground and I like that. I wonder if it is because I fear heights so much that I feel fear in a perch phaeton or even sometimes in a landau—although they are more substantially built and I don't often have the feeling that they will fall over."

"Do you dislike heights?" asked John, curious. "You didn't used to."

Fanny bit her lip. "It came upon me rather suddenly," she explained, a typically dry note to her tone.

"Ah. Very suddenly, I suspect. Does it still hurt so

much?" He asked the important question as casually as he could. When she didn't answer, he added, "Losing Gerard, I mean?"

"I still miss him occasionally," said Fanny slowly. "Something will happen and I'll think of how funny Gerard would find it or I will wish to ask his advice. The pain was terrible when I first went to live with my family, but it comes only rarely now."

"I wonder if you would have ceased mourning sooner if you hadn't shut all your friends from your life," mused Seward.

Fanny remembered she'd made a somewhat similar comment to Tacye recently and blushed. "Are you scolding me?"

"Perhaps." He thought about it. "Yes, I think I am. A bit. Do you have any notion how terrible it all was for me?" He glanced at his passenger. "Fanny, not only did I lose my best friend, but I lost my second-best friend as well."

"You did?" Fanny straightened in her seat. "Did someone else die that day and I not know it?"

"She might as well have died," said Seward. "She was gone from my ken as thoroughly as if she had."

Fanny was silent for a moment. "John, you promised?"

"I cannot tell you that I missed you? That it was as if I were in mourning for both you and Gerard?"

"You wish me to feel guilty," she accused.

He chuckled. "I suppose I do. I need a bit of revenge, do I not?"

"I couldn't cope," she said after a moment.

"Cope?"

"With Gerard's death, my blind eyes, everything . . ."

"After you vanished, Fanny, I wondered if you even allowed yourself to hear Gerard's will."

"Yes—I must have, I think." She wore a confused

look. "At least, I receive my little widow's portion each quarter and I would not if I had not told the solicitor where to send it . . ."

"Little . . . ?"

Startled, John frowned deeply, remembering the large and prosperous and unentailed estate in the Lake region where Fanny and Gerard had lived very nearly year round. Something was very wrong if Fanny wasn't receiving a more than adequate income from what was, if he'd not misunderstood something Gerard once said, hers for life.

"My needs are very reasonable, John. I am comfortable living with my nieces. We understand each other. I'm useful since they must have a chaperon and I fear they are not *quite* as other girls in such needs. Or at least my elder niece is not."

"Is she not in Bath?"

Fanny blenched. She'd rambled unthinkingly because her mind was again ruffled by Seward's hints as to the importance of her place in his life, but recovered almost immediately. "Tacye had no desire to do the pretty, as she calls it. She decided to visit her old tutor while I—and Toby—brought Damaris to Bath where, we hope, she'll make a reasonably good marriage."

"Ah, that explains the oddity you mentioned, does it not?"

"What does?" asked Fanny, wondering what she'd said now.

"Why, the fact that your niece had a tutor rather than a governess. I've met some progressive families in which that is the case and always there is that trifle of difference between girls raised with a tutor or a bluestocking instructress and those raised with a governess. Tell me about young Adlington?"

Fanny didn't know what to say. Would John remember anything of Fanny's brother's family. "The girls' half-brother . . ." she began, a sudden inspiration striking. She told herself she must not forget to have a word with Toby as to his new status—and thought the notion Toby was a bastard might be very good revenge on her niece who had, recently, put Fanny into several very difficult positions! Such as this ride . . .

Seward considered her long pause. "I see," he said. "I'm sorry to have embarrassed you."

"It isn't that. I call him my nephew, of course, which he is. No one need be informed he and Damaris have different mothers, I think. Toby is well educated and, generally, perfectly acceptable . . ."

"Of course. You mustn't worry, Fanny. No one else will be so rude as to ask about him. Don't let it concern you. It is far better that you have a man with you because there are a few gentlemen in Bath just now who will be drawn by Miss Damaris's looks but, thanks to her small dowry, will have something other than marriage in mind—if you know what I mean?" He paused long enough to note her worried expression. "I will give you a hint if I think someone who shouldn't is paying her too much attention."

"Thank you. Although I'm not certain that even then I'll know how to handle the situation."

"Have you not taught Miss Damaris how to depress the pretensions of the wrong sort of man?"

"I don't think *I* know how to do so."

I certainly, she thought, have not succeeded in depressing yours! Oh, John, if only I were not blind, if only I could respond as other women do, if only . . . oh if only!

The drive continued with Seward entertaining Fanny with verbal sketches of some of the Bath quizzes whom she would meet, making a game of passing on needful information in a humorous form. She was laughing gaily when they pulled up again in front of the Abbey Arms just as the bells in the Bath Abbey rang out. The clamor startled Seward's near horse. The animal hunched back on his haunches, surged forward and, when not allowed his head, rose to paw the air with his front feet, drawing his mate up with him. Fanny, not anticipating the problem and having no visual warning, screamed.

Seward, his attention required to sooth his nervous beasts, managed to put out one arm and settle her until she had good hold on the side. Then she was on her own until the bells stopped ringing and the horses, now sweating freely from their fright, calmed.

"Fanny, are you all right?" Once he was certain his pair would not, again, react in such a potentially dangerous way, he turned to his guest, his concern clear in his voice.

"I'll be fine in a moment," she said, but was very pale. She drew in a deep calming breath and went on rather ruefully. "Being unable to see—it is *such* a nuisance!"

"Yes."

Seward remembered the old witches words: *If she needs to see she'll see again.* But it hadn't worked in this potentially dangerous situation. What would it take? What sort of danger or need. . . . Holding Fanny's hand in his, he eyed his love . . . and plotted plots. Dared he . . . ? But no. Surely such a notion would be far *too* dangerous. But somehow . . .

"I think I'd better go in, John. Damaris and T-Toby will be home soon. I'd like to change before they come."

"I was rather hoping for an invitation . . . ," he began, coaxingly.

Fanny chuckled, her color almost back to normal and he relaxed that she seemed to be over the fright so obvious only minutes earlier. "I wouldn't dare invite you in for refreshment," she said. "We brought Cook from home and she is still muttering about how impossible it is to cook in such quarters as are available. Breakfast was edible this morning, just, so I believe she *will* conquer the difficulty, but until she is comfortable I daren't suggest we have a guest, even one so easily pleased as I remember you to be!"

"Then I won't press you. I know how difficult and temperamental a good cook can be and we mustn't make her more prickly than she is! You'll invite me in the future, however, when you become certain it will no longer upset your cook's sensibilities?"

"I'll be happy to do so." Fanny smiled.

Seward's grip tightened very slightly on her hand until he noticed that the smile faded as he did so. He sighed silently and told her to wait while he came around to help her down. He didn't try to explain to her where the narrow step was placed but grasped her waist and swung her to the paving, her hands going automatically to his shoulders.

"My arm, Fanny?" She found it and he led her dexterously into the house and up the stairs. Standing in the hall before her door, he asked, "You'll come to the Pump Room tomorrow?"

"We plan to be there."

"I'll see you then." He raised her hand to his lips, aborted a move to turn it so he could kiss the inside of her bare wrist, and lightly kissed her glove covered knuckles instead. "I enjoyed our drive, Fanny." She didn't respond. "We should make a habit of it, I think," he coaxed.

"Not too often," she said. Once again flustered by his behavior and her reaction to it, Fanny sought an excuse so that she'd not be able to see too much of him. At least, not alone as they'd been today. "I . . . I must not desert Damaris." She bit her lip. "My niece is my responsibility while we're in Bath and an important one. . . ." She stopped, aware she'd begun to say too much, nattering again, to cover her embarrassment.

"Hmm. We'll see. I believe, once Miss Damaris is known to her, you may rely on Lady Lawton to take her about and see to her comfort. Your niece will be safe under her ladyship's eagle eye."

"Very likely safer than under my not so eagle eye," said Fanny, a tiny smile hovering around the corners of her mouth.

"There is that," agreed Seward just as lightly without embarrassment or causing her embarrassment—something Fanny only realized later when thinking over their day. "Very well," added his lordship. "I'll try to restrain my impatience. We'll not make plans for the future, but take each day as it comes, then?"

"Yes. John . . ."

"Shh, love. I'll try not to push you, but you must remember that for many years I thought I'd never see you again." He chuckled. "Meeting you here in Bath has gone to my head like old wine and I cannot be calm and collected and simply take your arrival in stride. Not when I feel the veriest boy again."

Fanny bit her lip. "But you promised . . ."

"Friends. We can be friends, Fanny. At least that."

"I would like that," she said, blushing. "But you must understand that it can only be that."

"Because you are blind?" She nodded. "Funny Fanny," he said, a caressing note in his voice. "As if that made the least difference. Goodbye for now, my dear. We'll meet in the Pump Room," he said as he ran down the stairs.

After waiting for the door to close at the bottom, Fanny knocked on the door which opened promptly, her maid obviously waiting on the other side for just that signal, but Fanny stood there a moment longer, staring blindly in the direction John had gone. It made no difference? What could he mean? How could her blindness possibly not make all the difference in the world?

When the maid touched her arm, Fanny jumped, startled. "Sorry, my lady," said Mary.

"Hmm? That's all right—Mary! I wish to go to my room," said Fanny in the abrupt tone which meant she'd become disoriented and needed someone to show her the way. . . .

Chapter 5

The next morning, just after seating Aunt Fanny in the Pump Room with friends, the first person Tacye Adlington saw was Hereward Lambourn. She immediately turned her back and bent to speak to Damaris. "Maybe I should disappear," she said. "The Lambourn boys have followed you here. One of them might be smart enough to recognize me. What do you think?"

Damaris cast a curious glance across the room. "No, do not leave me. Please. We'll just explain you to them as we've been explaining you to everyone else, will we not?"

Curious, Tacye asked, "Just what have you told people?"

"Hmm? Oh." Damaris drew her sister down so that she could whisper in her ear. "Only that you're a very distant cousin, of course. I couldn't think of anything else. A long-lost cousin, of course."

"So lost no one ever heard of my existence until I showed up just now, hmm?"

"Why not?"

"Damaris, Damaris, you are such an innocent. No one will believe such a tale. My story is better." Tacye grinned the wicked grin which made her look exactly like her brother in mischief. "It's obvious I'm a half-brother who, because Terence——" Her jaw clenched for a moment, then relaxed. "—Is gone, you have need of. I've been adopted into the family."

For a moment Damaris didn't understand. When she did, a look of horror crossed the younger girl's face.

"I'm assured," soothed Tacye, the wicked glint still in ascendancy, "that if you and Aunt Fanny accept me, then society will not turn aside from me."

Damaris's horror faded quickly, but a trifle of disgust did not. "You always make up the worst possible tale," she sniped softly. "*I* will continue calling you cousin."

"Actually," said Tacye, thoughtfully, "that might not be a bad idea. It is likely that's what you would have been told. After all, one doesn't discuss bastard siblings with innocents barely of marriageable age, does one? Devil take it, here comes Hereward," added Tacye.

A big, rather bulky young man at just that awkward age where he easily embarrasses everyone, including himself, rushed forward and thrust a rather large bouquet at Damaris, then turned beet red and pulled it back when he realized she carried her parasol in one hand and a small book in the other and had no way of taking it from him. " 'ello Damaris," he whispered and blushed a still more fiery red.

His brother arrived just then from another direction. Herbert was a year older and, although he looked very nearly a twin to Hereward, he'd lost some of the adolescent gawkiness which marked his brother. "Morning Lady Tamswell," he said, bowing toward Fanny. He turned immediately to Damaris. "Walk with me, Miss Damaris?"

Hereward's huge hand tightened around the bouquet, strangling it. "Here now, Herbie, I was about to ask her that."

"But you didn't, did you?"

"Well, I thought," he hissed, "we was to do the pretty

for a bit before I stepped right in with a request like that. That's what you told me, you . . ."

"Shush!" squeaked Damaris, horrified by what she knew would follow. She hid her face with her quickly opened book because she also knew her warning would do no good.

". . . Bastard," whispered Hereward in what he thought a quiet voice.

"Call me names, will you? I'll . . ."

"Hush, the both of you!" scolded Fanny from her seat a few feet away. Her voice was cold when she added, "Herbert. Hereward. You were born gentlemen. See if, for once, you can act the part!"

Hereward's blush looked to become a permanent part of his complexion. He glanced around and saw that others were staring in a disapproving way. "Sorry," he muttered and hung his head. The bouquet began to disintegrate under what had become a nervous, twisting, two-handed grip. A rose and then a daisy drifted to the floor.

"Apologies, Lady Tamswell," said Herbert, moderating his tone. "And to everyone else." He made a creditable bow.

"I believe you boys should depart," Fanny continued, "and perhaps, by tomorrow, the good people of Bath will contrive to forget this contretemps. Then, if you can manage to behave yourselves, I will introduce you to a few people."

Hereward looked startled. "Leave? But I haven't walked with Miss Damaris."

"Nor have I, blockhead," hissed his older brother, "but we better do as she says if we don't want to find ourselves quite out of things. Have to have introductions, you fool," he added when Hereward would have balked. He reached out and pulled one bloom, a just opening rosebud, from the bouquet Hereward had nearly ruined. He handed it to Damaris with another and more graceful bow.

Damaris managed to accept the single stem in the hand holding her book and then didn't know what to do with it. Especially when Herbert gave his brother a superior grin which had Hereward gritting his teeth. Inspired, by desperation, Damaris stepped to where her aunt sat. "Aunt Fanny, the boys want you to have this rosebud." Fanny held up her hand and Damaris managed to slip the bloom into it.

"Thank you. Now you'd best go and give people time to forget today's unacceptable behavior. Remember, boys, it *will not do*. I have no authority to send you home, but I can and will forbid you Damaris's society if you cannot behave like civilized creatures."

"Yes, Lady Tamswell," said Herbert with only the faintest hint of a sneer. "I'll see Hereward toes the line."

"Hereward will have far less difficulty doing so if you cease to bait him. I will ban *both* of you if *either* of you misbehaves. Do not think you can trick your brother into a state of Coventry." When inarticulate noises indicated the boys would like to object, she continued. "Hear me, Herbert! I will consider you still more at fault in such circumstances because, as the elder, you are responsible—and I don't *merely* mean that you will, with malice, have tricked Hereward into a *faux pas*. Do you understand?" she finished on a stern note.

Fanny couldn't see him, but she guessed her words brought a scowl to the heavy features of the older and more astute of the brothers. Tacye, who had managed to remain in the background, but with a good view of the scene, made a mental note to describe how right on the nail her aunt's assessment had been—assuming Herbert's expression meant what she assumed it meant. She must remember to congratulate Fanny on her wit.

"Who," asked an already well-known voice over her

shoulder, "are those louts?" Worth stepped to Tacye's side.

"Unfortunately we must call them neighbors. They are Baron Lambourn's eldest sons. Poor Hereward has been competing with his brother ever since he managed to learn to walk and I don't think he's won a single round in all the years they've been sniping at each other. They fight constantly. At the moment they mostly fight over Damaris."

"And Damaris? She is amused by this?"

"She finds it most embarrassing when strangers observe the boys, but we are so used to their quarreling that that, in itself, is simply more of the same."

"Something must be done to make that chit understand it is essential she turn off unacceptable suitors! Those *boys* are fast becoming men. In fact I had *boys* younger than they come out to the Peninsula as responsible officers. Those two idiots obviously have no self control whatsoever and very little knowledge of proper behavior. They could easily get themselves and everyone else into serious difficulties over a girl they both wish to court. You know, Adlington, when she'll have neither in the end, it would be much kinder to make that known now."

"But she can't very well tell them she'll marry neither when she hasn't been asked."

"Surely you are aware it is possible to hint them away in ways other than words."

Tacye turned disbelieving eyes toward Worth. "With someone like the Lambourns? Nonsense. Oafs of that order don't take hints! They don't recognize them."

"A problem, that," he admitted with a grin.

Tacye met his eyes and grinned in return, but shook her head along with it. "Aunt Fanny discourages them as much as she can," she explained, "but it isn't wise to insult the Baron who has a temper which makes the boys' squabbles look like the playful attacks of one kitten on another. Since one never knows when Lambourn will take exception to something said to or about his sons, one puts up with them."

"You've known them from a young age. You do not see them as a stranger does. They are no longer kittens, Adlington, and they may be dangerous—to each other, of course, but also there is the possibility they may be a danger to Miss Damaris."

Tacye absorbed Worth's warning and nodded. "You mean that, if desperate, they might think to forcibly elope with Dammy. I'll tell Aunt Fanny what you've said. Thank you."

"It might be still more proper to tell Miss Damaris," said Worth on a dry note.

Tacye grinned. "She would look at me with big bemused eyes and ask if I'd been drinking." Tacye allowed a slight falsetto into her tone: " 'Why,' she'd say, 'the boys are just great big unruly puppy dogs and not to be taken seriously.' "

Worth grimaced and shook his head. "My boy, I suggest you attempt to convince your sister that they've grown far beyond puppy-dom and must be taken very seriously indeed."

Again Tacye fell silent. "It's a problem, is it not? I think you wish her to turn a cold shoulder their way. Say she does. How will such as they react?"

It was Worth's turn to remain silent for a thoughtful moment. "You fear it would goad them into the sort of behavior I predict they'll soon enough think up on their own?"

"Was I right, then, in what you predict?"

"If forcible abduction occurred to you, then yes."

Tacye, who had made the suggestion rather tongue-in-cheek, blanched at his biting tone. "Please. Do not suggest anything of the sort!"

"I've met young men of their character before. Take them seriously, Adlington—if you love your sister at all," warned Worth.

"I will," said Tacye with suppressed fervency—and wondered why she'd ever thought it an excellent notion to bring her sister to Bath!

Worth studied his new young friend. Although he'd wished to impress him—or her as the case might be—with the seriousness of his suspicion, he had no wish to upset her—him?—as deeply as he obviously had. In a lighter tone, he asked, "Now, shall we see who is newly arrived in town?" They promenaded.

Lord Cahill arrived with his family, Lady Lawton surging into the lead when she saw Damaris seated near a quiet-looking woman who must be the girl's chaperon. Lady Lawton was determined to discover as much as she could of the Adlington chit. Cahill had spoken of the girl *three* times the preceding evening, revealing more interest than he'd shown in an eligible for months. Lady Lawton had had some difficulty believing her ears. But, if Cahill continued interested, and assuming the girl were at all acceptable, the match must be promoted.

Lady Lawton hoped Miss Damaris would not be found wanting: Cahill must produce heirs and as quickly as possible. Her ladyship had been deeply shocked by the multiple deaths which led to Cahill inheriting. Too many had succumbed in a single accident to allow for mistakes now. A mistake which would lead to a mere third cousin inheriting which was far worse than Cahill who was, at least, the son of her younger brother and a first cousin to the previous heir.

"Good morning, Miss Damaris," said Lady Lawton, putting aside thoughts of the succession.

Her ladyship stood stolidly, eyeing a gentleman seated between the girl and the aunt. Suddenly realizing he was expected to offer his seat, Sir Davey Questerman did so, but with exceedingly bad grace. He took one glance at Lord Cahill who eyed him with a different but equally intimidating look and made his adieux. His spine rigid with perceived insult, Sir Davey walked from the Rooms.

Worth, watching the interlude from across the way, pointed it out to Tacye. "That fine gentleman, my young friend, may very well be a second and equally probable source of difficulty."

"Is there no end to it?" muttered Tacye.

"All will be well once she weds." Tacye gave him a speaking look and Worth grinned. "Don't concern yourself about that. She'll wed soon and I believe she'll wed well."

"I hope that is a true forecast, my lord, or I'll turn gray and become a palsied old man before my time."

Or perhaps, thought Worth, before it's even possible? Old man indeed. But then he paused. She—*he* had made that comment so casually it was difficult to believe it was not made by a male. And yet . . .

Inwardly, Worth sighed. *Was this or was it not Tacye Adlington!*

With Questerman gone, Lady Lawton seated herself. "Now that impossible creature has taken himself off," she said complacently, "you may introduce me to your aunt, Miss Damaris." Damaris did so with her usual quiet grace. "Very good. Now, Cahill, why don't you take Miss Damaris for a stroll around the rooms while I become acquainted with Lady Tamswell." She obviously felt she'd settled things for her nephew and the blushing Damaris because she nodded them off and immediately turned to her quarry. "I seem to recall a Tamswell who died in a climbing accident. Would that . . . ?"

Damaris was already too far from her aunt to help her. She felt sorry for Fanny, but how could she stay to protect her aunt when she'd so obviously been gotten out of the way.

"You are very silent," said Cahill.

Damaris didn't respond, her mind still worrying whether she could do something for her aunt.

"Are you wishing me to the devil and my aunt somewhere still hotter—if that is possible?" teased his lordship.

Damaris glanced up and smiled. "It isn't that, my lord. I am quite comfortable with your escort. I only worry that Aunt Fanny may find questions concerning her marriage upsetting. She has never quite recovered, I think, although it is all of ten years now."

Cahill smiled a reassuring smile. "My aunt," he said, "is blunt and a trifle overbearing, but she is not unkind and never completely insensitive. If she sees that your aunt is agitated, she'll turn her questions in another direction. You note, of course, that I did *not* say she'd cease to question?" he asked in a mildly humorous tone. Damaris chuckled and seemed to Cahill to relax. "Did you enjoy our pick-nick yesterday?"

"Oh yes," said Damaris, feeling much easier for his assurances. "I did. It was a delightful day . . ." She babbled on lightly, giving astute comments now and again about the personalities she'd met, some of which drew a quiet chuckle from the earl.

Elsewhere the day wasn't going so well: Herbert and Hereward bickered over whose was the greater responsibility for their recent exile from the Pump Room. They'd gone from there straight to the common room at their inn where they indulged their optimistic hope they'd someday relieve their unquenchable thirst. Long before the day was done it was quite likely the argument would escalate into a full-fledged battle. . . .

Still elsewhere, totally unaware that the fickle sun shone brightly, Sir Davey Questerman brooded darkly over ways and means of achieving his nefarious goal with the little Adlington. Such a lovely little tidbit she would be too . . .

On the edge of the group surrounding Lady Tamswell and Lady Lawton, the widowed Mrs. Lovett kept a wary eye on Worth who seemed deeply involved with the young man of the Adlington party. The Marquess had shown not the slightest interest in Miss Damaris or jealousy when Cahill walked off with her. The widow narrowed thoughtful eyes. Perhaps it would be wise, however much a bore, to become acquainted with the Adlington lad—especially if the young man were to be forever in the company of the Marquess . . . ?

And while all this was going on and while she smoothly parried Lady Lawton's questions—or answered where appropriate—Fanny wondered where Lord Seward might be on such a lovely day and why he did not come.

It finally occurred to her, when it was nearly time to return to their rooms, that, just maybe, no matter what he'd insisted to the contrary, his lordship had been forced, in the course of long night hours, to admit that her blindness *was* a barrier to any further friendship between them and his non-appearance today was his way of informing of that decision.

Since it was exactly the decision Fanny had wished him to reach, she couldn't for the life of her understand why she felt so deeply disappointed that he'd not come.

Thursday morning Tacye was particularly careful as she folded and tied her cravat into a simple but elegant knot. Damaris waited with her coat, ready to help ease the close-fitting back and shoulders into place. The cravat approved, Tacye turned, a slim figure in her soft shirt, starched collar points, and smoothly fitted vest, the latter having subdued stripes laid on a slightly darker background which matched her buff-colored coat.

Damaris withheld the coat, staring at her sister. She looked up from the vest to her sister's eyes. "You aren't *that* flat in front," accused Damaris. "I know you've more bosom . . ."

"I've bound up what little I have," interrupted Tacye abruptly. She turned back to the mirror. "I think I make a very nice-looking young man, do not you?"

Damaris covered her mouth with the coat she still held and giggled. "Hmm. That Tabitha surely thinks so."

"Tabitha?" Tacye fiddled with her hair, brushing it over and over again, attempting to tame crisp waves into something resembling a Brutus. Why was short hair so difficult? She wasn't achieving her aim or anything like, she thought ruefully.

"You know," said Damaris. "Lord Cahill's cousin. The small one. She has developed an everlasting tendre for you." Again Damaris giggled. "She assured me it was so when we were in the Pump Room yesterday and told me she desperately hoped you'd still be unwed in a year or two when she is finally presented."

Tacye scowled at the mirror. "That's the little yellow-haired flirt, is it not? Surely she's far too young for such behavior." Fiddle. No matter what she did, the hair simply would not lay right.

"Here let me," said Damaris setting aside the coat and pushing her sister onto a stool. Her fingers worked busily at the problem hair. "Tacye, her infatuation isn't funny. She asks me all sorts of questions I can't answer. What should I say, Tacye? I hate lying."

"Tell her I promised my father I'd not think of marriage until I'm thirty-five and that by then she'll be long married."

"But that's a lie, too. I asked what I *should* say."

"Damaris, sometimes it is far better to prevaricate a trifle than to allow a woman hope where there is none. Or," added Tacye, thinking of Damaris's inability to turn off her suitors, "for that matter, to allow hope to remain in a man's breast. You, for instance, play with fire when you allow Herbert and Hereward to brangle over you and it is my sincere prayer you do not find yourself burnt by it."

"Oh, Tacye! They never mean anything by it."

"Has it ever occurred to you that they could actually kill each other in one of their fights? Perhaps the one might knock the other into something so that he hit his head. . . . Oh, very likely he'd not be meaning to go so far as to kill his brother, but once something of the sort happens—like a broken head—it is too late, is it not?"

Damaris bit her lip. She met Tacye's steady gaze in the mirror. "You think I should do something to convince them they don't really wish to marry me, do you not?"

"Yes. I also think you need to be far less polite to that slippery creature, Sir Davey. I've been informed he must marry money—when he gets around to marrying at all. That being so, the very particular attentions he's been paying you cannot have an honorable motive."

At this suggestion, Damaris was truly shocked. "Not honorable!" Her eyes widened. "But he's a gentleman."

Tacye sighed. "Innocent child. Not all men born to rank have the sense of honor which makes a man behave, naturally and without question, in the manner that defines a gentleman." When Damaris only bit her lip, Tacye continued. "My love, I've been warned that Sir Davey has *no* sense of honor. It was suggested far more bluntly than ever would have been the case if it were known I'm *not* the young man I appear to be, that the monster desires only to seduce you."

A fiery blush rose from below Damaris's modest neckline and disappeared into her hairline. "That's a truly awful thing to say," whispered Damaris, her fingers trembling.

"Have you developed a tendre for the man?"

"Not at all." The pleasant comforting features of Lord Cahill rose into Damaris's mental vision, a man for whom she thought she might be forming a tendre. "No. Never! But, still, surely you cannot think the man would . . . would . . ."

"Why not?" When Damaris only shook her head, Tacye said, "Damaris, you are young and you have led a sheltered life, but even you have heard of the existence of rakes and rogues and that they are *not* to be encouraged. Knowing the type exists, why do you find it difficult to accept that you have now met with such a one?"

Damaris's blush, which had begun to fade, returned. "One doesn't know such people," she insisted. "I would never have been introduced to a man who . . . who . . ."

"Just who did introduce you?" interrupted Tacye, suddenly curious.

"At the pick-nick. One of the Cahill guests. I can't recall just which one . . ."

"Think."

"Maybe Mrs. Templeton?" Damaris tried to turn the subject and forced a giggle. "I think Mrs. Templeton wishes her daughter to catch Lord Cahill's eye. Did you notice how they were always putting themselves in his way? What do you think?"

"I think she thinks *you* a rival to those plans," said Tacye sternly. "If she introduced you to Questerman, she very likely did it maliciously, hoping you *would* be ruined by him and no rival to that bouncy daughter she tries too hard to push off onto *any* eligible male. She is, Damaris, interested in any unexceptionable man—not just Cahill. The earl is, most likely, her first, but not her only choice."

"I feel sorry for Merry Templeton," said Damaris, a frown marring her brow. "Her father is an invalid and only interested in his aches and pains and her mother only cares about marrying her off well." Then Damaris giggled. Her eyes twinkled. "Merry is another one who looks longingly in your direction—whenever her mother is looking elsewhere, at least. You are becoming quite the beau, Tacye!" Damaris caught her sister's eye in the mirror, her hands for the moment still. "I think she too has developed a tendre for you."

"Of all the ridiculous notions! Of course she has not."

"You are far too modest, *Toby*. You do, as you said earlier, make a fine-looking young man." Damaris frowned. "I can't help wishing there were something one could do for the poor girl. . . ."

"I know how soft-hearted you are, Damaris, but I don't think you should take her up. Believe me, her mother wouldn't like it." Tacye pushed her sister's hands from her barely tamed hair. "That's well enough, Dammy." She turned. "Tell me, how did we get lured away from speaking of your behavior toward unsuitable suitors!"

"I don't know," said Damaris, wishing her sister would drop the distressing subject, "but, however that may be," she added, suddenly thinking of a way by which she could cut short her sister's lecture, "if you do not finish dressing, you'll not be ready when Lord Worth arrives. Do look at the clock, Tacye," she coaxed.

Tacye glanced to where it crouched on the mantle, some indeterminate wild beast, the clock face set into its side. She sighed, rose to her feet, and, with Damaris's help, struggled into her coat. Once on, the fit was so excellent she could move freely in every way which counted—it was the getting into it which was the problem! One more glance at the clock and she strolled down the hall and into the front room. .

"Morning, Aunt Fanny," she said.

"Do you really think you should participate in this race?" asked her aunt.

"Do I have a choice?" Before Fanny could respond Tacye added, "What protection would I be to Damaris if I were to acquire the reputation of a coward before we'd been in town a week?"

"I cannot like it," confessed Fanny. "I cannot help but worry about you, Tacye."

"Toby!" reminded Tacye. "Do not forget even when we are alone, my best beloved aunt."

"Your *only* aunt! Toby . . ."

Tacye chuckled. "If I break my neck jumping a regular rasper and my secret is discovered, you must immediately make a run for home and marry Damaris off to the vicar before he can hear the least word of the ensuing scandal."

"Toby!" said Damaris, her hand clutching the frame surrounding the doorway. "You cannot mean it! Oh, do not allow anything to happen to you during the race! Perhaps Aunt Fanny is correct and you should *not* race." Her skin paled somewhat alarmingly. "I could not bear to have Bridget Connors for sister. I could not!"

Tacye threw a glance toward her sister, a scornful look. "Damaris, when was the last time I came off a horse?"

Damaris looked as if she were actually trying to remember.

"It has been so long even I cannot call it to mind," scolded Tacye. "Do not be concerned for me; I'll come to no harm." She looked from her frowning aunt to her obviously concerned sister. "Why will you not believe me?" Tacye felt a degree of bewilderment at their fears.

When Damaris would have argued further Fanny interrupted, asking, "When do you expect to return home?"

"Worth indicated it would be a long day. Do not expect me until you see me." That thought reminded Tacye she'd not discovered what her aunt and sister had planned. "And you? Have you occupation for today? Or will you find yourselves here alone and bored without my escort?"

"We will shop this morning for a couple of ball gowns for Damaris. What she owns were suitable at home for those few occasions when young people got together to dance, but will not do here in Bath. Lady Lawton was kind enough to warn me invitations to informal dances should be expected and, of course, we'll attend the subscription balls at the Upper Assembly Rooms. We will take Mary shopping, of course."

Then Fanny pursed her lips, her anxiety at the prospect obvious. "This afternoon we make calls—or, at least one. Lady Lawton intimated she is at home today and that she expects us to come by."

"Excellent," said Tacye in encouraging tones. "Do not feel you must stint yourself, Fanny. Thanks to your savings added to mine, we'll do very well, you know, so you must take a chair. That way you need not fear an uneven walking surface. If you will promise to do so, I'll not feel concerned for you." She glanced out the window. "And *there*," she added, before her aunt could demur, "is Worth. Don't forget! Take a chair. I must go now."

Tacye exited, a rising feeling of anticipation filling her which she put down to the fact she'd take part in a race later on and not at all to the sight of the broad shoulders and darkly auburn hair of the man sitting tall on a long-boned horse named Jackass. He waited for her to mount Numbskull so that they could be on their way.

Up in their rooms Fanny tentatively asked Damaris if she would sit a moment before they started on the rounds of the mercers looking for dress lengths, because she had something she must say to her. "I always hate to lecture you, my dear, but I fear, in this case, I must."

"If it is about Herbert and Hereford, Tacye has done so already. Or, at least, she spoke some nonsense about their being a danger to each other and perhaps to me."

Fanny hesitated before rushing on. "I don't believe it *is* nonsense, Damaris. Obviously—and so it should be— you are unable to understand the depth of passions those boys feel or the animosity they hold for each other. You grew up with love from those who are your family. Naturally you expect only kindness from those around you. The Lambourns have been raised far differently, Dammy. They've no love for each other, nor none for anyone else. Only a selfish desire to have their own way in all things."

"I *don't* understand."

Fanny sighed. "How can you? You have never known the negative feelings which are the only ones to be experienced by those poor lads. Damaris, I would not put it past one or the other—or perhaps the two together—to abduct you, expecting to sort out later who is to have you. Each would, of course, assume it to be himself." Her blind eyes stared painfully. "Can you not see how dangerous they could be?"

"No," said Damaris stubbornly. "I cannot believe any man would wish to harm a woman he loved."

"But," said Fanny, asperity beginning to creep through her usual patient tone, "that is exactly the problem as I've been trying to explain to you. They do *not* love you. Nor does that exceedingly oily Sir Davey. Even without sight, I'm not blind to *his* plans for you."

Damaris stared off into the distance, her eyes caught and held by a soaring lark swinging around the highest towers of the Abbey. She sighed. "Can no man love me because I am me?"

"An honorable gentleman will do so. Do not concern yourself about that."

"Is," she asked softly—so softly even her aunt's excellent ears could not determine her words, "Lord Cahill an honorable gentleman?"

"What dear?"

"Nothing." Damaris faced her aunt again, putting aside nonsensical dreams concerning the kind and thoughtful earl. "What am I to do, Aunt?" she asked, sincerely wishing to know.

"You are to be cool to them. Never laugh at their jokes. Look blankly at them if they make a suggestion you think a little 'off.' You know. As if you had not understood them. And *never* allow yourself to be alone with any of the three." Fanny frowned. "Or, come to that, alone with the Lambourn boys when they are alone together!"

Damaris thought about her aunt's advice. She sighed. "If you truly think it necessary, I'll do my best."

"I feel it strongly." Fanny paused, wondering if she'd said enough and decided, that for now, it was best to leave well enough alone. Instead, she asked, "Now, shall we call Mary and see what we can do about adding to your wardrobe? Lady Lawton gave me a hint as to where to look first and I think we'd be wise to follow her advice, do not you? She is knowledgeable about Bath as we cannot hope to be. I think a length of pale blue lawn would be nice, for instance. . . . Have you your hat and pelisse by you, my love?"

"I can be ready in two minutes," responded Damaris, again relieved to have ended the discussion of a subject she found exceedingly distasteful. "Do you need anything from your room?"

"No. I have it here. Do find Mary, however, and ask that she come to me. Your sister's advice—I mean, Toby's advice that I hire a chair is excellent. I wonder

I didn't think of it myself, but Mary will have to find one for us. I wonder what it would cost to hire the men for the whole of the day . . . ?"

"Shall I have her ask?"

"I think perhaps you should. If it is not above half a pound, which is, I think, excessive, I'll do it." Fanny thought for half a moment. "My dear, just send Mary here. And don't be long getting ready. She'll find a chair near the Abbey, you know. They are always there, or, if not, then in front of the Pump Room." Her worst fears calmed by the knowledge she need not walk far over uneven paving, Fanny, too, began looking forward to their shopping.

Tacye allowed Numbskull to amble along the country lanes beside Worth's Jackass. She had given his horse a good once-over when she exited the Abbey Arms and, although she now believed the contest between them would be close, she still felt she could win. "I saw nothing which looked like a race course when we pick-nicked the other day."

"If your walk took you toward the coverts, you went the wrong direction. The race course is laid out in rather rougher and more varied country to the far side of the property."

"I should have thought, should I not? No one would hold races near maturing birds! How long a course is it?"

"Having second thoughts?" he challenged.

"Of course not. Merely curious. And making conversation. I can well wait to see for myself, if that is your choice. Of what would you wish to converse, my lord?"

"And that sets me down quite nicely, does it not?"

"I do not mean it so."

He chuckled. "You will not rise to the bait, will you?

I admire that, your self control, I mean. I think it will serve you well while bear-leading that sister of yours."

"Damaris will do very well, I think."

"Yes. I agree. I've the feeling Cahill will not take long making up his mind."

Tacye turned a startled look toward her companion. "Cahill? I had not thought it!"

"Had you not?" He studied her. "Perhaps it has not occurred to you, but I assure you it's crossed Lady Lawton's mind and more than once!"

Tacye shook her head. "He is too far above my sister. Her fortune is too small and her birth, although perfectly respectable, is not suitable for so great a match."

"An earldom of a mere three generations!" Worth grimaced. "Not so very great a match," he said. "Believe me."

Tacye's eyes twinkled and she turned that half-smile, characteristic of the Adlington twins, in his direction. "Especially when compared to a nine-generation marquisate?"

A bark of sharp laughter met her jibe. "Was I so very pompous?"

"Oh, exceedingly so."

"I did not mean it so. All I wished to imply was that you should not make discouraging noises to your sister. Cahill likes her better than any other young woman he's met since he's become earl. He told me so," he added when Tacye's raised brow asked how he knew. "It's partially because she does *not* push herself forward as others do. He nearly ran from London like a fox during cubbing half way through the Spring Season. He's discovered," added Worth in that half-cynical half-amused tone Tacye was beginning to know, "just how much value a peerage has in the eyes of an unmarried woman. He has reason to know that those chasing him now would have had nothing to do with a mere vicar, even one with excellent prospects for advancement."

"The value of a peerage in the marriage stakes . . ." Tacye cast a curious glance at the man who was beginning to take up far to large a portion of her thoughts. "You must have discovered that long ago, I should think?"

"At a very young age, actually—but I had my father to guide my first tottering steps among the *ton's* more active huntresses. Cahill has not that advantage."

Tacye was thoughtful for a moment, wondering just how wary her companion might be—and then wondering at her wonderment! "I think our discussion has ranged a little far afield. May we return to what I think was your advice?"

"If you will."

"I think, assuming I did not misunderstand, that you suggest I not warn Damaris away from Cahill, that I not suggest she look elsewhere for a husband among more suitable young men who will not expect so large a dowry or demand so much of her in the position they'll be able to give her?"

"Had you someone in mind?"

Tacye felt unwanted spots of heat in her cheeks. "There were several who appeared to find her to their fancy—young men she met at the pick-nick and in the Pump Room, you know. I wondered if . . ."

"Too young," interjected Worth. "Assuming I've the same men in mind, that is. They are mostly at university or have just come on the town and will not think of marriage for several years yet at the earliest. No, your best bet is Cahill—and here we are."

The open gates loomed before them and they turned in. They had ambled halfway up the lane when a perch phaeton rolled up behind them. Tacye looked over her shoulder, met the eyes of the idiotic stranger who

seemed, for no reason at all, to find her so frightening—
and once again she had that effect on the poor young
man.

Grenville Somerwell sawed at the reins. His misman-
aged pair responded as one might expect, pulling one
way and then the other and, suddenly, Somerwell's
brand new high perch phaeton tipped itself to the right.
Grenville, thrown onto the overgrown bramble bushes
allowed to grow thickly along the side of the lane, could
be heard swearing with surprising fluency for such a
foppish-looking man.

Chapter 6

"You go along," said Worth, quietly. "There doesn't appear to be anything so very wrong—assuming all that swearing may be trusted! I'll see the idiot right again while you follow the racetrack—if you think it necessary, of course," he finished with twinkling eyes.

"I'll do that then," said Tacye, raising her chin at his teasing. She listened to the thrashing around going on beyond the hedge. ". . . If you're sure you don't need help here . . . ?"

"Quite certain."

Tacye nodded and trotted on. Near the manor, she paused, wondering which direction she should go. Worth had said the coverts were on the opposite side of the property to the track so that meant . . . She turned left behind the house, threaded her way through a stand of fir and soon came out near an elaborate set of stables and dog runs. These were, she thought, in far better condition than the house had looked to be!

But they would be. She'd heard the late earl had been hunting mad. From what she knew of the present Cahill, it didn't surprise her they were no longer in full use. Two of the stables had been closed and the third held no more than half a dozen animals. Only two of the dog runs were occupied. As she approached, a full-

throated baying from one black and tan throat brought
an irascible Stemper into view.

"Oh. It's you," said Cahill's keeper. He looked up at
Tacye through grizzled brows. His bald and spotted
head shone in the sun but his lean and well-muscled
body belied his true age.

"Yes. Me again. I'm invited to the races, but have no
notion where to go."

Stemper turned on his heel and started round the side
of the kennels. When Tacye didn't move he turned,
frowning. He motioned and Tacye, undecided whether
to laugh or scold, followed.

Behind the cottage attached to the dog runs, Stemper
stopped at the edge of a steep hill. Tacye stopped beside
him. "There. Ye see the whole of it," said the old man
and scowled up at her. "You'll be racing?" he asked.

"I've been challenged by Lord Worth to race my
Numbskull against his Jackass." The old man glanced
up, the faintest hint of humor evident in his faded but
remarkably clear eyes. Gently Tacye added, "I know. I
couldn't resist, could I? Not with those names."

A rumbling chuckle answered her. "Well, then," he
said when he stopped laughing, "you'd better step down
here, young fellow-me-lad and I'll give you a pointer or
two."

Tacye dismounted and looped her reins over her arm.
"Well?" she asked when she'd let her eyes range along
the course which was hinted at by riders studying its
various jumps and traps for the unwary.

"See you there just beyond the first stream." The old
man pointed.

"I see. It looks a bit marshy."

He laughed again, that rumbling laugh that was so
surprising from such a desiccated old figure. "Marshy,
he says. Marshy! Well, boy, that *marsh* is more than a bit
wet just there. Ye'll be floundering like a beached whale

if you get yourself well into that bog. Be sure you jump the stream below that whitish rock, see you?"

Tacye nodded, making a mental note of the rock. The stream was narrower above it, obviously more tempting to a rider who was unsure of his mount's ability to span the wider stretch.

"Then there, where you turn in under the wooded area?"

"Under those young oaks, you mean."

"Aye. Just in where you can't be seeing it is a low branch. Not so low your horse can't get under it—just low enough to catch an unwary rider about the shoulders."

"Thank you. I'd hate to be unseated by such a ridiculous trick as that."

"Then that first hedge—there's a hidden ditch. Not too wide but wide enough if you don't jump broad."

"I'll remember."

Tacye wondered why the old man had mentioned that. The marsh she might have missed, having waded across when walking the course, and then, when the race began, jumping where it looked narrow. The branch she also might have missed; walking one would be well below it. But a ditch beyond a jump? Surely she'd notice . . .

"Why do you tell me of that particular ditch?" she asked.

" 'Cause if you jump anywhere but just this side of the age bleached post, it's nearly half again as wide."

"I suppose anyone who has raced this course would know that . . ."

"Likely," was the old man's laconic answer. He continued moving his pointing finger along the complicated course. "Now there. That jump. Get it set in your mind there's a second jump just beyond it. 'Tain't a straight jump, neither. Don't know how many young idiots walk that course but forget that second jump. Don't know how many have gone off there making nice asses of themselves." The old man turned his beetling brows toward Tacye. "Wouldn't like a man who can walk as soft as you can coming off for such a damn fool reason."

"Thank you very much. I can't think of anyone who could say that, about my tracking, and it mean more to me," said Tacye with all seriousness. "Anything else I should know?"

"That's all the tricky bits. Walk the course. Find those spots I tell you about. You'll do all right." He eyed Numbskull, his lids lowering. "May just put a bob or two on you. Might just do that." He nodded.

"Worth will have raced this course before. He'll know it. I believe his horse is the equal of mine. Are you certain you should take a chance on my skill and courage about which you know nothing?"

"Yes." The man grinned. "Do know. Know you can sneak up on me even when you ain't trying. That takes a good man. Know you ain't overconfident. That's good too. Think you've a good chance of winning. Can't say fairer than that, now can I?"

"Well," said Tacye, wondering, now she'd seen the course, if she really did have a chance against Worth, "I hope you do win. I'll do my best not to disappoint you." She grinned and turned to mount. "Thank you again for the hints."

"Didn't think those fools below would think to warn you," he said, gesturing to the dust-stirring crowd of horses and men milling about in the valley near trestle-tables set with barrels of ale. He gave her a sly look. "Maybe they wouldn't want to?" he suggested, his finger laid knowingly to the side of his nose.

Tacye chuckled. "Maybe they wouldn't at that! Thank you again," she called as she headed for the lane which led down into the valley.

She was perhaps halfway down when Worth caught up with her. She turned in her saddle but saw no phaeton following. "Was Somerwell more badly hurt than you thought?" she asked.

"No. Nor did the carriage appear to be damaged, although I warned him he should have the wheels and axles checked for weaknesses. One of the horses got a bit scratched up in the brambles and Somerwell looks as if half a dozen cats had chosen his person as the arena for a cat-fight but insisted he was well enough, just too shaken up to enjoy the racing. He turned tail and went back to Bath, setting a rather brisk pace, I thought," finished Worth with just a hint of confusion in his tone.

"He is the strangest man I've ever met," said Tacye, frowning. *I wonder,* she thought—and not for the first time—*why the sight of me puts him into a panic. . . .*

Worth turned to look at her. He recalled Somerwell's confusing questions about Terence Adlington, whether he'd died or not. Then he recalled some talk just before Waterloo that Somerwell swore he'd seen the ghost of Nelson.

The hero of the naval battle of Trafalgar had, according to Somerwell, been pacing around Wellington's map table, studying the terrain and pointing now and again with his one arm to the Château Hougoumont after which he'd shake his head and sigh deeply.

The story had not been referred to after the battle: Hougoumont had been a focal point. The many men who defended it died honorably, but it had been the most bloody site of the bloodiest battle Worth had ever seen or ever hoped to see. If Nelson had really appeared to Somerwell . . .

Worth's mouth firmed and he pushed the thought aside. Even if the hero of Trafalgar had tried to warn someone of the importance of the château, the battle at Waterloo was now long in the past. And surely

Somerwell didn't think ... such nonsense. Worth shook away all thought of the battle and of ghosts.

"Would you like to slake your thirst or go over the course first?" he asked.

"How long until the first race?" asked Tacye, giving a quick glance to checking the sun's position.

Worth pulled a very nicely engraved watch from his fob and opened it. "We've half an hour—assuming nothing delays things, which likely *will* happen—in which case we've all the time in the world."

"I think I'll not chance that and take the course first."

"I'll come with you."

Worth debated whether it was dishonorable to hide the few oddities with which the course was booby-trapped. He watched the straight back of the young man he followed toward the first stream crossing and decided the boy would be competition enough without teaching him to suck eggs. Besides, if he were still so green he fell into what were, after all, obvious difficulties, then it would be a lesson for him!

For an instant the possibility Adlington was a she rather than a he crossed his mind. Again he pushed it away as he had whenever the notion occurred to him since leaving the Pump Room yesterday: women didn't race. No woman could accept a challenge as easily as Adlington had done, could she? Nor would she calmly ride down into the midst of the heavy drinking, wild betting, and, inevitably, the rather course stories which a woman must know would be the rule of the day—would she?

Surely not ...

Of course not, Worth decided, and wondered why he'd ever thought it might be otherwise. He kicked Jackass's side and caught up to where Adlington stood by the edge of the stream—right where the stream was its most narrow! Worth grinned slightly. This was surely going to be the easiest win of his life! The young man would be long behind him right from the beginning if he crossed there where he was standing!

They went on, Tacye moving her animal in behind Worth's when they forded the stream at the wider, shallower, place. The rest of their walk round the course convinced Worth he need have no concerns about their race—although he was glad to see Tacye studying the double jump.

Worth wanted to win. He didn't, however, want the boy to come to grief and that double jump was a tricky spot in the course. One was required to switch directions and take the second jump at an angle to the first with either no room for maneuvering if one didn't land correctly to begin with or, alternately, far too much room, which was time wasted when even fractions of seconds could mean the difference between a win or a loss.

They returned to the starting post to discover the first race had been postponed. Cahill, wishing to avoid the early eventuality of what was inevitable inebriation among hard drinkers, had ordered a huge roast brought out, the carved slabs of juicy meat served on thick slices of newly baked bread. Also available were several cold pies, slices of which were seen here and there among the men eating and drinking before the first race.

Aware that however she avoided most of it, she would still be required to imbibe far more alcohol than she liked, Tacye headed straight for the food. She could at least start her drinking with a full stomach!

"Slept late and missed my breakfast," she told Worth who was, himself, heading toward the barrels. "I'll get a tankard after I've eaten," she added when he suggested he bring her one.

The first race included half a dozen young men, some on half-wild horses which could not be brought up to the starting line—at least not all at once! Three times it was thought the race could begin and each time a horse would get away and have to be brought back. On the fourth line-up the starting gun went off without waiting to discover if everyone were ready. Some were not and the laughter at their expense obviously riled the handful of young red-faced riders left behind at the starting post.

Other races followed, some challenges and some open to any entry. Tacye told half a dozen different betting men that she wouldn't bet money she didn't have. She wasn't fool enough to find herself in debt, she insisted. She grinned at one persistent young man who tried to goad her into laying a bet—an obviously foolish bet at that.

"You wait until after I win my race—assuming I do. Then I'll place a bet or two with my winnings."

But the young man looked from her to Worth and shook his head. "You'll lose."

"Will I?" said Tacye. "I think not." She turned away and headed, again, for the table with food on it. She'd discovered, somewhat by accident, that, if she appeared to be eating, no one pressed her to refill her partially full tankard!

When time for their race was upon her, Tacye went to where she'd hobbled Numbskull and laid aside his tack. Knowing from Terence's tales the sort of tricks which could be played on one, she checked every inch of leather for loosened buckles—even half-cut straps. She checked the pad for sharp objects such as thorns. Everything was just as it should be.

As she tacked up, a graying groom came up to her to watch. "Don't need to check gear at one of Cahill's races. He don't allow such tricks. I been watching good. Had to turn away I don't know how many jug-bitten greenheads with silly notions in their noggins, but no one's been near anything while *I've* been here."

"That's good to know. I've been to races where they aren't so careful, you see."

"Right you are." The groom looked around to make certain no one was within hearing distance. "Don't know if anyone thought to warn you, but best to jump the wider stretch below that big rock at the first stream." Like Stemper, he laid a finger beside his nose and added, "Land you in the mire if you jump the narrow bit above it!"

"Thank you. I appreciate the word." Tacye mounted and, inwardly reluctant, tossed the groom a shilling for the information which she already had. "You can place that on me to win," she said, grinning.

The groom grinned back but shook his head and said, ruefully, " 'Fraid I can't do that. I'll be laying my blunt on Lord Worth. Know him for a bruising rider, you see. Ex-peri-enced—and that counts."

Tacye shook her head. "Mistake that. You'll lose," she said cockily and trotted off to where Worth sat his long-boned Jackass.

"Ready?"

"Whenever you are," she said.

"Cahill wants the track clear before we begin."

Tacye's brows rose. "Why?"

"There's too much money on this race," said Worth grimly. "He's sent some trusted friends out to see no one is lurking where they could interfere." He scowled. "I can't understand why this race has become a wild one but it has."

"Because you are racing, perhaps?"

"I always race," he said.

"Then perhaps, it's the names: Jackass against Numb-skull! If you'll recall, I couldn't resist it!"

"Perhaps." Worth looked down the course. "Here comes the last of them and look at his prize!"

"Prize?" asked Tacye studying the deeply tanned, dark-haired young man riding in behind the first.

"That second man has a reputation for being not quite the thing. He's been suspected of rigging races before and no one, who has the least bit of sense, will play hazard with him."

"He uses down hills?" asked Tacye casually, remembering the term from something her brother had once said about cheating at dice.

"Down hills, up hills, whatever . . ." Worth shrugged. "No one has had the impudence to challenge and break his die, but no one really doubts they are weighted, either."

"Why is he allowed to mingle with good company then?"

"His family. He's a younger son of his grace, Duke of Castelbourgh."

"So, where someone like myself would be ostracized for such behavior, one must put up with him?"

There was, thought Worth, no bitterness in that calm comment and he liked Toby Adlington all the more for his acceptance of his position in life. "I don't believe anyone ever said that life is fair, young Adlington." Worth replied, equally calmly.

Tacye's mind drifted to the fact her very special brother was dead and that the idiotic Grenville Somerwell had managed to survive not only the Peninsular war but Waterloo as well. It certainly *wasn't* fair. Such thoughts were pushed aside when Cahill walked over to where Worth and Tacye sat their horses.

He lay a hand on Worth's boot. "Ready?" he asked. He turned to look at Tacye. "It's a tricky course, Adlington. Are you certain you've made yourself familiar with it?"

"I walked it with Worth. I also studied it from up there near your dog-runs," she said, tucking her chin in the general direction—and by doing so, noted that not only Stemper watched. A whole group of men—servants and grooms and possibly nearby country people who hadn't enough status to join those in the valley below—stood around in small groups. Tacye, suddenly a trifle nervous, gave the signal that made Numbskull dance on his front feet. She let him go for a moment before reining him in.

"Terence's horses could do that," said Worth.

Tacye felt heat run up from her too tight cravat. "Yes. We all learned from the same groom. He said it brought good luck."

Worth's brows rose. "Then you were not unknown to the family before Terence died?"

"Did I give you the impression I was? I may have done. Although the family has always treated me with respect—even affection—I am not one of them. At home it was understood that I did not push myself forward. Until Ter—" Tacye found she couldn't say the words and swallowed hard. She looked away from the others.

"Until his death . . . ," said Worth quietly. "You must have been very fond of him."

Tacye recovered promptly. "I loved him like a brother." She spoke the words with only the slightest hint of dryness and then, thanks to the look in Worth's eye, wished she'd controlled her emotions better. But, although she'd feared he might, he didn't question her further—partially because Cahill called them to the starting line and partially, Tacye thought, because Worth had far too nice a manner to probe an obviously tender spot.

Tacye might not have raced since the last time Terence and she tested his new mounts one against another just before he'd returned to war after a winter leave, but she had, since his death, galloped again and again like the wind across wild moors, trying desperately to run from the deadness filling her, the part of her which was missing, the darkness which hovered over her month after month. Numbskull had profited by those long runs and now, due exercise after too many days in a stable, he lengthened his stride and flowed down the hillside toward the stream.

Tacye was a trifle ahead of Worth but not much. Just enough that when she gave Numbskull the order to jump, Jackass, with Worth on his back, was very slightly to the wrong side and, in order to avoid Numbskull, jumped just a trifle too far downstream and, for a moment, floundered in soft soil before finding his feet again.

Worth, realizing it had not been an accident, but that Adlington had carefully chosen his exact spot to jump, now suspected that, from somewhere, the boy had learned of the course's specific hazards. The so-called greenhead had deliberately forced Jackass into the wet!

His mouth set in a grim line, Worth settled deep into his saddle and tapped Jackass's rump with the tip of his crop. Jackass needed no such encouragement: a horse was ahead of him and Jackass had an aversion to following in another's dust.

Worth made up the lost yards until he was nearly at Numbskull's flank again, just before they entered the growth of young oaks—and when he saw his opponent duck beneath the tricky branch, he grew more certain his rival knew the points of danger or difficulty. He became absolutely certain of it when Tacye took the fence and broad ditch on the right side of the aged post and his jaw clenched. What had appeared the easiest race of his life was now certain to be a very close race indeed.

Tacye, past the fence and ditch, knew she had a stretch of good running with only a couple of hedges, the one including another hidden ditch, before the fancy jump-turn-jump came into sight. She leaned low on Numbskull's neck and spoke encouragement and expressions of delight and praise for Numbskull's effort. When they reached the tricky fence she was again a yard or so ahead of Worth.

Tacye wished she'd been able to school Numbskull for the coming jump. Too close to the corner and there would be no room for the second. Too far away and one had plenty of room, but lost too much time. There was, she thought one spot where one could land a little facing the new challenge and still have room to turn a trifle more if necessary before making the second jump. She turned very slightly wide toward the first fence, losing a little of her lead in the process.

Numbskull jumped, found himself facing a second fence and, putting his heart into it, jumped again. Jackass landed each time right behind him, the thuds of his hooves echoing Numbskull's. They now faced the long easy run back to the finish line with only the usual hedges and fences and the stream between them and a win or a loss. Again Tacye settled herself against Numbskull's neck and again she spoke encouragement and praise for the long-eared animal.

They made the first jump almost side by side. The second they *were* side by side, and Worth grinned at her. She grinned back, enjoying the day, the race, the man beside her . . .

They were still nearly side by side—first one pulling ahead and then the other—as they made the jump over the stream. The crowd awaiting them cheered wildly, the noise rolling across the wide meadow that lay between them and the finish.

"This is it, Numbskull. Do your best," yelled Tacye and crouched still lower in her saddle.

The animal's stride lengthened still more. He seemed to float across the grass which had become beaten down in previous races, dust rising from the dry ground beneath to stream out behind.

"One last effort, my love," shouted Tacye.

She got it and was half a head's length in the lead as she and Worth crossed the line. A double shout went up. There were those who had dared bet on the newcomer, or who always chose to bet a longshot, but most voices revealed surprise and a very few sounded a bit sour.

Glad she didn't have to face the losers immediately, Tacye guided Numbskull into a wide circle to cool him. A surprising emotion rose within her. Suddenly she felt closer to her brother than she had since his death. As she brought down Numbskull's pace slowly and then walked him it was as if she could hear Terence's voice saying, *Well done!*

Tacye patted Numbskull's neck and spoke loving words to him, knowing from his twitching ears that he heard and found the sound of her voice pleasing even if he didn't understand the meaning. The feeling of closeness to her brother faded slowly and, when it was gone, she could delay no longer returning to the others. She pulled her horse's reins around and headed him back to where Worth was walking Jackass in another circle. They met, facing each other.

Worth grinned. "An excellent race, my boy. Closest run thing I've experienced for a very long time."

"I wish I could afford to buy your Jackass, my lord," said Tacye ruefully. "He gave Numbskull the only close race *he's* ever run!"

"Ah. You didn't tell me that, did you? That Numbskull had won all his races?"

"You didn't ask, did you?" asked Tacye, grinning. She thought of the two or three races Terence had run against her oddly named mount and how Numbskull had easily won them all. But Terence hadn't chosen his horses for speed so much as for stamina and for a certain steadiness of temperament one needed in battle. Tacye hadn't been at all certain she could beat Worth—although she'd believed she stood a good chance.

"Here's your winnings, bratling," said Worth, handing over several crisp banknotes. "I've learned not to jump to the conclusion that every green-looking youth is as green as he looks!"

"Thank you." Tacye stuffed the money into the fob pocket at the top of her leathers. Even folded they barely fit. *I'm eating too much,* she thought and made a mental note she must either get more exercise or dine more frugally.

The men she'd agreed to bet with were soon crowding around hoping to take her winnings off her. Tacye was at a disadvantage because she knew neither the riders nor the history of the horses—but she had an excellent eye for horseflesh and she'd learned to judge men pretty well too.

She lost part of her winnings on the first race where her choice came in second—but she won the next two and, when the last race came up, shrugged and bet the whole on the man and horse she thought might win. The odds were not outstanding, only three to two, but there would be a nice little profit if she won—and she'd be out nothing, really, if she lost. After all, her whole bet was made with what she'd won that day, so she wasn't dipping into her savings.

"What will you do with your winnings?" asked Worth, coming to stand beside her.

"Hmm? If I win?" Tacye tipped her head, her eye following the challengers as they crossed the stream. "I think I'll buy Damaris a hat I know she's coveting."

"If she's been coveting it, she's been plaguing the life out of you to get it for her, has she not? If you win you'll no longer have to listen to her pleadings."

"Damaris plague me?" Tacye gave him a surprised

look. "Not at all. She knows we've no money to spare for extra frills and fripperies. We could, I suppose, take some of her dowry to pay expenses, but I don't think that fair, do you? As it is, we must budget carefully."

His brows rose. "Ah. There is a dowry, then?"

"Had you thought us so stupid as to have come to Bath, obviously looking for a husband for her and she have no dowry at all? We aren't so foolish. It isn't the sort of fortune one occasionally hears about, one of those where the young woman has more than any man could ever need, but I think it will please any sensible man."

"Good." Worth looked up at a shout from the young men watching the turning point for the riders in the last race. "Here they come. Should we find ourselves a better viewpoint than this?"

He gestured to the backs of the men standing between them and the approaching sound of pounding horses. Tacye followed Worth part way up the hill to where they were well above the finish line and with a good view of the coming horde.

"I hadn't realized so many were entered," she said, bemused by the number of horses strung out along the last meadow run, some still appearing around the curve.

"Hmm. There's a small purse on this race." Worth glanced at Tacye, a faint frown appearing on his brow. "I assumed you knew and rather wondered that you hadn't entered as well."

"I didn't know," said Tacye pensively.

"I'm sorry. I should have made sure you were aware."

"I wish I'd known, but I didn't and that's that. I'm sure Numbskull could beat *that* nag," she added and couldn't help the disparaging tone with which the words came out.

Worth grinned. "I think so too. Ah . . ."

They waited in silence as the last handful of yards

were run, Tacye's choice mere inches behind the nose of the lead horse. She held her breath, hoping. Just maybe . . .

"Congratulations!" said Worth, turning to shake her hand. "Your bet was won by a nose!"

He seemed almost as pleased as if he had placed it himself which seemed strange to Tacye. She soon collected her small winnings and then looked around for Cahill whom she found talking to several of the slightly older and more sporting Corinthians, those who had come a distance and just for the day's racing—and, she guessed, a convivial evening with old friends. She waited patiently until Cahill noticed her and excused himself.

"I must go now," she said politely, bowing. "I wished to thank you for a very pleasant day."

"I'm glad you enjoyed it. We'll be doing the thing again in a few weeks. You must be sure to come again."

"Thank you. I will."

Tacye turned on her heel so she didn't see Worth join Cahill. "He's leaving?"

Cahill nodded. "A very nicely brought up young man," added Cahill. "I wonder if any of the rest of these scrubs will thank me for a pleasant day!"

"Very likely not," said Worth. After a moment in which he stared after Tacye, frowning slightly, he added, "I think I'll be running along too." The expression faded and he grinned. "Thank you, Cahill, for a very pleasant day!" he added, his eyes gleaming.

Cahill laughed. "You won't stay for the evening?"

"I might be back." Worth was silent for a moment. When he spoke, it was softly. "Frankly, Cahill, I didn't like the look Castelbourgh's cub threw Adlington's way when he won our race. I think I'll just see the boy safely home."

Cahill looked around and frowned. "You are right in

so much as that young cully has left already! I hadn't noticed. Do you want me to send along some grooms?"

"I think not. He'll not try anything if I'm along, surely. He's far too much the bully to take on someone of my size, to say nothing of my status, is he not?" Worth's brows rose, queryingly.

"Very likely. But be careful."

"Of course." Worth's brows rose, his look one of surprise. "Am I not always careful?"

Thinking of some of the stories he'd heard about Worth's adventures when in the army, Cahill stifled laughter. "Oh, of course, Worth. *Always.* You would never take a chance, would you now?"

Worth smiled sweetly and strolled off to where Tacye was about to mount. "A moment, Adlington, and I'll ride with you. I've an appointment in town and am leaving now as well. My solicitor will have come down on the Mail and I have no wish to keep him kicking his heels any longer then necessary. You'll wait for me, will you not?"

They rode side by side up the hill to where Stemper awaited Adlington. Tacye stopped and looked down into the sour-faced old man's face. "I say," she said, surprised at the look, "did you decide to put your blunt on Worth after all?"

"Nah. Put it on you. Just shoulda had more faith in m'judgment and put on *more,*" grumbled the old man.

Tacye pulled another shilling from a pocket. "Here, old man. You have a brew on me the next time you take yourself off to the local inn. I wouldn't have done it without your coaching, you know."

"Thankee kindly," said Stemper, catching the spinning coin with no trouble. "Thankee very kindly." He looked from Tacye to Worth. "Think maybe you should keep your eyes open up ahead," he said softly.

"Oh?" said Worth, speaking for the first time.

"Hmm. Couple of young bully-boys looking for trouble, I think."

"What reason have you to think so?" asked Worth.

"Heard 'em. Lost a bundle on your race. A bundle they may have difficulty finding?"

"I see. So they want a little revenge. We'll be careful."

"Good." Stemper turned away.

Worth looked at Tacye. "You, my new friend, are turning out to be more trouble than I ever expected."

Tacye, who had been staring along the path through the evergreens, straightened, a proud, slightly defiant look crossing her features. "You needn't accompany me."

"Oh yes I do." Worth spoke with sudden firmness. He'd noted how pale Adlington had become at Stemper's revelation, how the youngster had straightened and bitten a lip. But he'd soon recovered himself and now sat firmly in the saddle. He'd do. He was a good lad. . . .

Assuming he *was* a lad.

Once again suspicions as to Adlington's gender rose to bother Worth. Surely he must be a he, must he not? A woman could never have ridden a race such as they'd fought. Surely not . . . and yet! His companion had gone far too pale at Stemper's warning for Worth's liking—at least, too pale if one assumed it was a young man! A woman, now . . .

Worth shook away the thoughts filling his head. He *did not* feel any special attraction to Toby Adlington. He *didn't*.

But if it were *Tacye* Adlington for whom he had that feeling which seemed to sneak up on him at the oddest moments? That desire to protect and aid? An even more ridiculous wish to take the slim figure into his arms; a need to touch and be touched?

If Toby were Tacye it made sense, but if he were not?

Worth shook his head. This was nonsense! He had never been one to find another male interesting in that way. Either he was losing his mind, or Toby Adlington was really Tacye Adlington—and, he decided, remembering the threat to his companion, whoever, he or she, there was need of protection against whatever Castelbourgh's spawn had in mind for her—him!

They were part way down the lane to the road into Bath when Worth, riding a pace or two ahead of Tacye, ran into a wire held chest high. He was trotting just fast enough he was pulled from his saddle, but not from his horse. It took a moment to regain control and those moments nearly led to disaster.

Numbskull squealed in outrage, bucked, and when that didn't rid him of the sting in his rump, he took to his heels, doing his best to out-run the pain, racing out of control.

Tacye, realizing an attack had been made on them, but unsure what had happened, leaned into Numbskull's mane and tried to talk him into calmness. It didn't work. Neither did her handling of the reins slow him. Finally she decided she'd have to ride it out, let the horse go his limit and eventually, exhausted, stop by himself. At least there was little or no traffic.

Or so she thought.

Jackass was only a pace behind Numbskull when the horses rounded a bend to see a gig, one wheel off the road, slid down to the axle in the steep ditch. A sweating nag took up the width of the road as it attempted to pull it out.

Tacye pulled sharply at the reins hoping Numbskull might finally be tired enough to slow. She studied the road on either side, hoping there would be somewhere where she could get off of it and around the obstruction. There wasn't. Not only were there deep ditches to either side, but beyond those, again on both sides, was a tangle of hedge and vines.

Just as Tacye despaired of averting an accident, Worth's steel-wristed hand grasped her reins and pulled both horses to a skidding standstill. Tacye told herself it was over and she'd be a damn fool to faint, so, she told herself, take a deep breath and thank Worth for his assistance. She took the deep breath.

"Are you all right?" asked Worth.

"I'm fine. Thanks to you." She looked at Worth, meeting his eyes, before admitting, "I simply wasn't strong enough."

"I know." Worth was looking over the trembling horse he'd just pulled to a stop. He was almost certain what he'd find and he did. "Hold him steady. There's a dart in his rump."

"A *what?*" Tacye grasped the reins firmly, but she twisted to see what Worth was doing. Numbskull was not happy to feel another twinge in his rear, but this time the pain was followed by relief and he was too exhausted to complain again anyway. "That . . . that . . ."

"I'll have a word with him. You are not to accost him, do you hear me?" Worth said, glaring at Adlington whom he again, and seriously this time, suspected of being Tacye.

"I'm sure he'll listen to me far less seriously than he would to you, but will I not appear to be hiding behind your coat?"

"Bantling, there are times when it is not stupid to appear sensible. Now, what have we here?" he added and turned to look at the gig. He stared at the unconscious woman, recognizing her as the widow, Diana Lovett. "Blast and bedamned," he added in a mutter.

Tacye dismounted and had to turn a desire to giggle into a chuckle. "Do you think she'll be long in her faint?"

"Long enough, I suppose," grumbled Worth. "Let's get that carriage back up on the road, shall we?"

Tacye saw, sticking out of the hedge, a long pole. "Do you think that strong enough for a lever?" she asked, pointing.

"We'll try it. A lever would make the job a great deal easier."

Tacye scrambled down into the ditch and up the other side. Reaching the pole proved difficult but she acquired only a few mild scratches and soon had her prize.

"We're in luck," she called. "I believe the wood is good ash."

"Then very likely it'll do the job. Hold it up and I'll help you up the side here."

Getting the gig back on the road proved far less difficult than expected once they had the long pole in place and a makeshift fulcrum set just so. The only problem was that the stupid carriage horse pulled so hard he very nearly stumbled down into the other ditch, an eventuality which was only just averted by the lady rousing herself and using the reins to advantage—but once safe, she proceeded to swoon off again.

Tacye looked from the woman to Worth and hid a grin. "It is Mrs. Lovett, is it not?" she asked.

"I believe that was the name," said Worth.

He spoke in such an indifferent tone one of the lady's eyes opened to glare at him—as Tacye noticed. So. As she'd expected—and as she suspected Worth believed—it was a trick on the part of the lady to put herself in the way of his lordship.

Tacye pinched Worth's arm. "She cannot be left here, of course, but you have an appointment in town, as I think you said? Then it is up to me, I believe. I'll just tie Numbskull to the back and drive her to town myself. Do you think that will do?" asked Tacye diffidently.

"Worth, is that you?" moaned the lady.

"Yes. Adlington and I have gotten you out of the ditch, Mrs. Lovett. We've decided Adlington must drive you back to town since I fear you are in no condition to do so yourself."

"Oh, I'd feel so much safer if you would drive me, my lord," she said, simpering and looking up at him from under her lashes.

Tacye, noting the lashes, felt a moment's jealousy. Why, she wondered, was everyone blessed with long lashes except herself. Her own were all very well, but they were nowhere near so luxuriant as those being batted at Worth—or so full as her own sister's even. It wasn't fair. Tacye sighed silently. Life, as she and Worth had agreed earlier, was *not* particularly fair.

But it was time to cut through Mrs. Lovett's attempt to coerce Worth into escorting her back to town. Tacye broke into the conversation between his lordship and the putative lady. "Worth, I think you've no time for this argument. Were we not racing into Bath because you've an important meeting with someone?" When they looked her way, she added, "Your estate manager, did you say?"

Worth looked at Adlington from under his tightly drawn brows. "My solicitor, actually. He's come down on the afternoon Royal Mail from London especially for this meeting."

"Then you've wasted far too much time as it is. I am perfectly competent to drive Mrs. Lovett back to Bath and you may assure her my character is good so she has nothing to fear. Do hurry. I know you hate to be late for an appointment."

"I do. In fact I find it a most irritating trait in others so am careful to never do so myself." He bowed to Mrs. Lovett. "I am afraid, madam, that I must go. Adlington will take great care of you."

He touched spurs to Jackass's sides and, although he didn't race off at the speed at which he'd chased down Numbskull, he didn't bother to get very far down the road before he urged his horse into a full canter. The dust rose behind them and floated closer. Tacye, tying Numbskull to the back of the gig heard Mrs. Lovett cough and hid a grin. Good for Worth. Lovett wouldn't like dust all over herself and might just find it irritating enough she'd turn a cold shoulder toward Worth in future.

"Now," said Tacye, as she climbed into the gig and picked up the reins. "I apologize for being the wrong man, but it was a foolish trick, was it not?" she asked in a kindly voice.

"You! You aren't suggesting that I did that on pur— How dare you suggest I'd do anyth—"

"You mean you did not back the gig carefully into the ditch? I apologize. When I saw the tracks, I was certain that was what you'd done and assumed it was so you might meet Worth under interesting conditions. I fear," said Tacye in a kindly voice, "that that is what his lordship suspected, too. You see," she went on as if telling secrets, "he has been chased for too long and tricks of all sorts have been played on him because he is such a great matrimonial prize. He has grown to be suspicious of every little thing, don't you see?"

"Don't speak to me. *You* are the trickster, providing him with that silly excuse so that he could ride off. Oh, if we'd only been alone where we could get to know each other better!"

"I assure you, Worth had an important appointment in town or he'd yet be at Cahill's," Tacye informed the fuming woman.

"You cannot know that."

"I can. There are a group of his special cronies, you see, who have gathered from some distance around and about and they expect to make quite a night of it—or so I heard. Worth, if he'd not had an appointment, would not have been coming along this road for hours, perhaps not at all—until tomorrow, I mean."

Mrs. Lovett bit her lip, looking once or twice sideways at her driver. She had no choice but to believe that, if there *was* a gathering of men who expected to play cards and drink far into the night—which, she assumed, was the case from Adlington's description—then perhaps Worth had truly had to leave her for an appointment and hurry on.

But that meant he'd not left because he'd taken her in disgust. She brightened. It meant she still had a chance.

"Please do not speak to me," she said again, but in a far less nasty voice. "I've had a shock and am not well and wish only to reach my home and my bed."

"Fine by me, but perhaps you'd best tell me your address—just in case you, er, swoon again?"

Mrs. Lovett had no intention of shaming another faint, but she did wish to think about her next approach to Worth. Given Adlington's hints, it must be far more subtle than anything she'd so far thought up. *Far* more subtle!

Which, she admitted, was a problem for the simple reason that she was not a particularly subtle woman. Always she'd been able to rely on her looks and her ability to please a man. And why, she wondered crossly, was that not enough in this case? If only she could contrive to be in a position where *pleasing* the man might do some good!

At last Adlington helped the lady from her carriage and up to her door in Henrietta Street. The door was opened by a rather slatternly woman—and shut in her face before Tacye remembered she hadn't a clue what to do with the carriage and horse! She rattled the door knocker and waited. No one came and she tried again.

And still again. Angry, Tacye turned, hands on hips, to stare at horse and gig.

"What am I to do with you? I could leave you here, I suppose, but you deserve a good feed and a rub down. Well, Horse? Where did she get you?" Tacye asked rhetorically.

" 'Cross Laura Place and down Johnston Street apiece," said an urchin of about ten years.

Tacye eyed the boy. "Know something about horses, do you?"

"Work in the stable now and then," said the boy, puffing up his thin chest. "When they need an extra hand or two," he added.

"Then I think you are just the lad I need."

"You do?"

"Hmm. I've a shilling here . . ." Tacye searched her pockets and finally came up with another one, "if you'll take the horse and gig back, compliments of the lady."

"Here now, you'll not be paying the shot?"

"I didn't hire the rig and see no reason why I should pay for it. Mrs. Lovett is no particular friend of mine," added Tacye, thinking of just how little a friend the lady must be at this point. It had been an odd day, had it not? Never before had Tacye made so many enemies in so short a period of time!

"Then why were you a-drivin' of it?" asked the boy, breaking into her reverie.

"The lady managed to get a wheel into a ditch and, as a result, felt herself too shocked to drive herself home. You might suggest the owner take a good look at the left wheel and the axle before he lets that gig out again. The way her horse was straining to get free in the interval before I and a friend intervened there may have been some damage."

As she spoke Tacye untied Numbskull. She grinned at the boy before leading her own tired horse off down the

street and across the bridge and on to where her own
stables stood in Corn Street. Tacye shook her head in
bemusement. She'd have quite a story to tell Damaris
and Aunt Fanny—not that they were great ones for gossip, but they'd enjoy hearing of Mrs. Lovett's comeup-
pance. And then there was the money for the hat for
which Damaris secretly yearned!

Actually a bit more than was needed for the hat.
Tacye decided she'd better save the rest in case she was
again challenged to lay a bet!

All in all, it had been a very good day, she decided—
and wondered, ruefully, just how much that agreeable
outcome had to do with the fact she'd spent most of it
with Worth. The man was becoming far too important
to her for her peace of mind.

And she hadn't a notion what to do about it!

Chapter 7

During those half dozen hours during which Tacye avoided drinking too much by using every trick she knew or could dream up, Fanny and Damaris finished their shopping, ate a light luncheon and went calling. Lady Lawton had suggested Lady Tamswell bring her niece to call during her ladyship's usual "at home" which happened to be that afternoon, adding, in her frank way, that Damaris would enjoy the young people who would gather there.

Fanny was a trifle bemused by Lady Lawton's gruff persistence in drawing the unknown Damaris into the Lawton set, but she was perfectly willing to give her younger niece the treat. Lady Lawton said there would be archery and lawn tennis and gardens in which to take one's exercise and that the young seemed to enjoy it all.

The men and chair which had been hired for the day were waiting when Damaris, dressed in a new sprigged muslin, the flowers printed on it just happening to match those on her second best bonnet, handed her aunt down the front steps of the Abbey Arms. Just then the bells rang out and, down the street, a horse reared between the shafts of a gig. The woman driving it had some difficulty getting the animal under control and shouts of encouragement or jeers of disparagement from the various urchins observing the contretemps were no help at all.

"What is happening?" asked Fanny softly.

"It's that Mrs. Lovett," said Damaris. "She's driving a gig and the horse objects to the bells."

"Not only the horse objects," said Fanny, covering her ears. "Will they never stop?"

And stop they did after another few long minutes. Damaris then seated Fanny in the chair without difficulty. They were both pleased by the facility with which Fanny managed it. Silently they cheered Tacye for thinking of it, because, with Fanny riding in the chair, they reached Lady Lawton's Bath residence on Brock Street just off the Circus with no stumbling or fumbling, the rough paving and steep hills delaying them not at all. The chairmen stopped, not even panting although Damaris, walking beside the chair, had found the way a trifle wearing!

"Lady Lawton's house is set a bit back from the street, Aunt Fanny," said Damaris when she'd extricated her aunt from the chair. "There is a short walk and no stairs. We'll enter directly into an entrance hall, or so I believe."

So it was. The Lawton butler bowed deeply after receiving their names and eyed Damaris curiously. Fanny, if she'd not been blind, would have noticed and understood that the servants, in that unnerving way servants had, knew that Damaris was thought by their mistress to be the young woman who would catch Lord Cahill's eye.

Damaris, who didn't understand such nuances, was merely embarrassed by his probing look. Her rosy cheeks, resulting from his rude stare, were nothing for which the man would dream of finding fault: a proper modest miss, was his considered opinion and so he'd tell them belowstairs at the first possible instant!

The butler was about to lead them up the curving stairway to the first floor drawing room when Sir Davey Questerman appeared from the back hallway. "Ah, Miss Adlington," he said in his too smooth voice. "Allow me to escort you to where the young people are competing with bow and arrow!"

Damaris's arm muscles tightened under her aunt's hand. "Aunt . . ." There was the tiniest hint of desperation in the single word.

Fanny, remembering the disliked voice, said, "I think not, Sir Davey. My niece has yet to greet her hostess. Come along Damaris. We are ready now," she added, turning toward where she could hear the butler shuffling his feet.

Questerman followed them up the stairs. This was the first opportunity he'd had to get the Adlington chit alone for even a moment and, although he had no real plans for discommoding her today, he wouldn't object to stealing a kiss if the opportunity arose!

Such a sweet fluttering bird, he thought, very nearly licking his lips. How trembly she'll be from fear when he finally held her in his arms—but not too fearful, he added silently. He was not one of those who cared for *that* sort of conquest—it was just that the natural fear and trembling which went with anticipating the unknown aroused him greatly.

But for that very reason, he must go slowly. Regretfully he decided that, today, there must be no kisses.

Lady Lawton, never one to pussyfoot around a fact, had pierced Fanny's reserve enough to ask if her vision was particularly poor. Fanny had admitted her blindness. Now, with a sensitivity Fanny found surprising in the blunt woman, Lady Lawton came forward to greet her new guests and gently took Fanny's arm.

"Child," said her ladyship to Damaris, "I'm very pleased to see you in my rooms, but you'll have far more amusement with those your own age than here with your aunt's generation and my own. Run along with you. Sir Davey, I see, is waiting to escort you. We'll be watching as you join the others, my dear. You may see where I've settled my friends there by the windows so we could sit in comfort and yet see how the archery goes on. Are you an enthusiast of the sport, my dear?"

"I've been taught," said Damaris, only half soothed by the knowledge Questerman would have little or no opportunity to get her alone.

Ever since her sister's lecture, whenever she thought of either Sir Davey or her old neighbors, the Lambourns, she feared even a moment alone with any of them! It was frightfully disturbing, the thought she could not simply trust her acquaintances to treat her as she should be treated, as she'd always been treated. It wasn't fair.

"But," she went on when she realized Lady Lawton was waiting for more, "I am not very good, I fear. My sister is." Her agitation led her to add, "I do wish she were here."

"Your sister is very likely enjoying a long boring coze with her old tutor, my dear child," said Fanny with just a hint of warning, "They'll be debating the merits of some obscure theory against the contrary merits of a second theory or something equally uninteresting to the rest of us. And, very likely," added Fanny with a smile, "she'd not find our diversions here in Bath half so amusing as we do."

"Oh, no. No, of course she would not! I did not mean . . . I only meant that she is far better than I with the bow!"

"Do not concern yourself, child," said Lady Lawton. "I'm certain you will do quite well enough. Now, off with you." Her ladyship gave Sir Davey a stern look which he had no difficulty interpreting before turning and leading Fanny to a chair near the windows.

"Shall we go?" asked Questerman.

Sir Davey had answered her ladyship's look with a wry one of his own. It was an expression which appeared to others to be half-laughing at his own faults, but he was, figuratively, gnashing his teeth that her ladyship seemed to discern his plans for the little Adlington. If he were to complete those plans to his satisfaction and dare the chit's abduction for his own purposes he must defuse her ladyship's suspicion as soon, and as completely, as possible. Perhaps he should seem to pursue other game so that when Damaris Adlington disappeared, as she would disappear eventually, *he* would not be suspected!

"When I have led you out, I believe I'll go on to my next appointment," he told Damaris just loudly enough he thought Lady Lawton might overhear. "I've several other calls to make and had best hurry on my rounds since, later, I am meeting friends for a convivial evening."

Once they were down the stairs and beyond her ladyship's keen hearing, he asked, politely, "Have you plans for this evening?"

"I think not. I would have to ask my aunt," said Damaris.

Cautious child, thought Questerman. Has she been taught so carefully, then? Ah, a challenge indeed. "You have not been in Bath for long but have you been to the Sidney Gardens and explored the maze?"

"We have mostly attended to our shopping, and attended, of course, the Pump Room each day." A silence ensued, a silence which bothered naive Damaris. "Have you been long in Bath?" she asked, to break it.

Ah ha! Not quite so well trained as he'd thought or she'd never have asked a question which would keep the conversation going!

"I come each summer. I've a crotchety old uncle living on Queen's Square on whom I batten. By the end of the London season I'm usually at fiddle's end if not actually in the basket."

There. Now she would, if she had an ounce of sense, know he would not court her seriously! Only someone with a great deal of money could afford to take the delightful little Adlington to wife.

"Sir?"

Could it really be that she didn't understand he was telling her he had no money and could not, therefore, court her with marriage in mind? Or was it, perhaps, the cant language he'd used without thinking?

"I am," he tried again, "without funds until the next quarter day. My uncle supports me until then. It is terrible when one hasn't enough in the funds to cut a dash as I like to do during the season. Fortunately, my uncle, who was a great rake in his day, doesn't object to franking me while I'm here."

"Fiddle's end? In the basket? And now your uncle is franking you? You speak words I do not know," said Damaris.

"Such words are called cant terms," he explained with only a bit of condescension. Could she really be so ignorant? "Most young ladies have picked up a great deal of it from their brothers or cousins. You are not among their number?"

"I am not allowed to know such things," fibbed Damaris, although it was true she'd never heard the phrase *fiddle's end* before. "Such language is not proper."

All the better, my dear, thought Sir Davey. If you don't know something so innocent as cant, then you are also unlikely to have been informed of the way it is between men and women—and it will be that much easier to entice you into a brief affair. There was almost a fond look in his eye as he glanced down at Damaris. You won't, he thought with satisfaction, know what is happening until far too late—from your point of view, at least!

"We've arrived," he said a moment later, pushing aside a swinging gate and allowing Damaris to enter a wide alley set between hedges, neatly trimmed to shoulder height. Several giggling girls and a few of the younger men were gathered there. The butts were set at not too great a distance and one young woman was being shown how to hold the bow and how to aim it by a gangly youth while the others stood by giving advice, both sensible and of an unhelpful if humorous nature.

Sir Davey asked if Damaris knew everyone and when he learned she had friends among the young women who could introduce her to those she did not know, he bowed and turned away. If she had admitted to knowing nothing of archery, he'd have dared Lady Lawton's suspicions and insisted upon teaching her himself—but she was apparently trained in the sport and there would be no sport of the sort *he* liked in merely watching!

Damaris didn't even watch him go, behavior which Questerman noted ruefully. Miss Adlington was definitely going to be a challenge. And Sir Davey rather liked a challenge—just not so much a one he wasn't assured of winning in the end. For just an instant, as he went through the house and out onto the street, Sir Davey wondered if, in this case, there was a chance he might lose. The moment didn't last. Questerman had never lost at this particular game and he could see no real reason why he should this time either.

Damaris's turn at the bow came quite soon. Long ago Tacye and Terence had taught her that they disliked girlish squeals and pretended incompetence and that they would not put up with it. Because of that, Damaris, unlike some of the other girls, merely took a bow and tested it. It was a trifle less taut than her own and she asked to try another.

The two youngest men—boys, really, and too young to be interested in her beauty—had not really noticed Damaris up to this point. Suddenly, when they realized she was an archeress, they found her worthy of their attention. They helped her find a bow which suited and she accepted her first arrow. Standing up to the mark, she carefully pulled back the string, holding the arrow as she'd been taught. Even more carefully she aimed. She let fly and waited for the dull thunk of arrow hitting butt.

"Very well done. Wait up and let me check it," enthused one young man, running down the alley. "Very well indeed," he called back, measuring with his fingers how close she'd come to the center circle.

"Thank you," she called and waited, her second arrow in hand, until he returned. She flew her third arrow immediately after. Neither hit the center but each one was closer to it than the first. Damaris thought Tacye would not be utterly displeased with her skill—especially considering she'd not practiced for quite some time.

One other young woman, an overly tall lady with a long face and intense manner, was an archeress of note. She challenged Damaris to a contest and the men immediately organized everyone into teams to join in, the less able with someone of more skill. Damaris retired into the background as the targets were reset even closer for the first round.

"You are not happy," said young Merry, joining Damaris off to the side. "Did you not wish the challenge?"

"It seems a trifle pushy, when I've just arrived in Bath, to become the center of attention this way." Damaris remembered Terence's scorn at her skill. "Besides, I'm not that good. Truly."

"Did Mr. Adlington teach you?"

Mr. Adlington? thought Damaris. Oh. She means

"Toby." "Not the Mr. Adlington you know. I'd a brother who died in Spain." Damaris wished she'd not thought of Terence. It always made her sad to think of him. "He and my sister tried to teach me, but despaired of my ever becoming expert. I believe Miss Browne must be very good indeed?"

Merry nodded. "Will it bother you to lose to her?" she asked, putting her hand through Damaris's arm and holding her close.

"Not at all."

"Then," whispered her new friend, "be sure you *do* lose. Because Miss Browne will *not* be happy if you win."

Damaris sighed and turned a wary eye toward her challenger, winced when the young woman's first arrow landed a good two inches from the center. "I hope she's better than I am, then. I'm not very good at pretending."

Merry giggled. "Well, do your worst!" she said and gave Damaris a little push. "There you go. Miss Browne is finished and you are up now for your first turn."

The rounds continued. At the end of each, the team with the lowest score dropped out and the butts were moved three yards farther down the alley. To her surprise, Damaris found she was rather evenly matched with Miss Browne and might, if she concentrated, be rather better. She did her best *not* to concentrate—doing just well enough that she and Miss Browne continued in each succeeding round.

They and another team, a pair of brothers who were really very good, waited for the last round. Damaris found her arms had grown trembly and told Miss Browne she didn't know if she would do so very well this time, that she was becoming too tired.

"I fear," she said to her partner, "that we may lose this round because I'm so out of practice. I'm so very sorry," she added when a frown formed on the taller girl's narrow forehead.

"I don't suppose you do it on purpose," sniped Miss Browne and turned away. "I will," she added over her shoulder, "simply have to do well enough for both of us, will I not?"

Damaris felt her brows climb her forehead. What an unpleasant young woman, she thought, and determined to do what she could, but not to feel guilty if she did badly. In fact, wondered Damaris, might it not be best if I did so badly we're disqualified for the last round when we must compete against each other? Let the brothers do that!

Unfortunately, one of the brothers actually missed the target with one arrow, thanks to another young man's teasing him at just the wrong moment. Damaris sighed. She didn't want to play the last round and asked Merry if it would be bad ton to simply concede the win to Miss Browne.

"I don't think she'll like it, because she won't actually have shown you up for being worse than she, but I don't see how, since one must be polite, she can demand that you shoot if you do not wish to."

Just then a diversion was made by the appearance of the Lawton butler. He cleared his throat, when he had everyone's attention, announced that refreshments had been laid out on the terrace and would be served as soon as the young people wished.

Damaris, drawing Merry along with her, walked toward the man. "I'm sure I'm not the only one who has become parched by our play. Miss Browne," she said, turning slightly and smiling, "I freely confess you the winner and admire your skill very much indeed. I'm not strong enough for that final distance and shall not even try! Shall we go along to the terrace?" she asked and suited action to words. She and Merry went out the gate and along the path in the wake of the dignified butler who led the way.

The others followed and, except for Miss Browne who had to be teased from her pouting by a friend who dwelt on each flight of her arrows which had been particularly good, everyone was ready for lemonade and several of the small sandwiches which had been prepared for their delight. Soon after, word was brought to Damaris that her aunt was ready to go and, calling goodbyes, she went to join Fanny who awaited her in the front hall.

As they went back to their rooms in the Abbey Arms, Damaris told her aunt about the archery match and asked advice as to how she should have dealt politely with Miss Browne who had character traits such as Damaris had never before met with.

"I truly didn't wish to accept her challenge, but the others seemed to think it a settled thing and it was all arranged before I gathered my wits enough to say no."

"I think you did as well as you could in the circumstances. There are some people who will not be put off. You were lucky, perhaps, that Ruggles arrived when he did to announce that refreshments were available. On the other hand, you say you were tiring, so very likely Miss Browne would have won and there would have been no difficulty in any case."

They were approaching the Abbey Arms and Damaris groaned softly.

"What is it?" asked Fanny.

"Hereward and Herbert. They are waiting by the steps."

"It has been such a nice day—up to now," said Fanny pensively.

Damaris giggled. "You are a complete hand, Aunt Fanny. Will it be necessary to invite them in?"

"No. It is too close to the dinner hour."

"Ah," yelled Hereward, bouncing forward. "We've been waiting forever, Dammy-girl."

More quietly Herbert added, "As you see, we've a carriage and thought to take you for a ride."

Damaris stared at the high perch phaeton in horror. "In that thing? No. I won't!"

"What is it?" asked Fanny, concerned by Damaris's tone.

"Nothing to worry anyone," said Herbert smoothly.

"Ain't she grand?" said Hereward in his too loud voice, but his pride in the rig obvious in his tone. "Didn't think we could manage such a thing, did you?"

"A high perch phaeton? *You* can't," said his brother, snidely. "Miss Damaris? We insist you take a turn with us."

"Crowded into that thing? No. It is too high. It is dangerous."

"Insist," echoed Hereward and went so far as to reach for Damaris's arm.

"Boys!" said Fanny, firmly. "Just what do you think you're doing? A high perch phaeton is for two at most. You cannot be thinking of taking Damaris up with you."

"Put her between us," said Hereward.

"Lots of room," said Herbert, knowing Fanny was unable to judge for herself.

"I won't go. Aunt Fanny, I don't have to go, do I?"

"Of course not. In the first place, it is a totally unsuitable carriage for you to be riding in and, in the second, it is far too late in the day for a drive. You'll have to go away now," she said sternly to the Lambourn brothers.

"We've been waiting forever," said Hereward with a scowl. "Don't seem right somehow we can't take Damaris for just a *little* ride."

"Of course there is time for a short ride," said Herbert smoothly and, in his turn, *he* reached for Damaris. "I'll just lift you up, shall I?"

"Here no! I'll lift her up," interrupted Hereward and shoved his brother.

"Neither of you . . ." began Fanny, sharply, but was interrupted by another deeper voice.

"What is the meaning of this?" asked the Marquess of Worth. He eyed the Lambourns, cowing Hereward, but leaving Herbert more defiant than ever. "Miss Adlington, are these oafs bothering you?"

"Yes. They asked me to ride with them and I've said no, but they will not take no for an answer."

"*Not* the mark of a gentleman. You *are* gentlemen?" asked Worth with just a touch of sarcasm.

" 'Course we are," growled Hereward, scraping a toe against a paving stone.

"You don't understand, my lord," said Herbert. "Damaris . . ." He trailed off at Worth's look of outrage and began again, "*Miss* Damaris is a very old friend. We've known each other forever, have we not?" He didn't wait for an answer. "We do not stand on points with her."

"You do not consider her wishes of any importance?"

Herbert flushed slightly but his younger brother looked confused. "*Her* wishes?" asked Hereward. "What have they to do with anything?" he mumbled, confused by the notion.

"Shut up," Herbert told him in a hissing tone. "You are correct, my lord. We are so used to arguing—old friends, you see—that we didn't take her objection seriously."

"She objected to riding with the two of you in a high perch sporting phaeton in the streets of Bath, of all places, and you were going to encourage her to do so? You have," asked Worth politely, "no care for her reputation?"

"What's that got to do with anything?" muttered

Hereward and was again shushed by the more knowing Herbert.

"You are saying, my lord," said Herbert, carefully, "that it is not the thing?"

"It most certainly is *not.*"

Herbert sighed. "I am very sorry that we almost did something which might have harmed Damaris—" His eyes flew to Lord Worth's. "—*Miss* Damaris, I mean. We didn't know."

"Here now," asked Hereward hastily, "does that mean we can't take Dammy for a ride?"

"Will you shut your bone-box," said Herbert. "I apologize, Miss Damaris," he said and bowed. "Come along, Hereward. We'd best be getting this rig back to its owner."

"But . . ."

"*Will* you stop making bad worse?" asked Herbert, dragging his brother to where the phaeton stood. "Now get up there and be still."

"But I don't understand. You'll explain what happened?" asked Hereward plaintively.

"I'll explain it to you, you knock-in-the-cradle! Just get up there," said his exasperated brother.

The high and unstable carriage made a slow way down the street under Herbert's somewhat inexpert guidance. Damaris turned to Worth. "Thank you, my lord," she said with a certain amount of fervency. "I almost thought I'd have to run into the building to get away from them, but I couldn't leave Aunt Fanny so I didn't know what to do."

Fanny carefully maneuvered out of the chair. "Damaris, pay these men, please, and we'll go inside. Discussing this contretemps here on the street isn't at all proper."

The men were soon paid and trotted off. Fanny invited Lord Worth to come in for a brief visit, but he told

her he was already late for an appointment and, therefore, unable to do so. From his tone, Fanny thought he
rather wished he might, that he regretted the appointment which would take him away. His disappointment
made her wonder if he were, perhaps, interested in her
niece, because, if so, that made two exceedingly eligible
suitors!

Lady Lawton, once her other guests were gone, had
told Fanny outright that she believed Cahill interested in
Damaris. Her ladyship had added she would do all she
could to promote the match if Fanny did not object.
Now Worth, too, showed an interest.

Could it possibly be so? Would two such wealthy and
eligible men court the child? Fanny, questing in that
strange way she had which almost involved a twitching
nose, wished desperately she could see. She accepted
Damaris's aid in entering the building and climbing the
stairs, but all the time she was worrying.

She could not see. She would never see. At the moment
she deeply regretted her disability, which, for herself, she
accepted stoically. But in these circumstances, for her
nieces' sake, she really *needed* to see. She could not be a
proper chaperon for Damaris when she could not.

The immediate case was an excellent example. She
wasn't certain what would have happened if Worth had
not arrived, but she feared the worst. It was not beyond
the Lambourn boys to simply pick Damaris up and put
her on the overly high seat of a style of carriage which
had been described as a flimsy sporting vehicle of im-
moderate height. And what could Fanny have done to
prevent them? Muttering more than a few inadequate
swear words under her breath, Fanny entered her bedroom and took off her hat.

This journey to Bath may have been an error in judgment, she thought—and then recalled, again, Lady
Lawton's encouraging words concerning a match with

Cahill. Now that would be just exactly the sort of offer Tacye had had in mind when she'd determined to bring Damaris to the attention of a larger world, was it not? If only those silly boys did not do something stupid and ruin all . . .

And speaking of Tacye, just were was she? She'd gone with Worth, so why had she not returned with him?

The swearing which passed Fanny's lips at that thought was less mild than that she'd indulged in only moments earlier and would have shocked even Tacye if that young woman had been there to hear!

One further thought crossed Fanny's mind and left her feeling depressed. Where, too, was John Stewart Seward? Why had Lord Seward disappeared with no word of his going? Especially when it had seemed he'd wished to pick up their friendship from where it had ended . . . or rather from a somewhat deeper position than when it had ended?

Fanny, disoriented by her thoughts, had to find her bed by feel. She lay down on it and, much to her disgust, a single tear ran down her cheek. Why should she feel the least bit sad at John's defection? After all, she'd decided nothing could come of his interest in her, had she not? So. No more tears.

Fanny wiped her eyes and propped herself up on her pillows, determined to simply rest until Tacye returned.

Chapter 8

Tacye ordered an extra portion of oats for Numbskull before she left the stables where she rented space for the animal.

"Did he win?" asked the boy with whom she spoke.

"He did." Tacye patted her horses neck. "He did magnificently."

The boy's impudent grin widened. "Wait until I tell Joey. *He* said you hadn't a chance."

"Put a shilling on him, did you?" asked Tacye grinning as well.

"A piddling bob? Pah! I sprung for a whole guinea."

Tacye smile faded abruptly. "You can't afford to lose that, surely."

"Didn't lose, though, did I?"

"And if you had?" Tacye frowned fiercely.

A sullen expression settled on the young features. "Bet you laid a wager or two without you counted the cost."

"I had one wager on Numbskull—but no more than I could afford to lose. When we won, then I bet that money on later races. If I had lost it, I would have stopped betting." The boy's lower lip poked out farther than ever. "I have a sister and an aunt who depend on me," said Tacye, holding the boy's reluctant gaze. "I would not hurt them by losing money which is needed for their support."

They stood there, silent for a long moment, and then the boy sighed. "All right, then. I'll remember." But, irrepressible as ever, his eyes lit and he grinned again. "But I'm still glad I put a good bet on ol' Numbskull, here. I tol' Joey it was a great horse! The greatest horse in all the world!"

"Perhaps not quite that and I hope Joey can afford a guinea! Don't forget the oats."

"I won't. I'll give him a good brushing too. Come along here, Stupid," he added, giving the reins a tug. "You're a good fellow, you are. I'll take werry good care of you, I will!"

Stupid. Was that what poor Numbskull got called by his grooms? Tacye chuckled and wandered out of the stables into the late afternoon sun. She strolled the distance to the Abbey Arms and neared home just as the bells began to ring.

At the sound, Tacye hurried her steps. Aunt Fanny very much disliked it when one was late for dinner and Tacye, after a long afternoon in the dust and dirt of the track—to say nothing of actually racing—needed to bathe and change before she sat down to dine. Running up the steps two at a time, she entered their rooms a few moments later.

Fanny called out as she passed the bedroom. "Ta— Toby? Is that you?"

"Yes." Turning in, Tacye strolled to where her aunt leaned against her pillows, her hands in her lap. "I can't stay, Aunt Fanny. I'm in all my dirt and must change, but did you want something?" She noted what she thought were traces of tears. "Aunt, is something wrong? Did something happen? Did you have an unpleasant day?"

"Hush now! A very good day, taken as a whole, but a surprising day in one respect—something which I'll wish to discuss later, but since," she added, sniffing delicately, "you must change, would you don evening clothes? We've been invited to an informal ball given by that Mrs. Templeton who is pushing poor Miss Merry Templeton at everything in pantaloons. I'd have said no but Lady Lawton added her encouragement so that I didn't feel I could."

Tacye decided she'd been reading too much into what was merely tiredness due to dealing with too much strangeness. She said, "Dancing? After the day I've already had?" Tacye groaned. "I was looking forward to dinner and an early bed."

"Are you tired, bright eyes?" asked Fanny, frowning. "I know no reason why Damaris and I may not go by ourselves. Damaris is looking forward to it, of course. She so dotes on dancing and has had few enough chances living isolated as we've done."

Tacye bit her lip. She *was* tired, but it was for this reason, so that Damaris could be brought out in society in order to bring her to the attention of suitable young men, that they'd come to Bath. She must not shirk her duty to her sister.

"Once I've had a soak and fresh clothes so I don't smell of the stables, I suspect I'll feel my old self again and wouldn't want my bed even if I had the chance at it." Tacye grinned at a sudden thought. "Actually my bed is likely the last thing I should want. I'll be stiff as a board in the morning if I don't get some exercise this evening. So, if Damaris comes in to you while I'm getting ready, you may tell her she need not concern herself. I'll find my dancing shoes!" Tacye started to exit and then stopped by the door, frowning. "There is hot water, is there not?"

Fanny smiled. "You can be certain I knew you'd want it and urged Cook to be sure to have plenty ready for you. I believe, from the mutters I heard, she is keeping cans warm to the detriment of her cooking and only because it is for you!"

"Good."

A couple of hours later Tacye stood behind Fanny's chair and watched Damaris going down the line. "She's an excellent dancer, Aunt Fanny," said Tacye with badly hidden pride. "Graceful and energetic, but without a single hint of the hoyden. And she doesn't pretend to that listless boredom too many of the chits don, believing it a properly elegant manner. I don't understand why that pose seems to appeal to some men."

"I suspect they wish to feel they are protecting and supporting and in all ways dealing with their women's life."

"I much prefer *your* lord's attitude—that you were expected to keep up with him, I mean."

Lady Tamswell pulled in the reins controlling her emotions. After all, she'd long ago accepted that Gerard was dead. It was just that instant in which she'd seen him fall from the cliff face that she could not accept.

Unfortunately, whenever he was mentioned, that was what she pictured in her mind, never the good things, the desirable memories. After a moment in which she assured herself her feelings were well curbed, Fanny said, "Gerard certainly didn't coddle me, if that's what you mean, but perhaps you'll look for a husband who doesn't expect *too* much of you."

Tacye looked around, but the music was particularly loud and no one was too close. "Careful, Aunt," she whispered. "Someone might have heard that. *I'm* not in search of a *husband*—or a wife for that matter!"

"Heard . . ." Fanny felt a flush rush up her throat. "Toby, I'm very sorry. I should not have forgotten . . . and I won't again. You say we are isolated?"

"Yes. For the moment."

"Then I think now's a good time to ask you about something which is bothering me. Do you think Lord Cahill has shown more than simple courtesy to Damaris?"

Toby groaned softly. "Who has been talking to you?"

"Lady Lawton, of course. She deliberately held me at her side today until her rooms were empty of other guests and then spoke frankly about her hopes that the interest he's shown will come to something and asked if I had objections."

"I can see no objection on our side, but isn't the match a bit unequal? Won't *his* family object? That's what worries me."

"Then he has shown an interest?" Fanny bit her lip. "Ta-Toby, I simply don't know. He came to his honors unexpectedly, I understand, and is appalled by what he finds in society. It might be that Damaris, raised quietly in the country as she has been, appeals to him for the simple reason she does *not* have the . . . the . . . airs and graces of someone who has been on the town—" A flush darkened Fanny's skin at the use of the cant phrase and she hurriedly added a caveat. "As they say!"

"*They* may say," said Tacye in a hushed tone, teasing her aunt, "but I am shocked to hear you say it! How often, I wonder have you warned Damaris that speaking such words is not *done?*" She chuckled at Fanny's renewed blush. "But that is not important. I think you are asking me if I think there is any chance Damaris might be hurt by our pushing her onto Cahill . . ."

"Exactly."

Lady Lawton approached just then like a ship in full

sail. "Dear Lady Tamswell," she said. "How good to see you again so soon."

Tacye, quietly fuming that their conversation had been interrupted, went to where another spindly chair stood near the wall and carried it back, setting it near her aunt. She held the back and looked at Lady Lawton, a question in her eyes.

"Thank you, young man. Very thoughtful. Now run off and . . . and ask that poor pimply child sitting so forlornly there near that palm if she wishes to dance. You needn't worry about introductions at such a paltry affair as this." Ice coating her tone, Lady Lawton added, "Mrs. Templeton very likely announced at the beginning that everyone was on their own and was not to stand on ceremony. She thinks it shows that she's up to every rig and row in town, but to my mind it merely indicates she is too lazy to do her duty as a proper hostess. Oh," she added, when Tacye hesitated, "I think the child's name is Miss Mary Jessup. No one at all, of course, but still, I dislike seeing her sitting there wishing she were dancing. There's a good boy," she added as Tacye, a wry look in her eye, went off to play the gentleman.

Fanny, too, wished she and Tacye might have completed their conversation before Lady Lawton arrived, but now, acceding it was not to be, she politely asked her new friend to tell her who was in attendance that evening.

"No one in particular," she was informed—again with that acid note. "The men who count are all Cahill's guests out at his estate. Just what one might expect of the Templeton woman: hold a dance when no one of importance will come! No, no one of interest will be here, but the children will very likely enjoy themselves. I think that Miss Merry Templeton is a nice girl and would do quite well for herself if only her silly goose of a mother would just let her be. I detest pushy match-making mothers."

Lady Lawton glanced at Lady Tamswell and sighed. "You are thinking that I am one as well and of course you have the right of it. I excuse myself by saying I worry about the family if Cahill's heir were to inherit. I have, I'll admit, suddenly realized how very mortal we are. It was a terrible shock when my brother and both his sons drowned that way. Cahill is a good man and he will do well even though he was not raised to it, but he must marry and he must fill his nursery." She sighed again. "If only he didn't have such an odd kick in his gallop! If he is to marry, he says, then it must be a match he can tolerate. He'll not agree to a fashionable marriage—as they call them."

"Merely tolerate?" asked Fanny. A coldness creeping up her spine caught her by surprise and iced her voice as well.

"I spoke without thinking. It is because he seems to like your Damaris that I wish to promote the match," continued Lady Lawton. "You see, the boy is stubborn. He was as much as handed on a platter several really brilliant matches last season, but he turned up his nose at all of them. He said he would as soon take a cold compress to bed as any of the young women thrown at him at balls and in the street and . . . and wherever he went, actually. He was quite angry, you know, or he'd never have said such a thing to me and he apologized very prettily, but it does seem he's looking for the impos-sible. So irritating of him."

"The impossible?"

Lady Lawton leaned a trifle nearer. "A love match," she whispered. "I know the ton has gotten away from a sane and rational approach to marriage, but I admit frankly I don't approve this modern tendency to think marriage a proper milieu for the nurturing of love. Love, to my mind, should be kept a game and, as one does with games, be kept for those special occasions when one wishes to relax and has the time for it. Marriage is far too serious and must be worked at, both partners knowing their duties and applying themselves to their accomplishment.

"Children," she continued, "are, of course, one such responsibility, and a very necessary one, but to achieve them requires little time, actually. The greater share of one's life is spent in seeing that estates are run properly, that one's various houses are kept up and well stocked, that one does one's duty to one's dependents and community and so on."

Fanny sat mumchance through Lady Lawton's lecture. She knew very well that this was how most marriages in Lady Lawton's generation had been arranged but she herself had fallen quickly and deeply in love and it had never occurred to her her nieces might marry for anything less. She cleared her throat.

"Have I run on?" asked her ladyship. "I do tend to get carried away. Did you wish to say something?"

"I firmly believe affection between husband and wife is essential. I do *not* believe in arranged marriages where the emotions of the two parties have not been considered carefully and where they may have such totally different values and interests and natures there is no meeting of minds at all," said Fanny, wondering at her bravery in the face of Lady Lawton's firmly expressed opinions.

"Oh dear, have I not made clear that that is exactly why I wish to help your Damaris to a match with Cahill? It has become clear he will *not* marry where there is no affection. I've seen signs he is intrigued by the chit. With careful tending, I think that intrigue may grow into the necessary affection. The child is a good girl and you have raised her well. I could approve this match. That Cahill might marry to disoblige his family, I freely admit, has begun to fret me.

"Cahill," she continued, "is just such a romantic that it would be our luck that he come to think himself deeply in love with an opera dancer or such like and forget himself long enough to bring her into the family! He is, as yet, unsure of his position and himself and that leads to trouble every time. I will do my best to prevent that, but one must be subtle . . ."

She trailed off. After a moment and sadly, she added, "I am not very good at subtlety, I fear. It is not my way."

"I wonder if we shouldn't simply let them go on as they've been doing?" suggested Fanny as tactfully as she was able for the agitation she felt. "Walking together in the Pump Room, for instance?" Could there really be a match for Damaris here? "Later, if they show more serious interest in each other, then perhaps we might ensure they are both invited to the same things so they have the further opportunity . . ."

"All very well if one had forever and a day," interrupted Lady Lawton, "but just how long are you staying in Bath? And how long do we have before Cahill tires of this down-at-heels, old-fashioned resort and goes elsewhere? Brighton, for instance? I'm surprised he agreed to come here at all and it is my opinion that if he did not have that estate just outside of town to tend to, he would not have done so. But it isn't a very large estate, you know, or a very important one. It cannot hold him for long."

"Still . . ."

"Still you think I should not obviously push them together." Lady Lawton sighed. "It is all so difficult, is it not?"

"We will be in Bath for nearly two more months,"

said Fanny soothingly. "Do not despair. If there is an attraction between them, Lord Cahill will find excuses to remain nearby." Again Fanny continued with what she felt was surprising firmness. "I think, as I've said, that for the next week or two—at least that long—we should do nothing."

The notion Lady Lawton might actually push forward Damaris's claims on an earl—even a newly raised earl who had been nothing but a country vicar—was a trifle frightening. Fanny feared to put such notions into the child's head. She might develop ambitions beyond their means to promote—assuming Lady Lawton did not succeed in making the match she obviously wished to make . . . and yet there had been that strange note in Worth's voice earlier today which had sounded very much like disappointment he could not join them for a few minutes. Was Damaris's beauty such that she simply drew men into her net? A honeypot as such a girl was called? Oh, if only she could *see*.

The older woman fidgeted. "I detest sitting back and doing nothing," she said, reminding Fanny they'd been discussing ways and means.

Fanny's fears rose again. "In this case . . ." she began.

Lady Lawton sighed again. "I know. I will do my best not to meddle. At least for the coming week! But it *will* be difficult."

Fanny forced a chuckle. "Think of it as a task set you by your governess."

Lady Lawton's answering laugh was far more robust. It drew eyes. "My dear, it has been so long since I was under a governess's care, I don't believe I remember how it was." She looked around. "Now, let me see who is here that you've not met. . . ."

Her ladyship described Mrs. Templeton's guests. As she'd suggested earlier, no one of any importance was attending, but, if the noise level were anything to go by, the young people would, before the night was over, turn the informal dance into a romp. Her ladyship commented on Mrs. Templeton's lack of control and Fanny made a mental note to tell Tacye to collect Damaris and herself and get them away if any signs of laxity appeared.

Finally, after a long monologue to which Fanny attempted to pay attention, Lady Lawton said, "Ahh. Now there is a fine young gentleman—I *don't* think! Lord Andrew, Castelbourgh's youngest. The duke, you know. His grace is an excellent soul and I dearly love her grace, but the children . . . and that one in particular. Well! The rumors I've heard . . ." She paused. "Oh dear. Should I warn the Templeton woman, do you think? Surely she would not attempt to . . . but I do believe she *is!*"

"Is what?"

"What? Have I not said? Mrs. Templeton has just taken her daughter over to meet Lord Andrew. Now she's suggesting they dance and she is waving her fan in the oddest way—behind her back, you know? What can she . . . oh dear!"

"A waltz?" asked Fanny, hearing the first notes.

"How can that woman be so foolish?"

"That she's signaled the orchestra to play a waltz?"

"No, that she allows her daughter to dance it! She'll never get the chit vouchers for Almack's if it becomes known the girl has waltzed. Even here in the provinces one must be careful of the proprieties."

"I don't understand," said Fanny, confused. "Why may the child not waltz? I know there is some controversy, but I've also been told it is a very invigorating new dance."

"You don't know!" Lady Lawton thought about that for a moment. "Ah. I'd forgotten. It's been over a decade since you've been to London, has it not? The

Almack's patronesses have become quite tyrannical in their rules and their regulations for entry into what has become known as the Marriage Mart. I don't know why the ton puts up with it. . . .

"For instance," explained her ladyship, "no one may be admitted to Almack's without a voucher provided by one of the patronesses. For that matter, one cannot be admitted at all after eleven of the clock! Proper knee breeches are required for gentlemen, of course, and I approve of *that* particular rule, but what I referred to here, is that a proper young miss *does not waltz*. Once a patroness is assured the girl is properly trained in all ladylike behavior, permission will be granted. It is often done by the patroness herself introducing a partner to the girl as perfectly acceptable. That is what I meant when I said Mrs. Templeton was surely not so foolish as to allow the chit to waltz. Allow, did I say? Actually encouraging it!"

"Lady Lawton," asked Fanny worried by her ladyship's revelations, "where is Damaris!"

"Do not concern yourself. She is with her, er, cousin." Lady Lawton had, obviously, heard the rumors concerning Tacye's purported birth! "Adlington has turned down two importunate young men who had the gall to ask Miss Damaris to dance."

"I wonder how T-Toby knew Damaris should not," muttered Fanny.

"Perhaps it was the child herself. Does she not read fashion magazines such as Ackermann's *Respository?*"

"His monthly edition which discusses the arts, literature, and such things?"

"Yes."

Fanny still felt surprised, but responded, "Why yes. She does. In fact my nieces read it aloud to me."

"Then they must have skipped the articles on London modes and manners. Miss Damaris will have read the rules herself, of course, and knows she must not be seen to know how to waltz."

Greatly relieved and able to relax, Fanny chuckled. "I wonder if she does. Know how, I mean!"

"I had not thought there was anyone who did *not.*" Lady Lawton drew in a deep breath and left it out with a huff. "Many of my friends think the dance merely an excuse for embracing in public, but I wonder if they feel, deep down inside, as I do."

"And how is that?"

"Jealous," said her ladyship with a chuckle. "How I wish I were even twenty years younger and I'd soon show these cawkers how the dance should be done!"

Fanny made a signal which she hoped Tacye would see. Soon Toby and Damaris approached. "Aunt Fanny?" said Tacye. "May I get you and Lady Lawton a lemonade? I am about to find a glass for Damaris, you see, and thought perhaps one or the other of you might like something to drink as well?"

"I'll not muddle my insides with lemonade, young man, but if you can find me a light wine . . . ?" Lady Lawton stared at Tacye, obviously wondering if the boy would object at bringing such an unsuitable drink to a lady. Tacye merely bowed.

"Aunt Fanny?"

"Lemonade sounds refreshing," she said quietly, realizing her notion of suggesting Tacye ask Lady Lawton to waltz was likely quite ridiculous. Still, the idea continued to tease at the back of her mind and, when the waltz drew to a close more quickly than a dance usually ended—due to the fact so few were on the floor—she made a mental note that she would suggest it to Tacye as a possibility for future consideration.

Tacye approached the room where Mrs. Templeton had set out liquid refreshment. No servant presided over the table as one might expect and Tacye entered just in time to see Lord Andrew shake the last drops from a flask into the punch bowl which held the lemonade. She waited for a moment while the young man hid the bottle in the pocket in the tails of his coat. Then she came forward, choosing a clean wine glass and filling it with wine from one of the bottles. She filled a second and turned to go but was jostled by Lord Andrew.

"Careful!" said Tacye.

"You'd best be careful," hissed Lord Andrew. "Worth won't be around to save your bacon the next time."

"Next time? I haven't a notion what you mean," said Tacye. "Excuse me. Lady Lawton awaits her wine." Tacye bowed and moved on and out of the room, leaving a fuming Lord Andrew to glare after her seemingly oblivious back.

Once returned to the ballroom, Tacye moved quickly to where Lady Lawton and Fanny sat. "I don't know what to do about the fact I just saw Lord Andrew dump the contents of a flask into the punch bowl," said Tacye quietly as she bent to hand her ladyship her wine. "Aunt Fanny?" she added, handing over the other glass. "The lemonade was not quite what you like, so I brought you wine instead."

Lady Lawton surged to her feet as Tacye spoke to Fanny. "Excuse me, Lady Tamswell. Must see to something," said her ladyship.

"What did you tell her?" asked Damaris. "I saw you speak to her as you gave her her wine."

Tacye quietly explained about the tampering and her suspicion that gin had been added to the beverage which would be drunk by many thirsty young people as soon as the patterns of the Lancers quadrille currently in progress ended. "Lady Lawton has gone to see that no damage is done, I think," she finished. "Can you imag-

ine what would be the result if several of these young ladies were to speedily drink one or two glasses?"

Damaris giggled behind her fan, but Fanny frowned.
"Lady Lawton told me that young man was not quite
the thing, but you are telling me he deliberately did
something which might result in undoing a girl's training in restraint and make one or more young woman
behave in a way quite beyond the pale! That was surely
unthinking behavior on his part."

"I doubt it unthinking at all. Quite deliberate, in
fact."

"Ta-Toby, you cannot truly mean that he *hoped* to in-
ebriate some young woman?"

"Why not?" asked Tacye casually. "It would make it
easier to seduce her, would it not?"

Fanny paled. "Toby, would you point out our hostess?
I believe it is time we leave."

"Do you fear that things will get out of hand?"

"It is only that I have not my sight and I cannot
judge for myself. Besides, it is late and you have had a
long day, Toby. I think we should leave."

Tacye looked to her sister. Damaris glanced around,
looked slightly forlorn for a moment and then, recover-
ing herself, nodded. "I'm quite ready to leave, Toby,"
she said quietly and with a sincerity Tacye could not
doubt.

Had Damaris been looking for someone who was not
there? And if so, for whom had she searched? Lord
Cahill? Or Lord Worth perhaps . . . ?

Tacye wondered why she felt a tightness in her chest
at that latter thought. But she obediently led her sister
and aunt up to a flustered Mrs. Templeton and said all
that was proper, explaining they were not used to very
late hours yet and thought it best to leave now so that
Damaris could adjust slowly to Bath ways.

"Must you go?" asked Mrs. Templeton, but she didn't

urge them to stay. She had a worried eye on Lord Andrew who, earlier, she'd been pushing at her daughter.
"I do hope you'll come again," she said, added an "excuse me," and headed toward where Merry Templeton
giggled at something Lord Andrew said to her.

Tacye watched, saw Lord Andrew look up, his eyes
narrow and a look of extreme dislike cross the young
man's face. Tacye nodded. Andrew simply turned his
shoulder, the cut direct. Tacye, knowing Lord Andrew
was not watching, grinned and turned her small party
toward the door. Little she cared if the fellow never
spoke to her again! In fact, all to the better, if he did
not!

On their way home Damaris told Fanny and Tacye
that plans were being laid for an afternoon of explora-
tion in Sidney Gardens. "I know you will not wish to go,
Fanny, but I thought perhaps Ta-*Toby* might chaperon
me? There are grottoes, I'm told, and a maze and all
sorts of things and we'd finish by having refreshments at
the hotel there. Do say we may go, Toby. Aunt Fanny?
Please?"

It was unlike Damaris to plead in such a determined
way and Tacye frowned slightly. "You seem to wish to
do so very much indeed," she said, the faintest of questions in her tone.

"Oh yes. Lady Lawton will be there, if you are worried no one of responsible age will come, and Miss
Browne says it is very likely Lord Cahill and his set will
come. Merry says Miss Browne tries very hard to hide
it, but has a tendre for Worth and watches his every
move when he is near. Merry says it is quite funny, but
I think it sad. Miss Browne is not at all the sort to catch
Worth's eye, or so Merry says, but she cannot bring herself to look elsewhere where she might be capable of
finding a match. I told Merry it was not something
about which we should laugh, but Merry just chuckled

and said I was far too soft-hearted for my own good, that Miss Browne would laugh at me under similar circumstances and that I shouldn't be such a silly goose. But it isn't maudlin to feel sorry for someone who loves in vain. Is it?"

Fanny, who had, with difficulty followed Damaris's rush of words, agreed that it was a sad situation but added that perhaps Miss Templeton had never felt the softer passions and didn't know how deeply one could hurt.

"I think it must be that," said Damaris, seriously. "But she is so light-hearted and so full of fun it is very hard to scold her or to make her see that not all of life is a game."

"Surely her mother . . ."

"Merry," confided Damaris softly, "doesn't really know her mother. Until this last year she's had very little to do with her parents, keeping to the nursery and then the schoolroom, her governess ruling her every move. I don't see how she has retained her sense of humor or her love of fun and games."

"What you are saying is that she will pay little or no attention to her mother's wishes for her and will go her own way?"

"I suppose there is a bit of that. She thinks her mother too pushy by half and does what she can to avoid her."

"Damaris," began Fanny, "I wonder . . ."

"What I wonder," interrupted Tacye, a warning in her tone, "is how much longer it will take for us to reach our rooms. I have not been so tired in a very long time."

Fanny, realizing that the recommendation Damaris not become quite such a bosom beau to Miss Templeton was not something she should say in public, relaxed. They'd be home soon and then she could and would have a serious talk with Damaris. But in the meantime . . .

"My dear," said Fanny, "if Lady Lawton is to be with the young people in the Park, I think it very likely you may attend. I will discuss it with her first, however. I've found her a very good source of information and she seems willing to help me see you are safe and properly guided. Do not get your hopes up, but I suspect you'll be allowed to go!"

Damaris thoughts turned back to the possible treat and the dream in which she was allowed to explore the maze under Cahill's guidance. She forgot about her friend Merry.

And, while Damaris dreamed of Cahill, Tacye wondered if Worth would come to keep his friend company and if she would be allowed to spend time at his side. She sighed. This was a problem with her masquerade which hadn't occurred to her: to fall in love with the man of her dreams and find it impossible to give him the hints a well-bred woman was allowed to give was an unexpected difficulty; to know it was out of the question to dress in an enticing fashion which might draw his attention; and worst of all, to find it impossible to even let the man know she was female . . . !

Tacye sighed still again and looked up to find they'd arrived home. She paid off the chairmen and helped her aunt up to her room. She left Damaris there for what she guessed would be a kindly meant lecture and went on to her own room.

There Tacye readied herself for bed. She pulled the covers up, rolled on her side, rolled back, and eyes wide opened, stared at nothing in the dark room, while her thoughts roiled and boiled.

Finally, a long ineffectual hour later, Tacye sighed once again, turned on her stomach, and fell into a trou-

bled sleep where she raced on and on and on with
Worth half a pace behind or half a pace ahead—but
never, never, right by her side.

Chapter 9

Two more days passed while the wonderful plans to visit Sidney Gardens were put in order by Lady Lawton who took the notion in hand and made it hers. Damaris spent those days pleasantly, meeting friends in the Pump Room each morning, going for fittings for her new ball gowns or shopping for trim for an older dress, and visiting—usually under Lady Lawton's gruff escort—with those same young people at various homes in the afternoon.

She had the felicity of speaking with Cahill each day, and once, she promenaded with him in the Pump Room. On one memorable day, she and several new friends were again in competition at the archery butts. On that occasion, Miss Browne was unaccountably absent and Damaris allowed herself to do her best and enjoy every flight of arrow. It was icing on the cake when Cahill stopped by and, with others, shouted his encouragement to her when she reached the final round.

Tacye, on the other hand, saw very little of Worth. An old friend, another survivor of Waterloo, arrived in town for a day or two to benefit from soaking in the baths and the two men spent many hours together. Tacye had to fight off a certain unexpected and unwanted lethargy, an unusual degree of disinterest in

what went on around her. She didn't understand why
Bath seemed suddenly boring when, earlier, it had held
her interest quite well.

Or, actually she did, but refused to admit, even to
herself, how important Worth's mere presence had become to her happiness.

Fanny, too, was distracted when at home and, when
away from their lodgings, seemed to strain every sense.
Tacye, who wasn't completely preoccupied with her
own silly affaires, noticed, and worried that Fanny was
overset by all the strangeness and her need to pay attention to every move for fear she stumble over something,
or miss something important concerning Damaris.

"Are you all right?" asked Tacye, leaning over her
aunt's chair at an evening rout to which they'd been invited.

"All right?" asked the startled Fanny. "Why, of
course, I'm all right. Why should I not be?"

"I thought perhaps this was too much for you. You
seem very tense and as if you were constantly on the
alert."

Fanny instantly forced herself to relax. "Why should
you think me overly tense? I'm fine, I tell you."

The response, which was *almost cross*, worried Tacye
still more, but if Fanny refused to discuss her problem,
there was nothing to be done. Fanny, on the other hand,
realized she must not continue to concern herself about
Lord Seward's whereabouts. By now it should be obvious to the meanest observer, he'd had second thoughts
and taken himself off so that he would not be tempted.
Fanny determined to forget how happy she'd found herself when in his presence and how safe she'd felt when
he was there to help her.

She'd almost convinced herself she was no longer listening for his voice when she heard it! It was the morning before the jaunt to Sidney Gardens, a treat she'd

decided to forego—for her usual reason that walking in strange areas was difficult and she didn't wish to make a fool of herself. But now, she, Tacye, and Damaris were moving to leave the Pump Room when Lord Seward stepped into their path.

"My dear Fanny," he said softly. "What is this? I go away for a few days and return to find you looking as if you yourself were in need of Bath's medicinal waters!"

"Lord Seward? Is that you?" Fanny, convinced he'd taken himself away to avoid her, felt her usual confusion—only more so. If only she could *see*, she told herself.

"You called me John when last we met. Here, let us move aside. We are blocking the entrance."

And so they were. Questerman followed by Lord Andrew entered, both men scowling at the short wait, and scowling still more to see who had held them up. Neither was finding it easy to carry through with plots against the Adlingtons. Neither Eros, godling of love, nor Ares, god of war, could find an opening to take a hand in the Adlingtons' fate.

Lord Seward, shepherding Fanny and her young relatives to one side, turned his back on the two younger men, but Tacye saw, and ignored, their animosity. Since Fanny seemed unable to speak, Tacye welcomed the baron back to Bath.

"It's good to see you again. You have traveled far?" she asked.

"Not so very far, but a momentous journey to my mind. It is done now and, I am pleased to announce, a success. Lady Fanny ... Fanny," he said, turning to his love, "when may I bring a certain gentleman around to see you? It is important," he added before she could respond with the negative he could guess was on her tongue.

"My aunt will be at home this afternoon," said Tacye slowly. "But if she does not wish to be disturbed . . ."

"Fanny," said John urgently, "please. Do not deny us. I have been on a quest, you see, to fight dragons for you, but it appears it was all a mistake, the dragon a pussycat and everything easily straightened out, but you must speak with Mr. Thawle before we may do so."

"Thawle? That name . . . have I met him?" The characteristic questing motion of her head indicated Fanny was seeking enlightenment. "I feel I should remember him."

"Yes Fanny, you *should* remember him," said Seward dryly. "Please say we may come by this afternoon."

"If you think . . ."

"Fanny, it *is* important."

"What dragons," asked Damaris, a question Fanny and Tacye had felt too impertinent to voice.

Seward grinned down at the girl. "My child, I remembered that Gerry—Lord Tamswell, that was—once told me his wife would be well cared for if anything ever happened to him. Since it is obvious she is *not*, I thought I'd just see for myself what villain had stolen her widow's portion! But," he went on when Damaris gasped, "that was not the way of it. At the time of Gerry's death Fanny, it seems, had no particular need of funds and suggested some ridiculously low quarterly stipend for pocket money. She's never contacted her solicitor to increase it!"

Damaris gasped. Tacye gave Seward a wary questioningly look. Fanny, her blind eyes staring blindly straight ahead, merely blinked.

Seward grinned, pleased to bring her his startling news. "You have, as a result, a nice little fortune invested in the funds, Fanny, monies on which you may draw to very nearly any sum you might wish!"

"Good heavens," murmured Fanny. She wavered and

Seward grasped one arm as Tacye moved in to put her arm around her aunt's waist. After a moment Fanny recovered her poise. She clasped the steadying hand holding her arm. "Oh dear. A fortune, you say?"

"If you aren't too greedy!" Seward chuckled softly. "And you are not, so I think you'll agree."

Seward could not help but feel like a good fairy and his beaming face made several observers wonder if he'd just proposed and been accepted and if so, to whom had he proposed: Miss Damaris or Lady Fanny!

Cahill found himself particularly curious as to that point, much to Lady Lawton's amusement and secret glee: His Lordship muttered unanswerable questions and biting comments into her ear for some time. Lady Lawton relaxed, certain Cahill would come up to the mark where Miss Damaris was concerned!

"Aunt," said Tacye, after a moment in which they each silently mulled over the news, "I think you must agree to see this Mr. Thawle. Do you wish Damaris and myself to stay home with you while he explains the situation this afternoon?"

"No, no," said Fanny distracted. "I'm certain Lord Seward—John—means to remain at my side while I discover what I obviously should have known for years now. How stupid I feel!"

"You must not. Mr. Thawle is the stupid one. He should, and he admits it, have sent you regular reports even though you told him you didn't wish to be bothered by any of it. It seems you told the poor man that he was to go away and take care of everything himself."

Fanny's expression turned to one of curiosity. "He has been an honest caretaker then?"

"You've been lucky in that respect, my dear," said Seward very gently. "So far as I could tell by the brief inspection he insisted I make of his records, he has been honest to a degree one could hardly have unexpected, given the temptation you placed in his way!"

Fanny drew in a deep breath, plans and possibilities already swirling through her mind. "Very well, John. If you would bring him about two?"

"We'll be there. You were just leaving when I nearly ran you down?" Fanny nodded. "Goodday, then, until this afternoon," he said, bowing over her hand. He nodded to Damaris and to Tacye and moved on into the Pump Room, looking around himself for friends.

"Let us go quickly," suggested Tacye, "before someone comes to see what this has been about. We've been watched by half a dozen different pairs of eyes, Fanny—and some of them will not be reticent about asking questions. This way. Yes. Just a few more steps and we'll reach the door. There. Damaris has opened it for you . . ."

Tacye continued talking her aunt's way from the Pump Room to where the chairmen waited.

Fanny was partially in shock and moved as she was directed. She could not seem to assimilate the notion that she had a great deal of money while at the same time she plotted a trip to London for a season for Tacye and more clothes for all of them and, her head in a whirl, the revolutionary notion they *immediately* move to a house farther from the cathedral and the sound of the bells and not care a jot for the funds wasted renting their current rooms!

If John were correct, she was rich and could do any or all of those things. Was it possible, she thought, wonderingly, that it would be sufficient she *could* give Tacye and Damaris, if necessary, a *London* season! She must suggest that to the girls, and explain they need no longer worry about finding Damaris a husband here and now, that there could be a further opportunity. . . .

Or perhaps it was better to wait until she knew for

certain she could do all that? No need to raise expectations . . . but a real house instead of cramped rooms and farther from the frequent torture of peeling bells. . . .

Fanny's delightful daydream lasted all the way to the Abbey Arms where, once again, Herbert and Hereward awaited them, a pair and somewhat less sporting carriage standing nearby. "Morning, Lady Tamswell," said Herbert. "Fine day, is it not? We've come to take Damaris for a ride."

"Not today," said Fanny coolly. "She is invited to take part in Lady Lawton's gala at Sidney Gardens this afternoon and must prepare for it. Please excuse us."

"Not again!" said Hereward. "We even went to the trouble of finding a proper carriage."

"You consider that proper for taking a young woman for a ride?" asked Tacye, stepping forward for the first time.

"Oh, hello Tacye," said Hereward, barely glancing at the boyish figure. "You here?"

Herbert eyed the straight-backed figure facing them. "It *is* Tacye, is it not?" he asked a trifle hesitantly.

"No," said Fanny crossly. "It is not. It is a young cousin you've never met. Herbert and Hereward, be pleased to meet Mr. Tobias Adlington. He has come to Bath with us to provide us with consequence. Now, we really must go in. Toby?"

"Now one little minute," said Herbert. "If we may not go for a ride now, then when may we?"

"I haven't a notion," said Fanny.

"Certainly *not ever* in a *sporting* carriage," added Tacye, her voice as low as she could make it and cold in tone.

"What's wrong with this one?" whined Hereward.

"There was another one?" asked Tacye. "Why was I not told?"

"Maybe because it's none of your business," said Herbert. "Lady Tamswell, this is not fair behavior to old friends."

"Perhaps," said Fanny, slowly, "if you were to rent a *proper* carriage, a phaeton or, better, a landau . . ."

"Not that. Can't spring 'em in a landau," complained Hereward.

"But you will *not* 'spring 'em,' will you?" said Fanny severely. "Not when driving out with a young woman *and her chaperon.*" Fanny glared blindly in the direction of the boy's voices.

Hereward mumbled something about not asking Fanny, but Herbert shushed him. "Of course. Delighted to have you with us. Didn't think, did I, that you might wish to go along."

"Herbert," said Fanny, exasperated, "we are in Bath now. There are rules of behavior which must be met. Damaris may not go riding alone with you. It is not done. Surely you are aware of that?"

"Wanted Damaris to ourselves," muttered Hereward and was again shushed by his irritated brother.

"We've been friends for so long," said Herbert, "we didn't believe such restrictions applied. Goodday," he added and poked his brother who bowed jerkily. "Get moving," said Herbert.

"You mean we can't take her *again?* But our pla—"

"Shut up, will you?" Herbert, completely nettled, shoved Hereward roughly toward the curricle. "We'll discuss our plans for this afternoon later."

"Don't mean plans for . . ."

This time Hereward found his arm pulled up behind his back. He was marched toward the curricle. "Will you mind your gab?" hissed Herbert just before he half-lifted, half-shoved Hereward up into the seat. He bowed again toward the Adlingtons, a greasy, placating, smile on his face and then climbed up to take the reins.

"I didn't like the sound of that," said Fanny.

"I didn't either," said Tacye, frowning, and gazing thoughtfully after the vehicle's traffic-impeded movement along Milsom Street.

"Surely Hereward wasn't referring to a plan to kidnap me?" asked Damaris, her skin white and her voice hushed.

"I think perhaps he was. Fanny, under the circumstances, I'm not certain you are sufficient chaperon. Do you think perhaps I should ride with you if you accept an invitation from them?"

"When I can no longer put it off, I'll make up a larger party," said Fanny. "It will be all right."

Tacye hesitated, then said, "You say that last as if you weren't quite certain."

"Toby, I can counter any plot the boys evolve, but I admit I'm worried about Hereward. He was too certain it was you when he first heard your voice. He was confused when I introduced you as Tobias, but he'll think about it and I fear he'll come to the conclusion you *are* Tacye. His mind works in simple ways. He thinks it's you and he'll decide it *is*. And then what?"

Tacye was silent for a moment. Then she shrugged. "We'll face that if it happens. The best thing to happen, of course, would be for the Lambourn boys to leave town." Tacye brightened at the notion. "Now, I wonder how that might be arranged. . . ."

"Let us go in," said Damaris. "Too many people are round and about!"

Tacye agreed. "So there are." She paid off the chairmen who had gone some paces away and were waiting further orders as well as their money. They trotted off, back to their usual place between the Pump Room and the Abbey, where, if they were needed again today, they could be found.

Fanny, who was becoming quite comfortable with the floor plan of the Abbey Arms, went up the stairs, through their door, and turned down the hall to her room without a thought of where she was or where she was going. She was far too busy worrying at the question of why Lord Seward—John—had not walked her home, why he had left her side and gone on into the Pump Room.

Was this another indication he'd given up all thought of courting her? Even if he'd gone to London and brought back a solicitor whose existence Fanny had forgotten and even if he'd made that trip for her, perhaps it was a sop to his conscience. A sop necessary now he'd seen her and discovered he was *not* nourishing strong feelings for her as he'd believed true until they'd met again?

After all, nursing a tendre all these years had kept him safe from other women and, for some men, that was an important consideration, was it not? An excuse which could be trotted out to protect themselves from importuning females?

Fanny entered her bedroom faultlessly, moved to her dressing table without hesitation, where she dropped her gloves on its shining top without her usual touch—one made to be sure. She removed her hat just as decisively and let it drop to the padded seat of the stool—again without feeling for it. She turned and, while unbuttoning her pelisse, moved to the armoire where she hung the outer garment. She turned again toward the door.

Tacye and Damaris, who stood in the hall watching her, looked at each other and, quickly, moved out of the way.

"Are you there?" asked Fanny, feeling their presence in that odd way she had.

"We're both here," said Tacye. "I had no idea you had learned your way around these rooms so thoroughly. I think I may stop worrying about you quite so much."

"I have never," said Fanny with the faintest of acid bite, "suggested you *should* worry about me."

"But," soothed Tacye, a frown creasing her brow, "you need *not* suggest it. It is the duty of fond nieces to worry about loving aunts. Aunt Fanny, what is it I *should* worry about, since it is not how you feel in our new surroundings?"

"I think you should let me worry for myself, Tacye. I can do it very well all on my own."

Again the girls heard that unusual and unexplainable acid in her voice. Tacye looked at Damaris who stared back, her eyes taking on a worried expression as well.

Damaris tried. "Is it perhaps what you'll learn from the solicitor Lord Seward mentioned? Is there some problem you have guessed which we cannot know?"

Fanny opened her mouth to reply, closed it. "I think you should change for your afternoon outing, Damaris. As for you, Ta-Toby, you can run along and do whatever it is young men are supposed to do at this hour."

Tacye eyed her aunt thoughtfully. "Perhaps I will," she said, and immediately left the Abbey Arms to return to the Pump Room where she breathed a sigh of relief to discover Lord Seward had not vanished. Unfortunately, he was talking to Lord Worth and Tacye, reluctant to feed her tendre in that direction, didn't wish to interrupt.

"Well, if it isn't the little man," said Lord Andrew from behind Tacye. "I'm laying my plans, you know," he hissed. "You'll be sorry."

"Do you often throw *your* races, Lord Andrew?" she asked just as softly.

"That's an insult. How could you suggest such a thing?"

"How can *you* suggest it is my fault you lost because I won my race?"

For a moment there was silence. "You should have lost. Worth is the far better sportsman."

"Perhaps I should have done, but I had a very good horse and I was lucky. Nor did I lay your bet for you."

"Damn you. You should have lost."

Tacye sighed. There was no arguing with someone like Lord Andrew and she should have remembered it. "Excuse me. I wish to speak with Lord Seward now he's free." She walked away from Lord Andrew feeling his eyes on her back like a burning brand.

"Lord Seward, a word or two?" she asked as she approached him.

"Hmm? Oh. Adlington, is it not? Is your aunt excited and happy?"

"My aunt," said Tacye dryly, "seems confused and worried and I don't understand it."

The confusion and worry must have been catching because Lord Seward's expression revealed just those emotions. "Now that makes no sense at all. I thought she'd be pleased!"

"I was hoping you might clarify the situation. The whole situation?" Tacye took the impertinence from that with a wry grin which brought a grin to Seward's face as well.

"If, you are asking my intentions," said Seward, his features relaxing, "I'll admit I'm desperately hoping to steal your aunt away from you and take her off to my own home."

"I assume you mean to wed her first?" asked Tacye, a touch archly.

Seward's face burned a brilliant red. "Of course," he said stiffly. "Was that not clear?"

"Not in so many words." Tacye grinned—something more than the half-smile so common to her. "Sir, if you can make our aunt happy, I'll shake your hand and wish you well. Just be very sure you make her happy."

"Make whom happy?" asked Worth from just behind Tacye's shoulder. "Has this to do with Seward's recent discoveries? He's been telling me about them."

Tacye felt herself tense. She turned on Seward. "You've been telling all and sundry my aunt is so stupid she did not know she was a reasonably wealthy woman?"

He looked horrified. "No. Certainly not."

"Not," murmured Worth, humor in his tone, "unless you consider me all and sundry."

"Worth is an old friend. I'll admit my excitement was too obvious and Lucius asked me about it and I could not refrain from telling him of my genius in remembering what Gerry said and putting two and two together. I freely admit to a trifle of disappointment there was no dragon to fight, that it had all been a mistake—but I'm happy Fanny will not go in want, whatever her decision about my suit."

Tacye nodded, accepting the apology and understanding how difficult it must have been to have no one to discuss one's great achievement with. "I should not have accused you of gossiping, but Aunt Fanny is so easily hurt and I feel it my duty to protect her."

"A duty I hope will soon be mine."

Tacye bowed.

"We were also discussing," said Worth, changing the subject, "the notion of indulging in a good beefsteak or an excellent raised pie at York House. Will you join us and we may go on to Sidney Gardens later?"

Tacye wavered and her worst nature won. She should not agree. She knew that. For her to go to a hotel and dine with two men was outside of enough—if she were caught and unmasked, that is. But she would not be. There was no reason why anyone should guess she was

not a he. Fanny's suggestion Hereward would, somehow, give her away was—must be—ridiculous.

Still, she berated herself for giving into her desire to
associate as much as possible for as long as possible with
Worth. The growing romantical dreams she indulged at
night in the privacy of her own bed were becoming embarrassing and she must, she reminded herself, be very
careful she not give those feelings free rein so that they
become obvious.

After all, the sight of a young man mooning around
after a *gentleman* would soon cause all the talk Tacye had
feared Seward was spreading. Merely, the *subject* of the
gossip would be different!

When the three were seated around a table in
Worth's private sitting room, Tacye diffidently asked
Seward if he would mind telling the story of his adven-
ture.

"I only wish it were an adventure," said Seward, ruefully. "I find myself in the oddest situation. This meeting
Fanny again after so many years, I mean. I feel young
again and alive as I haven't in forever and a day. I went
off in the spirit of knight errantry so, it was all quite
anticlimatic. Instead of my dragon I found a horrified
and embarrassed solicitor who had, he felt, badly mis-
handled one of his clients. It had never occurred to him,
you see, that when he talked to her after Gerry died
Fanny didn't care about the future and paid him no attention whatsoever, merely wishing him to the devil, so
she need not be polite to this intruder on her grief—at
least that's the way we worked it out while traveling
down from London."

"Was Lady Tamswell so very much alone that there
was no one to see to her interests?" asked Worth, ad-
dressing his beefsteak with knife and fork. He lifted a
bite to his mouth and looked at the other two—
surprised to see Toby flushing bright red. "Not you

bantling. You'd have been far too young ten years ago to have known anything about it."

Worth's teasing comment gave Tacye time to remember she could not refer to Fanny's brother as her father—even if Worth did believe it to be the case. One did not make reference to one's father when one was a bastard. Not in polite society, at least!

"Her brother was alive then," said Seward, obviating a need for her to say anything, "but the solicitor says he saw Fanny immediately after the funeral and Adlington had not yet arrived. When Adlington appeared, Fanny had him take her away. Immediately. I don't think she gave the poor man time to make proper murmurs of regret to Gerry's relatives and certainly there was no time to explain to him the will in which Gerry left Lady Tamswell the Lakes District's property as well as the insultingly small Widow's portion which was part of her marriage settlement. I never understood why there was such a small settlement originally. It didn't make sense."

"Family history says, that Aunt Fanny's father-by-marriage did not approve the match," said Tacye. "He insisted, it is said, on the small settlement in the hopes Aunt Fanny would break the engagement, but she was far too deeply in love to care about such mundane things as settlements."

"Gerry made things right after his father died, but evidently, no one knew he'd done so." Seward sighed. "It is too bad the solicitor handles several very large estates and Fanny's relatively small inheritance was rather lost in his more important duties—not that he skimped his responsibilities, but, since she never contacted him, he assumed everything was all right and never again checked that all was truly as it should be. He is a very chagrined man just now!"

"As well he should be," said Worth. "Adlington, has Lord Andrew been causing you difficulties?"

Tacye, her mouth full, shrugged. She swallowed. "He blusters occasionally, makes stupid but vague threats, so no, no particular difficulty has arisen."

"Blast. I hoped I'd frightened that particular bully into behaving."

"You would fight my battles?" asked Tacye, surprised.

"What battle?" asked Seward. "What have I missed, being out of town as I've been?"

Worth outlined the problem with Lord Andrew as they finished their meal with a large tankard of ale. "I had a word with him later, but it appears it did no good."

Lord Seward looked at the clock on the mantel and rose to his feet. "Is that truly the time? I must collect Thawle and go on to the Abbey Arms at once. If our business doesn't take too long, perhaps Fanny and I will join you later in the Gardens. Thanks for dinner, Worth!" He disappeared out the door.

Tacye's eyes followed his rapid departure. He'd given her no time to tell him how unlikely it was that Fanny would agree go to Sidney Gardens. "I too must leave, since I must escort Damaris to the party," she said, setting aside her half-full tankard.

"If you do not object, we may go together. It is not much out of the way to stop at the Abbey Arms." Worth tipped up his tankard and drained his ale. They left the York House minutes later and strolled down the street, meeting up with Lord Cahill who was, obviously, headed for the Arms as well. "Seeking to escort the little Adlington?" asked Worth.

Cahill blushed. "M'aunt. Suggested that perhaps it would be a nice gesture if I were to go along with the young Adlingtons. Said they didn't know too many people yet and might feel shy about coming along by themselves." He glanced at Tacye who did her best to look retiring. "Hope I'm not pushing in where I'm not wanted?" he asked diffidently.

Tacye hid a grin. Shy? It had never occurred to her, and very likely not to Damaris, to feel shy about going where they'd been invited. "Your aunt is a thoughtful woman. Damaris in particular will appreciate your support and I know Aunt Fanny will feel happier that we arrive in your shadow and therefore acquire a patina of your consequence!" she said, smiling. She spoke quickly, forestalling Worth, who she guessed, was about to tease his friend. She caught his eye and shook her head. Worth's brow arched, but he shut his mouth and forbore to embarrass Cahill.

The three trooped into the Adlington sitting room where they found Damaris awaiting Tacye and, with a trifling agitation, Fanny, the imminent arrival of Seward and the solicitor.

"You're all right?" Tacye asked her aunt.

"I'm fine. What can possibly be the problem when I am about to hear I'm a wealthy woman?"

But, obviously, something bothered Fanny and Tacye looked to Damaris to see if she'd a clue. Damaris, however, was looking into Cahill's eyes as his lordship greeted the girl a trifle more effusively than might be thought quite proper. Tacye sighed. Damaris would be no help at all in discovering what had upset Aunt Fanny so badly. That something had and that whatever it was was important could not be denied.

Somehow Tacye must find time to gently urge her aunt to confide in her . . . but not now. It was time they left and with a few more words they did so.

Fanny wished she'd had an opportunity to ask Damaris if she looked a perfect guy, which she feared must be the case. Gently she patted her hair, resettling the lace-edged cap she'd worn since returning to her brother's home a widow. She retied the ribbons just under her left ear. Had she done that right? Were the bows too large and floppy? Were there wrinkles?

And speaking of wrinkles, should she have changed her gown? Was *it* badly crushed and in need of freshening? Agitated, Fanny rose to her feet and without thought paced around the small sitting room. It didn't occur to her to wonder that she'd been moving with surprisingly assured steps ever since returning that morning from the Pump Room.

She stopped by the table and reached out to touch a flower in the bouquet centered there. The petals were soft under her gentle fingers but the fact barely registered before she turned away and moved to the window which she immediately abandoned in order to return to her chair where she settled as comfortably as her growing but ill-understood apprehensions allowed.

But, this was the behavior of a skitter-witted woman with no more sense than an infant in arms! Why *was* she so very upset by the knowledge she had money?

Fanny forced her mind to stillness and then thought why? Perhaps it was simple: she was upset because she felt her new security would give Seward one less reason for continuing the suit he'd begun. Because now he could abandon her and feel no guilt.

But surely she wasn't so foolish as to believe anything *could* come of his idiotic notion they marry? She'd already informed him it could not be, so why should she act like an agitated duck whose nest had become an object of interest to the kitchen cat?

She could not, in honor, marry. No man should be forced to take on the burden of a blind wife who could not even take on the simple duty of overseeing servants in a proper manner, checking that they did their work as they should! And that was only a minor problem when one was blind because one could always have a trusted housekeeper to take up that particular burden.

There were other duties, far more important duties she *could* . . . but it would not do. She must *not*, as she'd been doing somewhere deep in her mind, dream of wedding John Stewart Seward, Lord Seward, Baron Seward . . . John . . .

A knock interrupted the daydream which followed her self-inflicted scold. She started, then composed herself and called permission to enter. Mary opened the door and, a bit awed by the knowledge her mistress was about to become a wealthy woman, carefully announced Lord Seward and the solicitor, Mr. Thawle.

After profuse apologies which Fanny, a trifle rudely, finally cut short, Mr. Thawle proceeded to outline exactly what Fanny's situation was at that moment. Her life interest in the Lake's estate didn't interest her, except to ask that all was well there, that no one was in need, and that the property was in good heart.

"I've no interest in ever visiting that region again, especially since I can no longer appreciate its beauty," she explained diffidently. "I fear there is too much I only wish to forget."

"If you are concerned that all is not as it should be," said the solicitor a trifle stiffly, "you could send an agent to see that all is well." He was obviously a trifle insulted that she might think he'd not done all that was proper. "Now, as to what you own outright—the result of what has been saved from the income from the estate, you know—" He pulled papers from a capacious pocket and looked them over. "Let me see. . . . First, let me explain . . ."

It took nearly half an hour for the man to outline how he'd invested her income over the years. The bulk of it had been put in the four percents which were safe and solid. The rest had gone into various investment propositions, nearly all of which had come safely to maturity.

"I have done *some* investing in shipping, but not

much. One cannot predict storms at sea whereby everything is lost instantly. No, no, careful analysis of such projects as canals and the prospect of proposed mines are far better, as you can see—I mean," he said, embarrassed when he instantly realized she could *not* see, "as I will explain to you. There are two mines which are doing well, although I think I'll sell out of one of those . . . but you're not interested in the details, surely, only in what you have. Now let me see: the total income per year has, for the past three years, averaged around sixteen thousand pounds. . . . My Lady!"

But Seward was before him and caught Fanny before she could fall over. He lifted her and held her until she began to come to and then carefully seated her, sitting on the arm of her chair and holding her hand.

"Are you all right, my dear?" he asked, anxious.

"Did he say . . . ?"

Seward chuckled when she trailed off her blind eyes lifted to stare him in the face. "Sixteen thousand pounds," he repeated slowly and distinctly. "Per year. Fanny, you must not swoon again. It is," he said, tongue in cheek, "merely money."

"Sixteen thou—" Fanny shook her head, put a hand to her forehead. "Sixteen thousand po—" She couldn't say it.

"I'm very sorry to have startled you," said the solicitor, not certain just why, when she'd been warned she was wealthy, she'd found the actual figure such a shock.

"And I'm very sorry to be such a silly fool, but when one's family and oneself have occupied a small estate and lived on less than three hundred a year for more years than one likes to think, the notion we need never stint ourselves again is more than merely shocking!"

"My poor dear," said Seward, now somewhat in shock himself. "If only I had known . . ."

"It's my own fault. I've tried, ever since you told me of Mr. Thawle's existence, to remember the interview you tell me we had. I cannot recall a thing about it—except the vague knowledge I'd heard the name before. . . . But you would have been Gerry's solicitor, would you not? Of course I'd have heard it." She shook her head, regretfully. "What a fool I was to be so wrapped up in my grief and my blindness that I could not even listen to the gentleman explaining to me that which would give me security in future!"

"Perhaps it was that you felt you would *not* have a future?" asked Seward, diffidently. "I remember how, for a time we feared . . ."

"Oh yes," interrupted Fanny. "I was that low. For a time. A brief time. But my brother needed me. And his children were without a mother . . . one adjusts, forgets such nonsense. One only need allow oneself to remember others and *their* needs."

She said that with such off-handedness that John breathed more easily. "Is there more?" he asked the solicitor.

"Only that some arrangement should be made so that Lady Tamswell may draw upon her funds." Mr. Thawle explained how she could do that and, after a few more words, departed, saying that if he hurried, he thought it possible he might still be able to make arrangements to catch that evening's Royal Mail back to London.

"Well, Fanny?" asked Seward when they were alone.

"Is it well, John?" She wrinkled up her forehead. "I cannot tell yet if it will be a blessing or merely raise new problems altogether! Not that it will not ease life a great deal. That is a certainty, but . . ." The frown deepened. "I just don't know. . . ."

"There will be changes you cannot foresee, is that not it?" he asked kindly—and suddenly, with a lurch in the region of his heart, wondered if lovely Fanny, who would soon be known to be a wealthy woman, might not look much higher than a mere Baron for a husband.

"I'm sure there will be," she said and squeezed his hand which still held hers. He squeezed it back, holding on tightly. "Many problems as well as many advantages, I think."

The bells rang tentatively, once or twice and neither spoke until the last peal drifted away.

"Now there is *one* advantage to my newfound wealth! And the more I think on it, the more I like the notion! I must immediately look into finding a house situated in a far corner of Bath! And," she said, smiling, "I may do it with no concern for wasting the rent we've paid in advance here. Moving may now be accomplished with no problem."

"*I,*" he teased, "think the immediate problem is that we're missing the fun at Sidney Gardens. Will you come with me?"

Fanny hesitated. "I do not usually attend such parties. I'm awkward and too likely to make a fool of myself and I do not like it when I do that."

"If I promise to take very good care of you and watch every step for you?" he coaxed.

"And for you, where would the fun be in that?" she asked, rueful.

"Where you are, there I wish to be. Since it is not proper for me to stay here alone with you—at least not until you agree to wed me—then I must somehow make you agree to go elsewhere where it will be proper. . . ." Again he lightened the tension with his teasing. "Perhaps I could hire you a Bath-chair and push you around the gardens!"

Fanny felt her spirits rising. He was *not* suggesting he have nothing more to do with her. In fact, quite the reverse! After only half a moment's hesitation, she agreed to chance a walk in the gardens. "But not all the way

there! If you'll ring the bell, John, I'll send Mary to order up my chairmen. You'll not have to half-guide and
half-carry me all the way to the entrance!"

"I would be quite happy . . ."

Suddenly the bells rang out again, full voiced and
running in peels from the smallest to the largest and
back again, and again. They drowned out the rest of his
sentence—which, decided Fanny, was just as well. She'd
momentarily forgotten that nothing could come of her
friendship with John. Except, perhaps, friendship?
Would that be enough?

Her maid entered just then and Fanny gave Mary her
orders. A very short time later Fanny and John left the
Abbey Arms for Sidney Gardens.

Chapter 10

Tacye and Worth followed Cahill, who had Damaris on his arm, into the hotel which was the entrance to Sidney Gardens. They wended their way through the high-ceilinged lobby and onto the terrace which overlooked the gardens themselves. These stretched out before them, enticingly laid out with flower beds, hedges, and shrubbery, small groves of trees and paths, offshoots of which, led to well-constructed bowers or small grottoes. And, of course, there was the much celebrated maze. Neither so old nor so large as the maze at Hampton Court, still it provided much amusement for those willing to go into it without the key to its solution.

The Lawton party was gathering at the bottom of the stairs leading down from the terrace. As the Adlingtons descended toward them, Herbert and Hereward broke from a small group of young men and approached with long strides.

"We've been waiting for you, Dammy," said Hereward, grinning widely, his friendly open face glowing with anticipation.

"We'll see you have a good time today," said Herbert, ignoring the fact Damaris clung to Cahill's arm—actually seemed to move more closely to his side.

"Come along now, Dammy," urged Hereward.

"We've found the most beautiful thing in all the world. Truly lovely . . ." he said enthusiastically and then turned an almost guilty look toward his brother. "At least, *girls* would think so." One more glance at his brother and he hung his head, digging his toe into the gravelled path.

"Hereward is correct," agreed Herbert. "It's a water grotto with ferns and flowers and interesting rock work. I found it fairylike and think you'll enjoy it, Miss Damaris."

Hereward stared in outraged surprise at his brother. "When I said it was pretty and fairylike you told me not to be a nick-ninny!"

"Lickspittle!"

"I'm not tellin' tales. I'm tellin' the truth. You called me a nick-ninny!"

"Boys!"

"Yes, Tacye?" Hereward looked around and his expression turned to one of blank confusion. "That you, Tobias? I thought it was Tacye. Sorry. You wanted something?"

"You cannot fight it out *here*. If you wish to settle your dispute, you'd best leave the gardens."

"But we want to take Damaris to see the pretty grotto," insisted Hereward.

"Why do not we all go?" suggested Cahill, putting his hand over Damaris's where it lay on his arm. "Will you not lead the way?"

Herbert scowled, but bowed and, grabbing his brother's arm, pulled him around. They turned down one of the side paths, Cahill and Damaris following. Tacye looked around, fearing the Lambourn's dispute had made them conspicuous. Besides, Cahill's suggestion meant they were going on before they'd properly greeted their hostess. No one, however, among the rather large group, appeared at all interested. In fact, the gathering was breaking up, smaller cliques moving off in various directions.

"Shall we go?" asked Worth, a pensive look following the quartet's backs.

"I'm tempted to let Cahill handle it, but I suppose I must not." Tacye sighed, and moved off slowly in the wake of the other four. "The Lambourns are such great loobies," she said.

"More like the Devil's own," said Worth dryly. "Get it out of your head they are a pair of Dandy Prats! They are not to be considered insignificant and you must not believe they can be easily brushed aside! Especially the elder. Hereward, poor boy, merely follows, I think, in his brother's path."

"But what am I to do? I am not of a size to take them on in a bout of fisticuffs and even if I were up to their weight, I'd not take on the two of them together. They may fight each other at any and every turn, but let either be set upon and the other jumps in to his brother's defense. The only alternative I can think of is forcing a duel—I do not, however, believe that particular solution an answer to any problem. Beside, they'd have to have done something far more serious than they've yet done for me to suggest a duel, something like running off with Damaris out of hand. I'd rather they were sorted out before it came to that!"

"So would I."

Worth gave her a curious look. Hereward's innocent response to Tacye's voice had convinced him, finally, that he *was* dealing with Tacye Adlington. On the other hand, her calm statement she wasn't up to the weight of the Lambourn cubs, was just such a statement as a slightly built youth who knew and accepted his limitations would have made—but no. Voices were individual and rarely did two people sound exactly alike. Hereward had, to Worth's satisfaction, proved Tacye Adlington was indulging in an outrageous, a *scandalous,* masquerade! Worth was very surprised to discover he was not particularly shocked by it.

"Would you duel if it were necessary?" he asked, curious at just how far Miss Tacye Adlington would go to maintain her chosen role.

A grim line of jaw gave him answer almost before she spoke. "The provocation would need to be great and no alternative available, but I love my family and I would do anything necessary to protect them."

"Bravo," he said softly.

"Do I sound like a prating verger? I don't mean to, but you asked and I said what I felt."

"I meant no insult, bantling. I like it that you support your family in whatever way you deem necessary." Worth eyed Tacye's well-fitting trousers and repressed a twitch to his lips as he thought of just what contravening of conventions Tacye Adlington had already felt necessary! "I believe we've nearly arrived at the water grotto," he added. "At least, I assume those ohs and ahs I hear come from Miss Damaris's lips?"

They rounded a last turn in the path to find Damaris peering into a shallow manmade cave from which a narrow stream trickled over and around fern-shrouded rocks. Herbert, a brooding look in his eye, watched Cahill laughingly prevent Damaris from falling into the water as she stood upon a wet boulder, slippery from the spray. Hereward had moved farther away and was swinging his cane at the heads of swaying flowers, occasionally nipping one from its stem. Occasionally, his large blue eyes trailed toward Damaris and away again and his countenance drooped sadly.

Tacye joined her sister and Cahill, but Worth approached the younger Lambourn. "You were correct, Hereward," he said softly. Hereward looked up, saw who had approached him and looked wary. "When you said the grotto was beautiful," Worth explained. "It is. I haven't a notion what your brother said to you concerning your feelings about it, but you've no call to feel ashamed for being affected by such loveliness. It does not make you less a man to realize that true beauty makes one's heart beat faster and allows one's soul to soar."

"You feel that too?" asked Hereward, wonderingly.

"Yes. There have not been many occasions when it's happened, but I treasure each such moment. I remember, for instance, a time in Scotland. The mist was heavy over the brae and we could barely see our feet on the path that led to where we meant to cast for salmon that day. Then the sun rose. As the mist thinned, the view revealed is one I'll never forget. For a long long moment I stood and stared. My friend," he added, "twitted me for being a twaddling poet, but I contend such moments prove we're human and not mere animals."

"You didn't care when your friend called you a poet?"

"If it is being a poet to see the beauty around us, then I'm proud to be called such," said Worth, firmly repressing the fact that in his immaturity at that time, he'd pushed his friend into the stream for his teasing. "One simply ignores—and feels sorry for—such crass fellows who will never allow themselves the privilege of seeing in just that way."

The philosophy was true enough—although it had been hard won and very likely Hereward would have to win through to it himself. One couldn't *tell* another. Or perhaps one could? Worth eyed Hereward, feeling sorry for the lad who was neither a boy nor yet a man.

"Are you really a suitor for Miss Damaris's hand?" asked Worth, swinging his own cane at an innocent flower.

"Oh yes." Hereward nodded several times. "I want her. Desperately. She's so beautiful . . ." he finished, trailing off.

"Are you sure you want, at your age, to be tied down with wife and children and responsibility?" Worth adopted a horrified expression only long enough for Hereward to note it and then quickly wiped it from his face. "But, of course, I've no business saying that, have I? I merely thought that young bucks like you and your brother would look forward to London and your grass time there—and now that Napoleon is gone for good, perhaps you'd wish to see Europe and the, hmm, fun and games our grandfathers enjoyed on their grand tours."

"A grand tour?" Hereward's eyes gleamed. "Travel on the continent? I never thought of it. I wonder . . ." He caught sight of Damaris's laughing face. "But . . ." He sighed. Another flower was decapitated and Hereward looked up to face Worth squarely. "I haven't a chance with her, have I?" he asked and a fleeting impression of maturity briefly shadowed his features.

"I think, although you'll not believe me now, that in a few months you'll be very glad you do not," said Worth kindly. "One suffers a great deal from first love. It is very real while it exists. The trouble is that it rarely does for long. It doesn't last, I mean."

"Truth?" Hereward stared into Worth's eyes, a strained, begging, needy look.

"Truth. I can't say first love is *always* ephemeral, but almost always it wanes and disappears in new interests."

They watched as Tacye stepped on one rock, put her other foot on another, carefully straddling the tiny stream. She reached down for a particular stone Damaris had admired.

"It won't look the same when it's dry," warned Tacye.

Damaris giggled and looked up at Cahill who took

the dripping stone from Tacye and wiped it with his handkerchief before giving it to her. They bent their heads close over the drying stone.

Herbert, watching, seemed to swell with anger.

Hereward sighed. "I don't think Herbert even likes her," he said softly. "But he's determined to wed her."

Worth blinked. He stared at his young companion. "Doesn't *like* her! Then why would he wish to wed her?"

Hereward again eyed the toe of his boot as he scraped gravel around in shallow arcs. "Maybe because I said I wanted to? So he said no, *he* wanted to and he would. And now he's too stubborn to say otherwise. Herbie don't like to lose." He looked up at Worth. "I don't like the notion of Herbie leg-shackled to Dammy. I don't think he'll treat her right." The lad's face fell into thoughtful lines, and he said slowly, "It's rather like when he wanted a toy I was given by my godfather. He had to have it. Finally Papa made me give it to him. Then, once he had it, he didn't care about it and he broke it. It would be the same with Dammy, I think."

"You know, Hereward," said Worth slowly and thoughtfully, "I think you spend far too much time in your brother's company. You are a good lad and he isn't. Don't try so hard to be like him."

Hereward looked toward where his brother glowered at Cahill's back. "Perhaps you're right," he said sadly, "but I don't know how else to be . . . and he's my brother."

Worth mulled over the revealing comment. "Loyalty is a good thing up to a point, but, Hereward, don't let him do something you know wrong. Come to me, will you, if he plots . . . something he shouldn't?"

Hereward shot him a startled look. "How'd you guess?"

Worth looked startled in turn. "He's already planned . . . ?"

"He's only suggested maybe he'd . . ." Hereward shut his mouth, the wary look returning to his features. "I'd really be the lickspittle he called me if I told you *that*, wouldn't I?"

"Sometimes it is better to be a telltale then to regret what happens because one wasn't." They were becoming far too serious again, thought Worth. The only way to get through to this particular type of boy was to keep it light. Attempting a more jocular note, he suggested, "Just remember if you will, that saving a fair maiden from a villain is time-honored behavior." He observed Hereward's grimace and doubted if he'd been successful.

But then Hereward seemed to think again. He bit his lip. "Maybe . . ."

"You were perfectly correct, Toby," said Damaris, and the boy swung around to look at her, his heart in his eyes. Damaris dropped the stone back in the water. "It is not half so pretty now it's dry. Shall we go on?" She looked around, cringed slightly closer to Cahill at the look she surprised in Herbert's eyes. "Please?" she asked in a small voice.

This time Cahill and Damaris were smoothly separated from Hereward and Herbert by Worth and Tacye as the six strolled along one of the narrow paths, stopping occasionally so Damaris could admire some particularly fine show of blooms or could comment on a vine-covered bower protecting secluded seats or on another grotto, each different from the last.

Before too long they came to the maze. Laughter could be heard from behind the high hedge. Voices calling from one part of the maze to another. And then, once, a panicked cry for rescue which was followed by contradictory advice until someone found the lost lamb.

"Shall we attempt it, Miss Damaris?" asked Cahill. "Or has the lost lady put you off?"

Damaris looked up at him trustingly. "I'm certain,

with your help, I can find the center. I would like to try."

Herbert shoved by the others and Hereward followed. "We'll find the center first," called Herbert, his competitive instincts roused. "We'll show you the way."

Damaris also entered the maze with Cahill on her heels. Tacye frowned when Worth held her back. "Is that proper?" she asked. "Allowing them to go alone, I mean? Shouldn't I stay with them?"

"There's a guide seated in a tall seat who overlooks the whole of the maze. They are alone together, but not unobserved and it is considered permissible as long as that official is in his place."

"And he *is* there? I cannot see him."

"One cannot from here but Lady Lawton would not forget such an important point of propriety as that! Shall we too attempt to find the middle or do you find mazes a bore?"

Tacye gave him a look and strolled under the living green arch of the entrance. Worth followed, running his cane along the hedge as he walked along. Once, when Tacye would have turned left, he took her elbow and turned them right. Later, when she'd have turned right, he again, gently, forced her the other way. It wasn't long before they reached the empty center and Tacye looked around, surprised.

"You knew the way!" she accused.

He grinned. "I knew the trick for finding the way," he admitted, chuckling. "*You* may not find mazes a bore but I do. I get in and out as expeditiously as may be!"

"What's the trick?" asked Tacye.

Again that quick grin. "I wonder. Should I reveal my secret?"

"You are teasing me," said Tacye. She shrugged. "Keep your secret if you will." She strolled over to the statue centered in the sun-filled open area. When she looked back, she surprised a tender look on Worth's face which had her turning immediately to the statue, confusion welling up inside her. What could he mean by that look?

Surely she'd misinterpreted it? Perhaps it was only been the sort of look a man gave a friend when he knew his teasing had hit a nerve? Surely only that!

Worth, on the other hand, wiped all expression from his face the instant he realized he'd revealed emotions he should not at this point reveal. He'd been flirting, he realized, not teasing when he suggested he'd not tell. Of course, the two behaviors *were* closely related and perhaps Tacye Adlington had not realized . . .

But such behavior would not do. Not so long as Tacye Adlington insisted on playing the buck, something she'd done very well so far.

No one else joined them although there were voices all around. Worth moved to one of the benches placed there for the convenience of those who reached the center exhausted and in need of a rest before working their way back out again. He seated himself, mulling over possible topics of conversation, something which would put Tacye at ease.

"Adlington," he said drawing Tacye's attention, "I don't know if you noticed, but I had a rather interesting conversation with Hereward Lambourn back at the water grotto. Much to my surprise I believe he's not such a complete lout as his brother appears to be—Herbert has acquired enough bronze he doesn't appear so rough and ready on the surface, but Hereward has, I think, gentlemanly instincts his brother lacks, if one could only bring them into being!"

Tacye strolled nearer, struggling to maintain an even voice and to keep her complexion clear. The fact he sounded calm and merely friendly helped. "How did you reach that conclusion?"

Worth told her of the conversation relating to Damaris and Tacye nodded. "Your hope is that Hereward will come to you if Herbert decides to do something drastic? Why not to me?"

"I think he'd find it easier to come to me," evaded Worth. Once he thought about it, however, he decided that might actually be truth—if not all the truth. He had no intention of allowing Tacye Adlington to go after Herbert Lambourn if the young fool *did* attempt to run off with Damaris! It was time Tacye discovered there were some things she, as a woman, must not chance. That some gambles were beyond her was also truth, but bringing her to that realization might, perhaps, take a lifetime!

Ah well, they had a lifetime. Once he unmasked her and took her into his arms where he already guessed she'd fit perfectly. After he'd convinced her to wed him, of course!

Worth cast a look at the heavens. Terry, ol' man, he thought, did you know I'd find her fascinating when you told me all those tales? Did you guess she'd be just the woman for me?

Worth chuckled silently, his moving shoulders evidence of his repressed humor. Oh yes, Tacye Adlington. Young Lambourn would find it much easier to come to me than to the sister of the chit his brother was kidnapping with the intention of wedding her out of hand!

They were interrupted just then by the entrance of Cahill and Damaris. "You found it first," said Damaris, pretending to pout. "I was certain I would do so."

"You have found it before either Hereward or Herbert—but here come other guests, I think," said Tacye.

A whole bevy of brightly clothed young women trooped into the center followed by a handful of smartly dressed young men. The group pretty much filled the open area with their laughter and giggles, swirling skirts and parasols, pointing canes and raised quizzing glasses.

"Shall we go?" asked Worth.

He rose to his feet and bowed one coy young woman into his place, before turning to Tacye for her answer. Tacye seemed not to have heard him; she was looking to where Questerman had, somehow, succeeded in separating Damaris from Cahill. Unfortunately, Cahill was speaking, with frequent glances toward Damaris, with one of his many cousins. Worth followed as Tacye moved toward her sister, catching her up at the same moment Tacye reached her quarry. He touched her shoulder lightly and she glanced up at him.

"Good day, Sir Davey. You here?" asked Worth, the faintest suggestion of insult in his tone. It worked. He drew the man's eyes from Tacye to himself.

"As you see," said Questerman tightly.

"Well, well," said Worth, lightly, "one never knows whom one will see in a public place."

Questerman scowled. "I was invited," he snapped.

"Did I say otherwise?" Worth looked at his knuckles. "Miss Damaris, I believe it nears the time when everyone is to meet near the terrace. Will you come along with Toby and myself?"

He held out his arm and, with eyes glowing with thankful appreciation, Damaris placed her fingertips upon it.

"Enjoy yourself," said Worth, nodding slightly to Sir Davey. He turned Damaris toward the arched exit on the far side of the circle.

Tacye, following, actually heard Questerman's teeth grit and repressed a shudder. Perhaps Herbert planned to abduct Damaris, but at least he actually believed he meant to marry her. Tacye, knowing Questerman's need to marry money, was equally certain the man had only Damaris's ruin in mind.

Worth might have talked Hereward into ratting on his brother if it came to the pinch, but there was no one who might do likewise if Questerman came the ugly. Damaris, decided Tacye, must be watched.

Closely.

Always.

It would, thought Tacye a trifle grimly, not only be endlessly wearing, but exceedingly boring as well! She stared at Worth's back, a hungry look in her eye and a great deal of wanting in her heart.

Almost instantly Worth paused and looked around, a questioning look in his gaze. Tacye averted her eyes quickly and hoped he'd not seen what she feared had been revealed in them.

"Coming, Adlington? Don't dawdle. I find myself thirsty beyond bearing and I'm certain Lady Lawton is just the hostess to have thought of that problem when she made her plans. Lady Lawton never forgets such things," he finished.

Although he spoke a trifle sharply, something inside him soared. He had *not* missed the look in Tacye's eyes. Nor was he a green'un who had difficulty interpreting such things. On the other hand, he was almost certain Tacye herself didn't know exactly what it was she felt.

Besides, nothing could be said or done until Tacye came out of her ridiculous masquerade, but when she did . . . ! Ah *then*.

Then he'd show her exactly what she'd meant by that look. He frowned. Just when would she doff her trousers and get back into her proper skirts? Soon? Or not until the Adlington family removed from Bath to return to . . . to wherever it was they'd come from. Worth reminded himself he must discover that particular bit of information—before something sent the Adlingtons hightailing it back there and he didn't know where *there* might be! Such idiocies happened. But, he swore, not to himself.

They exited the maze with no more difficulty than he and Tacye had had finding their way in. Damaris was loud in her admiration and Tacye believed she'd discovered his secret. She reminded herself that at some point she should ask him if keeping in touch with one side and not deviating from where that led would lead one through any maze. She was pretty certain, following along behind and watching as his cane grazed the hedge that that was what he'd been doing.

Worth led Tacye and Damaris to the central alleé and the direct route back to the terrace. He wished to place Damaris under the protection of Lady Lawton as quickly possible. Questerman would not try his tricks under that good lady's eye. She was far too wise to rakes such as Sir Davey was known to be and would allow him not one inch in his pursuit of Damaris.

At least it appeared Miss Damaris had taken someone's warnings to heart: she had been anything but reluctant to come away when he'd suggested it to her. On the other hand, that resistance on Damaris's part might just add fuel to Questerman's determination to have her. Some men became stubborn in the face of opposition.

Worth sighed. He wanted children. He even wanted daughters. But the thought of their growing to the age Damaris had reached and becoming prey to such predators as Questerman was almost enough to make him hope he had nothing but sons. That *he and Tacye* had nothing but sons . . .

Worth swallowed. Hard. He must put such thoughts away until it became proper to act on them. At least until Tacye became a woman in looks as well as fact!

"Oh look! Aunt Fanny has come!" Damaris released Worth's hand and skipped toward the chairs which were set in an arc in the shade near a long table.

The table was graced by flowers, but also held a small keg, a large punch bowl, and pitchers of lemonade. Among the liquid refreshments were bowls piled with fruit and plates with delicate little cakes. But Tacye wasn't looking at the table. Her gaze followed her sister's progress toward the chairs.

"I don't believe it!" Tacye stopped in her tracks and very nearly goggled.

"What do you not believe?" asked Worth.

"My aunt. She is sitting beside Lady Lawton."

"So?"

"But she *never* comes to parties such as this where she must walk on uneven ground and maneuver so much unknown territory! She very much fears making a fool of herself in such situations."

"It appears she managed all right today. Is that Seward I see bringing her a glass of lemonade?"

"Yes."

"That's rather abrupt." He gave her a questioning look. "Do you disapprove his wooing her?"

"Do you too know that he is?" Tacye's eyes widened. "No, I don't object to *that.* Just that he encourages her to do something which tires her terribly. He cannot know, of course, how very tense she becomes when she must go into strange places. She'll be exhausted tomorrow."

"Is that so very bad?" She appears to be enjoying herself," he said as Fanny laughed at something Lady Lawton said. "Surely to occasionally be tired is a small price to pay for the happy times."

"She does seem far more secure than I'd have thought possible. . . ."

"Perhaps that is because she is seated and does not have to stroll around?"

"Possibly." Tacye's eyes narrowed and she studied the

stairs and route one must take from the hotel. "But she had to reach that chair!"

"You must believe that Seward loves her far too much to put her to any trouble. I'm quite certain he arranged things so she had to walk as little as possible."

A muscle jerked in Tacye's jaw. "We'll see. Tomorrow. If she is not prostrate, then I'll agree Seward has taken very good care of her! I wonder how her talk with the lawyer came out. . . ."

"Ah yes. Her solicitor. Do you suppose part of her relaxed attitude is because she need never again worry about paying the bills?"

Tacye wondered if her aunt ever had worried about such things. It was true she had, when Tacye came to that age, complained because she could not take Tacye to London for a season, but that was nothing like Tacye's constant concern about such problems as providing a tenant with a new and badly needed roof or paying a tradesman in a timely fashion for some necessary purchase.

They'd been lucky in that the estate provided most of their daily needs, but there were always some few things one had to purchase or must have done for one and those expenses could, if one were unlucky, add up to an amount which it was sometimes difficult to find—especially when one was determined one would not touch what one had carefully set aside for this summer in Bath with Damaris!

"You think it something else . . . ?" asked Worth when Tacye didn't respond. "If not concern over bills, then perhaps it has occurred to her she needn't push Miss Damaris into a match here and now, but may take her to London for a season if no one comes up to scratch before you must leave Bath. Not that she *need* concern herself about that, I think."

"You think, then, that Cahill will offer?"

"I think it very likely. I'm not certain he has, himself, quite decided on that course, but I don't think it will be long before he recognizes that what he feels for Miss Damaris is something more than mere friendship!"

After a long moment, Tacye looked up, discovered Worth was watching her with a speculative look she could not read. "You were thirsty, my lord, and must wish to satisfy that need. I, however, should pay my respects to Lady Lawton before I head for the tables. If you'll excuse me?"

Worth watched her move away and wondered how he could actually believe that slim youth was female. Tacye Adlington had the boyish stride and suppressed energy of any lad of her seeming age and temperament. Could he be wrong? He recalled how Hereward had turned at her voice, thinking it was Tacye, how confused he'd looked when it wasn't. Surely there couldn't be two Adlingtons with exactly the same timber and tone . . .

Worth shook away his thoughts and headed to where Cahill was accepting a mug of beer from a liveried servant. A long cool wet would taste very good right now and, besides, it might settle his mind and keep it from going in circles, as well!

Sir Davey Questerman arrived shortly thereafter, a young lady on each arm. The girls were, almost immediately, tactfully removed from his side by careful chaperons. Sir Davey grimaced, but was otherwise philosophical about the loss of his companions. It was, after all, the way of the world that he search for prey and the chaperons be watchful against just such depredations. He strolled toward the tables where he too was handed a mug of beer and moved from there to a position where he could see Damaris who was laughing at something her brother said.

". . . Fortune, you know," said one of the gray-haired matrons seated on a nearby bench.

Casually, Questerman moved nearer. A fortune, after all, was just what he wanted and it behooved him to find out what cit or manufacturing mogul had brought his daughter to Bath in search of a title. His was not a particularly high-sounding title, but what could a cit or a manufacturer expect?

"She hadn't a notion?"

"That's what I hear. A total surprise to her."

Her? Of whom were they speaking? Questerman turned his back so he would not appear to be listening, but he strained to hear every word.

"Seward remembered his friend telling him his wife would be well off if something happened to him," said the first lady, "so his lordship was surprised to find she was not."

Why, wondered Questerman, did they not use *names?*

"Do you suppose she'll leave it to her family?"

"Don't be a goose. She is quite young enough and attractive enough to catch the eye of some man— probably a widower who already has an heir, of course, because she isn't so young one may presume she'll be capable of having children."

Sir Davey looked around and his eyes lit on Lady Tamswell, her face tipped up to look into Lord Seward's laughing features as she accepted a glass of lemonade from him. Was it possible . . . ?

"But it's rumored she's blind," hissed the second woman. "Surely no man would wish to take on that sort of responsibility."

The first shrugged. "I expect it'll depend on just how large the fortune, do not you?"

"Doesn't it always, actually?" said the other, equally dryly.

Questerman had heard enough. Lady Tamswell was blind. He had determined that to his satisfaction early in his pursuit of Damaris. Lovely, lovely Damaris. If he pursued the aunt, he'd have to give up the niece. He sighed. It *was* too bad. A notion struck him and he brightened. *First* he'd make sure of the aunt and *then* he'd return to his pursuit of the beauty!

So lost in thought was he, that Questerman strolled toward the stairs and away from the laughing happy crowd enjoying Lady Lawton's hospitality without a thought to making proper adieux to his hostess. He had plans to lay and he didn't need distractions while he thought through to a solution to this particular problem.

Lady Tamswell must be his. Must soon be his. The sooner the better, actually! Before Miss Damaris found a husband he'd not wish to offend!

Chapter 11

Tacye drank from her wine glass and searched among Lady Lawton's guests until her eyes fell upon Worth. He was in a group of men, his head thrown back and laughter pouring from his throat. Tacye wondered what tale had brought him so much enjoyment—and concluded it was very likely unsuitable for her poor female ears! For a moment she considered joining his circle, but then realized it was not what she wanted. Oh, she wanted to be at Worth's side; what she did *not* want was for anyone else to be there, too.

She turned away and pretended to listen to the gossip entertaining her aunt. What she was feeling for his lordship was totally unsuitable to her current situation. But what could she, would she, do if she were *not* playing the part of Toby Adlington? Would she attempt to attach him? Would she try to bring him up to scratch? Tacye repressed a wry grin. Even if she were to dress again as a woman, it would be useless.

No man would want a tall lean woman with skin too brown and hair too short. A woman who had outridden him and could very likely outshoot him. A woman who could, when she would, swear as fluently as any stable boy and hated her skirts and the restrictions that went with them. Tacye sighed. Whatever this was she felt for

Lord Worth, it must be rooted out and thrown away and forgotten.

It would not do.

But curiosity concerning Worth's reaction to her in her feminine form, returned to tease Tacye off and on for the rest of the afternoon. The only distraction she had was toward the end when Lady Baggins-Keyton arrived, Mr. Grenville Somerwell in her train. Halfway down the steps from the hotel, Mr. Somerwell saw Tacye and would have bolted if Lady Baggins-Keyton hadn't clutched his arm in iron-hard talons.

It was almost a game after that. Lady Baggins-Keyton moved majestically from one small group to another; Mr. Somerwell skittered and slithered until he was on her ladyship's side farthest from Tacye—who watched him with the half-smile so like her brother's. Finally, Tacye touched her sister's arm and told her to watch the young man's antics, that she'd be amused.

Somerwell seeing Tacye touch Damaris and then look back at himself cringed. Already pale, he turned ashen and sat with a thump in a convenient chair. He shook his head, horrified at the notion which had suddenly taken up residence in his head.

"No," he mouthed, almost silently.

"What's that? What do you say? Speak up, you ninny-hammer!" ordered his aunt.

"I didn't say anything."

"Poor Grenville doesn't look well, Lady Baggins-Keyton," said Lady Lawton kindly. "Perhaps he's such a one who cannot sit for long in the sun?" Her ladyship smiled at Grenville.

"Don't feel well? Nonsense. The boy's just playing up. Didn't want to come. Doesn't want to go anywhere. Nonsense, I say." But Lady Baggins-Keyton actually looked at her nephew. "Or perhaps not. What's to do with you, neffy?"

"Don't feel so good," mumbled Grenville with another furtive glance toward Tacye.

"Fiddle. Nothing for it, I suppose. You'd better go home. Can't have you spoiling the party for everyone else, can we?"

Grenville bolted and Tacye's one bit of amusement went with him.

Soon after Lord Seward came to ask her aunt if she were ready to leave. When Fanny nodded, Tacye decided it would be best to discover, at once, just how Lord Seward handled the situation. She stepped back although she wanted to play her usual role in easing Fanny's movements.

"Come along then," said Lord Seward. "I've had the chairmen come to the top of the stairs. They begin just a few feet away, if you remember?"

"Yes. We counted my steps and it was ten from the bottom of the steps to here." Fanny stood, bit her lip and squared her shoulders and then smiled. "I'm ready if you are."

Lord Seward laid her hand on his arm, smiled at Lady Lawton and nodded. "It has been a very pleasant afternoon. You are the premiere hostess in Bath, my lady!"

"Thank you for inviting us," said Fanny and was echoed by Damaris's enthusiastic agreement.

Tacye watched Seward lead her aunt to the stairs, talking softly as he did so. She saw his pause, saw Fanny lift her foot and take the first step. Tacye didn't watch beyond that. She too made her goodbyes to Lady Lawton, took one last glance to where Lord Worth was still being well amused, and she too took the stairs to the terrace. She was strolling through the hotel lobby when Worth caught up with her.

"Hold up, m'boy!"

Tacye paused and turned, her heart pounding at the

sound of his voice. "Yes, my lord?" she asked, her gray eyes meeting his steadily and seemingly calm.

"We've organized a fishing party for tomorrow. Do you fish?"

"I enjoy it very much, but I didn't bring any rods or lines."

"I suspect such can be found for you. If you'll be ready at four, I'll join you at your lodging and we'll ride on from there. The best fishing won't occur until about dusk, of course, but we can reach our destination and ready our lines and practice a cast or two, perhaps."

"May I ask where we're going?"

"I've a friend with property to the south of Bath. He has the best-stocked streams this side of Scotland!"

"Then I'll not wish to miss it, will I? 'Til tomorrow, then," she said and, her pulses beating, she watched him stroll back out toward the gardens.

So much, she thought, for forgetting her feelings for him. That would be impossible. Until they left Bath and returned home there was no hope of weeding out her emotions and freeing herself of such idiotic dreams as Worth roused in her—dreams she'd long ago decided, that in her case, had no possible hope of fulfillment.

But *would* Worth react as had other men she'd found attractive to her senses? Would he, too, take one look at the bean-pole figure and faintly browned face and turn to Damaris with her peaches-and-cream complexion or another like her? But there was that look she'd surprised in his eyes when they'd been in the maze. *Had* it been only a look of friendship?

And if it were not? If it had meant exactly what she'd thought for an instant it had meant? Then that was wrong too, was it not? Tacye grimaced: she certainly didn't want or need *that* sort of *friendship* when the man thought her a boy!

Still, a chance to discover for herself how Worth

would treat her when she *was* herself was tempting. Was there a way? Could she devise a scheme where Tacye Adlington could be in Bath for a few days while Toby was required to be elsewhere? Stepping out with long strides down Great Pultenay Street toward Laura Place and the bridge just beyond that which spanned the Avon, she put her mind to work.

Surely there was a way . . .

Tacye, tossing the keys to the Abbey Arms and their suite, waited outside for Worth to arrive. Numbskull stood nearby, his reins hanging loose. The street was nearly empty for a change—or perhaps because of the time of day? Many chose to forego luncheon and have a light meal at this time, something to hold one until the rather late hour which was considered proper for dining.

Because the streets were empty, the somewhat distant presence of Mrs. Lovett was glaringly obvious. The woman kept turning slightly, looking back down the street toward York House. Tacye wryly surmised the widow was watching for Lord Worth and wondered what game she'd play today. It wasn't necessary to wait long. A horse and rider appeared, approached, and just as he neared Mrs. Lovett, that lady put her hand to forehead, moaned, and, gracefully swooned.

Tacye shook her head, chuckling. Was there no end to the machinations of determined women? She strolled down the street to where Worth was dismounting, a frown creasing his forehead.

"Trouble, my lord," called Tacye.

Worth looked around at her and grinned. "The lady appears to have fainted again although this time I can see no reason for it."

"Perhaps she's increasing," said Tacye tongue-in-cheek. "My aunt has told me that often causes women to swoon for seemingly no reason."

Tacye's comment had Mrs. Lovett's eyes opening and a glare turned her way. "I am not enceinte!"

"Are you not?" Tacye reached for the woman's arm. Mrs. Lovett tried to evade her grasp her eyes going to Worth. "If you are not breeding, then I think you must have another common disorder. I call it by its common everyday name." When Worth looked at her questioningly, she added, "Beau-diddling, my lord." Tacye forcibly lifted the slight woman to her feet and held her there.

Worth stifled a chuckle at the notion that catching a man by trickery was a sort of illness.

"You are no gentleman," screeched Mrs. Lovett—and stamped her foot.

"You are no lady, so we're even, are we not?" asked Tacye politely and wondered what Diana Lovett would think if she knew that Tacye *really* was *not* a gentleman. She grinned at the thought.

"You think that humorous, young man?" Mrs. Lovett scowled. "That you are no gentleman?"

"That you think me ungentlemanly doesn't bother me one whit. The lady appears to have recovered, Worth. Shall we be on our way?"

"We must go or we'll be late—and Mrs. Lovett knows how I feel about that. Good day, Mrs. Lovett."

Worth bowed and turned to lead his horse up the street to where Numbskull still waited, but Tacye put her hand on his arm and stopped him. She whistled and Numbskull raised his head. She whistled again. He twisted his neck slightly to keep the reins from under his feet and paced the few yards toward her. Tacye reached for his reins where they arched away from the bit. She patted the animal's neck.

"Well done, Numbskull," she crooned.

Jeanne Savery

"You've trained him well," said Worth.

Tacye shrugged. "It is very quiet where we live. I've had many hours to spare for Numbskull's training, have I not, my love?" she asked into the horse's ear when he lowered his head just then. The horse appeared to nod agreement and Worth chuckled. "Oh, do not laugh, my lord. Teaching the poor creature English took up much of that time. He's Irish, you see, and knew nothing but the Gaelic when I first acquired him."

Worth laughed outright. "You have a wonderfully dry sense of humor, Adlington. I like it well."

Tacye mounted as he spoke and both looked back to Mrs. Lovett who still scowled at them. Tacye shook her head. "My dear Mrs. Lovett, do not, I pray, allow your features to fall into lines like that. You'll find yourself old before your time."

She gasped, smoothed out her expression, and turned on her heel—only to turn back. "You, sir, have spoiled my whole visit to Bath. I wish you bad cess!"

"Cess! Ah! Another from Ireland, is the lady—if she refers to luck that way. But now I believe I understand. Surely that explains all, does it not, my lord?"

"No—not if you refer to her blatant attempts to catch my eye—and, still more likely, my purse. English women can be just as tricksy, as all of us in my position know to our cost."

"Cahill?" asked Tacye remembering what he'd said before.

"Yes. I think I explained to you that he'd been chased last season until he wanted to leave town in disgust."

"I guess you'll just have to find a woman you can tolerate and wed her out of hand, my lord, so that you need not put up with machinations such as Mrs. Lovett's."

"Perhaps I'll do just that," he said. He turned a smile her way.

Such a smile! What, she wondered, could he be think-ing! Since he didn't know she was female, it wasn't that he had made a suggestive comment to her as a woman. But if it were not that, and not a yearning for an illicit relationship with a boy—which she'd concluded was nonsense or the other men would not admire him so— then was it some form of male joshing of which she was unaware? Tacye sighed. Softly. But not softly enough.

"What is it, bantling?"

"Hmm?" Tacye improvised an answer that went with her wishes. "I was regretting the fact I must leave Bath for a few days."

"How so?"

"We've had a note from Ayerst Hill. Someone must see to a problem with one of the tenants. It cannot wait, but I'll be gone no longer than need be." Tacye cast a quick glance toward Worth. "What makes it particularly untimely is that our older sister will be in Bath for a day or two on her way from visiting her old tutor and going on to visit some distant cousins who live in Devon. I'll miss seeing her unless we catch each other on the road."

"You and she are close?"

"We're very close to each other."

I'll just bet you are, thought Worth. Wondering how Tacye perceived herself, he asked, "Is she as attractive as her sister?"

Tacye forced a laugh. "They are nothing alike. Tacye has no interest in her rather plain looks. Nor is she tiny and perfectly formed as is her sister. She is much more interested in her books than her needle and not at all in-terested in flirtation or the usual behavior one expects of a young woman." Tacye bent another look his way, a twinkle in her eye. "In fact, my lord, if you are looking for a woman who will not fall at your feet and attempt to rush you to the altar, then I suggest you meet my sis-ter when she arrives."

Worth's mouth twitched. What a gull-catcher Master Adlington thought himself to be! "I will certainly wish to meet her. I liked her twin brother very much, remember."

"Ah. That is why you have been so kind to my insignificant self. I have wondered."

"That was it at the beginning, m'boy, but your lively intelligence and your willingness to accept the responsibilities placed on your shoulders through Terry's death, and any one of half a dozen other reasons have held my interest. Come along now. Put that excuse for a horse to an effort, or we'll never arrive."

Worth put his heels to his own mount and they surged ahead. Tacye and Numbskull soon caught up and the horses cantered along side by side, the miles flowing under pounding hooves, the wind burning skin a trifle browner and ruffling hair below the brims of hats. Tacye enjoyed it immensely. When at one point she turned and met Worth's sparkling look, she knew he did too. She grinned and he smiled in response. Soon after they arrived at the Pembrook estate and before long were choosing their sites along the bubbling river where they'd try their luck.

Worth took a small box from his saddle bag after unsaddling and rubbing down his horse. Now they were beside the river, he set the box beside himself and opened it, looking over the contents carefully. His next move was to glance around, test the wind, feel of the air, and such like, just as gravely. Sorting through the box, he chose the fly with which he'd begin his casting.

Once he'd chosen he pushed the box toward Tacye. "Take your choice. Anything I have you may try."

Tacye pulled the box nearer and looked into it. "I see you've supplies for tying new flies. Do you mind if I make my own?"

"Not at all."

"Then let us see what these southern fish think of a north country fly!"

Southern fish didn't think much of it and eventually Tacye gave it up and tried another from the box. She did better then, but even so, she only had four nice salmon when the evening ended, their host calling that supper awaited them at the house. She held up her string and asked if they were to release them.

"Not at all. Brook will want you to take them home with you. They'll be cleaned and put into iced moss for you by one of his servants and we'll not forget them when we leave." He busied himself with his own string, swinging it around and looking carefully at those he'd caught.

"And yours, my lord?"

"The hotel will fix one or two for me, but I'll put the rest back." He slipped several from his string and watched them swish away into deeper water. The last two he lifted, along with his gear, and started along the path toward where other men gathered in the dim light from a rising moon.

"You enjoy fishing, do you not, my lord?" she asked as they sauntered along in the tail of the near dozen headed for the house.

"Very much. Our days are generally filled with too much activity and become rather hectic. They leave no time for reflection. Fishing, on the other hand, is something one must do alone. Silence is not only the rule, but the rule is enforced! One has time for quiet thought."

"I too have found that true. I enjoy casting as we did tonight, but I much prefer to find me a certain tree that bows down practically to the water and about whose roots a certain old granddaddy of them all hides. I lay in a line for him three or four times a summer."

"You've never caught him?"

"Oh yes. Once or twice."

"And then you let him go," said Worth with a chuckle. And why do you do that? he wondered. "But if you let him go how can you prove you've caught him, this granddaddy of a fish?"

"I don't *wish* to prove it. I don't want anyone else to know of his existence! Someone else would not consider it a contest which sometimes one wins and sometimes the other. They would take my old granddaddy home and eat him!"

"Usually the fish wins?" asked Worth, smiling but still more curious about the way Tacye Adlington's mind worked.

"Yes. He's very good at stealing my bait and leaving the bare hook there to taunt me."

"And this does not bother you?"

"Should it? I think not. When I go to that particular spot, I go not for the fishing, but for the quiet, what I call my unlonely alone time." She glanced at him from under her lashes and wasn't surprised to see him nodding. "I thought you might understand."

"Everyone needs such moments in their life—usually far more often than one realizes."

"Some never realize it, I think," mused Tacye.

"Very true. *Our* time alone has ended, I fear," Worth added as they came through an arch and into the cobbled yard at the back of the big square manor house. Pembrook was not Worth's friend's family estate, but a minor property which had come into the family with his grandmother. It was kept primarily for the fishing, although the two farms that came with it were prosperous and did very well.

Later, when the men settled down to cards, Tacye demurred. When their host jovially insisted, she stood straight before him and held his rather bleary eye. "I have this strange fancy, my lord, that I never bet where

I cannot afford to lose. This particular summer, all our funds must go to Miss Damaris's care. Please do not force me to something which I know is wrong." Tacye didn't move or smile or in any way force an answer. But she waited.

"Alackaday, cub!" The baron, not often meeting with straightforward admission of lack of funds, shook his drink-muzzled head. He remembered that his friend, Worth, was sponsoring the boy and, instead of throwing the boy out, which was his first impulse, said, "I guess you may watch if that is your will."

"It is."

"So be it." His lordship immediately joined a table and forgot all about his nonbetting guest.

As the drink flowed faster, Tacye became more bored. She wandered away from the group and explored the house, running into a servant who showed her to a small library. It was not terribly well stocked, but there was an old copy of *Tom Jones* and she settled down with it, skipping passages she knew were rather tedious and finding favorite scenes.

She was chuckling over one of those when Worth, a trifle more tipsy than he'd thought before getting to his feet, found her. A glow of lamp light caught her mahogany-colored hair and found reddish tints in it. His hands itched to run into the clean healthy curls and feel them wind around his fingers. He was just barely sober enough to restrain himself.

"It's later than I'd thought, bantling," he said, more gruffly than he'd meant to do. "Shall we be off?"

Tacye looked at the clock ticking quietly on the mantel and immediately laid aside her book. "*Much* later than I'd thought. I should never have picked up a book. I lose myself, you see. Do let us go. My aunt will be worried."

"Does she keep you so closely under her thumb then?"

"No, but she is of a nervous nature," said Tacye, sacrificing her aunt to her momentary need to explain why a young man's late arrival home would surprise anyone. "She has been very kind to me and I do not like setting her to fidgets."

"Come along then," said Worth, and humming quietly, set off toward the back of the house and the quickest route to the stables.

"Should I not tell my host I've had a pleasant day?"

"Some other time. Last I looked someone had laid him on the couch and covered him neatly with a blanket. He was snoring loudly," said Worth, chuckling. He returned to humming.

Tacye smiled. The song was off-key and barely recognizable, but Worth obviously cared not a whit. After a bit she joined him, singing in a contralto which was just low enough it barely kept her secret.

They were singing a catch and nearly back to Bath when a shot rang out taking Tacye's hat from her head. She immediately closed with Worth's horse and reached for his saddle holster, praying he kept his pistols loaded. Another flash of a gun and she sighted carefully, gently pulled the trigger. A scream of outrage come from the bushes.

Worth, sobered by their danger, lifted his other gun and spurred forward. He forced a way into the bushes, coming into a small clearing where a young man was attempting to mount, one of his arms hanging useless, blood streaming down it.

"I might have known," said Worth. "Lord Andrew, you have gone too far. No. Don't move. We'll see what your father has to say to this escapade. I said you aren't to move!"

"Damn you." Andrew spoke in sullen tones. "You would have to be around to protect that bastard."

"That bastard protected himself. An excellent shot it was too."

Worth approached to where Lord Andrew leaned against his horse, the blood still dripping from his fingers. "Adlington?"

"I'm here." Tacye had stripped her neck-cloth from her throat and now used it to bind up the wound. "I think that'll hold. What do we do with him now?"

"The idiot has finally gone his length. I'll have him held by the local magistrate until his father can be contacted. I don't think the old man will be pleased by his cub's latest attempt to overset the ton. Up with you, Lord Andrew."

"Can't. Too weak."

"Then perhaps we should just let you lie here and bleed to death. That would perhaps be the best solution all around," said Worth acidly, and started to walk away.

"Don't leave me. I'm wounded." There was a sudden desperate note to Andrew's voice. "You can't leave me here."

"Why can I not?"

"Because . . . because my father wouldn't like it."

"Your father has indulged your every vicious whim for years, but I do not think he'll indulge you in attempted murder."

"It is not me who has been the murderer. If you don't get me to a sawbones it is your illegitimate sycophant who will hang."

"You aren't going to die. You were barely touched." Worth half-lifted, half-shoved Andrew up onto his horse.

The young man instantly started forward, only to find the hated Adlington riding into his path, a gun aimed for his heart. The filth which tumbled from Andrew's mouth included words and phrases Tacye had never heard.

"Fluent, is he not?" she said when he began to run down.

"Yes. One must wonder where he picked up some of that gutter language. Come along Andrew. Lord Montloft is not going to like being knocked up at this hour, but I see no alternative."

"Let me go. I promise I'll not . . ."

"Do you really believe I'd take your word for anything?" asked Worth, his brows arching.

Andrew swayed in his saddle. "I'll do anything," he mumbled.

"Do you think he's going to pass out?"

"He'd better not. I'll let him lie and send Montloft's men back for him—and hope the fall opens that wound and he bleeds to death before they get here."

"You don't really wish him dead, do you?"

"It would solve several problems, bantling," said Worth, his jaw firm and his mouth a straight line. "I don't think you wish to give evidence in court. Nor do I think his father will wish it to come to that. But the boy cannot be allowed to go free after this. Next time it may not be the hat which has the hole in it. Do you know just how close you were to death tonight?"

"Yes."

"And you can still sit your horse as calmly as if we were out for a pleasure jaunt?"

"It is over, my lord. Terence taught me that once a thing was done, it is done and there's no use crying over it." Tacye shrugged.

"Yes, I've heard him say that. Terry was a damn good man, Adlington. I still miss him."

"As do I." Tacye suddenly realized she could say that without *quite* so much pain as references to Terence usually brought her.

The three turned up a tree-lined lane and Worth pounded on the Montloft door. They had to pound again and wait, but soon the soft glow of a lamp approached and then any number of latches and locks were undone. Finally the massive door swung open.

"We must see Lord Montloft. We've business with the Justice of the Peace."

"Yes, sir. Wait here, sir."

The servant shuffled off and Worth pushed the sulky and weakened Andrew into the porter's chair. The wait was not too long, Lord Montloft clattering down the stairs half dressed, a robe thrown over his trousers and half done-up shirt. "What's all this? What's so important is can't wait for a man to get his sleep, hmm? Ah. Lord Worth." Montloft's brow's climbed as he noticed the wounded Lord Andrew. "Foot pads? What next. Well, well, don't need me, my boy. Need the sawbones."

"You don't quite understand, Montloft. Lord Andrew set up an ambush. He shot the hole in Adlington's hat." Worth handed over Tacye's hat and watched as Montloft pushed an inquiring finger through the hole. "Adlington waited for the next shot and returned a shot at the flash. He hit Lord Andrew in the arm."

"Lord Andrew, hmm? Turned bad, has he?" Montloft's eyes narrowed. "Not surprising. He's been heading that way for a long time now. Castelbourgh isn't going to like it, of course."

"Castelbourgh is going to have to lump it. Andrew has gone too far this time. Look again at that hat!" Worth pointed to how close the shot had come.

Tacye colored up as both men stared at her.

"Another inch or two lower and Adlington would be *dead*. Andrew cannot be allowed to get away with this— not as he has with other vicious pranks." Worth lowered his voice a trifle. "Have you heard that one of his victims will have a bad limp for the rest of his life?"

"I hadn't heard about that. So. What to do with him?"

"Lock him up. As JP, it is your duty, Montloft!"

His lordship sighed. "So it is. So it is. Well, Castelbourgh will just have to understand I had no choice."

"The duke is a good man. He'll not blame you. Whether he'll see his way to doing something about his son, though, is another question entirely. You'll see to that arm?"

"Yes, yes. Must have a doctor in. And then put the lad where he'll do no one any harm. I'll tuck him away safely, Worth. And I'll let you know Castelbourgh's decision. You go along now. You must be tired." He glanced at the clock. "Three in the morning! Won't Dr. Drench just love to be roused from bed at this hour!"

"Three . . ." Tacye tugged at Worth's arm. "I really must go, my lord. Aunt Fanny . . ."

"I understand. Montloft, don't let that animal talk you into anything. He has a smooth tongue but is a known liar. You can't trust his promises. Do *not* give him an inch. You are responsible, man!"

"I'll see he's safe. Good night."

The horses cantered on into Bath. Tacye worried every step of the way about her aunt's feelings. After telling Worth good night, she rode straight to the stables where she left Numbskull with a sleepy groom and walked home at something just short of a run. As she feared, Fanny was waiting her arrival, sitting alone in the dark in the sitting room.

"I'm sorry, Aunt Fanny. I'd have come sooner but there was a problem."

"You're all right?"

Damaris, yawning, strolled into the front room. She saw Tacye's hat and screeched softly. "Tacye! What has happened?"

Tacye scowled at her sister, her lips compressed. "Shush, Dammy."

"But it's a great big hole and your hat is *ruined*, Tacye!"

"Tacye?" asked Fanny, anxiously.

"Relax, both of you." Tacye had hoped to avoid the truth, but Damaris had forced her hand. "Truly. Everything is fine. I was shot at, but I shot the villain and he's in the hands of the Justice of the Peace and, really, all is well."

Fanny blanched, her hands tightening around the arms of her chair. "You didn't kill him?"

"No. A flesh wound. It bled a lot, but he'll survive."

"To hang."

Tacye sighed. "Very likely not." She explained about Lord Andrew and his belief Tacye's win over Lord Worth had lost him his bet, how he'd vowed to get even and she described his first attempt when the dart had made Numbskull run wild. "I think Worth once spoiled another plot Lord Andrew had laid, and tonight ... well, it's over. I'm fine and Lord Andrew will not be laying any more plots."

"I've heard talk ..."

"About his father's tolerance? Worth assures me attempted murder is beyond what the duke will tolerate. The question is what his grace will decide to do. Perhaps Andrew will be sent to the colonies or the islands or India—somewhere far away."

"You are certain it is all over?"

"Quite certain." Tacye yawned a jaw cracking yawn. "Now, may we all go to bed? I'm exhausted."

"I think we're all exhausted. Come, Aunt Fanny. Let me help you. You must sleep in in the morning."

Fanny stopped. "No, no. We can't do that. I have such plans for the morning!"

"What plans?"

"Why," said Fanny, a huge smile lightening her expression and pushing aside the last of her fears, "I fully intend to go out and spend lots and lots of money—on all of us!"

Tacye chuckled. "If you truly mean that, my first purchase must be a new hat! Lord Andrew's bad aim ruined mine for future wear."

Damaris shoved her finger through the hole. She looked at her sister, her own eyes sober and fear showing.

Tacye mouthed, "It's over, Dammy. It's all over."

Damaris nodded, set the hat down with overly careful hands, and, taking Fanny's arm, led her toward the door.

"By the way," said Tacye casually. The others stopped. "I believe Tacye will be visiting one day soon. Too bad I won't be here, is it not? But that business at home concerning one of our tenants simply won't wait. I have to go see about it, do I not?" Damaris looked over her shoulder, bemused. "I won't be gone long, of course," continued Tacye, "but very likely *Tacye* will have gone on to our cousins in Devon before I return. . . ."

Tacye looked at her fingernails and waited.

Fanny finally responded. "It will be very good to see Tacye again," she said with a completely sober face. "We've so much to tell her, have we not, Damaris?" She continued on and Damaris, willy-nilly, went with her.

Tacye, however, moved to the table on which her hat sat, put her own finger through the hole and moved to the side table where a decanter and glasses rested.

It was over, Lord Andrew was under restraint and Worth promised he'd never again have a chance to bother her. Tacye truly meant to put it behind her—but first, she'd have a good-sized drink. Her fingers trembled very slightly as she poured and drank the medicinal dose down. She set the glass on the table with special

gentleness and walked toward the door wiping her
hand, boy-fashion, across her mouth.

Now she'd forget all about it.

She hoped.

Chapter 12

Toby Adlington strapped a second saddle bag to Numbskull's saddle. He turned back to where Damaris stood in the Abbey Arm's doorway and moved up the steps to speak to her. "You take care now."

"I will. Ta-Toby, you'll be all right?"

"I'll be fine. Tacye will be here tomorrow or the next day at the latest. In the meantime, you and Fanny stick together. I didn't like the way Questerman stared at you this morning in the Pump Room."

"Did you think he stared at me?" asked Damaris, a faint frown between her brows. "I thought it was our aunt. What I truly didn't care for was the way Herbert glowered when I wouldn't speak more than a word or two to him. I didn't used to be, but I think I'm afraid of Herby, Tacye. He's . . . he's changed."

"Watch what you call me," hissed Tacye, but continued her lecture without looking to see if they'd been overheard. "I don't think he's changed so much as he's seen that in the wider world he hasn't the prestige or the power he has at home. Here in Bath he's next to nothing. He doesn't like it that other men are better than he at almost everything. Nor does he like that his name draws contempt instead of the respect—of a sort—it gets at home. Hereward, on the other hand, seems to me to be changing for the better. Have you noticed?"

"I haven't, really. But then one doesn't notice Hereward, does one? Ta-Toby, please come back soon." Damaris held out her hand and Tacye took it between her own warm palms. "I don't know why it is, but for some reason, I'm so nervous I jump at my own shadow."

Tacye bit her lip, her eyes narrowing. "Perhaps I shouldn't go at all," she said slowly.

"Nonsense," said Damaris, straightening her shoulders. "I don't know why you wish to come to Bath as yourself, given how you said you'd hate your skirts and having to behave yourself, but I'm rather glad you want to. I'd very much like to present you—as yourself—to Cahill. I'm proud of you, Tacye. Even when I'm mad at you," she added sternly, but the twinkle had returned to her eyes.

Tacye relaxed in part, but part of her was still concerned. "I won't be long, Dammy. No longer than need be."

Frowning, she turned toward Numbskull and found Worth with his hand resting on the pommel, one foot tipped, the toe resting to the far side of the other foot, watching her. Tacye stopped. What might he have heard!

"You startled me, my lord," she said, watching him closely.

Worth unwound himself and stepped forward. "You're leaving now?" was all he asked.

"Yes."

"You didn't mention it this morning in the Pump Room."

Tacye was faintly surprised at the waspish tinge stinging through Worth's tone. "I wasn't aware anyone would be interested. Besides," she added quickly, "I'll be

gone no more than a few days." She looked back to
where her sister had slipped into the house. "I'll be no
longer than need be, because, to be frank, I'm a trifle
worried about my sister's safety. If it weren't
essential . . ."

Tacye trailed off. It wasn't essential. Very likely she
was a fool to leave just now. Not only did she not trust
Questerman's motives for hovering around the
Adlington party, she feared Herbert, too, might be just
foolish enough to think he could run off with Damaris.

"If you're worried about your sister, I'll keep an eye
on her. So will Cahill if I suggest to him you'd appreciate it." Worth's brows arched in that way they had.
"Lady Lawton, for that matter, is a dragon of the best
sort. Should I have a word with her as well?"

"Would you? I don't know what it is which concerns
me so, but I'll freely admit I've a feeling I should not be
leaving Bath just now!"

"Your womenfolk will wish to attend the Upper
Rooms tomorrow evening, of course. I'll arrange to escort them."

Tacye instantly decided she'd be back and herself for
that occasion! To be escorted to the subscription ball by
Worth, even if it was merely as a favor to Toby
Adlington, was something she'd not miss.

"I'll ask your aunt," he continued, "if there are any
other occasions for which she'd like an escort. I'll receive any invitations which will come to her and may
accept and reject as she does."

"Thank you. You ease my mind a great deal."

"If your other sister arrives, I'll also see to her,"
added Worth, no hint of the humor he felt at that offer
in his face or voice—although he couldn't completely
restrain a faint sardonic look in his eyes.

Tacye glanced quickly to check that he was serious.
When it appeared he was, she again said, "Thank you.

I must be off. The sooner I'm gone, the sooner I'll return."

"Very true."

Again Tacye glanced at him. There was no hint he'd guessed her secret, and yet there was something in his manner toward her that made her wonder. *Did* he know she was not what she appeared to be? And if he did why did he not denounce her as any other member of the ton would do? Why did she feel safe and secure and . . . happy . . . when she was near him and what was it about him that made him different in her eyes from any other male she'd ever known—except for Terry, of course.

Tacye mounted, looked down at Worth. She filled her mind with the look of him, the sun glinting off his auburn hair, the intense blue of his eyes holding her gaze for a long moment. Then he nodded and she looked away, pulled gently at Numbskull's reins, and trotted off down the street toward the road north and home.

Not that she'd go far, of course. Somewhere to the north she'd turn off the main road until she found a well-run local hostelry where she'd feel it likely Numbskull would be kept safe. Then she'd walk cross-country until she'd returned to the main road and a coaching house where she'd hire a carriage for the return trip to Bath. She hated the thought of leaving Numbskull—even for the few days of her Bath "visit" as Tacye Adlington. But it couldn't be helped. Numbskull could not masquerade as anything but the striking animal he was. He, as well as Toby Adlington, must disappear.

All went as Tacye planned—including her transmogrification from Toby to Tacye—and she arrived back in Bath less than twenty-four hours after she'd left it. All charming smiles, she convinced Mrs. Armstrong she was Damaris's sister come for a few days visit before going on to friends elsewhere, and that she should be let into the suite of rooms the Adlingtons still, if reluctantly, rented since it had been discovered that suitable housing was unavailable elsewhere.

Tacye soon settled herself into "Toby's" room, hanging the few items of feminine clothing Fanny had insisted be brought for her although they'd not previously been unpacked. There was a morning gown, a walking dress, a habit which became her very well, but was hated because it required a much detested side saddle, and one evening gown. She hated that last as well, but it, too, looked well on her tall lean figure, the slightly gathered skirt hanging beautifully straight, and the small sleeves barely capping her shoulders, leaving a smooth expanse of skin across her back and a reasonably modest decolletage in front which flattered as much as was possible her small breasts.

Tacye changed from her travel gown to the morning gown and brushed her hair until the curls clustered forward over her ears onto her cheeks and made parentheses marks at her forehead. She moved into the sitting room where she'd decided to await the arrival of Fanny and Damaris who were, very likely, nearly ready to leave the Pump Room and return home.

Unable to settle she wandered to the window where she automatically fell into the posture she adopted as Toby. After a moment it occurred to her a well-brought-up young woman would not stand with arm upraised against the window frame, hip-shot, and staring at the passing humanity.

She forced herself to proper posture, sent one last look down the street in the direction from which Fanny's chair would come, and went to sit in one of the comfortable chintz-covered chairs where she picked up the book Damaris had been reading.

Tacye grimaced. Her taste and Dammy's was far different and a Gothic romance was *not* something for

which Tacye had ever developed a liking. She thought
the heroines portrayed were so many ninnyhammers
and the heroes far too idealistic to be either believable
or interesting and, too often, she'd thought the villain
the only titillating character in such books.

She lay it down and looked around the room. She'd
almost forgotten its comfortably shabby appearance, becoming so used to it during the weeks they been in Bath
it had become a background one didn't see. Now she
felt a certain amount of shame at the lack of decoration.
They'd rarely thought to spend even a single shilling to
improve the looks of the room with something so simple
as a bouquet.

Of course, to begin with, they'd thought they didn't
have the money for such things. And, of course, they
hadn't—until Fanny was found to have an income beyond their wildest dreams. Now they could and they
should do something to improve their milieu. It was in-
sulting, bringing guests into such a bleak and threadbare
room. The only thing which could be said in its favor
was that it was spotlessly clean!

Tacye's thoughts were interrupted by a clatter of
shoes on the stairs. She wondered if it were Damaris
and Fanny, but thought there were far too many persons
coming up to be them. Perhaps the family which lived
on the floor above . . . ? But no, that was Damaris'
voice, laughing at something which had been said to
her.

Something inside Tacye tightened to the point of
pain. Was Worth out there? Was he about to enter and
was she about to be introduced to him as the woman
she was? The extremely tall, far too thin, too tanned, a
too-everything-a-man-did-not-like-in-a-woman
woman . . .

The door opened and Fanny strolled to her chair
near the table. She was followed by Lord Seward who

pulled a straight-backed chair nearer and was about to seat himself when he noticed Tacye.

Damaris was followed by Lords Cahill and Worth and, sullenly, by Herbert who was trailed by Hereward who smiled when he saw Tacye. "You here, Tacye? Thought you were at your tutor's. Much better to be here. More fun, don't you know?"

"Hello, Hereward," said Tacye, smiling.

"Tacye! You've come," said Fanny. "You must meet everyone at once, my dear. Damaris, will you introduce Tacye around, please?"

Damaris did. Herbert scowled still more but said all that was proper. Seward gave her a quick but thorough look and nodded. Cahill was also polite, but very obviously, far more interested in Damaris than in the too-tall sister who had unexpectedly arrived. Worth, on the other hand, came to her side and lifted her hand. He bowed over it, his eyes catching her apprehensive gaze and holding it.

"Young Toby said you were coming for a few days," he said softly. "We must see your visit is everything you could wish it to be. I knew your brother—your *other* brother—very well, by the way. Terry spoke of you often and I am very happy to meet you at last."

Tacye relaxed an increment or two. She was still not quite certain Worth hadn't guessed her secret, but if he had, he wasn't going to betray her. "I remember you from Terry's letters, my lord," she said equally softly. "He admired you a great deal."

Worth didn't release her hand and Tacye's emotions roiled from the contact.

"I understand," he said, "that you'll be here only briefly, but I hope you'll allow me to become acquainted with you while you're here?"

"I would like that, my lord," Tacye said, and amazed herself at how shy and maidenly she sounded even to herself. She felt heat come up her neck and into her cheek.

At least, she thought, a bit of her more normal cynicism returning, I am presenting a proper picture of young ladyhood—even if it is for all the wrong reasons!

The men left soon after. Even Herbert realized he could not prolong his stay when no invitation was forthcoming for luncheon as it would have been in the country. But he was the last to leave, his brother waiting impatiently in the hall while Herbert cajoled Damaris into promising him two country dances at the ball that evening.

"You should not have agreed to two," scolded Tacye when the door was finally closed behind him.

"He would not go. I finally agreed just to be rid of him. Oh, Tacye, I'm glad you're back. I don't know why I'm nervous, but, every day, it gets *worse*."

"You must simply never do anything which will put you in a position where one of the men you don't trust could harm you."

"That's easy enough for you to say, Tacye, but you don't know how difficult it is," pouted Damaris.

"I noticed Cahill seemed very nearly unable to take his eyes from you," said Tacye, hoping to introduce a lighter note. Before she'd left Cahill had been attentive, but he'd not hovered as he'd seemed to do today. She wondered if Worth had pointed out her sister's problems. It seemed he had.

Damaris blushed. "He says Worth warned him that I might be in danger and he says he won't allow anything bad to happen to me. But he has said nothing . . . nothing which would indicate he feels those warmer passions which . . . which would lead to his proposing. . . ."

"And you wish for him to do so?" asked Fanny quietly.

It was, thought Tacye, far too easy to forget Fanny's

presence. Now she turned to her aunt. "Should she not?"

"I want very much to protect you both from hurt," responded Fanny slowly. "I know Lady Lawton wishes for the match between Damaris and Cahill, but I wonder if the young man is truly ready to settle down. He only recently acquired his honors. Perhaps he is still attempting to find his feet amid such a torrent of new responsibilities as we cannot even imagine. Would he be willing to take on still more responsibility in the form of a wife . . . ?"

When Fanny didn't continue Tacye brusquely asked what it was she truly feared.

Fanny held out her hand toward her younger niece who took it and was pulled close to her chaperon's chair. "Despite the interest he shows her, I fear to encourage Dammy's attachment to the young man. You do feel such an attachment?" she asked, turning her face up in Damaris's direction, actually seeming to look at her and see her—although that could not be, of course.

Damaris burst into tears. "Life was so much more simple before we came to Bath," she wailed and, jerking away from her aunt's loose embrace, ran from the room.

Again there was silence. Finally, on a dry note known well to Fanny, Tacye said, "Somehow I think perhaps she may just about be feeling some trifling something which might be the attachment or something very like it, of which you spoke."

"Somehow," said Fanny, sighing, "I think you may just possibly have the right of it." She sighed again. "I should not, perhaps, have been quite so frank?"

"I don't know. I agree that we don't wish to allow her to assume he will come up to scratch—but he has shown signs that he may. So," grinned Tacye her spirits lightening, "does *your* suitor, Aunt Fanny. Seward

couldn't take his eyes off you and, if he'd not been restrained by all of us standing around you, I think he'd
have eaten you whole right here in the sitting room."

"Don't tease, Tacye. You know nothing can come of
it. No man should be allowed to take on the responsibility of a blind woman! It would be totally unfair to even
suggest such a thing." Fanny bit her lip. "I'm certain
John understands that."

"Are you? I'm not at all certain! And I think you may
be wrong about what would or would not be fair,
Aunt—but I'll not push you now. We've got Damaris to
worry about. Your romance can wait until she's settled."

Fanny found herself wishing they might *not* change
the subject from Seward to Cahill . . . but she did.
"Tacye, would she feel better, do you think, if I were to
remind her we may now go to London for a season if
she does not find a husband here in Bath? That this is
not her only chance?"

"I'm sure she'd like a season in London, Aunt, but I
wouldn't mention husband-hunting at all. Your warning
to her, though well meant, is, I fear, far too late. At the
moment our Dammy has set her heart on one specific
man. Until he comes up to scratch, or, on the other
hand, she recovers from the pain that he does *not*, I
think the mention of any other suitor would be superflu-
ous."

Fanny sighed again. "There is the ball this evening. If
we are to go to it, and it seems we are, then I think I'll
lay down for a bit."

"You don't wish a nuncheon?"

"No. Nor, I think will Damaris, although she should
be asked."

"Then I'll eat alone. However repulsive you lovestruck ones may find it, I am disgustingly hungry."

Fanny blushed. "I am not lovestruck. Not at all.
Don't even suggest such a thing!"

"Why not?" asked Tacye and chuckled when the blush deepened. "And do not say it is because you are blind, my beloved aunt. What you decide to do about it is one thing, but do not try to bam me that you have not fallen deeply in love with Lord Seward!"

"Tacye Adlington, do watch your language. You are not a young man who may say what he pleases."

"Sorry. Instead I will suggest that you not attempt to flim-flam me into believing you are not in love."

"That too is outside of enough, Bright-eyes, but it seems you are set to tease me into a better mood and, as usual, you have succeeded. I'll tell Cook you are in your usual good appetite, Tacye. She'll have something for you before the cat can lick its ear."

"Good."

Tacye watched her aunt leave the room, her steps as sure and certain as when at home. Then it occurred to her that Fanny had walked through the door Damaris had left open without feeling for it. She frowned. How had Fanny known the door was open? How often, at home, had Tacye watched her aunt fumble at a door, testing to see if it were open . . . but not this time?

The maid came in just then with a heavily loaded tray. Tacye was immediately far more interested in what was on it then in solving a mystery which was very likely no mystery at all: her aunt had, very likely, heard that Damaris left the door open. There was no mystery. At least none greater than wondering what the intriguing aromas rising from the covered dishes on the tray might mean.

Now there was a mystery which could easily be solved! And was.

After she'd appeased her appetite, Tacye also returned to her room, and went to take a second look at the gown for that evening. Never had Tacye Adlington worried about how she looked. Never had it occurred to her to check to see if something needed pressing—which her gown definitely did. Never had she wondered if ribbons needed freshening or whether a bit of lace might look well. . . .

Tacye held the gown up to her and looked in the mirror set over the washstand next her armoire. When she could see nothing but a bit of the bodice, she took the gown and, knocking for permission, entered her sister's room. Here there was a narrow full-length mirror and Tacye walked directly over to it, again holding the dress against herself.

"Will it do, Dammy?" she asked, a single deep crease in her brow and her eyes on her reflection.

Her sister rose slowly from her bed and, dawdling, approached. "I don't know, Tacye. It looks as plain as your gowns always do because, you say, you are too much of a rake-handle to draw attention to yourself with decoration of any sort." She lifted the pale blue ribbon which, when tied in the front, trailed down to knee length. "I wonder if a darker blue would look well with the peach color of the satin . . . or perhaps a light-weight lace overskirt in pale honey with ribbons a shade darker?"

"There isn't time for that," said Tacye, something a touch sad in her tone. "New ribbons perhaps?"

Damaris took a closer look at her sister. This was a Tacye Adlington Damaris had never seen. Her sister was usually completely impatient with any suggestion she might do something with her wardrobe, pooh-poohed any notion that she could look very well if she would only pay attention and think about what looked right on her. Now Damaris put aside her own concerns in the sudden hope she might, just once, convince Tacye something *could* be done.

"You are wrong. It wouldn't take any time at all to add an overskirt of lace because we'd not have to hem it. The finished edge would lay against that satin and be beautiful. What is more, I know just where we may find the exactly right piece of lace—if it has not been sold. I looked at it the last time Aunt Fanny and I went shopping, but I remembered what we read in Ackermann's that a girl my age would not wear it, but you, Tacye, I think you are old enough it would raise no eyebrows and it is so very lovely. Let's go get it. . . . Do come!" she urged when Tacye bit her lip and, again very unlike the Tacye Damaris knew, actually dithered.

Tacye, thinking of the warmth of what she thought must be friendship in Worth's eyes that morning, decided it would not hurt if she were to encourage that friendship. She trusted Damaris's sense of fashion in a way she'd never have trusted her own and if Dammy said they could add an overskirt to the gown in time for the ball that evening . . . then they'd do it!

The sisters left the Abbey Arms together only minutes later, having located pelisses and parasols—Damaris loaning one of the latter to Tacye who had not thought to pack one—and the maid, Mary, walking a few steps behind. Damaris talked volubly of the lace, and a ribbon she remembered at the same shop which would be just the thing. . . .

Across the street a sharp-nosed urchin looked up from some game he played by himself which looked to be a variation of taw in which he must remove other marbles from a circle he'd drawn on the pavement. The boy's marbles appeared to be the cheap-baked marrididdles he'd likely made himself from clay, but he gathered them up as if they were as valuable as antique alabaster. He followed along until he saw the small group traipse into a mercer's well-lit shop, the merchandise set below lamps and near windows so as to be seen in the most flattering of lights.

"Here, Tacye," said Damaris, moving to one side and

pointing up at a bolt of material. "See?" she added when a young clerk pulled down the lace and flipped out a length of it in the very best approved fashion. "The color of the satin will glow behind this in a way it would not under white. White, I think would kill the delicacy of the peach. We'll take a half length," she added decisively and turned to the shelves where ribbons were arrayed so that each color proceeded from the palest tint to the deepest which could be managed for that particular color.

Very soon Damaris had chosen lengths of ribbon in varying widths as well and the girls and their maid returned, at once, to the Abbey Arms. They noticed an empty chair approaching, Sir Davey Questerman strolling along behind it. Damaris, seeing him, hurried Tacye on into the house with a brief comment that they must have every instant to remake the dress.

Because they wished to avoid the fortune-hunting roue, they didn't see him tell the chairmen he'd not need them after all. He gave the boy a few small coins and the boy returned to his circle across the way and again set out his marbles.

Questerman wondered why the Adlington women could not be like other women: having set out to squander the hours shopping, why had they not done so! Ah well, another opportunity would come and he'd be ready. He just hoped it would be before the feisty Tobias Adlington returned. He'd just as soon not face that bantam cock's rage before he had all settled to his own satisfaction—not that it would be his own skin which would suffer in such a confrontation!

Later that evening, Tacye stood before Damaris's mirror and couldn't believe she looked so well. She'd combed her short hair upward from her face and neck and encircling her head with a wider ribbon the same color as that of the narrower one which replaced the old blue. The band around her head forced her curls into an oddly attractive crown which she stared at disbelievingly.

"Damaris, I have never understood why you have a deep interest in such things, but I'm very glad you do. You've done wonders with my dress."

"Your hair looks well too—I had feared we'd not be able to arrange it in a fashion which would make you look different from your Toby image." Damaris put her hand to her chin and pondered. "I wonder if I should send Mary out for some flowers. A cluster affixed at the side to the ribbon would, I think, complete the change."

"Me? Flowers?" asked Tacye scornfully "You know I don't care for such things!"

"But you do care that you not embarrass Aunt Fanny and myself, do you not?" Tacye nodded. "Flowers would make you very different from the boyish figure that Bath quizzes have met and come to know!" Damaris turned toward the door, determined to send the maid out for some.

But just then, Mary knocked and was told to enter. She held three small bouquets, tightly bound and carefully framed by silver paper tied off with long trailing ribbons in varying colors. "These just come," said Mary. "I don't know which is for which of you, though."

Dammy carefully took two from the maid and looked at the attached cards. "This one is for Aunt Fanny from Lord Seward. Isn't it lovely, Tacye?" The next, she discovered, and blushed to find it so, was from Cahill and her own, which meant, she assumed that the third was for Tacye. She had Mary take it to her sister.

Tacye, her heart pounding, reached for the tiny card. Was it from Worth? Could it possibly be?

"This too is for you," she said, her voice absolutely neutral as she hid her disappointment with care. "It's from Herbert, of course. He must have seen the others buying theirs and done likewise—he'd never have thought of it on his own, I'm sure."

"We'll tear it apart to use in your hair," said her sister still admiring the posy Cahill had sent her.

"I don't believe the colors will do." Tacye set the bouquet aside and returned to look in the mirror. She really couldn't believe it was herself looking back! She had, she decided, never looked so well. Perhaps she should have cut her hair years ago—but she'd always been proud of the long heavy length and rather enjoyed the feel of it against her back and shoulders when she'd brushed it. Tacye sighed. However much she'd liked that sensation, her hair was gone and it was as well it was. Short hair suited her.

Another knock took Damaris to the door and there she accepted still another bouquet. This time she checked before taking the posy to Tacye and then stood by while Tacye read the card inside the envelope with her name on it.

Tacye read the words—reread them—and tucked the card down her bosom next to her skin.

"What did it say?"

"Hmm?" She wasn't about to tell her sister that Worth wished there was a waltz he might request but that, unfortunately, such was not allowed in the rooms! "Only that Worth would find it agreeable if I were to save him the supper dance and that, if I did not object, the opening dance as well."

"How nice of him." Damaris looked at her sister. "You'll be all right dancing the formal opening dance? You know it is just you and your partner going through the steps? And everyone watching? I don't mind when Cahill leads me out, but I wouldn't like it at all if it were anyone else."

"Why should I worry? I'm certain Worth knows the

steps so well he could do them in his sleep. I needn't be concerned my partner will make a foolish misstep."

"Is that all which would worry you?" asked Damaris, curious.

Tacye glanced around, that single frown line back. "Why? What other reason could there be?" She studied her sister's blushing cheeks and chuckled. "Oh. You mean I should feel shy and unsettled on the floor with no one else but my partner? You forget how ancient I am, Damaris. Much too old for such missish thoughts. Besides, you know how much I like to dance. And how rarely I find a partner who is not shorter than myself! Dancing with Worth will be a treat."

Damaris had never considered how awkward it must be for her sister. "Perhaps Lord Seward and Lord Cahill will ask you to dance."

"Lord Cahill is barely my height and Lord Seward appears to have eyes and time for no one but Aunt Fanny. Should we see how she is doing?"

They found their aunt her hair up and her shoes on, debating between two gowns. "Tell me again exactly what each looks like," said Fanny as they entered.

"The one on the right will make you look a fairy queen," said Tacye, making her aunt swing around in surprise, "and the one on the left will turn you into a se-ductress . . . no, no. Do not blush. I was only teasing, truly. Either will make you unforgettable, but I like the gray-green which matches your eyes and brings out the best of the gold in your hair. Did Damaris choose those for you?"

"One of them matches my eyes?" asked Fanny, ignoring the question, although Damaris nodded a response.

"It matches exactly."

"Then I think I'll wear it."

"The bouquet will look best with it, too," said Damaris softly. "It is full of tiny pink rose buds in all shades from the palest possible to the very dark and will contrast nicely with the green."

"That settles it. You two run along if you're ready and I'll be finished in a few moments now."

"Don't take long, Aunt Fanny," warned Damaris. "Our escorts will be here any time now."

They were and the six of them went down and out into the street where not one but three chairs awaited them. "For us?" asked Damaris, surprised.

"We would not ask you to walk to the upper rooms in all your finery," responded Cahill, "but a coach, in Bath, is more a nuisance than a help. You'll see that most of the women arrived tonight in chairs."

"It makes me feel like a queen," said Damaris, as he helped her into her chair.

"And so you should feel!" he responded gallantly.

Tacye waited to see Seward help Fanny into her chair before turning to the third. It unsettled her when Worth offered his hand to aid her in sitting back into it. Again his warmth was apparent even through their gloves and the shivers it set off up and down her spine were both desirable and yet should be avoided at all costs: Worth might treat her with respect and kindness, and might even like her, but she must keep in mind that she was not the sort of woman a man fell in love with or wished for his wife. Terence, with brotherly kindness, had been brutally frank about that when she'd first reached an age where she found herself interested in the differences between men and women.

The chairmen picked up their burdens and trotted off up Milsom Street toward Bartlett and thence to Alfred Street which led around to the front and the chair entrance. The women stepped from the lowered chairs, each handed out by the appropriate gentleman. Hands were placed on arms and, to the sound of Seward's quiet description of the vestibule and corridor Fanny must traverse to reach the famous Octagon room, ante-chamber to the ball room, they strolled amid the crowd of people arriving for the ball.

"Whose are the portraits?" asked Damaris of Cahill when they reached the small Octagon. She looked from one to the next around the upper walls.

"That," said Lord Cahill, nodding toward the one straight across from the entrance, "is Captain William Wade who was the first Master of Ceremonies. Gainsborough, as you might guess from the style, painted it and made a present of it to the Rooms. The others are succeeding Masters."

They were already nearing the doors to the ball room, again moving with the crowd, when Herbert stepped away from the wall. "I'll take the first and the supper dance, Dammy," he said gratingly, and glared at Cahill.

Damaris drew strength from Cahill's presence at her side and said, "I know I promised you two, Herbie, but I meant country dances. I think the second and the . . ."

"The last," he insisted, his voice a trifle loud and drawing eyes.

Since the dance was free Damaris reluctantly nodded, her face averted. Cahill led her on into the ballroom and looked around to see where Seward had taken Fanny to sit among the chaperons. "That was not well done of Lambourn," said Cahill, frowning slightly.

Damaris sighed. "He is not to be blamed for his rough manners, I think. His mother died when he was young and his father pays no attention at all to the boys. He has four brothers other than Hereward, you know."

"There are six of those louts!" Cahill put on a look of alarm and Damaris giggled. "Dear me," he added, "will society ever manage to survive it? Hello, Hereward," he added, a tinge of color along his cheekbones indicating he'd not thought he'd be overheard.

"If you mean me and my brother," said Hereward, complacently, "I don't know that it will. But *maybe* we'll learn how to behave—if we've good sense." He glowered to where his brother leaned, arms folded, against the wall, ignoring the Masters of Ceremony who was attempting to lead him to where a young girl sat, obviously in need of a partner. "Dammy, may I have a dance? Or have you given them all away?"

"Of course you may have one, Hereward—the third? I don't mind dancing with *you.*"

Hereward sighed, giving her a surprisingly gentle look. "Thank you, Dammy." He strolled off and asked the wilting wallflower to dance, making her brighten up and look almost pretty.

"That young man has come a very long way in just the short time he's been in Bath," said Cahill, watching the younger Lambourn's behavior.

"Yes. But he'll very likely revert to normal when his brother gets him home. Herbert is much the stronger personality, I think," said Damaris, frowning.

"I suppose. But why do we discuss them? There are far more interesting things to talk about . . . like, are you going on the ride which is planed for tomorrow?"

"Oh dear." Damaris's expression changed to one of chagrin. "I forgot, what with Tacye's arrival. Because I forgot, we've not arranged for horses and will have no mounts." She sighed. "I don't see how we *can* go."

"I'll talk to Lady Tamswell and see if she'll trust me to provide horses for you and your sister. I believe you'll enjoy our plans. We expect to see a folly and enjoy a pick-nick—assuming the good weather continues, of course."

Strictly by rank the Master of Ceremony organized the couples who were to start the ball. Couple followed couple onto the floor, most performing with some skill and only one pair forgetting their steps to the point they left the floor in disgrace. Damaris, her cheeks rosy, did very well, but the most graceful couple by far, arousing murmurs of curiosity among the Bath quizzes, were Tacye and Lord Worth. Amused by the old-fashioned display dance, they played the flirtatious parts required by the classic French form and never once looked away from each other's eyes or missed a step. Coming off the floor, Worth commented on how well they'd managed.

"Ah, but it was easy with you for partner. Only Terence has ever managed to lead me through any dance without a single misstep." When she didn't immediately feel searing hurt at using his name, it again occurred to Tacye that the hard cold center that was her lost brother had eased, that a knot or two of sorrow and loneliness had come undone.

Had her aunt been correct? Would a season in London have given her a few friends who might have made Terry's loss easier? And if that *were* the case, if knowing Worth and enjoying his company had helped her over some of her grief, then how much worse would it be when he too was gone from her side, when she was faced with both the loss of her twin and the loss of her love? A suddenly roused fear for her future sent an icy cold shiver down her back. She hunched her shoulders in reaction to it.

"What is it?" asked Worth, noticing—as he noticed every little thing about the woman he found more and more intriguing with every meeting—whichever role she chose to play.

"What? Oh. I believe it is called a goose walking over one's grave," said Tacye as lightly as she could—and was thankful when Cahill and Damaris arrived at their side, Damaris wondering if it would be proper for Lord Cahill to provide mounts for them for a day's pleasure in the country.

"If Lady Lawton were to offer them, I'm certain it

would be all right," said Worth. "Here comes Seward. While he and I see to the ladies, why do you not arrange something with your aunt?" Worth suggested to Cahill.

Seward had come to ask Tacye to dance and Worth watched Damaris reluctantly take the floor with Herbert. Herbert was, he thought, becoming more of a problem then one liked to admit. He noticed Hereward did not have a partner and went to join the younger Lambourn.

"Good evening," he said to the boy. "Are you not dancing tonight?"

"I just did and I'll have the next with Dammy and then . . ." Hereward frowned. "Then I think I'll go. I don't want to stay and be embarrassed by Herbert's foolish behavior. We'll only have an argument if I do. So I'll leave. . . ."

"Tell me, Hereward, he hasn't firmed up his equally foolish plans for her, has he?"

"For Dammy? Not yet." Hereward sighed and turned to look into Worth's eyes. "I cannot allow him to harm Dammy, can I? If he does intend . . . something foolish, then I'll come to you. It isn't loyal to my brother—but then I think about how I believe he'll treat Damaris and I mustn't let him do that to her. . . ."

There was a pleading look in the boy's eye and Worth reached out to grasp his shoulder. "You will be doing just as you ought. Hereward," and added, "have you ever thought you might like an army career?"

Hereward shrugged, a sullen look returning to his eyes. "Don't think of it, do I? Can't afford it. Every cent the old place will raise—and then some—goes to the old man's gambling." He stared toward where his brother danced with Damaris.

"If a commission were arranged for you in a regiment about to leave for India, would you take it?"

Jerkily, Hereward turn a disbelieving gaze Worth's way. "You don't mean it could happen, do you?" Worth nodded and Hereward's eyes lit. *"Would* I like it?" Then the glow left him and he slumped. "Don't see that I could. Herbert wouldn't like it. . . ."

"It would have nothing to do with your brother. He is your father's heir and a man's heir usually does not join the army. It is, however," suggested Worth, ignoring his own career as an officer, "an honorable choice for a younger son, especially when the estate will not afford him a living. . . ."

Again the glow could be seen in Hereward's eyes, but then, again, it faded. With a wary look, he turned again to Worth. "Why me?"

Worth grinned. "Good question. I think because I believe there is a good man in you which will be lost if you continue to follow your brother about. The officer I'd see you under will teach you to be the man I think you could be."

Hereward looked thoughtful for a long moment and then drew in a deep breath. "If I could do as you suggest I'd be forever grateful. I don't see how it could be arranged so that my father would allow it—or my brother accept it—but I would like it of all things," he finished in a simple manner which pleased Worth still more.

"Be patient then, and don't get yourself into trouble. I'll see what I can do—including organizing things so that your father is willing to accept them. I won't, however, promise that your brother will be happy about it. On the other hand, you'll be far away and he'll not be able to say much, will he?"

"At least not to *me.*" Hereward actually grinned at that thought. "Ah. The dance is over. . . . Blast! My stupid brother isn't bringing her back to Lady Tamswell!"

"Then we'd better go and get her, had we not?"

Worth was already working his way through the crowd and actually cut across the corner of the dance floor against all proper usage, in order to reach Herbert before he managed to maneuver Damaris from the room.

"Ah, there you are, Miss Damaris," said Worth, his eyes meeting and holding Herbert's defiant ones. "Hereward will take you back to Lady Tamswell since he has the next dance with you." He looked down to where Herbert's hand tightened around Damaris's arm to the point the girl had actually to stifle a sound of distress. "You have a problem with that, Lambourn?"

Very slowly Herbert released Damaris and her hand went to where he had squeezed her arm so tightly. "This is none of your business, Worth," snarled Herbert.

"But it is. It is any man's business when another gentleman forgets himself to the point he would harm a young woman."

"I don't wish to harm her. I wish to marry her."

"You don't, you know. You've only taken a silly notion into your head and are now too stubborn to take it out again. You are far too young to be thinking of marriage!"

"If you think to have her . . ."

Worth broke into this snarling would-be threat. "I don't. I only wish to see her happy. Do you?"

"Do I what?"

"Wish to see her happy."

"Of course I do."

Worth cast him a disbelieving look. "But every time I see you with her you are making her *unhappy.*"

Herbert gnashed his teeth. "Nonsense."

"Is it?"

Herbert couldn't answer and turned on his heel to go in search of what mild refreshment was available that evening.

Worth looked after him and shook his head. He

turned to find Grenville Somerwell at his shoulder. "Evening, Somerwell."

"Evening, Worth. Is that Terence's other sister with Lady Tamswell?"

"That's Miss Adlington, yes."

Grenville looked around, studying the room with a baleful but sly stare. Gradually he relaxed.

"What's the matter, Somerwell?"

"Nothing." The overly thin man took another look around and relaxed still more. "Nothing at all." He glanced again at Tacye. "Looks like her brother, don't she?"

"So she should. His twin, you know."

"Twin? He had a twin?"

"You didn't know?" When Somerwell didn't respond, he asked, "Want an introduction?"

Grenville backed away. "No, no. Not at all. See my aunt wants me," he added, rushing to Lady Baggins-Keyton's side where he hovered for some time until she sent him away. He went with wary glances left and right.

Even with Adlington's ghost not in evidence, Grenville wanted nothing to do with either Miss Adlington or Miss Damaris Adlington. He'd come to the horrendous conclusion the ghost expected him to court the younger Miss Adlington and ask her for her hand in marriage and the last thing in the world Grenville wished to do was to wed at the behest of a ghost!

Why he might *never* be rid of the specter, who for the rest of his life, might hover over his shoulder seeing that he treated Miss Damaris right. No, no. It wouldn't do. He couldn't chance it. Never.

Just then the moment for which Worth had been waiting arrived. He moved quickly to where a laughing Tacye was surrounded by young men and deftly removed her from their center. It was time for their second dance, and then, finally, supper with her in the Tea Room. Even with others at their table there should be an opportunity to find out more about the young woman when she *was* a young woman!

And more and more, Worth wanted to discover all he could about Tacye Adlington.

Chapter 13

"I wish it were a waltz," said Worth as he led Tacye to a place in the set nearest the musicians.

Tacye gave him a quick smile, but refrained from responding to his teasing comment. It wouldn't be at all proper for her to tell him she also wished it. Instead she asked him what he'd said to make Herbert so angry—something she'd observed from her place by her aunt.

"I suggested he was too young to marry and asked him if he truly wished to make Miss Damaris happy. He couldn't seem to find an answer," was Worth's dry answer. "Ah," he added. "We begin."

The steps called by the Master of Ceremony were complicated and required concentration. Tacye was pleased when she managed, without putting a toe wrong, even the somewhat complicated *Tour de Main* with its *Temps Levé*, multiple *Chassé*, and finishing with the *Jeté* and *Assemblé*. She curtsied at the end, smiling up into Worth's equally pleased countenance.

Again the quizzes muttered behind their fans. Who was this young woman to make such a hit with the elusive Lord Worth?

The tea room was crowded by those who had not waited the end of the set, but had gone in early. Worth, looking around, saw that Seward guarded a table with determination. He led Tacye to join her aunt, seated her, and joined Seward in watching for Cahill and Damaris. the last two came and they were soon served the meager tea and sweet biscuits which were all one got at the upper rooms.

"Not that it isn't sufficient," said Damaris. "The rooms close so early in the evening one is not ready for more than what will quench one's thirst."

"In London during the season," agreed Cahill, "one would only be starting out for a ball when, here, we are nearly ready to go home!"

"Personally, I like this better," said Fanny softly. "Even though day and night mean little to me, I continue to be a person who is happier and more energetic in the morning. I fear the hours kept in London would not suit me at all."

"Yet you suggested we might take in the season this year," said Tacye in something of a panic. Where the panic came from she could not tell—until she turned slightly and met Worth's steady gaze.

So that was truly it? she thought. I have been so foolish not only to fall in love, but to have hopes in that direction? Terence, Terence, where are you when I need you to laugh me out of my foolish dreams?!

"I think you'll find London interesting for a time, Miss Adlington," Worth said a trifle pensively, "but soon your good sense will intervene and you will see through the glitter and fine show to the overly rigid manners and the ridiculous attention to just who is whom. You'll chuckle when some lady gets upon her stiffs because another, whom she feels beneath her, is taken into dinner before her, for instance. Also," he added thoughtfully, "I believe you'll find it sad that so much time and effort is put into the too careful shaping of bon mots and that true and natural wit has fallen by the wayside."

He eyed her for a moment. "But, of course," he continued, finally, "you'll enjoy patronizing the very best shops and libraries and expect the attention of the highest genius among those who are available to design your gowns—but I predict you'll tire of all that, too.

"Even the delights of the opera and theater will pall when you discover the boxes are, for far too many, merely smaller stages than the professional performers occupy in which tonnish actors may show off those gowns of which I spoke and their jewels and their daughters." Worth looked around, found all eyes on him. He flushed slightly. "Have I surprised you, Miss Damaris, that I do not believe the Season perfection? That I find flaws in those who would tell you they are the very arbiters of fashion and all that is proper?"

"It has always been my dream to go to London for a season," admitted Damaris softly. "Not that I ever thought to do so." She turned to Fanny. "Did you, indeed, tell Tacye we might go?"

"Now that I can afford to take you, I will certainly do so," said Fanny firmly.

"But you just admitted you thought you'd not enjoy it," said Damaris, confused.

Fanny chuckled. "Am I so selfish I would insist on my own interests before yours, my dear?"

"No, never, but am *I* so selfish I would ask it of you," retorted Damaris half-joking and, yet, half-serious.

Everyone chuckled and, having finished their tea, they rose to their feet to return to the ballroom.

Tacye found herself overly aware of the muscular arm beneath her hand. It was worse when Worth laid his other hand over hers and the heat through their gloves seemed to almost burn. She controlled an urge to pull away and then trembled from the effort.

She glanced up, found Worth looking down at her, a curious light in his eye. Tacye felt heat in her cheeks and knew she blushed. She never blushed. How Terence would laugh, she thought.

She realized, the thought had once again come without the accompanying pain normal to such musings. Instead there was a gentle warmth of the memory of a love shared. Bemused by the revelation that her grief for Terence was fading to manageable proportions, Tacye joined her aunt, unwilling to dance again that evening when she could not take the floor with Worth.

When he saw her settled he sighed, grimaced slightly, so that only she could see, and took himself off to do his duty by a partnerless young lady hopeful of taking the floor.

Tacye watched him do the polite—as a young man would say. She smiled slightly, that half-smile so reminiscent of her twin, when she realized that she had so far sloughed off her role as Toby that she was even thinking as a proper young woman should! Chiding herself that way, as if it were only young *men* who used the phrase rather than that only men were *supposed* to use it.

But whatever one called it, Worth did it very well. He was not supercilious. Nor was he overly friendly. He managed that mid-point between raising hopes and setting at ease with a facility Tacye envied. The young woman with whom he danced would, she thought, remember him with respect, remember the dance with enjoyment, and never in her most secret dream think he would ever ask more of her!

Ah, she thought, if only he would ask it of me!

A logical being, it then occurred to Tacye that, if he could deal so easily with the green young miss without raising hopes, why had he not dealt in such a manner with herself? Or was it that she'd first been attracted to him when he'd known her as a young man—and because of that he'd not realized she was a stranger. He'd have been on his guard against any tendency in her toward a tendre if he'd known she was him? Did that make sense? Tacye rather thought not, but wasn't feeling rational enough to think it through.

A little later that evening when the Adlingtons were escorted to their temporary home Tacye was still confused and wary and wondering if she dared hope? Just a little? Or if she was acting the fool altogether! Tacye sought her bed that night after deciding it would hurt no one if she were to dream a little!

Unfortunately she dreamed a a very great deal—and none of it likely to come to pass. But, or so she decided upon waking a moment during the blackest hour of the night, the only person to be hurt by such dreaming would be herself, so why not . . . ?

A heavy-eyed Tacye, dressed in her habit, joined the others for breakfast. Fanny wasn't exactly her usual lilting self, either. In fact, the only one of the three who looked forward to the day with no question was Damaris. She had not put on her habit, however, and Tacye asked her why.

"I discovered we'll be going too far for me to find it enjoyable, Tacye. You know I prefer my equestrian efforts to be of the milder sort." Damaris carefully spread preserves from one edge to the other of her toast as had been her habit from childhood.

"There will be carriages as well as mounts?"

"Oh yes. Lady Lawton told me I could have a place in hers. Are you going, Aunt Fanny?"

"I believe so," said Lady Tamswell, a flustered color whipping up her complexion. "It seems so strange to find myself doing things I have sworn I'll never do again!"

"Lord Seward has urged you to attempt new things?" asked Tacye just as if she had not been in town for weeks and watched, amazed, her aunt's growing confidence.

"Yes." Fanny picked up her tea cup and held it in both hands, set it down again. "I cannot seem to say him nay. He asks the impossible of me and, willy-nilly, I find myself doing it!"

"But isn't that a good thing?" asked Tacye softly.

"I don't know, do I?" Again the cup was picked up and again returned to its saucer. "I came to Bath because I believed Damaris would need me. I did not come to . . . to . . ."

"Fall in love and find a new husband for yourself?"

"Don't tease, Tacye."

"Husband?" asked Damaris, putting her half-eaten piece of toast back on her plate. She looked from one to the other. "Has Lord Seward asked you to wed him?" she asked.

"Have you not noticed how attentive he is?" asked Tacye.

"Yes, but I thought that was because he was an old friend. I thought—" She blushed rosily. "—That old people . . ."

Tacye scowled a quick warning, but Fanny merely chuckled, her frown disappearing at Damaris's half-told belief which touched her sense of the ridiculous. "You did not think that old people," she said, "such as myself and Lord Seward were interested in romance?" Fanny drew in a deep breath. "Joh—Lord Seward has been very complimentary, Damaris, but I believe he must be indulging himself, merely, in an odd sort of flirtation. Perhaps my blindness raises difficulties which require solutions and he finds me less than boring for that reason?"

Fanny reached out and grasped Tacye's wrist when Tacye would have objected. She nodded to where Damaris was obviously relaxing. Tacye frowned. Was

Damaris upset by the notion Fanny might marry again? But why? Surely not because Damaris feared such a marriage would interfere with their going to London! Damaris couldn't be so selfish—or so foolish. Fanny would be in a better position to chaperon Damaris around the ton if she were married to Lord Seward! Money, which it seemed her aunt now had, was not enough; one needed position as well, the sponsorship of some great lady, or marriage into the sort of company one wished to join. Still bemused by the unanswered questions, Tacye looked down to where Fanny was releasing her wrist and reaching for her teacup.

It struck her how deftly and with what confidence Fanny had grasped her wrist and then moved to pick up the cup. Quickly Tacye raised her eyes to Fanny's face. Had a miracle happened? Could her aunt see? But if she could, then why had she said nothing to those who loved her? More questions, thought Tacye with that wry half-smile so common to her.

Was there no end to questions . . . ?

The cavalcade which left Bath some time later was very nearly worthy of the gawping housemaids, cheering clerks, and shouting, racing, urchins who followed along behind for a distance. There were six carriages for the ladies, three curricles for young men who wished to show off their driving skills and a myriad of dancing horseflesh, mostly ridden by men, but several women, including Tacye, braved the disapproving gaze of such quizzes as Lady Baggins-Keyton and sat atop their mounts with straight backs and the anticipation of a good ride.

As the dust rose Tacye worked her way toward the front of the parade, Worth keeping to her side. Soon they were somewhat ahead of the others along with a few other ladies and their escorts. "Ah! I can breathe again! I feel sorry for those in the carriages," said Tacye as they cantered along the tree shaded lane.

"We need rain, 'tis true," said Worth, quirking a brow. "Are we, then, to discuss the weather, Miss Adlington?" He paused for half a moment before clearing his throat and saying, portentously, "The sun shines brightly, does it not? And the breezes are just right, I think, to cool blood heated by ... exercise?"

"But not," she said, her brow arching much as Worth's was wont to do, "that heated by thought of ... exercise?"

"Definitely not." He laughed, but the faintest of red tinged his ears at her daring response. "Shall we race to that far corner? Everyone? Shall we race?" he asked, raising his voice.

Soon the terms of the impromptu race were decided and, with the six of them lined up across the lane, the signal was given. Tacye had silently stigmatized the horse chosen for her that day as a slug; the race proved her judgment sound. She pulled up with the others from some yards behind and asked what the forfeit was for coming in so far in the rear.

"Perhaps a new horse?" asked Worth.

"That would be a *forfeit?*" she promptly asked in return.

The others chuckled and they rode on to where servants lay out the paraphernalia to a day in the outdoors. Drinks were already available and the others rode on to where servants would bring them glasses of lemonade or mugs of ale. Tacye, on the other hand, was struck by the view. Across a valley rose a wooded hill. At the top, visible through and over the trees, a castle stood, its outline stark against the blue sky.

"I didn't know there was a castle this near to Bath," she said, staring. "Is it still inhabited or a ruin? May we explore it?"

Worth grinned. "Would you care to see it more closely?" he asked, a mischievous light in his eye.

She nodded and they rode down the trail which led to a path across the valley. Very soon they were wending their way through the trees toward the top of the rise with no thought to the fact they'd left behind their chaperons. Or at least, Tacye had no thought to it. She was too used by now, to riding off with Worth.

They topped the hill and the stonework began only a few yards beyond. "Would you enter?" asked Worth, still smiling broadly, his eyes still twinkling in that odd fashion.

Tacye eyed the door. "May we?"

"Would I suggest it if we could not?" He dismounted and came to her side while she still stared at the monument. "Tacye?" he asked softly and she looked down at him. He reached for her waist and lifted her down, setting her on her feet with a lightness she'd not expected. She thought of herself as over-sized and not a woman a man would easily move about but Worth had no difficulty. His hands remained for a moment at her waist and then, slowly, just as she'd wondered if he were about to kiss her, he released her, offering an arm for her comfort across the rough ground.

They reached the door surrounded by granite which, grinning, Worth opened. Tacye, all unsuspecting, stepped through—to be faced by more woods. She looked to each side, turned on her heel and looked up. Then she too grinned, turned to Worth and they laughed.

"But it is nothing but a folly!" she said, still chuckling and turning on her heel to look first one direction and then the other. "How unfair when I looked forward to dungeons and I don't know what else."

"The gentleman who had it built lives across the valley. It is his contention that, from the beginning of time a castle was supposed to have topped this rise. He swears that he has, in his imagination, seen it like this from earliest childhood. So, when it became popular to add ruined abbeys to one's parks where abbeys never stood, or a Grecian temple in a countryside where the sun could never warm it as such temples should be warmed . . . well, he had his folly erected here. He is happy, now with his view, and need no longer pretend to see what is not there."

"Grecian temples . . . have you been to Greece, my lord?"

"Not yet but it is an ambition of mine to see the places about which one reads in school, to see temples to gods and goddesses who no longer walk the earth, to walk where the fathers of philosophy trod the markets—yes, I hope to travel there. And you, Tacye Adlington? Do you too dream of far places?"

"My dreams stopped in Italy. I've read all I could find of the wonders to be seen there."

"Perhaps some day you will see them," he said from behind her. He reached for her and turned her. "I think," he mused softly, "I'd rather enjoy seeing them with you. . . ."

This time when his hands clasped her waist Tacye gasped softly. But she didn't pull away. When he tugged gently she stepped closer and when one arm circled her and his other lifted her chin the small bit necessary for their lips to meet, she allowed it.

His mouth touched hers, lifted, touched it again. Tacye wanted more and pressed into him, lifting her hands to his shoulders. When his lips touched hers again, slanted slightly, pressed warmly, her arms slid on around his neck, holding him.

The kiss deepened, Tacye unshocked by the feel of his tongue following the line of her closed lips, finding the brush of rough texture intriguing, exciting. Very carefully she allowed the tip of her own tongue to participate in this new act in the play of mouth against mouth. For a moment tongue tip touched tip—and then his pressed forward, inward, and his arms tightened, hardened.

Tacye pulled back, her eyes wide and wary. She paled at the hard planes of his face, the tension around his eyes, the fact he did not release her. "My lord?" she asked.

His arms dropped away and he drew back, turned. "I should not have done that."

Tacye found herself bereft and wished she'd not objected! "Perhaps not. Neither, of course, should I."

"I won't apologize."

There was an intriguing note to that which set Tacye pondering. Something of a warning in it. Something stern and unyielding. And yet something, too, of anticipation.

"Did I ask you to?" she said after a long moment.

He turned. "Terry said you were something special, Tacye Adlington. He spoke no more than the truth."

"Special." Her eyes narrows. "I know what Terence would have meant by that. I wonder just what *you* think he meant!"

"Someday, perhaps I'll tell you. For now—unless you have no objections to continuing the delightful experiment we just ended—I think we'd better join the others."

There was still something of that sternness. Something warning her—or daring her and she discovered, for the first time in her life, she hadn't the courage to accept a challenge. She sighed softly.

"Tacye?"

This time the questioning note asked something else and she looked up to meet his gaze.

"Are you all right?"

She smiled the smile shared between herself and

Terry, her half tipping the right side of her mouth where his had tipped the left. "Am I? I wonder. Oh, yes, I think I'm quite all right, my lord." She turned and went back through the doorway to where they'd left the horses. She was mounted before he joined her. "Shall we go?"

Again she didn't wait for him, but turned her mount and walked it down the steep path to the valley where, with Worth just behind, she trotted back across to where the carriages were just pulling up near the chairs and blankets and pillows strewn around a perfect little glade.

Tacye was almost hectically gay that afternoon. Damaris commented on it to Fanny.

"Don't concern yourself, Damaris," said Fanny, kindly.

"But it is so unlike her."

"So it is . . . recently."

Damaris was silent for a long moment. "You mean since before Terence went off to the army."

"Even longer. I believe they argued about it for nearly a year before Terence actually bought his commission."

"I had almost forgot."

"So had I. If there weren't such a brittle edge to it, I'd shout hurrah."

"I don't understand."

"I don't know that I do either, Damaris. Is that Lord Cahill I hear calling you?"

"Hmm. Aunt Fanny . . ."

"Not now, my dear."

"No. Not now." Damaris turned away and called. "I'm coming."

"Was that a private conversation or may anyone join in?" asked Lord Seward softly, once Damaris was beyond hearing.

"I'd forgotten you were there, John."

"Should I pretend I didn't hear a word of it?" he asked whimsically, touching the back of her hand with one finger, tracing the embroidery decorating her glove.

"I don't think you need go so far as that. Instead tell me what Lord Worth is doing. . . ."

"Ah. I wondered. He doesn't take his eyes off her. There is a complacent almost possessive air about him and your Tacye avoids him, or tries to."

"I hope very much she doesn't succeed," said Fanny, an earnestness deepening her normal light tone.

"There was something in the way you said that which intrigues me, my dear."

"Was there?" asked Fanny. "Well, perhaps there was. If he may convince my stubborn Tacye she is not unattractive, then I'll be well satisfied."

"That tall lovely figure? That wonderfully bright hair? She thinks herself unattractive!"

"Should I be jealous?" teased Fanny, and then bit her lip. Hard. Such teasing led to just the sort of word play she most wished to avoid. She must *not* encourage John in his nonsensical notion they might marry. She would *not* burden him with a blind wife. Never.

"You never need be jealous, my love. My one and only love," he said slowly. When she turned her head away, he drew in a deep breath and said, "It is only that I find your Tacye as nonsensical as her aunt if for differing reasons. Why has she taken such an odd notion into her head?"

"Her brother," said Fanny, not hiding bitterness. "Terence's word was, of course, law, and he died before he could tell her she'd changed, that she was no longer a gangly colt of a girl, but a lithe and lovely woman." She paused, sighing. "She *was* a gangly sort of girl. She blossomed late, long after Terence went off to war and left her behind. Because he never told her otherwise, she still believes herself to be the oddling he once told her

she was. I have been unable to convince her otherwise—and, of course it was complicated when Damaris
grew up to be so *very* lovely so that the young men in
our area never looked at Tacye. Only at Damaris."

"But Damaris is beautiful with the beauty of youth,"
objected Seward. "Your Tacye's sort of loveliness will
last the whole of her life."

"And she is supposed to just *know* that?"

"Perhaps not." After a thoughtful pause, he added,
"Tell you what, Fanny, if the opportunity arises, I'll tell
Worth to inform her of it."

Fanny chuckled. "I can just see how *that* conversation
will go!" Fanny lowered her tone: " 'Here, now,' you
say, 'if you ever want that Adlington girl to come to you,
you'll just have to tell her she's beautiful and will always
be beautiful.' " She laughed again before continuing in
her own voice. "You know you cannot do it."

"Oh, yes I can."

"Don't be silly. It simply isn't done."

"Fanny, my love, I know you very well. Until you've
settled Miss Adlington and Miss Damaris suitably, you'll
not think of your own future. Since I very much wish
you to think of that future, I'll do all I can to see those
two married and off your hands! Anything, even to
guiding Worth in how to court Miss Adlington!"

"John! You distress me beyond bearing when you per-
sist in thinking I can have any sort of life other than
what I have now."

He patted her hand. "We won't discuss it, but you are
wrong and I'll convince you of it eventually . . . ahhh!"

"What? What have you seen? Don't tease me, John."
Fanny quested with her blind face, wondering in what
direction she should look.

"While we argue, so too do Miss Adlington and Lord
Worth. I wonder what she is saying to him to make him
look so grim."

What Tacye was saying was that she did not appreciate being made to look the guy.

"And in what way do I contribute to such an illusion?"

"By the way you look at me, as if you wished to . . . to . . ."

"Eat you? But I do."

"What?" she asked, startled from the line of her argument.

"Wish to eat you." He smiled, that warm, warming smile she'd come to watch for. "Don't you know how desirable you are, my dear?"

"You go too fast."

"Do I? I suppose, Miss Adlington, that since we met only yesterday, that perhaps I do. But I feel as if I'd known you forever."

When her eyes darted to meet his, a worried look in them, he realized she thought he was alluding to her masquerade. He wasn't ready yet to reveal that he'd seen through that.

He added, soothingly, "From your brother's stories, don't you know? He loved you very much. He knew you well, and he made me see you for who and what you were. And now I see you as you've grown to be, why you are even more intriguing and lovely and wonderful than I ever thought any woman could be."

"Nonsense. What my brother said was that I was a bean pole and awkward and would never be attractive to a man—which he thought a very good thing, because he was determined *he'd* never marry and when we got old we could keep house together."

Worth chuckled, still more amused when his laughter irritated Tacye. "And how old was he when you had this conversation?"

Tacye thought back drawing out memories she'd buried deep. "I suppose fourteen or fifteen." She shrugged. "I don't know. It makes no difference to the truth of what he said."

"Tacye—Miss Adlington!" he added when she glowered. He drew in a deep breath which helped to push aside his irritation at her sudden prudishness. "What I began to say was that you've forgotten that at that early age girls *are* awkward, coltish creatures and boys are often convinced girls more a nuisance than a boon. Did it never occur to you that you'd grown beyond that stage?"

Tacye's chin rose. "I am still too tall. I am still too thin."

"How I'd like to prove to you that you are wrong on both counts. Unfortunately this is neither the time nor the place. But remember how well we fit each other when we kissed beyond the folly there—" He gestured and watched with interest as her cheeks bloomed with color. "—Because we did, Tacye Adlington. Very well, indeed."

"A gentleman would not remind a woman of her fall from grace," said Tacye on a choked note.

He chuckled. "You fell only a very little distance, my dear. Nowhere near so far as I wish you might fall!" He looked thoughtful. "And perhaps it is true that I'm no gentleman for insinuating ... much. . . ." His brow quirked, but Tacye wouldn't meet his eyes. "However that may be, you are to be in Bath only a very few days. I'm compelled to push you as far into a corner as I can get you, trap you with silken promises and loving caresses, because, my dear, my opportunity to do so is so short!"

"But why would you wish to?" Utterly bewildered, Tacye stared at him.

"Because, having found you," he said softly, "I'm not about to let you go." He smiled. "Don't look so frightened, Tacye. I'm an honorable man as I'm certain you must know by now."

"Ah." Tacye relaxed.

"What does that mean?" he asked warily.

"Why, that now I believe I understand you. Terence, the fool, must have asked you to look after us if something happened to him. Now you've met me and have remembered that promise and, being an honorable man, you'll . . ."

Tacye stared as Worth turned a stiff, angry-looking shoulder her way and stalked off.

"Now what did I say?" she asked the empty space where he'd stood moments before.

Worth didn't approach again until they were riding home. Once on their way, the cavalcade which had stayed pretty much together on the way out of Bath, strung out so that there were long moments when individuals and pairs could ride pretty much alone. Worth caught Tacye during one of those periods. He was, she discovered, still angry.

"Don't you ever," he said as if their conversation had not been interrupted by several hours of would-be entertainment, "accuse me of such a thing again. Terence did *not* ask such a thing of me and if he had, do you think I'd have waited one minute longer than need be before coming to you and putting you and yours into my care?"

Tacye tossed her head. "If I've insulted that ridiculous thing called male honor which even the best of you are burdened with, than I am sorry for it. But if it is not that, then I can only believe you have one of those sad humors which delights in making a May-game of poor innocents such as myself."

He growled. "You are making the May-game of yourself when you deny that you are attractive."

She looked around. "How odd. Here I am, an attractive woman, and the men stay away in droves! It is a mystery, is it not?" she finished in a sarcastic tone reminiscent of her Toby incarnation, if she'd only known.

"They stay away because I have made it clear that any man approaching you will have me to deal with."

Tacye turned, finally, to look at him. "I wish I could believe you," she said, simply.

"Believe, Tacye Adlington. And extend your visit here in Bath for more than a few days so that I may prove to you what I say, what I feel."

"Feel . . ."

"You think it too soon. And yet you kissed me."

"You once again remind me of what should be forgotten," she said sharply.

"*I'll* not forget." He was silent for only a moment. As another gentleman maneuvered his horse nearer, he added softly so the other would not hear, "I think you'll not forget so easily either. . . . Yes, Ransome? Have you been introduced to Miss Adlington . . . ?"

They had no more privacy that day. But, later, when the darkness of her room pressed heavily against her prone body, Tacye had to admit that Worth was correct.

It would *not* be easy to forget that kiss!

Chapter 14

Worth walked out of his favorite library the next morning just as the bells tolled. He'd risen early, gone for a long ride before breakfast—and wished that Tacye might be riding with him—gone to the Pump Room where he'd again sparred verbally with his elusive love and then gone to read yesterday's papers which he'd missed due to the riding party.

Tacye was, he thought, going to drive him crazy before he won her trust and, even more importantly her hand! He should never have kissed her. From her behavior this morning, Worth guessed she now believed him to be merely one of those men who took advantage of any lone female. Worth sighed. That belief he could change. He could win her trust later—but not if he lost her to some muddle-headed thinking put into her head by her twin.

Terence, he thought, a trifle grimly, you did me no service, convincing me of her value—and, on the other hand, convincing her she has none. You make it exceedingly difficult to win her!

He was musing ways and means when the huffing and puffing of someone coming up behind him caused Worth to turn. He was nearly run down by Hereward who, wild eyed, could barely stop in time to avoid hitting his quarry.

"Herbert . . ." panted Hereward, and bent to put his hands on his knees. He breathed deeply. "Herbert . . ." he repeated, looking up beseechingly.

"Herbert has done the unthinkable and kidnapped Damaris?" asked Worth softly.

Hereward nodded his head rapidly, several times.

A grim expression made Worth's features hard and unrelenting. "When?" he asked.

"Don't know," panted his informer.

Worth looked around. There were too many curious eyes watching them although he thought no one had actually heard their words. "We can't talk here, Lambourn. Come along to my rooms where we may be private." He took Hereward's arm and the two continued on down the street at a casual-looking but distance-eating pace.

Once they reached Worth's hotel, his lordship beckoned a waiter and placed an order that a good brandy be brought to his room. He then took the stairs as quickly as he could and was already unbuttoning his jacket before they reached his rooms. As they entered, his valet—his batman when he'd been in the army—was crossing the parlor carrying a stack of newly pressed cravats.

"Good man! Boxer, lay out riding clothes and send down for Jackass to be brought around and a good horse for yourself." His valet bowed, and continued on into the bedroom. "Boxer," added Worth, "be sure you put loaded pistols in the saddle holsters, if you please."

"Here now, you won't shoot him, will you?" asked Hereward, horrified. "He's my *brother.*"

"I won't shoot anyone and, no matter how much the idiot deserves to be horse whipped, I'll not do that either. But I may have to shoot over the horses' heads to get the driver to stop."

"He's driving himself."

"Blast. I've seen his driving so that's something else about which one must worry!"

"My lord?"

"Sorry, Hereward—just a comment on your brother's driving skills—or lack there of!"

Worth had stripped off his coat and was down to his shirt and trousers when the waiter arrived with a bottle and two glasses. Worth took his and went on into the bedroom. Hereward, hesitantly, followed him, holding his own exquisitely blown glass in an unpracticed way.

"Very good, Boxer, I believe I'll find those moleskins comfortable if we must ride far, but the green hacking jacket, please. Roll up a great coat just in case we're on the road late and the the weather changes. Now, Hereward," he said, sitting so that Boxer could pull off his half boots, "tell me what you know."

"But I don't know much at all. I didn't know he was going t'do it today." Hereward suddenly wore an expression of disgust. "He *foxed* me. I'll bet he guessed I didn't approve. In fact I know he knew I didn't because I told him so!"

"Which tells me nothing of his plans. Stop ranting and give me facts, Hereward."

The boy sighed. "I found a note. I'd been gone most of the morning looking for a tavern were there was to be a cockfight and couldn't find it . . ." Hereward straightened and looked outraged. "Do you think he told me to find it knowing there was no such place?!"

"Very likely. You found a note." Worth stood while his pantaloons were stripped from his narrow hips and pulled on the moleskins himself. Then he reached for his first boot. "You go order the horses, Boxer, and ready yourself. What did the note say, Hereward?"

"Only that I'd have a new sister in a very few days and he knew how much I'd like that."

"Blast. So we don't even know whether he left by the London road or went north."

"Yes we do."

Carefully Worth caught and held onto his temper. "Hereward, I need to know everything if I'm to catch him and rescue Damaris."

"Think I should go too," said the boy sullenly, looking away from the guns Boxer, who had just returned, was laying out along with ball and powder—and then back as if fascinated by them. "He's *my* brother."

"Which is why it will be better if you are not involved. You can pretend you know nothing of how I discovered he went off with Damaris."

"And her maid."

"And her maid." Worth shut his eyes and counted, silently, to ten. "How are they traveling, Hereward?"

"He'll have taken a post chaise and four as far as Gloucester. There he'll leave the maid behind and find a lighter rig with only two horses when they go on from there."

"I don't know how you know all that, but if you also know the style and color of the chaise, Boxer and I can be on our way."

"I went to ask that before coming to find you, o'course," said Hereward as if it should be obvious. "Panels are green. The wheels are picked out in green as well. The trim is black, mostly, with a bit of gold fancy stuff on the panels."

"And the horses?"

"Four good'uns, big strengthy sorrels."

"Very good staff work, Hereward. I think you've proven you'll make a good soldier." Worth put his hand on the slumped shoulder nearest him. "Buck up, lad. You have, although very likely you can't quite believe it, done the right thing."

"He's my brother," repeated Hereward for the third

time. "Ain't his fault we ain't been raised right," he added sullenly. "Father should have seen to us, seen us right."

"Maybe he should have, but *you* are turning out better than one might expect and you were raised the same way your brother was reared. No reason why he must live *down* to expectations, is there?"

Hereward sighed again and straightened his shoulders. "Better go tell Tacye now."

"No!"

Hereward raised bewildered eyes to meet Worth's. "But, Damaris—she'll want to help."

"Exactly." He met and held the boy's eyes. "She'll want to help, but we won't allow her to do so, will we?"

Hereward again looked bewildered. "We won't?"

"No, we won't," said Worth a bit grimly. "It is just the sort of thing she *would* do, race off after your brother—and very likely challenge him to a duel or some such nonsense. We'll brush through this much more easily without her and with far less noise." He stared at Hereward, commanding him with his look of sternness. "You stay right here and wait for my return. I'll tell them downstairs you are to order whatever you like and put it on my bill—just don't go dipping too deep," he finished more lightly. "It never does to drown one's sorrows in a bottle."

"I'll remember," said Hereward and followed Worth back into the parlor. He dropped into a chair and stared at the empty grate. "Not much of a drinker anyway. Might order some supper if you're late. Do like my food regular, like. Only drink when Herbie's there pushing it and I'm arguing with him, don't you know? Don't really like what it does to my head the next day. Sick as a dog, mostly, you know . . ."

For a moment Worth wavered between laughter and sadness at the boy's words. He wondered if he should say more, but decided there was no time to spare. He motioned to Boxer and the two left the room, the hotel, and, very soon, Bath itself, at which point they gently urged their mounts up to speed.

Worth did some calculations and decided, that if they didn't push too hard, he'd come up with Herbert in no more than three stages—assuming they didn't lose the trail at the point where the young lout changed carriages or come to grief with a thrown shoe or something similar.

At about the time Worth left Bath, Tacye turned from the window in the Abbey Arms. "When did Damaris say she'd be back?"

"Not for hours, Tacye. She's shopping with Mary for chaperon and then going on to visit a friend."

"Then, if you do not need me, I think I'll take Cook and go choose the new dresses for the maids about which we spoke last night. We can get much better quality material here and for a better price than at home. If that's all right with you . . . ?"

Tacye gave her aunt a quick look. This being dependent on her aunt's newfound wealth was already becoming irksome—and yet Fanny had been dependent on the Adlingtons for years and had not once appeared to feel beholden. Tacye bit her tongue and decided she'd just have to learn to live with her new status vis-a-vis her aunt and with no grumbling and no feeling sorry for herself.

"Aunt?" she asked when she missed her aunt's response.

"I said that that's an excellent notion. We've that ball to go to tonight, so I think I'll rest while you're gone."

"Good."

After finding a pelisse and bonnet, Tacye collected

Cook who, at home, was also housekeeper and went off to their favorite mercers. There the two quickly chose the print stuff which the maids could sew into a best dress but were rather undecided about the plain.

"Gray is always good," said Cook gruffly.

"Blue is prettier but it fades so quickly," said Tacye, fingering a lovely clear blue.

"Might be daring and go with a pink," jested Cook and chuckled at the look of horror the stiff-backed clerk gave her.

"Not pink, but what about that nice yellow up on the next to the top shelf."

"Yellow?" asked the clerk, sneering. "For *maids?*"

"Why not? Do you not think they'd work better if their lives were cheered a little by pretty dresses? Yellow with white collars and cuffs. Well, Cook?"

While Tacye was baiting the clerk, Cook chose a red-brown which the clerk seemed to find more suitable if still a trifle out of the way for mere maids and another argument ensued.

While Tacye and Cook argued amiably there was a knock at the Abbey Arms front door. Mrs. Armstrong found a ragged urchin waiting there and very nearly slammed the door in his face.

"Message," said the lad quickly and thrust forward a piece of paper.

"I'll take it."

"Not on your life," said the boy, putting the slip of paper behind him. "I'm t'give it direct into Lady Tamswell's hand, I am."

"I can't allow a dirty little rag-tag like you entrance to my nice clean house. Now hand it over, I tell you." When he only shook his head and grinned, she added, "Impertinence! You're a cunning shaver, you are! You just want to see if you can gull a tip from the poor lady and you already been paid!"

"Haven't then," said the boy sullenly. "Don't get paid 'til I give the lady the note."

"Nonsense," said the manager of the Abbey Arms. "Give it to me and I'll give it to the lady and that's that."

The lad looked toward the corner of the building and then shrugged. After an instant, he handed over the note and jumped to the paving from the top step. "Have it then, but give it over to the lady *at once*. It's important."

"I will then," said Mrs. Armstrong with a harumph that anyone would think she would not.

The landlady immediately went up the steps to the first floor and knocked. After a brief interval the door was opened by Lady Tamswell herself. "Lad brought you a note, my lady," said Mrs. Armstrong, flustered at finding her ladyship doing such a minor chore as opening her own door. She extended her hand.

"A note." Fanny frowned.

"Yes. Seemed to think it rather urgent." Mrs. Armstrong thrust the paper forward but still Lady Tamswell didn't reach for it.

"Mrs. Armstrong, can you read?"

The landlady blushed rosily. "Some. Not very well."

"Do come in. That you can read at all will be better than I can do." Mrs. Armstrong boggled at such an admission from a lady-born, but followed her ladyship into the front parlor where Fanny seated herself.

"Now then," said her ladyship, "tell me what the note says, please."

The twist was carefully untwisted and the landlady lay it on the table. She bent over it. "Begins, I think, with your name."

"Lady Tamswell, correct?"

"Yes, my lady. Then it says . . . says . . . My lady, it's such a scrawl I don't know if I can make it out at all.

Something here, I think, about Miss Damaris. She's hurt herself?"

"Hurt? Damaris? Call Tacye . . . oh, you can't! She is not here. . . . " Blinking rapidly, Fanny rose abruptly. "Give it to me."

The landlady handed over the wrinkled sheet and watched. Fanny spread the sheet and began reading. "Broken her leg! In pain! Well, of course she's in pain! Oh, that poor child. I must go at once. Mrs. Armstrong, will you see that my chair is brought around?"

The landlady left the apartment and Fanny peered at the rest of the note. There was something about hurrying and something else about need for haste—but Mrs. Armstrong was correct that it was a terrible scrawl. Worst of all, there was no indication of where she was to go! Fanny paced the room once, twice—and turned when the landlady panted into the room.

"My lady, there are a pair of chairmen waiting. Say they've been sent for you."

"Ah." Fanny, who had been wondering what she was to do next, dropped the useless note and hurried after the landlady, down the stairs and out the door and, moments later, down the street carried by strange chairmen she knew not where—only that she must get to Damaris as soon as maybe.

"I've decided," said Tacye, finally. "We will get the yellow and will take twice the yardage for collars and cuffs. That way dirty collars and cuffs may be changed for clean and the dirty washed without having to wash the whole gown. That should do."

"But Miss Tacye," said Cook, exceedingly upset, "yellow will show every bit of dust every time a maid dribbles ashes over her skirt or drops a coal down it!"

"*That* is why the girls wear aprons, is it not?" asked

Tacye stubbornly. "Add three times the yardage for aprons and a bit of that lace for across the bib," she added, pointing to a narrow lace.

"Too fine by half for maids. They'll get uppity," said Cook. "Ayerst will never be the same again!"

"Aunt Fanny would wish to gift them with something which will give them pleasure. We've stinted everyone for too many years, Cook. And now I think we must choose a new Sunday dress for you. Would that taffeta be too bright, do you think?" asked Tacye, pointing to a deep blue which had caught her eye. Blue, she knew, was Cook's favorite color.

Cook drew in a deep breath and shut her eyes. "Bribes, now. Never thought you'd sink so low, Miss Tacye."

"But do you like it?" coaxed Tacye, her eyes twinkling.

"How could a body not like it? But that black beneath it is much more the thing."

"Very nicely spoken. We'll take the blue," said Tacye to the clerk. "I like to think of it surrounded by maids in yellow. What a bright happy bevy it will make when you walk to church of a Sunday!"

"I thought the yellow was for everyday," said Cook crossly, wishing to hide her gratification.

"I've changed my mind. The print with white aprons will do nicely for everyday and the yellow for Sunday. The lace is for the collars, not the aprons and don't you dare say one word, Mrs. Cook. I know you don't approve, but allow us this tiny bit of generosity. You may tell the girls that it will not be a regular thing, but this once, in celebration of our good fortune, we wish them to benefit as well."

Arrangements for sending on the material were made and Tacye signed the bill. It would be sent to Fanny's

man-of-business here in Bath as had been arranged after
they'd learned of her fortune.

Tacye and Mrs. Cook strolled back toward the Abbey
Arms, stopping now and again to look in windows, in no
hurry to return to the closed-in feel of their small rooms.
Tacye was staring at a pile of new books just in from
London in the Meyler's window when a young lad si-
dled up to her. She looked down and recognized the
young groom from the stable where "Toby" stabled
Numbskull.

"You know Mr. Adlington, maybe?" asked the lad
when he saw he had her attention.

"Yes."

"Maybe you'd tell him that Sir Davey is up to tricks?"

"How so?"

"Heard him making arrangements with a couple of
lowlife chairmen who'll do anything for a meg as to how
they were to make off with Mr. Adlington's aunt."

"You—" Tacye looked around and lowered her voice.
"—What?"

"He's gonna take her off somewhere and compromise
her and then make her marry him. Heard him."

"My God . . ." Again Tacye looked around. The trio
was drawing curious eyes. "You come along with us,"
she said sternly. "Cook? We must hurry. I must tell Toby
what this young man has discovered."

"You can't . . ."

"Cook, don't argue. Toby must be informed at once."
Tacye, to avoid the argument she knew Cook wished to
begin took off at a rapid pace, her skirts swishing in a
way no lady's should be allowed to swing! The stable lad
followed, panting, a pace or two behind.

Cook waddled along but hadn't a hope of catching up
with her wild young miss. But, what to do? If the boy
were correct, then someone must go after the villain.
But not Miss Tacye. It wasn't right. So who . . . ?

While Cook muddled through her inner argument, Tacye, with the boy following, took the steps to the first floor as quickly as she could, wishing all the while for her trousers. Skirts were so *damnably* restricting! She went down the hall to her room and, turning, told the boy to wait in the hall. Bemused, he did so.

"You can talk through the door and tell Toby in your own words," She stepped into her—and Toby's—room and closed the door in the lad's face.

"Quality," muttered the boy, disgusted. But he obliged, repeating what he'd already said with embellishment which added nothing to Tacye's knowledge.

While he talked to the closed door, she stripped out of her dress and petticoat and reached for the silken strip with which she bound her breasts. Soon she was into shirt and pantaloons, the straps tight under her stockinged feet and reached for her boots.

"You can come in now," she called, tired of not being able to see the boy as he spoke—or when she asked him questions.

"Where's the moll?" asked the boy, looking around.

Tacye swore softly for not thinking of that problem. "She's shy. Hiding while I dress, don't you know?"

The lad looked at the big armoire which Tacye glanced at and shook his head. "Quality!" he said again, thoroughly disgusted. "Never know what them will get up to."

"No one doesn't," agreed Tacye. "Now, did Questerman say anything about his plans once he had my aunt?"

The lad drew his speculative gaze away from the armoire and back to the young man questioning him. "Said he was gonna take her to a house in Back Street. Keep her there until she agrees to wed him."

"Ah. At least, then, he's not taking her out of town. I don't know if that's good or bad." Tacye pulled on her second boot and stamped her foot down into it. "Now, my whip . . . wish I had a pistol, but one can't have everything, can one?"

Cook opened the door and stood, arms akimbo in the door. "You can't do this."

"Can't rescue my aunt? I'm to allow that dastard to have his way with her, to force her?"

Cook's whole face turned cherry red. "Well and away with you! You watch what you say to me!"

"Cook, I must go. You must see that there is no alternative."

Cook, still bemused by it all, followed Tacye down the hall and into the sitting room where the crop was found. "What's this here?" asked Cook, picking up the note Fanny had dropped.

"So. That's how he tricked her," said Tacye, reading it quickly. "Except—" Tacye looked up. "—How did she read it?"

Cook looked as curious as Tacye felt. After a moment she suggested, "Mrs. Armstrong, maybe."

"Ah," said Tacye, nodding. "That'll be it. Young man," said Tacye turning to the stable boy, "can you show me the way to that street? Back Street I think you said?"

"That I can," he said sounding self-important.

"Then let's be off."

Cook followed, closed the door and then, treading heavily, went down the hall to her tiny kitchen. She slumped against the work table and took off her bonnet, all the while mumbling that it just weren't right and that Tacye was certain to get herself into a bumble-broth and it would serve her right . . . except that, of course, like all the staff, Mrs. Cook loved the girl and truly wished her only well.

So what could a body do? she wondered. " 'Twarn't Miss Tacye's place to go running off that way. Twarn't her what should rescue Lady Fanny," she told the closed stove, which, secretly, she'd grown very fond of and wondered if, now Lady Tamswell had come into money, if just perhaps she might request that one be installed in the kitchen at Ayerst Hill.

No, not Miss Tacye's place—but maybe that Lord Seward's who had been hanging around Lady Fanny and reeking of April and May?! Cook reached for her bonnet and then laid it back down. Where would she find Lord Seward at this time of day? She didn't even know where the man lodged! But someone would. Determinedly, she again reached for the bonnet.

One way or another she'd find Lord Seward and send him after Miss Tacye. Plopping the bonnet on her head, she didn't take time to tie the ribbons, but went immediately in search of Mrs. Armstrong who, if she did not know Lord Seward's direction, would know how to discover it!

Chapter 15

"Well, Boxer? What did the grooms have to say?"

"Maybe an hour ahead of us, my lord."

"As much as that. Damn."

"But only the two horses, as was told us it'd be. If you want to chance going crosscountry, we may be able to cut that to half an hour or maybe less—*assuming*—" Boxer grimaced. "—One can trust the jobernowl who gave me the directions, o'course."

"You're usually a good judge of that sort of thing, Boxer. Do you think we can?"

"Trust him? Oh, aye. I just don't know if we can follow the way if it gets dark soon now—and the weather do not look to be cooperating, do it? It may be dark far too soon."

Worth cast a look at the boiling clouds blowing in from the west and rapidly covering the formerly blue sky. He sighed. He never complained through all the campaigning he'd done in Spain—whether heat or snow or rain. Then and there one expected miserable conditions. But home again in England, he'd assumed he'd never again need be so uncomfortable!

"Assuming," he asked, "we don't catch them sooner, where do you think the Lambourn lout will lay up for the night?"

"Very likely at Stratford-upon-Avon," said Boxer promptly. "If not there, and he's pushing it to get as far from Bath as possible, then at Royal Leamington Spa."

"Or, and I suspect this by far the most likely," sighed Worth, "somewhere in between. I'd guess his pockets are much to let and he'll be forced to choose a hedge tavern—whatever Miss Damaris may think of it—which means we'll be stopping all along the way and wasting more time." His lips compressed, Worth added, "Let's go."

Boxer grinned but didn't respond. They'd just finished the meal of bread and cheese they'd ordered and were returning to where their somewhat rested horses awaited them.

"Jackass is willing and able, but what of that nag you're crossing?" asked Worth, mounting as he spoke.

"He'll do for another stage, then I'll find me something fresher."

"In that case, Boxer, lead the way. Find me this short-cut which may or may not cut Lambourn's lead in half!"

Meanwhile, Tacye, hands on hips, looked up and down Back Street. "Now what? Do we knock at every door?"

The stable boy, who should have been back at his work long before, chuckled. "Don't see how that'll do much good. The doors only open on halls and stairs, Mr. Adlington, sir, and you'd have to knock on all the inside doors as well."

"So. What do you suggest we do?"

"I could ask if a chair brought a lady anywhere here abouts today," suggested the boy after a moment.

"That sounds an excellent notion. Whom do you think you might ask *first.*" Tacye, her concern for Fanny making her irritable, scowled.

* * *

Mrs. Cook, also frowning a ferocious frown, left the Pump Room. Lord Seward, it seemed, was not in lodgings but was living with a relative or friend. The Master of Ceremonies had *not* been helpful, although grudgingly, he'd suggested Mrs. Cook might apply to Lord Cahill, Lord Seward's friend, for the information she insisted she needed.

Mrs. Cook had no more notion where to find Lord Cahill than how to discover Lord Seward's direction, but she did know that Lady Lawton lived near The Circus and that Lady Lawton would very likely know how to find Lord Cahill who, it seemed might know where Lord Seward might be found. It seemed a round about way of going on, but Mrs. Cook had no choice and, having gained rather confusing directions for finding Lady Lawton, she set off once more.

Mrs. Cook had never had reason to go into the better part of Bath where The Circus was to be found and was thoroughly lost before she again found her way—this time thanks to the kindness of a little housemaid scrubbing a doorstep. It was far later in the day than such work *should* have been accomplished, but Cook forbore to scold. The girl had, after all, done her a service and, thanking the child, she retraced her steps for a block and turned the right direction.

Having finally arrived at the proper door, she then found herself dealing with the most top-lofty butler she'd ever met.

"*You,* my good woman, must go to the scullery door," said Ruggles, his nose reaching for the sky after the most cursory look and before he even inquired why she'd come at all.

"Which will no wise change my errand which is merely to discover the direction of Lord Seward." He tried to shut the door in her face, but she put a foot in the way and pressed against the panels.

Ruggles sniffed. "If such as my Lord Seward wished such as you to know his direction then no doubt my Lord Seward would inform you of such!"

"Ruggles? Did I hear my name?" asked Seward, coming, cue in hand, from the billiards room to the back of the large entry hall. He studied the overly plump woman, recognized that she was an upper servant from her dress, and came forward, curious. "You wished to speak with me?" he asked.

"Lord Seward! At last." The door was allowed to open and Mrs. Cook caught her breath. "Yes, my lord," she said, "I wish to speak with you." Then she glared at Mr. Ruggles who had not taken himself away from the door. "But not where this squeak-beef can hear my words!"

Seward hid a grin. "Perhaps you would come with me into this little room just here?" he suggested and motioned to where tradesmen were asked to wait just beside the door. Mrs. Cook swept past the butler, her nose elevated to a position at least as high as his, and through the door held open for her. "Now, first perhaps, you tell me who you are?"

"I'm the Adlingtons' cook, my lord. Mrs. Cook by name and cook by profession." She touched her breast with one hand. "Thank the good Lord I've found you," she added in a worried tone.

"And now you have," Seward soothed the agitated woman, "perhaps you'll tell me the problem?"

Mrs. Cook dug into her capacious pocket and found, crumpled almost beyond legibility, the note which Lady Tamswell had dropped and Tacye, too, had left behind. "This came while everyone was out. Lady Tamswell must have gone off to see what's what—but a stable laddy who recognized Miss Adlington, told her some tale about a man who would trick our Lady Tamswell into a compromising situation so that she must marry him. The boy heard the villain plotting how to go about it. Miss Tacye—" Mrs. Cook blushed rosily. "—I mean Mr. Tobias Adlington went off with the boy to find them."

"Mr. Adlington has returned? Good. But you feel more help is required?"

"Yes, sir." Mrs. Cook clamped her lips tightly against the desire to rant that Miss Tacye was in danger as well, since she was play-acting at being Mr. Adlington again.

"Then I'll just call Cahill in and you will tell us where we may find them, will you not?" He strode to the door, told Ruggles to fetch Cahill and turned back. "Now. Where *are* we to find them?"

"Heard the boy say in Back Street, but he didn't know what address."

"That's not exactly the best part of town. I believe rooms may be rented along there by the day or week?"

"I wouldn't know, sir, not being a resident of Bath in the usual way of things."

"No, I see that you wouldn't. Thank you very much, Mrs. Cook. You've done just as you ought, coming to inform me, but you may now return to your duties." A muscle jumped in Seward's cheek and a certain tension could be read in his stance. "Lord Cahill and I will go at once to aid Adlington in the rescue."

"Rescue? Who is in need of rescue?" asked Cahill entering just in time to hear those words.

"Fanny. Lady Tamswell, that is. Do you have pistols, James?"

"Not here. Do you believe them necessary?"

"Not just at the moment, perhaps . . . but before another dawn is up?" A muscle jumped in his cheek. "Yes. I very much think *so!*"

* * *

"Which way now, Boxer?" asked Worth, a faint line creasing his brow. He was slowly becoming resigned to being lost for the rest of the day and, very likely, the ensuing night.

"My *guess* would be that way—which likely means we should go *that.*" He pointed first one way and then the other with his crop.

Worth sighed. "Then shall we flip a coin?"

"Sorry about this, my lord," said Boxer, guiltily. "Should have stayed with the main road."

"No, it is not your fault. I agreed to try this route. Let's go that way," said Worth, and gave Jackass a nudge.

The two men trotted down the narrow lane but hadn't gone far before the heavens opened. Worth, rain dripping from the brim of his hat to hit his nose decided things couldn't get any worse. He wondered what Tacye would have to say to him if he didn't come up with Damaris before nightfall and didn't like to think of the language she'd likely use.

He grinned. Tacye's language would *not* be that of a properly brought up young lady, that was for certain.

Would Damaris be forced to marry the lout if they didn't rescue the girl or would everyone do their best to forget what had happened? Worst of all, what would Cahill do? It had been obvious to Worth, at least, that the young earl was working up to a proper proposal. If Damaris was not back home at some more or less decent hour, would the two still manage to make a match of it?

Worth doubted it. Perhaps he should have sent a message to Cahill even though he'd deliberately avoided sending one to Tacye. Cahill might have been thought to have his own stake in the success or failure of this mission.

Worth, pondering the problem of Cahill—mainly to avoid thinking of the problem of Tacye—rode through the rain getting wetter and wetter and only looked up when Boxer cried, "Aha!"

"Yes?" he asked politely.

"I do believe we've managed it after all, my lord. That looks very much to be the hedge tavern my informant described. It lays just off the main road, he said."

"Do you suppose we'll have still better luck— miraculous luck!—and find our quarry awaiting us there?"

"I haven't a notion, my lord, but I'll tell you this: M'spirits been raised now I know my judgment hasn't gone totally to hell in a hand basket!" Boxer grinned.

"I never thought it had." Jackass, obviously hoping for a nice dry, and with luck, warm barn, picked up speed. "Even if you'd not been correct about our route, it wouldn't mean you'd made that great a mistake!" Worth pulled into the yard and stood looking around. "Boxer, does that gig with the broken axle look like the one described to us?"

"It surely do!"

"Then, if you'd be so kind as to see to the horses, I'll just see to the horse's ass who ran off with our little lady!"

"What do you mean you can find no trace of her?" asked Seward, anxiously, looking from Cahill's frown to Tacye's. His own frown was the deepest of all.

Tacye sighed. "I've had that stable boy asking questions of everyone in sight. No one has seen a chair arrive or seen a lady go into any of the houses along here."

"He's certain he heard Questerman say Back Street?"

Tacye beckoned and the boy trotted closer. "Yes, sir?"

"You are absolutely certain the man said Back Street?"

"Could he," asked Seward, "have said back to the street?"

The young groom looked confused. "Thought it was Back Street," muttered the boy, looking down to where he scraped at the paving with the side of his shoe.

"There's a Milk Street," suggest Cahill.

The boy's eyes widened. "The back of Milk Street!"

"What makes you suddenly so certain?" asked Tacye.

"I 'member they said something about a proper place for such a milkmaid as the lady were!"

Seward gritted his teeth at the insult to her ladyship and wondered just how he was going to manage to force a duel with no taint attaching to Lady Tamswell. Somehow he'd do it, he decided.

"There's a sort of terrace there, is there not?" asked Cahill.

Tacye had the boy by the ear and was walking off. "Come along, you scamp. Quickly now. Which way, lad? We've wasted far too much time as it is."

In a moment she'd disappeared around the corner headed toward the river and the walk along it to the top of Milk Street.

Before Seward could follow, Cahill caught his sleeve. "Also Bath Square, you know. Back. Bath. Sounds a bit the same."

Seward wavered, undecided. "I don't know what to do."

Cahill, guessing at Seward's fears, made the decision for him. "You follow Adlington, which seems the likeliest, and I'll go check out Bath Square. That may be difficult, since a lot of women will have been arriving by chair to go to the various baths for whatever cure has been ordered them by their doctors—but perhaps the chairmen she uses daily will be there and remember if they've see her! Either Lady Tamswell will have been there or not and, if it's the latter, I'll come find you."

Seward, not waiting for more, set off after Tacye and Cahill turned in the other direction toward the baths. Cahill, even though it had been his own decision, felt a trifle out of things because he didn't think he'd discover anything to help.

On the other hand, it was best to try every possibility as quickly as possible. Questerman, the only fortune hunter they could think of who might be the man involved, was not to be trusted. It was not difficult to guess how he might compromise Lady Tamswell—although the fact she'd been married and was no longer a virgin might dissuade him from that particularly nasty plan.

Actually, although Lady Tamswell might not know it, she had only to refuse consent for the marriage to make it impossible for Questerman to carry it through—whatever threats he might make to her reputation or her person. Unfortunately, that clause in the various laws which governed marriage, both civil and ecclesiastical, was not widely know. But, if only Fanny remained adamantly against it, in the face of all her abductor could do, he could not legally marry her. Surely she'd not agree to a marriage . . . Cahill fumed and, inwardly, the whole time he questioned people who might have seen her ladyship in Bath Square. . . .

Tacye turned into Milk Street and looked down its length. Even longer than Back Street, she thought. Now what? Do we begin again asking everyone in sight if a chair has brought a lady here? Tacye went back to the corner and on up the street a bit—and discovered the mews between Milk Street and Richmond Terrace which was the next over.

The back of Milk Street. Could it be? Tacye decided it very well might be and disappeared up it just before Seward came into view—which meant he didn't see where she went.

Seward went up Milk Street, surprised he couldn't see Adlington somewhere along its length. Had the boy already gone inside? But, if so, then *where?* How had he discovered, so quickly, which house Fanny was held in?

Again Seward dithered, anxiety growing with every minute. He wished that, on their way to Back Street, Cahill hadn't suggested it was Questerman who had kidnapped Fanny. If, for some reason, the man were balked or foiled, Seward didn't like to think of the villain's response. If his reputation were at all accurate, it would undoubtedly be as nasty as possible. So what did one do? How did one find a woman who could be anywhere at all in Bath—or, if the stable boy were a dreamer or, for that matter, a foil, somewhere out of it?

"Lord Worth!" Damaris jumped to her feet and ran to meet him as he bent to enter the low door to the tavern. "I knew someone would come. I told you, Herbert! I said I'd be rescued."

A sneer decorated Herbert's face, but it seemed to Worth, who observed him closely, that he was a little frightened. "I keep telling you we'll be married," he said, as if he'd said it a million times. "Just tell that gentleman to be off and, as soon as our new carriage arrives, we'll be on our way."

"I keep telling you I don't wish to wed you." Damaris stamped her foot. "Why will you not listen to me?"

"Perhaps," said Worth, coldly, "because he is one of those animals who listens only to his own will and his own interests. He is also a stubborn beast: he has said he will marry you and will not say other even though he no longer truly wishes to do so."

Herbert colored bright red. "That's a lie," he forced through a tight throat.

"No lie. You've had a taste of Bath society. You wonder what London would be like. Yet, you are too pigheaded, too lacking in self-discipline to admit an error and withdraw your suit as any sensible gentleman would do. Did I hear you say you've a carriage coming?"

"A closed carriage," said Damaris, witheringly, "although I told him I'd not ride with him alone in it. He left my poor Mary with the first carriage and with no money!" Damaris, feeling much braver now that Worth had arrived, glowered. "You called him pig-headed, but I say he's just a pig."

Herbert growled at her and raised a hand. Worth caught it and, in a grip of iron, restrained Herbert from hitting Damaris who shrank back, white to the point of looking faint—and immediately changed his grip so as to keep the young man from retaliating against himself.

"You would strike a woman." Worth said it sadly, shaking his head slowly. "It is not done, you know. You'll never be accepted in polite society if you go on this way."

"Because you'd tell," sneered Herbert.

"You think it would be necessary for me to tattle?" asked Worth thoughtfully. He shook his head. "Wrong. Your own behavior would soon make you persona non grata—and if you have so little Latin you can't construe that, it essentially means you'd be found to be totally unacceptable. By the way, Miss Damaris, we came up with your maid and, since a stage was just leaving for Bath, put her on it and sent her home with a message that no one was to worry, that we'd bring you home as soon as we could. . . . Ah. I think I hear the arrival of a carriage?" he asked, turning his head. "Good. Miss Damaris, if you will collect your things, we'll be off for Bath."

"You can't go with him!" howled Herbert. He pulled against Worth's restraining hold. "We're going to be married, I tell you."

"You are not going to marry anyone ever, Mr. Lambourn, if you do not cease this nonsense immediately. You become a dead bore!"

At the last words, Herbert ceased struggling, seemed to shrink, and turned to stare at his captor. "Bore."

"A dead bore. Now behave."

"A *bore!*" Herbert threw back his head and howled like a dog. "A bore, he says! Damme, I'll have your skin for that insult!"

"The truth is never an insult," said Worth, tiredly. "And you are too young to call a man of my status out, but if you insist . . ."

"He doesn't," said Damaris, firmly. "He is merely blowing and crowing and trying to make himself feel big again when he has been proven to be small. Herbert, if you have any sense at all—which I begin to doubt—you will go home and study a good book in etiquette and then, nicely, ask your father to take you to London where you may receive some town bronze. But read the book first!" she scolded.

Herbert bit his lip. "I want to marry you."

"If I do not wish you marry you, and I do not, then the proper thing for you to do is to bow out gracefully. You are not allowed to have your own way in this world merely because that is what you want. It simply isn't the way the world works."

Since it had been very much the way his world had worked up until then, Herbert, with some reason, looked confused.

"Besides," continued Damaris, sternly, "Lord Worth

is quite correct. You do *not* wish me to marry you. What you *do* wish is that I not marry Hereward. Well, be easy. I do not wish to marry Hereward, either—"

Herbert's expression lightened briefly, darkening again as Damaris continued her scold.

"But if I were to be made to choose to marry one of you, let me tell you, Herbert Lambourn, it is your brother I'd choose to wed. You are a pig and an ass and a great looby and I hate you."

Damaris had managed to control herself up to that point, but the day had become too much for her. She burst into tears and turned away, sobbing into the handkerchief Worth unobtrusively handed her.

"If I were you," he said to the suddenly flabbergasted young man, "I'd leave quietly and at once before she manages to stop being a watering pot and goes on with her scold. Something of a termagant, is she not?" he asked, a note of humor barely hidden.

"Termagant! She's a terror." Herbert shook his head and looked soulful. "What a lucky escape I've had!" he said in a man-to-man tone.

Herbert turned and walked out of the parlor before Worth thought to tell him to leave the carriage which he would need to transport Miss Damaris back to Bath. When he heard the horses start up, he turned to stop them, and then shrugged.

Where Herbert had gotten a post chaise, he himself could do likewise and he'd like a short rest and a meal before riding out again—especially since it looked as if it were lightening up and might stop raining soon.

Tacye strode down the lane between carriage houses and stables. Every so often her cohort, the stable boy, would stop to talk to a lad about his own age, asking if anyone had seen a gentry mort—by which designation

he meant Fanny, or so he explained to Tacye when she
asked—delivered somewhere along here by chairmen
and taken into one these here kens—by which, he explained, when again asked, he meant a house.

Finally, toward the far end, they met with success. A
chair had brought a woman who seemed distraught.

"She were met by a flash cove—by which I mean
that Questerman—who escorted her up the garden path
and into the back of that there ken—er, house," he corrected himself.

"Have them describe the woman." Tacye wasn't
about to get this close and have it be the *wrong* woman
and not Questerman at all. The description fit and
Tacye opened the high gate which was, luckily, unlocked
and went into the rough garden which had not, obviously been attended to in years. She studied the back of
the house and saw a two-story building about twelve feet
wide bounded on each side by identical houses. The
back had a door and window at ground level, two windows above that and another, even smaller above that.
In the roof was a dormer with a small four-paned window. Tacye eyed it, wondering if that were where her
aunt was held and if so how she was to get her out.

But, even as she watched, glass spattered from a window on the first floor. A hand carefully pulled remaining
splinters from the surround, then peered through.
"Tacye!" called a soft voice.

"Fanny? But how did you know I was here?"

"Never mind that. Questerman has gone out," said
Fanny softly. "I was going to see if I could climb down,
but I don't think I dare. Have you a plan?"

"Well, I'll try the door. Maybe it isn't locked." It was.
Tacye looked up. "Patience, my best of aunts. We'll find
a ladder."

She sent her young friend in one direction and she
went the other. She returned shortly with a pair of

grooms following along behind with their master's ladder.

"Set it there," she said.

"Don't know if we should."

"Do as she says," called Fanny.

"She?"

"I mean *he*, of course," said Fanny with an apologetic look toward Tacye. "Just do it. I've been locked in here against my will by a fortune hunter. Now help get me out!"

The men were slow and awkward and Tacye wished she were strong enough she could set up the heavy ladder herself. It was in place when her stable boy returned, Seward and Cahill in tow.

"Fanny," called Seward. "Are you all right, my dear?"

"I couldn't be better. Do wait until I get down from here and I'll tell you all about it."

"No. Wait." Seward scampered up the ladder and gently and carefully helped his love come down the awkward rungs.

They were halfway down when Questerman burst from the back door waving a gun. "How dare you! Leave at once! How dare you break into my house! Be off or I'll call the watch!"

"I think that's the *last* thing you'll do. How dare *you* kidnap my aunt?" Ignoring the long muzzled gun, Tacye strolled closer, slipped off her glove and, in classic manner, slapped him with it across the cheek. "I'll meet you whenever you say, wherever you say. Such villainy cannot be allowed to go unpunished."

"Here now, Fanny! You're almost at the bottom. Don't you dare faint!" Seward, stepping from the ladder, lifted his love off and enveloped her into his embrace. Over Fanny's head, he glared at Questerman. "When Adlington has had his turn, I, too, challenge you! You unmitigated gallows bird." Fanny squirmed but Seward would not let her go. "Shush, my dear. I know you do not like it, but this must be done."

"I'll have my seconds call on you," said a white-faced Questerman with an evil look toward Tacye.

"Here now," said Cahill, looking around. "None of that. We've enough right here to see to it with dignity. Much as I dislike doing it, Sir Davey, I'll second you. Seward can second Adlington, and then Adlington can second Seward."

"You assume, of course," said Questerman with a sneer, "that Adlington will be capable of seconding Seward."

Fanny moaned.

"I don't believe any of us wish to make this a killing affair—even you, Sir Davey. It wouldn't suit you to leave England just now, would it?" suggested Cahill, who was aware of the little-known fact that Questerman's uncle was slowly dying and that there was a good chance Questerman was named in the will.

His lips compressed, Sir Davey bowed, but the look he cast at Adlington was full of venom and Cahill sighed softly. The boy was pluck to the backbone, but would he actually be able to stand up to Questerman who was a practiced dueler?

"John," said Lord Cahill, "I think Lady Tamswell should be removed from here. You and Adlington take her home and I'll see to the details here and consult with you as soon as we are in accord. Lady Tamswell, you must not worry. I assure you, all will be well."

He heard a snort from Questerman and hoped Adlington's aunt, who looked pale and worried, hadn't heard it as well. He took Sir Davey's arm and forced him to return to the house, leaving the others in the yard to decide on the best way to get Fanny back to the Abbey Arms.

"I could maybe find you a chair," offered the wide-eyed stable boy who had observed the forgoing with awe.

Fanny waved the notion away. "That isn't the problem. You see, I don't need a chair. I can walk on my own. That was my great news, my wonderful wonderful news—which has been spoiled. Ta-*Toby* why did you do it? *Why did you have to play the fool?*"

"What news, Aunt?" asked Tacye ignoring her aunt's question.

"What news?" For a moment Fanny looked as if she'd forgotten her own words. "News? Why that I can *see*, of course. Am I to regain my sight only to use it at your *funeral?* Stop it." She turned to Lord Seward. "Somehow you must stop this at once. I tell you, my n—"

"You'll tell him nothing of the sort," said Tacye, interrupting before her aunt could reveal her feminine identity. "Terence would expect it of me, Aunt Fanny. And you must remember Damaris. She would suffer from my *not* doing what is expected. A duel is scandal. *Not* to duel, in a case such as this, is a *worse* scandal. To say what you were about to say would be the *worst* of all," finished Tacye softly and finally reminding Fanny that Tacye's masquerade must not, even now, be broken.

"The boy is right," said Seward when, after a moment, he decided not to probe that last statement. "I just wish I'd gotten my challenge in first," he finished, rueful.

"Fanny, truly, it will be all right. I swear it."

"I don't believe you. That man . . . I don't trust him."

"We'll not let him do anything irregular," soothed Seward. "Now, come along, my dear. Let us take you back to were you may rest from your ordeal."

They arrived at the Abbey Arms just after a hysterical Mary had been slapped by Mrs. Cook into sensibility.

The maid's news concerning Damaris, that she'd been abducted by Herbert, was a final straw to all that had gone before. It was nearly enough to make even the strongest wish for her bed. . . .

Tacye longed for hers—and a cover to pull up over her head.

Chapter 16

Fanny, however, at this newest disaster, ignored the rising voices, the wondering, and the exclaiming and calmly moved into the sitting room where she still more calmly ordered cook to prepare a good meal for them all.

". . . But you must remember," she finished, "to save back enough for Damaris and Lord Worth who will, surely, be not too late arriving."

"Aunt, do not order anything for me. I must go after them," said Tacye already moving toward the door. Her aunt's voice stopped her.

"And just where will you go? What route? And by what conveyance?"

Tacye turned and stared at Fanny. "I cannot just sit here, doing nothing."

Fanny sighed. "Toby," she said, obviously exasperated, "you rescued me and not happy with that outcome, you forced a duel on that awful man. I think you've done quite enough for one day and would prefer that you *not* come up with Herbert, too. We must trust in Worth's ability to outwit the boy—and yes, you *may* very well sit and, for once, do nothing, but twiddle your thumbs!"

Tacye, after stalking from one side of the room to

the other, finally, when she'd decided there was much in what her aunt said—not about the rescue and duel, but that she'd no notion in what direction to set off—sighed and seated herself, ostentatiously twiddling her thumbs.

"I find it strange that it was *only* Herbert," she mused after another long moment. "I've assumed that both boys would be in it together if they did it at all."

Seward had listened to this with little patience and now that it seemed settled, asked, "Toby, my boy, do you think you could go to my rooms and ask my valet for a certain wine which I'd like to have served with our supper tonight?"

"Wine? But we've . . . oh."

Seward had looked at Tacye, then at his knuckles and finally cast a significant look at Fanny before looking back to Tacye.

Tacye, finally finding something worth smiling about, was not slow at picking up the clue that Seward wished to be alone with Fanny for a bit. "Oh well, it would be better than sitting here or pacing a hole in that rug which does not belong to us—which I *would* do, since I find it unhelpful to twiddle thumbs! Would you write your valet a note please?"

The note was soon written and, much to Tacye's surprise, she was allowed to leave with no objections from her aunt. Did her aunt know why Seward wished to be alone with her? Did she guess he'd ask for her hand in marriage? And what would she answer?

Tacye hoped with all her heart that Fanny said yes. There had been too many lonely years and now, if it were true her aunt could see again, there wasn't even that as a reason for holding back. It wasn't as if Tacye weren't old enough to chaperon her sister—even dressed in her skirts, she was old enough!

Aunt Fanny, decided Tacye, had no excuse at all.

Perhaps *Tacye* thought herself old enough to take care of Damaris, but Fanny disagreed. "I must see them both wed," she insisted. "I will not marry myself until they are settled. It would not be right."

"Nonsense. There is no reason at all why they may not live with us. I've a house in London, you know. It's been leased for several years—well, ever since Gerry died and you disappeared, if you must know the truth—so it will need redecorating before it will please you, but there is time to see to that and then we may all go there for the season. Or, you and I and your elder niece may go. I'm certain Miss Damaris will be wed long before spring comes."

"And my Tacye?"

"Fanny, if you had seen Worth's expression whenever he looks at your Tacye, I think you'd cease to worry about her as well. But I cannot say with such certainty that Miss Adlington and Worth will wed as I can that Miss Damaris will."

"Cahill?" asked Fanny, after a short hesitation.

"He hasn't confided in me, but he is deeply enamored of her—although I'm not altogether certain he's yet admitted that to himself! Unless I read the signs wrongly, Miss Damaris is equally attracted to him."

John reached for Fanny, pulled her from her chair and into his arms.

"Tell me you'll wed me and that you will not be such a silly clunch as to insist the girls wed first?"

"Oh, John . . . I don't know what is right."

"Then believe that I do." He shook her gently, lovingly. "Say you'll allow the bans to be called and that we'll wed at the end of the month right here in the Abbey. . . ."

Before either could say more all talking was forced to a stop by the sound of the Abbey Bells.

". . . assuming you can survive that racket for so long," he finished ruefully when they'd ceased to ring.

"Oh John," she said and chuckled. "I have already tried to find a house elsewhere, but there is nothing available. . . ." She ducked her head into his chest and he put a hand under her chin, lifting it until their eyes met.

"Do you truly wish to say me nay?" he asked.

"Have I ever *wished* to say you nay? Since we've met again, I mean?"

"Say yes, Fanny."

"Yes."

For a moment the meaning behind the simplicity of her answer eluded him. Then with a whoop of joy, he lifted her face still more and bent to kiss her. The embrace lasted until the sound of the outer door opening brought them to their senses and, red of cheek, they broke apart just as Tacye returned with the bottle.

She looked from one to the other and grinned. "So? I think I should feel insulted, my Lord Seward. I do not believe you asked my permission to address my aunt, but if my eyes have not deceived me, you have done so, have you not?"

"Cut line, boy!" growled Seward, coloring still more, but chuckling along with his embarrassment at being caught like the veriest greenhorn. "I suppose it would have been proper to have asked you, but I'll freely admit it didn't occur to me, that at our advanced ages, it might be necessary. Your aunt has, by the way, done me the honor of accepting me. So—" He moved to where Tacye had set the wine on the table. "—You'll now understand why I asked that you fetch this. It is a very good wine and quite suitable to celebration. . . ."

He was interrupted by Cahill's entrance, who, when all was explained to him wavered between wishing to run off after Damaris as Tacye had wished to do and the force of good manners which told him to congratulate Seward with proper gravity and wish Lady Tamswell happy!

He was convinced to stay by the same logic which convinced Tacye. Supper arrived and, soon after, a round of toasts to the new couple. They all sat at the round table eating family style so that it would not be necessary to have the maid serve—which was just as well because Mary occasionally tended toward still another bout of hysterics every time she remembered her frightening experience of being left penniless in a strange place—to say nothing of her fear for Miss Damaris and therefore, wasn't in the best shape to serve. As a result she was not present to inhibit their various discussions which ranged from the wedding to the duel—which Cahill had arranged for the following morning, pistols at twenty paces.

When they finished and rose to their feet, Cahill asked Tacye to take a short walk with him. "I think we should give those lovebirds a few moments alone, do not you?" he asked, nodding to where Seward obviously longed to take Fanny back into his arms.

Tacye wondered if that were Cahill's only reason for a walk, but went readily, whatever his motivation. Anything was better than a quiet period during which she would think about the duel she'd forced on Questerman. Its reality had settled into her when Cahill told her the details. It was no longer merely something the character she played must do at that particular moment. She would, on the morrow, face the rogue across greensward.

And perhaps die.

Suddenly the prospect of her own death was not so happy a one as once it had been. The never ending depression she'd felt over Terence's death had lifted—if not totally, then to a degree that it no longer left her so lost and alone and hurting. No longer could she welcome the notion of joining him in whatever afterlife he now led. . . . Because it was just possible she now had a life to lead which did *not* include him and she didn't wish to die if that were so!

When they exited the Abbey Arms, she drew in a deep breath redolent of summer and horses and the husky, musky, sometimes nasty smells of the city. She looked up and saw the spires of the Abbey silhouetted against the darkening sky. She looked down Milsom Street where promenaders still strolled, pausing to look into a shop window here, stopping to talk to friends there, or greeting an acquaintance further along.

Life was good and she discovered she did *not* wish to die. For a moment a soothing wind seemed to blow right through her, touching her innermost soul and easing her, lightening her feelings, dissolving all negative premonitions.

A determination gripped her. She *would* not die. Whatever *Questerman* might have in mind, her time had not yet come and she would face him fearlessly. What she'd just felt told her so. Terence was, somehow, still looking after her. She wasn't and, perhaps had never been, alone. She wished she'd known.

"Shall we walk in the Orangery?" asked Lord Cahill, looking wonderingly at his silent companion who seemed, at the moment, to be communing with another world.

"What? Oh, yes."

Tacye strode out, turning away from the prospect up Milsom Street toward Westgate which led toward the

Abbey and the paved surface called the Orangery. There would be people there, as well, but, at this time of day, they would be going into evening services and, very likely, Cahill and she could find a corner in which to be alone. It was too bad that their lodgings were so restricted there was no room where she could invite guests to be private. Not that she knew that a need for privacy was on Cahill's mind. Very likely he only meant, as he'd said, to give the new lovers some time alone.

They did find a bench apart from the few strollers and Cahill suggested they sit. After a moment he cleared his throat. "I've never done this before," he said, "and I'm not certain of the correct phrases, so I'll merely say I wish to pay my addresses to Miss Damaris and would like your permission to do so. I am," he hurried on, "well able to support a wife. I love Miss Damaris and will treat her well. If you wish a summary of my circumstances before you decide, I can call in my solicitor who will lay it out for you far better than I yet can," he finished with a rueful simplicity.

"What it is to be so wealthy one doesn't know its source!" teased Tacye.

"If you'd been dropped into the shoes I'm now forced to wear as suddenly and unexpectedly as I was, you too might find it difficult," said Cahill with a trifle more heat than he'd meant to use.

Tacye laid a hand on the arm next to hers and squeezed gently. "Softly, my friend. I fear that if you are to join your fortunes to our small wealth, you must quickly discover we have learned to laugh at our poverty, ourselves and, all too often, at others. I accused my aunt of being a jokesmith recently, but it is a family failing." Tacye took a deep breath. "I think, before *you* make a final decision, Lord Cahill, you should know Damaris's circumstances."

She explained about the moderate dowry and the income from the small estate which seemed to be eaten up by the estate needs as fast as it was produced and, therefore, did not add to Damaris's wealth.

"And, too," Tacye went on slowly and with some pain, her concern for her sister returning to the fore, "we cannot know what is happening to her this very instant."

Cahill sighed. "It is that circumstance which has led me to speak with you a trifle prematurely. I expected to do so before you left Bath, of course, but I had thought to wait until I was more certain of Miss Damaris's feelings. Now I think she'll need the protection of my name. If you agree, I propose to buy a special license and marry her immediately. Before you can warn me that we do not know how that Lambourn rogue may have treated her I do not care. Truly, I do not." His voice began to rise in his agitation. "What may happen, may *have already* happened to her, won't be with her permission." Tacye placed her hand on his arm, this time warningly, and he took a deep breath before adding, more quietly, "She dislikes and fears Lambourn. If Worth does not rescue her in time—" His jaw clenched, unclenched. "—Adlington, I will not see her forced to marry that creature and forced to live a life of misery because he . . ."

He could not say it. Nor could Tacye. They sat in silence for a long moment, each wondering what Damaris might be suffering at Herbert's less than gentle hands. Finally Cahill turned a little and peered through the golden glow cast by recently lit lamps set in a row within the area. "You've not given your permission, Mr. Adlington."

It suddenly occurred to Tacye she had nothing to do with settling Damaris's future! "I fear I have, unthinkingly, led you on, Lord Cahill. Lady Tamswell is Miss Damaris's guardian and it is her permission you must have—but, if it eases you, I'm certain you'll have no difficulty obtaining it. She has told me when she's wondered about the possibility, that she would gladly give Damaris's future into your hands if you were to overlook how unequal the match would be, asking Damaris to marry you despite it."

"But it is not unequal in one sense. In fact, if I'd not had the bad luck to inherit the title and all which goes with it, you might very well think me somewhat beneath her," said Cahill with that diffidence which did not imply weakness, but an appealing modesty. "I was, after all, nothing but a poor vicar."

"I'm told that even as a mere vicar, you had prospects to rise within the church and that you might have risen as far as you pleased," said Tacye in that dry tone she used so often. "I doubt, even then, when you were a *mere* vicar, we'd have felt it a bad match!"

"Well, fine compliments, those, but my future is still unsettled. Shall we return to your aunt and I'll take my courage, once again, into my hands and this time," he added on a note almost as dry as that Tacye had used, "I'll not be so coy as to suggest a stroll, but will simply ask—whatever the company."

But the company was increased. Lord Worth and Damaris had returned and were eating the meal Cook kept warm for them. Cahill stopped short as he entered the room and his heart was in his eyes as he studied the girl seated at the table.

For a moment Damaris didn't realize Tacye had not come in alone. Then she saw Lord Cahill and blushed rosily as she rose to her feet. "My lord," she said, a trifle breathlessly, her heart's desire also revealed in her expression.

"Damaris," he breathed and took two steps closer, his arms rising to her. She stepped into them and pressed her head to his shoulder as his arms closed around her. Cahill dropped a kiss on her hair and looked, rather defiantly, over the top of her head. "Lady Tamswell," he said, "Mr. Adlington tells me you are the proper person for me to ask permission that I might ask Miss Damaris for her hand."

Fanny chuckled. "I think, my lord, you do not much care if you have my permission or no!"

"I do not, but there is a reason I must do this in form. You see, I wish that we wed as soon as a license may be obtained and for that I *do* need your permission since my love is under age."

"You have not even asked how she fared during her adventure."

"I do not care."

Fanny drew in a deep breath. "You say that now in the heat of passion, but once passions cool, your opinions may change. I would have you know that Damaris returns to us in the same condition as when she was taken from us."

"Good—but I do not think I am a man who is ruled by his passions. I would *not* have changed toward her— even if our first child were not mine, I'd not change!" When Damaris would have pulled away from him, he held her close, tipping up her face and staring down into it with a certain sternness. "My dear, truly, you must not feel insulted. I have been told it will not happen and I believe it, but I would accept your child for my own if it were necessary. And I would not resent the child. It would be ours in all ways and if a boy, would inherit."

"Honor is all very well," said Worth, dryly, "but that is too idealistic for my thinking! I wouldn't want anything of Lambourn's blood stepping into *my* shoes."

"It is not a problem. Let us drop this disgusting conversation since it is all theory and will not be tested," inserted Tacye, speaking firmly. "Dammy, my love, you have not answered Lord Cahill's request for your hand."

Damaris frowned slightly, only increasing her beauty, had she known it. "But Ta-*Toby*, I have not been asked. No one says anything to me, but only speaks about me to others!"

Cahill smiled down at her drawing a reluctant smile in response. "My love, will you be mine?"

"Yes," she said, unknowingly echoing Fanny's response to Seward.

It seemed the Adlington women were of few words when accepting proposals. Seward, inwardly chuckling at the thought, eyed Tacye Adlington but could believe the slim youth was truly a woman only because Fanny had admitted it when worrying about the duel. Before the evening ended, he must, he decided, find a moment in which he'd speak to Adlington—to *Miss Tacye*—explaining why she must not meet with Questerman. And also to come up with a reason acceptable to Questerman why he and she could not meet which would be the far more difficult task, he thought.

His determination to stop her duel lasted very little longer than it took to maneuver Tacye into a corner where he put it to her that she could not meet the man.

"I must."

"Nonsense. Your secret is no more, young woman." He looked down her trousered legs and winced. "You, a female, cannot meet Questerman. It isn't done. I think perhaps I can substitute for you since I am to marry Fanny. It would be natural for me to insist, I think, since Questerman and I are more of an age."

"Terence would expect me to go through with it,"

said Tacye stubbornly. "Neither you nor anyone else will substitute for me."

Seward frowned. "Now, you know that is nonsense. Women do not duel. I have told you, it is not done."

"Lord Seward, I appreciate your concern, but I have taken my brother's place in all ways since his death. I have shouldered his responsibilities willingly and in this too I will take his place."

"What if you are hit? Killed?" Seward shook his head. "Don't you see that the scandal following the discovery you are a woman will be worse than if you do not meet Sir Davey?"

"There will be no scandal."

"You cannot know that. I cannot allow you to do this. You must see that I cannot," said Seward a trifle desperately.

Tacye chuckled. "Has Aunt Fanny made you promise to dissuade me? Fear not. I'll explain to my aunt that she is a peagoose and must not be such a lackwit as to ask you to attempt the impossible. I swear to you, she'll not blame you."

Seward mopped his forehead. "Perhaps she is wrong and you are a man after all. You do not act at all as a woman should!"

"Thank you."

"My God, woman, I did not mean that for a compliment!"

Tacye grinned. "I know you did not, but I'll take it as one anyway. Terence would as well." She nodded to where Cahill and Worth were gathering up their hats and canes. "I must play host, Lord Seward. I'll be ready to leave at the appointed hour. Do not pretend to forget to pick me up! That I would never forgive."

Seward turned and, rigid with disapproval, said goodbye to Fanny, giving his head a slight negative shake. He joined the other men in leaving. Once on the pavement, the three stopped for a few last words.

"Cahill, I must speak to you," said Seward after a few moments desultory and unsatisfactory discussion of where they might go.

"About tomorrow? I had forgotten that," said Cahill, sobering.

"What?" asked Worth, hearing nuances which raised suspicions which were immediately confirmed.

"Adlington challenged Sir Davey." Cahill told Worth, who had not heard of Sir Davey's plot to wed Fanny. "The time is set for tomorrow morning. The boy had no choice but to issue the challenge. One could not have expected him to do otherwise—but I don't like Questerman's attitude." He shook his head. "Seward and I are seconds," he went on, "keeping it all as quiet as we may, you know, but I'm not happy with my principal's attitude. Not happy at all."

"I would be on the ground with you," said Worth abruptly. Worth knew very well there would be no dissuading his stubborn and impulsive Tacye from standing up against Questerman. What he feared was that Questerman's honor could not be trusted to do the thing fairly. "Have you asked a decent doctor—just in case?"

"A very discreet man," said Cahill. Himself unaware of Tacye's masquerade, he had no conception of how relieved both his friends were made by that news—neither of whom knew the other was in on the secret. But, if the unthinkable happened, each felt that discretion might be of more importance than the man's ability as a doctor!

They discussed travel arrangements for the morning and Worth decided to ride out separately, fearing the knowledge of an additional presence might unsettle Tacye—the last thing he wished to do.

* * *

"Tacye, please don't do this."

Tacye, tired of the argument, felt a muscle in her cheek twitch. Her teeth actually hurt, she'd compressed her jaw so tightly against the tirade with which she wished to lash out. Damaris, had, thank the Lord, gone to bed soon after the men left and so had not been made party to what Fanny called her stubbornness.

"That men duel at all is foolish beyond permission. That you intend to do so is an idiocy of which I didn't think you capable!"

"It *is* necessary. He must not be allowed to joke to his cronies about running off with you."

"And how will you shut his mouth if you do not kill him—which you do not intend, I think?"

"He will look the fool when it is shown how he failed," said Tacye.

"But that can be made clear without you meeting him," insisted Fanny, watching her pacing niece with worried eyes.

"No. Aunt, don't you see that if it is revealed he was allowed to get away with no punishment, than he will *not* look foolish."

"It is all nonsense from beginning to end! I am safe. Nothing untoward happened to me. I am engaged to marry a wonderful man. This will all pass off without raising a stir if you don't get yourself killed and your nature revealed to the world!"

"I will not be killed. I think I shall not even be wounded. You must not fear for me, Fanny." Tacye spoke quietly, firmly, and with complete belief in what she said.

"You cannot know that."

Tacye smiled the half-smile so characteristic of her. Her eyes held a certain sadness when she met Fanny's strained look. "But I can, Fanny. Believe me. I can."

Fanny studied her niece's face. "Terence . . ."

"I feel him close." Tacye's smile blossomed. "He wishes this, Fanny. I must do it—for him."

Fanny bit her lip as it occurred to her that if Terence's ghost was urging Tacye into danger, it might not be, as Tacye believed, because he had foreknowledge she'd survive—but foreknowledge she would *not*. Would a ghost have retained the conscience of the living man? A man Fanny *would* have trusted to protect Tacye? Or would a ghost be freed from such considerations and, selfishly, wish his twin, his other half, to join with him in death?

Those were considerations Fanny could not reveal to Tacye. Facing Questerman, as she was determined to do, would take all the courage of which the young woman was capable—and Fanny would not undermine her by suggesting a contrary interpretation of Tacye's revelation.

"Go to bed, Tacye," said Fanny on a sigh. "I'll call you in time to prepare yourself to leave."

"Thank you."

What she was saying thank you *for*, Tacye didn't explain. Perhaps, between the two women, there was no need to explain.

It was not the offer to wake her but that Fanny had taken very good care of her nieces over the years, which went without saying. That Tacye knew her aunt would continue to watch over Damaris until the girl married Cahill also went without saying.

Tacye could face Questerman on the morrow without concern for her relatives' futures and for that she was exceedingly thankful.

Tacye stepped from the carriage and looked about her. The grass was wet with dew under her feet and smelled of life where it was crushed. The copse of young trees between themselves and the chosen ground shielded her eyes from the brightening horizon and shaded the path, making it deeply mysterious.

Seward joined her and the doctor followed, fussing with his bag and pretending he was merely out for a morning stroll. He spoke too heartily about the early birds cheeping and chirping in sleepy fashion, obviously reluctant to leave their little nests and about the slight haze rising between the trees, obscuring the view still more, going on to quote more than one poet's work on the subject.

Seward finally shushed the man's effusions and Tacye was glad. She'd listened politely, but had no heart for quotes in poetic form about nature or the man's enthusiastic enjoyment of what might be her last sight on earth. It had occurred to her during the night, as it had earlier to her aunt, that Terence had soothed her fears, not because he knew she'd live, but knowing full well she would not! Could Terence do such a thing to her? Urge her to her death?

She strolled down the path to the ground—and discovered Questerman had already arrived. He and Cahill stood apart from one another, neither happy with the other's company. Cahill brightened at Seward's arrival and immediately the two second's went to pace off the ground, check that the light was fair to both participants, that there was no roughness which might trip up an unwary man and, all in all, did just as was proper to a second's duty.

The guns were next examined. Tacye was offered first choice, but she waved the case toward Questerman who lifted both pistols before making his selection. Tacye took the other casually and let it hang loosely gripped at her side.

She took her place back to back with Questerman

who spoke softly for her ears only. "You're dead," he said.

"Then I suspect you'll quickly follow me into hell, Sir Davey," she said calmly—but inside, she again wondered at her twin's odd reassurance that all would be well. Well for whom? she questioned silently—and again a wave of peace and comfort swept through her. She relaxed. Terence would not trick her to her death. He *would* not.

Cahill read the rules to the principles, stating that they must take their paces in time with the count, that they must not turn until the last count was reached and that they must not fire before the handkerchief was dropped.

"Is it understood?"

Tacye nodded.

"Questerman, is that understood?"

"I have been out on several occasions. Do you think I do not know the rules of dueling?" sneered Sir Davey.

"I've no fear that you *know* them."

"Get on with it," ordered Questerman.

The count began and Tacye stepped out firmly, but even as she clung to the belief her twin watched over her, Tacye could not completely repress the shivers of fear climbing up and down her vulnerable spine. She'd not missed Seward's not so subtle hint that Questerman might not abide by the rules and again she wondered—but only momentarily—if Terence had tricked her. But still again she felt that soothing, calming, wonderful sense that he was with her.

". . . Eighteen, nineteen . . ."

"No!"

Even as Cahill shouted his horror and Tacye turned, a shot rang out followed by a second as Questerman's gun spun into the air, his hand a bloody mess—his scream of pain overriding all.

Tacye blinked, unsure what had happened. She looked toward the seconds and found herself facing Worth, who held his pistol to his mouth, blowing away the drifting smoke from the powder. The doctor walked to where Questerman was swearing fluently, grasping his right wrist with his left hand, trying to stop the flow of blood from his ruined hand.

"You'll never again fire before the signal, will you, Sir Davey?" said Worth.

"Before the signal?" asked Tacye, still holding her pistol to her side. "He intended to shoot *before* the signal?"

"It is rumored, bantling, that he did so once before. I wondered if he might not make a habit of it and came prepared to see no evil ensued in the event that he did so again today." Worth strolled toward Tacye, continuing his conversation over his shoulder to the doctor. "Take that animal away, sir. The creature has no business consorting with human beings, but he cannot be allowed to bleed to death if we are not to become animals of the same sort."

The doctor, who had tied on a tourniquet which slowed the bleeding to a less worrying seepage, was binding on a temporary bandage. He spoke in a disgusted growl. "I've done what needs doing for the moment, but I'll have nothing further to do with this rogue. His second can see him to town or to the devil for all I care. We aren't so far from town—I think I'll walk home, and it offends no one?" No one objected and the man left.

"Cahill, see your man to his carriage," ordered Worth, "and then you may wait and go to town with us. Questerman's coachman will see he is delivered wherever it is he pleases to go—but I'd suggest," he added, catching and holding Sir Davey's gaze, "that it pleases you to leave England and not return. Word of this day's work will not be repressed as was news of your last duel.

This time there will be nothing so subtle as rumors: the scene will be described again and again and your name will be black with the horror attached to it. That a man would fire before the count was ended—not even to wait for the turn when excitement or fear might have excused one for firing before the signal—Questerman, you are finished in England."

Questerman, growling and holding his bandaged hand to his chest, shook off Cahill's helping hand. "I knew that pup was to be my bane," he snarled. "I knew it and I did not heed it!"

"Do not fail to heed *this* warning," said Worth. "Get yourself out of England and do it quickly. You'll find yourself unwelcome everywhere from this day forward."

Questerman strode away, again swearing, but more softly. Cahill followed to give the man's driver orders and see that the carriage got off and away.

Worth barely waited for Questerman to disappear before he reached for Tacye's shoulders. "You damn fool you. You little idiot! How dare you put yourself into such danger?" He pulled Tacye into his embrace and kissed her roughly. "You, my stubborn lady," he said when, for a moment he paused for breath, "will marry me just as soon as I can get a license allowing the deed to be done."

Tacye had, in her relief that the duel was over responded enthusiastically to Worth's kiss, but once it was over she realized he knew who she was. "Worth . . ."

"And you will never again frighten me to such a degree," continued Worth, giving her another shake. "Do you hear me?"

"I should think the whole world would hear you, my lord," said Tacye. She was rather glad to be held close when he pulled her back against him since she didn't have to rely on her own rather shaky legs for support.

She looked up at him. "Worth? How long have you known?"

"That you are a woman? Forever, I think." He immediately recanted. "No. I suspected from the beginning, but it has only been the last few days I've been certain."

"What did I do to give myself away?"

"I think it was more that Hereward gave you away."

Tacye swore softly.

Worth chuckled. "I should do the swearing, Tacye. You, my love, are enough to make a saint swear."

"Then you cannot wish to marry me."

"Oh, yes I can."

Seward came up to them a trifle diffidently. "My lord, Miss Adlington, do you think I might put away that pistol?"

Tacye realized that, when she'd put her arms around him, she'd laid the gun in such a way the barrel pointed right into the nape of Worth's neck. She blushed and gently moved it away, handing it over to Seward. "Terence would have my hide for such stupidity."

"This whole thing has been stupid," insisted Worth.

"No. You don't understand. It was necessary."

In that inner self where he'd recently revealed himself, Tacye was certain that Terence was chuckling just the way he'd often done in the past. In response she could not help smiling in the lopsided way which distinguished the twins for who they were.

"You smile at such serious thoughts?" asked Worth dangerously.

Tacye blinked. "What thought?"

"That you've been in great danger!" explained an exasperated Worth.

"That I've been in danger? No. Of course that's not why I smile."

"Then why?"

"My lord, I think you would not believe me."

"Try me."

"No," she said, turning stubborn. "Some things are too private for even one's dearest love to hear."

Worth's angry response that that was not so was forgotten as his mind caught up with her revelation. "I am your love, then?"

"Oh, yes. I believe it *must* be so, although I've never before suffered from the disease and I cannot be certain it is more than mere infatuation, of course."

Worth's mouth twitched. "So demure."

"Cahill comes," hissed Seward, not wishing Tacye's secret to be spread still further. He'd been surprised to discovered Worth knew it and, thinking of all the hours Worth and Miss Adlington had spent alone together, wondered just *how* he'd discovered the truth.

"Good. We can get organized, then. The first thing to do is to get Tacye back into her skirts—" Tacye grimaced at that. "—And the next is to get a special license and the third . . ."

"Is," interrupted Tacye, "to ask the lady if she would wed."

Worth laughed outright at that. "Do you think I dare? Oh, no, my love in britches! There is no way at all you will get a proposal from my lips. You, my stubborn dear, will marry me, willy-nilly, and with no nonsense at all. Do you hear me?"

"Yes."

Tacye said no more, but not because she did not have more to say. She said no more because Worth's mouth upon hers left her no breath and no way to say it.

Cahill arriving to find the slim youth in Worth's arms goggled. "Er . . . Seward?"

Seward sighed. "You may as well know now as later. Your future sister-in-law, Tacye Adlington, has the very bad habit of dressing and acting like a man," he said acidly. "Today has been an extreme example of it, of course, but do you remember that Worth lost his race with Adlington?" When Seward pointed, silently asking a question, Seward nodded. "Yes, that was Tacye. There is no guessing what she'll do next. We must pray Worth is strong enough to keep her in line and that we who love our own women do not have to protect them from the scandal that wench will otherwise cause."

"What she'll do next," said Worth, lifting his face for his bemused love's, "is return to Bath and to her skirts and, as soon as possible, to my bed."

"My lord, you would put me to the blush," said Tacye, her rosy cheeks proving her words.

"My dear, it is up to you. Whenever, in future, you put on your trousers, something I'll not deny you the right to do, you must accept that you will be treated like the man you pretend to be. I will moderate neither my behavior nor my words to suit a female's more tender ears. And, now, I tell you frankly, my dear, that I cannot wait to find you out of them and in my bed. If that embarrasses you, my beauty, you know very well what you can do about it."

"Wear skirts in perpetuity?" Tacye raised a horrified look to meet his grim expression. *"Wear skirts all the time!* My lord, do your worst. I'll be damned if I'll give up my trousers—" The Adlington half-smile tipped her lips. "—Except to join you in bed, of course."

It was Worth's turn to blush and he did so, chuckling. Living with and loving his Tacye, he decided, would never lead to boredom! Irritation, aggravation, annoyance, and perhaps the occasional befuddlement, confusion, and perplexity, but never ever again would he suffer from boredom.

"My lord?"

"Marry me," he said, breaking his word he'd not ask her. "Soon."

"Yes."

All the Adlington women were women of few words—when it counted.

Epilogue

Some days after Sir Questerman left Bath in something of a pelter, Grenville Somerwell watched the Duke of Castelbourgh's coach set out from Bath along the Bristol road. Inside sat a sad-looking duke and a sullen-looking Lord Andrew. Gossip was rampant that Lord Andrew was to leave, at once, for an island in the new world, one wholly owned by His Grace and one the boy would not escape. He was to stay there forever—or take his chances in the world without his father's consequence behind him to save him from his folly. Grenville, who had once gotten on the wrong side of Andrew and suffered for it, was pleased his old enemy had finally gotten at least part of what he deserved.

"That's very good, is it not?" asked a well-remembered, if ghostly, voice from behind Grenville. "There goes the last loose end, all tied up."

Grenville turned warily. His eyes started from his head and he began to shake.

The faint figure dressed in a dirty and torn uniform grinned in the old way. "What's the matter, Grenville? Did you think I'd forget to say goodbye to you?"

Grenville shook his head.

"I think you did. Or you hoped I would? But all has ended well, has it not? Not only is Damaris going to be very happy with Lord Cahill and my Tacye with Worth, but dear old Aunt Fanny will find all the happiness she deserves with Seward and I'd not thought to contrive that."

"Cahill . . . ?" Grenville's fear was very nearly overcome by that one piece of interesting news: If Miss Damaris was to marry Cahill . . .! "Lord Cahill has . . . ?"

"Had you not heard?" A ghostly chuckle fell into the air. "My family is settled now and I'm free to go. Sorry if you were a trifle upset along the way, old boy, but I wanted you to know it wasn't my fault and I'll not be blamed for it." The ghost talking to Grenville grinned. "If you're curious as to my meaning, you might turn and look at the couple riding up the street . . ."

Grenville turned, saw Worth on his Jackass . . . and Terence Adlington on his Numbskull . . . except he'd just been talking to Terence Adlington's ghost, had he not?

Grenville swung back, just in time to watch Adlington fade away, the old quirk to his lips and a wink in his eye. Grenville, whirling back to check the riders, thought he heard the well-remembered laugh as well, a laugh gradually fading away to nothing as Grenville, thoroughly confused, stared at the riders.

Worth pulled to a halt. "Something the matter, Grenville?"

"The . . . the matter? No. Nothing. Nothing at all."

Worth wondered, but, a sardonic look in his eye, asked, "Hmm. Have you met Tobias Adlington?"

"Tobias you say?"

"*Not* Terence," said Tacye softly. She'd been told of Grenville's fear of specters and felt a trifle guilty for frightening the poor man so badly.

"Uh . . . hear your, er, sister's to marry Lord Cahill," said Grenville, taking his worst fear in hand and hoping for the best. If he didn't have to marry the girl, then perhaps he really had been talking with Terence's ghost and perhaps all was really well. . . .

Tacye looked at Worth, back to Grenville. "My sister is to wed Cahill, but it hasn't been announced yet. How did you know?" asked Tacye.

"How did I know? Uh. Well . . ." Grenville looked around, but the ghost was gone. "Er . . . a good guess?"

"A good guess," agreed Tacye and smiled. They nodded goodbyes and rode on out of town. "I feel sorry for him," she said.

"For a moment I feared you were going to reveal your deception just to sooth him."

"My daring deception? No. For myself I'd not care, and I think you'd shrug and go about your way as well . . . but for Dammy's sake and my aunt's . . . ? No." Tacye grinned. "I'll dare most anything when I feel it's necessary, but I think, perhaps, the necessity has passed." They smiled at each other and Tacye set Numbskull to dancing on his forefeet. "Race you," she said.

"To that gate?"

"To the gate."

"Go!" he yelled.

Tacye turned her face from the dust raised by Jackass's heels and grinned quietly. Worth had warned her he'd give her no quarter when she dressed as a man. And he had just proved it, setting them off that way!

Tacye Adlington hunched down into Numbskull's shoulder, crooned words of encouragement into his ear, and settled to enjoying this first indication that life with Worth would be just what she would like and not some namby-pamby society existence where she was expected to pour tea to the ladies while he had all the fun!

Dear Reader:

I enjoyed learning about Tacye Adlington and Lord Worth as I wrote this book. Ending a story is always difficult for me. The characters become so real and letting them go is never easy. I think that's why writers like books in which characters from one story return to play a part in another. Maybe someday there will be a story in which Tacye and Worth have cameo roles . . .

My next book, CUPID'S CHALLENGE, is a Valentine's day story . . . although it looks as if Cupid will have a real struggle convincing this heroine she is lovable to say nothing of loved. You see, a villainess had a hand in raising our heroine and the villainess hated Lady Anne's mother. *That* problem is solved when Anne is convinced the villainess was indeed steeped in villainy, but there is still another to overcome. What self respecting heroine would burden the man she loves with a woman incapable of standing on her own two feet? Anne is paralyzed, you see. She believes the hero, Sir James, feels responsible for her accident and that he is only being kind to her because of guilt. So. A second problem for Cupid to unravel!

And while Cupid solves those problems, our young godlet must untangle the complications of a couple he'd thought well settled: Anne's brother and sister-in-law have become estranged. What might have been a minor difference is fostered into something far more serious by Lord Runyon, the villain of the piece, and Lady Fustor-Smythe, daringly called Lady Fussy-puss by Sir James, only complicates an already complicated situation with her well meant interference . . . Or is she, perhaps, an elderly and irascible incarnation of Cupid himself?

I enjoy hearing from my readers. If you enclose a stamped, self-addressed envelope, I'll be sure to answer. My address is:

Jeanne Savery
P.O.Box 1771
Rochester, MI 48308

ZEBRA'S REGENCY ROMANCES
DAZZLE AND DELIGHT

A BEGUILING INTRIGUE   (4441, $3.99)
by Olivia Sumner

Pretty as a picture Justine Riggs cared nothing for propriety. She dressed as a boy, sat on her horse like a jockey, and pondered the stars like a scientist. But when she tried to best the handsome Quenton Fletcher, Marquess of Devon, by proving that she was the better equestrian, he would try to prove Justine's antics were pure folly. The game he had in mind was seduction—never imagining that he might lose his heart in the process!

AN INCONVENIENT ENGAGEMENT   (4442, $3.99)
by Joy Reed

Rebecca Wentworth was furious when she saw her betrothed waltzing with another. So she decides to make him jealous by flirting with the handsomest man at the ball, John Collinwood, Earl of Stanford. The "wicked" nobleman knew exactly what the enticing miss was up to—and he was only too happy to play along. But as Rebecca gazed into his magnificent eyes, her errant fiancé was soon utterly forgotten!

SCANDAL'S LADY   (4472, $3.99)
by Mary Kingsley

Cassandra was shocked to learn that the new Earl of Lynton was her childhood friend, Nicholas St. John. After years at sea and mixed feelings Nicholas had come home to take the family title. And although Cassandra knew her place as a governess, she could not help the thrill that went through her each time he was near. Nicholas was pleased to find that his old friend Cassandra was his new next door neighbor, but after being near her, he wondered if mere friendship would be enough . . .

HIS LORDSHIP'S REWARD   (4473, $3.99)
by Carola Dunn

As the daughter of a seasoned soldier, Fanny Ingram was accustomed to the vagaries of military life and cared not a whit about matters of rank and social standing. So she certainly never foresaw her *tendre* for handsome Viscount Roworth of Kent with whom she was forced to share lodgings, while he carried out his clandestine activities on behalf of the British Army. And though good sense told Roworth to keep his distance, he couldn't stop from taking Fanny in his arms for a kiss that made all hearts equal!

TODAY'S HOTTEST READS
ARE TOMORROW'S SUPERSTARS

VICTORY'S WOMAN   (4484, $4.50)
by Gretchen Genet
Andrew — the carefree soldier who sought glory on the battlefield,
and returned a shattered man . . . Niall — the legendary frontiers-
man and a former Shawnee captive, tormented by his past . . .
Roger — the troubled youth, who would rise up to claim a shocking legacy . . . and Clarice — the passionate beauty bound by one
man, and hopelessly in love with another. Set against the back-
drop of the American revolution, three men fight for their
heritage — and one woman is destined to change all their lives forever!

FORBIDDEN   (4488, $4.99)
by Jo Beverley
While fleeing from her brothers, who are attempting to sell her
into a loveless marriage, Serena Riverton accepts a carriage ride
from a stranger — who is the handsomest man she has ever seen.
Lord Middlethorpe, himself, is actually contemplating marriage
to a dull daughter of the aristocracy, when he encounters the
breathtaking Serena. She arouses him as no woman ever has. And
after a night of thrilling intimacy — a forbidden liaison — Serena
must choose between a lady's place and a woman's passion!

WINDS OF DESTINY   (4489, $4.99)
by Victoria Thompson
Becky Tate is a half-breed outcast — branded by her Comanche
heritage. Then she meets a rugged stranger who awakens her
heart to the magic and mystery of passion. Hiding a desperate
past, Texas Ranger Clint Masterson has ridden into cattle country
to bring peace to a divided land. But a greater battle rages inside
him when he dares to desire the beautiful Becky!

WILDEST HEART   (4456, $4.99)
by Virginia Brown
Maggie Malone had come to cattle country to forge her future as
a healer. Now she was faced by Devon Conrad, an outlaw
wounded body and soul by his shadowy past . . . whose eyes
blazed with fury even as his burning caress sent her spiraling with
desire. They came together in a Texas town about to explode in sin
and scandal. Danger was their destiny — and there was nothing
they wouldn't dare for love!

*Available wherever paperbacks are sold, or order direct from the
Publisher. Send cover price plus 50¢ per copy for mailing and
handling to Penguin USA, P.O. Box 999, c/o Dept. 17109,
Bergenfield, NJ 07621. Residents of New York and Tennessee
must include sales tax. DO NOT SEND CASH.*

Taylor—made Romance From Zebra Books

WHISPERED KISSES   (3830, $4.99/5.99)
Beautiful Texas heiress Laura Leigh Webster never imagined that her biggest worry on her African safari would be the handsome Jace Elliot, her tour guide. Laura's guardian, Lord Chadwick Hamilton, warns her of Jace's dangerous past; she simply cannot resist the lure of his strong arms and the passion of his *Whispered Kisses*.

KISS OF THE NIGHT WIND   (3831, $4.99/$5.99)
Carrie Sue Strover thought she was leaving trouble behind her when she deserted her brother's outlaw gang to live her life as schoolmarm Carolyn Starns. On her journey, her stagecoach was attacked and she was rescued by handsome T.J. Rogue. T.J. plots to have Carrie lead him to her brother's cohorts who murdered his family. T.J., however, soon succumbs to the beautiful runaway's charms and loving caresses.

FORTUNE'S FLAMES   (3825, $4.99/$5.99)
Impatient to begin her journey back home to New Orleans, beautiful Maren James was furious when Captain Hawk delayed the voyage by searching for stowaways. Impatience gave way to uncontrollable desire once the handsome captain searched *her* cabin. He was looking for illegal passengers; what he found was wild passion with a woman he knew was unlike all those he had known before!

PASSIONS WILD AND FREE   (3828, $4.99/$5.99)
After seeing her family and home destroyed by the cruel and hateful Epson gang, Randee Hollis swore revenge. She knew she found the perfect man to help her—gunslinger Marsh Logan. Not only strong and brave, Marsh had the ebony hair and light blue eyes to make Randee forget her hate and seek the love and passion that only he could give her.

Available wherever paperbacks are sold, or order direct from the Publisher. Send cover price plus 50¢ per copy for mailing and handling to Penguin USA, P.O. Box 999, c/o Dept. 17109, Bergenfield, NJ 07621. Residents of New York and Tennessee must include sales tax. DO NOT SEND CASH.